AWESOME

a novel by

Abigail Arrington

Capricorn ☆ Star ☆ Publishing

This is a work of fiction. The events and characters described herein are imaginary and are not intended to refer to specific places or living persons. The opinions expressed in this manuscript are solely the opinions of the author and do not represent the opinions or thoughts of the publisher. The author has represented and warranted full ownership and/or legal right to publish all the materials in this book.

AWESOME

Capricorn Star Publishing
http://www.capricornstar.com

ISBN: 978-0-9849140-1-2
eISBN: 978-0-9849140-2-9

PRINTED IN THE UNITED STATES OF AMERICA

Awesome is dedicated to all
who have weathered the storm.

ACKNOWLEDGMENTS

The author extends heartfelt appreciation to:
Stratis, for knowing where to look;
Danielle, for helping me to remember;
Kent, for his inspiring sarcasm;
Jeff, for helping me talk the talk, and;
Dave, for lending me his car.

CHAPTER 1

"Testing. Testing. Calibrating auditory reception."
The pock-faced, overly-eager clerk at the dilapidated spy shop on Highway 50 assured her the device had a signal with ample range. He also said it could transmit back to the receiver as long as it was within a one-mile radius. For someone who acted like he knew everything, that little dork did not want to know what kind of hot water he would be in if this foreign made piece of crap didn't do everything she expected of it.

A sudden sensation caused Bunny Keiler to clutch her chest. The flutter she felt near her heart was a sign. She pulled her cell phone from the breast pocket of her slim-fitted jacket, and held it in several directions while trying to read the message in the late afternoon sun.

Big words don't make u smart.

"Subliterate plebeian," Bunny muttered quietly, before adjusting the button on the front of her jacket one more time to ensure the lens on the micro-sized button camera remained unobstructed. She pulled a tube of lipstick from her purse and tilted her rearview mirror downward to monitor its application. First one, and then a second generous coating of crimson made the rounds on a practiced pout.

Under ordinary circumstances she would have blotted away some of the excess, but she would be in a more forgiving, low-light environment in a few minutes. She could get away with a darker look.

After pressing her lips together a few times to muddle the freshly applied goop, she briefly considered a third go-round. Some of the color was likely to be lost to a Judas kiss before the night was over. Then again, too much of a good thing could leave a stain somewhere it didn't need to be. With one last glance in the mirror, she was ready. Time for the show.

Before crossing the parking lot toward the entrance, Bunny turned back and pressed the remote on her key fob to ensure her car doors were securely locked. This wasn't exactly the best part of town, and she stood out from the rest of the crowd like a rabbit in a fox den. That was just on the way in. On the way out, those same night feeders would be hungry for her kind and hunting in packs.

She waltzed past a group of people waiting in line at the front door and bypassed the entry checkpoints with nothing more than a wave directed at a familiar face. She'd been to The Polling Place before, too many times. In her case, no photo ID was required.

It was a Tuesday, but not just any old Tuesday. This was the first Tuesday of the month, which meant it was a "Super Tuesday" and there was about to be a raucous "election." Bunny surmised that to be enough to bring the usual local power players to The Polling Place early. Once inside, she wasn't disappointed. She spotted a few well-known faces settled into prime seats, front and center, surrounded by those of like mind.

She took her time weaving through the series of tables that faced the center stage. To some, a stage in the middle of a room might seem oddly placed. It worked here, or more to the point, it *was* worked. The inside joke brought a wry smile to Bunny's face. It was shortly supplanted by a look that reflected her growing confidence.

The Polling Place was not, as its name might suggest, a designated public location for exercising the inalienable right of suffrage. It served the community in far more colorful ways. The business conducted here had a historical reach that predated the founding of this nation and a few others. This place with polls and poles was an exclusive gentlemen's club, its name chosen as a forked-tongue-in-cheek throwback to another time when the owner and proprietor, Vincent Mikles, had been deeply involved in Florida politics.

In some respects, however, The Polling Place was not unlike its namesake. For one, those in charge of such things placed numerous impediments to access on "election nights" and continually heightened the requirements for voter participation. Also, for a number of reasons, whatever suffrage might take place here was generally beyond the grasp of the last group of Americans grudgingly bestowed the right of the other constitutional variety. Admittedly, in this case, it was unlikely any of her gender counterparts cared. There was an irony in that, somewhere, but not the kind Bunny favored.

While still on the first floor near the main stage, she made a slow 360-degree turn, as one might when looking for a seat, thus allowing her hidden camera to capture the faces of some of the men presently enjoying themselves to the fullest. She liked to call their type "very inebriated perverts." At this club, some of them were also known as "VIPs" albeit in the more traditional sense of the term.

The club's regular patrons were also quaintly referred to as "registered voters," a venue requirement for those attending the monthly election night events. That term, however, was used in anything but the traditional sense. In keeping with the theme, the dancers participating in the various campaign events and in the election that would take place sometime later in the evening were referred to as "candidates," each chosen to represent the ideology of a "political" party.

Since none of the early guests in attendance wore the glazed-over look of a depravity neophyte, Bunny decided they were regulars. She even recognized a few of them as the upper echelons of the local business community, whose pictures were frequently in the paper to announce their involvement in some merger, acquisition or other business deal of ridiculous proportion. Despite their wealth and success in the outside world, here they were no different from all the other men who came to play with the girls, except for the fact they played longer, and usually a lot harder.

The men who frequented this club liked to drop their considerable money on expensive liquor, more expensive cigars and equally expensive women. A few of them just liked to drop their money. Literally. Bunny had the pleasure, or displeasure from her perspective, of watching and hopefully recording one stout, middle-aged patron waive the promise of a hundred dollar bill in front of his young server only to conveniently release it just before she took hold. Gradually succumbing to the forces of gravity, the government-drawn note fluttered like Forrest Gump's feather until it found a resting place on the floor in front of the young woman. Dutifully, the server, wearing little more than she might on a hot day at the beach, bent over to recover it while her calculating benefactor enjoyed the view from behind.

Bunny rolled her eyes in disgust. How many times had she been forced to smile sweetly while some well-to-do patron pulled that tired gag? This time was different, though. This time someone else was picking up the Benjamin while she had the distinct pleasure of recording it for posterity. This was good stuff—the type of thing that could be highlighted and looped.

She turned slightly to her right to face the nearby velvet-upholstered booths just in time to catch a high-ranking state law enforcement officer frisking one of the dancers. Not in the ordinary course of his business, of course, and certainly without having read her any rights. In here, Miranda was just a name, and likely a fake one.

Not far away, a conservative candidate for the state house of representatives was enjoying a very personal lap dance from Ginger, one the club's famously endowed attractions. Only voters who contribute heavily to the Super Tuesday events get that type of access to a candidate before the election. Bunny made sure she captured the scene from an angle that clearly revealed the man's face. It would do wonders for his "family values" platform.

Upon a second scan of the room, it occurred to her that far too many of the club's regular VIPs, like the two she had just encountered, were seated on the lower level. Those guys usually stuck to the box seats up in the balcony. In those seats, they were less likely to be seen doing things they didn't want the public to know about.

The anomaly presented a question that begged an answer. If the roosters were in the yard, who or what was in the hen house? There was only one way to find out.

Bunny made her way around the right side of the stage and then to a far corner where a private stairway led to the second floor balcony. Along the way, she occasionally stopped to capture whatever debauchery conveniently fell within the purview of her hidden lens.

The stairway she was seeking wasn't in plain view or easy to find. You had to have been at the club when the lights were up, probably more than once, to even have an inkling of where to find it. Fortunately, she had. She had traipsed up and down those very stairs in the dark more times than she cared to recall—certainly enough to know which ones squeaked and which didn't.

Access to the balcony was limited to very exclusive clients and a select few employees and dancers chosen to serve them. The club's bouncers routinely patrolled the area to keep any uninvited guests out. Although her presence on the lower level wasn't likely to ring any bells, the same couldn't be said for the balcony. For that reason, it was best to make a quiet entry and keep a low profile.

Bunny unhooked the velvet rope—a symbolic advisory to the dwellers of the lower level they were not important enough to pass— and took the stairs two at a time without making a sound. When she reached the top, she paused to consider her next move.

Along the back wall of the second story balcony some of the best seats in the house were largely shielded from view by heavy velvet curtains that matched the curtains on the center stage below. When the show started, the front curtains would be opened to allow the occupants to watch the show, but the side curtains would remain in place, shielding the neighboring VIPs from view. Judging by the hectic pace of the servers as they ducked in and out, all of the curtained VIP booths had occupants. Unfortunately, there was still no way to see who the occupants were from where she stood. Whoever they were, they had to be heavy hitters because they had somehow managed to displace the regular balcony big shots.

It had been a while since she'd been up here, but it didn't look like much had changed. If her memory served her correctly, there was a sweet spot against the back wall where, if you stood in just the right place, you could see what was going on behind some of the curtains. Bunny crept over to an area on the far left of the balcony and leaned casually against the outer wall.

Through a small opening in the curtains that hung perpendicular to the wall, she could now see and record the nocturnal activities of some of the middle-aged, pattern-balding customers who were taking respite behind the velvet shield. At first, only the shiny tops of their heads were visible as they bobbed and weaved over a low beverage table in a scene oddly reminiscent of the teetering plastic birds that sit on the side of children's sippy cups. These balding birds appeared to be taking part in a different ritual; one that required them to douse their beaks into a white powdery substance dispensed on a mirrored tray. She knew what it was. Those viewing the recording would have to reach their own conclusions.

The men's full faces came into view a few seconds later when they settled into the thick cushions of the overstuffed, leather upholstered booths. Bunny wasn't sure who some of the guys were; of two other things she was certain. First, they were all very rich–Vincent didn't entertain anyone in the "99 percent." And she now had them on film doing something they shouldn't be doing.

Triumph lifted the corners of Bunny's lips. "Gotcha."

Once upon a time, although not in the fairy tale sense of the phrase, she had been a hostess for parties like this, mingling with and engaging the guests in whatever fashion they might prefer. As a former hostess and dancer for Vincent, and later a business manager at this very club, Bunny knew all too well what he was serving his VIPs tonight–a few overpriced but undercooked steaks with all-you-can-eat sides of sex, drugs, and whatever other vices might appeal to their warped appetites.

Most of the club's regular VIP patrons were extraordinarily wealthy men with prominent businesses or political careers—major league players in the world of power and influence. They were the lucky ones who always seemed to stay one step ahead of the turns of fate that frequently derailed their lesser counterparts. Some were from old money, but most were self-made men. One thing they all shared was an uncanny winning streak in the game of life. It was as if they alone were privy to a clandestine handshake that opened the door to the world's vault.

Although she didn't recognize them, the men now inhabiting the usual VIPs' playground couldn't be much different. If anything, they were all that and more. Vincent wouldn't have relocated his loyal customers otherwise. He had too much invested in them.

Vincent knew the secret lives of the wealthy businessmen who patronized his clubs because it was his job to indulge them. He also knew the value of keeping those secrets. His business was to mind his own, and he had proven himself time and again on that front—at least when it suited his interests to do so. When it didn't, the club's hidden cameras ensured Vincent had everything he needed to defeat any customer who challenged him.

Everyone is hiding something. The key to staying on top is to learn their secrets without giving away any of your own. That was the speech Vincent gave her when she became a manager and he showed her the inner workings of the club, and the hidden cameras, for the first time. To this day, she was fairly certain she was among the elite few who knew of their existence. Owning the information when dealing with powerful people was just one of the many valuable insights she gained while working under Vincent.

We did work "under" him, in every sense, didn't we?

Bunny's immediate thoughts were betrayed by the angry smirk that crossed her face. Her visceral response was directed at the vision of the many nights she and Cayren, a former dancer who had since become Vincent's wife, spent in forced intimacy with Vincent or with each other for his amusement. Although she and Cayren had ultimately become good friends, those early experiences did not make fond recollections.

At the time, she was young, considerably attractive, and believed she had nothing to lose. With none better among the few alternatives she had to choose from, she had decided to go with the flow. Putting up with the wandering hands of her boss and the ogling eyes of a few boorish men was a small price to pay for a job that in return paid four times what she could have made at any other part-time gig.

Looking back, she recalled reminding herself, more than once, that the job was simply a means to an end. Having a broad perspective, something foreign to most of her young counterparts, and a few lofty goals seemed to shield her from the types of things that destroyed many of them. As she later discovered, that shield had done nothing to keep scars from forming over the unavoidable emotional wounds. Still, unlike most of the other girls, she had made it out of this place. Just barely, though, and not for long. She was back now, in a different capacity, revisiting a past she longed to forget.

Bunny's dyspeptic expression smoothed into a look of quiet resolve. She recalled something Vincent had often repeated–"Keep your enemies close; there is no such thing as a friend." It was good advice, although she had come to discover something her mentor had overlooked, or at least failed to mention. The premise was flawed in that it failed to account for the various shades of grey. There's a lot of open space between an enemy and whatever else a person could be.

Vincent's singular vulnerability might well be the very thing that gave him his strength–women. He seemed to think boobs made one incapable of anything more devious than a cat fight, so he foolishly allowed women privileges he would never afford a man. Historically, that same mistake had taken down quite a few powerful men. Despite the lessons they should've learned, they always came back for more.

As a club manager, Bunny not only learned Vincent's business from the inside, she also earned enough money from bonuses and tips to pay for law school. She had not been the best student, but grades were only relevant if you didn't have connections or the means to make them. She had both.

She had continued to work at the club while attending classes at the nearby law school. By the time she graduated, she had enough on a few of the local lawyers and judges to garner glowing references, which in turn helped her to secure a position at a prestigious law firm. That had been her ticket out of the adult entertainment industry and into a career that required a different type of dance.

It was that different dance in a different venue that brought Bunny under the wing of her next mentor and current co-counsel, Sam Stone. That tall drink of troublesome man had helped write a whole other chapter of her story; one that carried her all the way to the present moment.

Although, upon reflection, she concluded giving Sam credit for any of this was a bit of a stretch. What she was doing at the moment wasn't exactly in line with anything he had taught her when she worked as an associate at his firm. Sam wasn't above bending rules into pretzels, but she had never seen him actually break one.

Vincent Mikles couldn't even spell the word "law" without looking it up. If, or rather when, he found out what she was up to, he of all people wouldn't have any legitimate basis to complain. Sure, there were laws on the books that might cause someone less clever than her to be concerned about the possibility of a fine or even prison if caught secretly taping people. Under those laws you can't intercept voices via wire and you can't record communications without giving notice. Blah, blah, blah. None of that applied here.

Hell, she not only knew about the law, she was the one who had advised Vincent about the existence of the state wiretap statute after researching it for an assignment in her first-year criminal law course. She had also advised him that the annoying little proscription made his creative home video collection illegal, unless of course he took measures to provide some sort of notice to his patrons and had a legitimate business purpose for the cameras.

As would any good attorney, she had also suggested the solution: a small sign with thin silver letters pitted against a black background, placed just before the hostess desk at the front of the club. The sign she created politely advised, "These premises are under video surveillance for security purposes." It was a clever enough remedy, and one Vincent still utilized mostly because his patrons, distracted by an attractive, strategically clad hostess, rarely noticed anything on their way in that wasn't flesh-colored and heaving.

Of course, after she took the time to enlighten him and provide a reasonable solution, Vincent, in typical fashion, came up with another way to turn the matter around entirely to suit his interests. He started streaming the club's events over the Internet. At that point, highly visible cameras recording events in the club were expected—just another part of the show. The other not-so-visible cameras that recorded more intimate, behind-the-scenes moments were simply corollary to the observable end.

It was announced a few times during each show that the event was streamed live on the Internet. That way, everyone knew why the cameras were there and that they might be seen or recorded by them. Indeed, the well-known fact the shows were recorded and broadcast was one of the many reasons most VIPs took to the second floor, where they assumed the cameras were not. Of course, like most who assume without inquiry, they were dead wrong. Their error in judgment wasn't Vincent's problem, however, and likewise, wasn't hers.

Should the venture she was presently undertaking come under scrutiny, the argument there was nothing illegal about it would be easy enough to make. Vincent runs his own cameras and the club's patrons are on notice they are being recorded. As such, neither have grounds to complain if someone joins Vincent in the enterprising measure—so long as the byproduct is not used for pecuniary gain. In this case, it most certainly wasn't. She had no intention of selling the rights to *this* film.

Bunny donned a wide, self-satisfied grin curried by the notion of besting Vincent at his own game. She quelled it before it peaked and with the apparent benefit of a sixth sense stepped out from the shadows as if returning from an upstairs lavatory just in time to greet him. He had likely been in his office on the lower level when she arrived, and had watched her move through the club and then sneak upstairs via his hidden cameras. She had expected nothing less. The Bunny Show was still running from her script.

"Bon Buns, my favorite former candidate. How good to see you," Vince Mikles acknowledged as he leaned over to greet her with a kiss. "I thought we'd seen the last of you at one of my VIP events. Are you here to do a private show? I've got clients that would still pay top dollar for a girl like you."

Still? Bunny's disdain welled within her, but never surfaced. Instead, she wore the same pleasant, internally vacant look she had perfected when having to entertain Vincent's guests in the past. No one called her "Bon Buns" anymore. It was once a term of endearment between them—a clever pet-name Vincent had crafted from her given name and her penchant for scant French lingerie.

His invocation of her past served only one purpose. It was an intentional reminder to her that she didn't have the same lithe, twenty-something body she sported back in the day—the one that had always gotten her what she wanted from men and managed to get Vincent paid handsomely in the process. What he was really saying without saying was that she wasn't as valuable to him in that way anymore. She knew it, and he knew she knew it, which meant he was actually being facetious.

Fuck him. She was going to get what she needed out of him and hold him eternally by the balls, all before the end of tonight's happy hour. The best part was he would know nothing about it until she wanted him to.

"Hello, Vincent, it's good to see you," Bunny replied, with forced emphasis on the "good" part. It was the easiest lie she would tell today. She purposefully called him by his full given name, as she always had. It was her thing.

"You know why I'm here. It's about the case," she explained. "These days, I only dance in court."

Vince raised a single brow with his reply. "Is there a new development? I thought Sam was keeping me up to date."

He stepped behind a small bar tucked neatly in a corner across from the VIP booths, pulled a bottle of aged malt whiskey from a high shelf, and examined the label. "You want one?" he asked, before pouring a tall one into an elegant cut-crystal highball.

Bunny shook her head. "I've got a few more billable hours before mine get happy. This isn't a development Sam would be privy to."

She took a step closer to the bar while she continued her explanation. "Actually, I'm here to suggest you consider using just one attorney on the case; that being me, of course. I'm a seasoned litigator. I've handled more than a few high-stakes cases for clients like you, and you know I know this business better than anyone."

"Can't argue with you on the last part, Buns," Vince responded. His gaze extended the length of her with familiarity before he drew a long sip of amber liquid from his glass. He nodded toward the stairs as he swallowed. "Let's talk about this in my office, shall we?"

"Of course," Bunny replied. "After you."

She followed him down the dark stairs to the lower level of the club and then down a long corridor into a room she knew all too well. Once inside, she closed the door behind them.

Vince opened with a suggestive wink. "I'm all ears, Buns. What are you proposing?"

Bunny had neither the patience nor stomach for more of his condescending saccharin. She met his gaffe with silence and a stern expression. It took a minute, but he eventually caught on. She was here as his attorney, not as a former dancer.

"Ah, I get it. This is business. All kidding aside, Buns, you think you can close the deal better than Sam's firm? How do you plan to pull that off?" Vince inquired. "More importantly, what's in it for me?"

Bunny continued to hold his gaze steadfast. She knew him well enough to know solid eye contact garnered high regard. He often said the truth, if there was such a thing, could be found in a person's eyes. Men were so easily duped. She could fake honest eyes as easily as an orgasm.

"A lot's in it for you, starting with protection of interests you don't want disclosed. We're going into the discovery phase now. That means Audra's snippy little attorney gets to start asking you all kinds of questions about your business and gets copies of all sorts of documents you'd rather he not have. Her attorney also gets to talk to the other girls. All of them. And they have to answer his questions, *under oath*."

Bunny drew out the last part to illustrate the importance of her request. She paused to ensure her words had made their mark. Vincent appeared to be giving them fair consideration, so she continued.

"Up until now, you've only had a few low-ranking government employees from the EEOC poking around in your business. They were easy enough for me to distract. But that part is over," she advised. "The lawsuit was filed in federal court. We're now playing the big game with a lot more at stake."

Vince smirked and intentionally turned away. "None of my girls are gonna rat on me. You know that."

Bunny took a step closer, placing herself well inside Vince's personal space. She took hold of his chin, and forced his face and his attention back toward her. "Do I?"

Still holding him rapt with a steady glare, she slowly removed her hand from his chin. This time she spoke in a lowered voice. "We go way back, Vincent, so I'm going to be very frank with you. Your girls are only here because they need money. For the right amount of it they will talk to anyone about anything."

Her confidence bolstered by a compelling start, Bunny stepped away from Vince, waltzed over to the oversized leather sofa against the back wall and plopped down. She lingered in the pause for emphasis before continuing her advisory.

"All Audra needs is one corroborating witness and you could get hit with a multimillion-dollar verdict. Could be a record-setting number, given the nature of your business. It's not like a jury is going to understand or approve of the way things work around here," she added, hoping the not-so-veiled insult to his seedy empire stung, at least a little.

Vince's face was quiet, which made it hard to read. Bunny continued her pitch anyway. "But I do. My understanding of the business comes from a perspective you'll never have. I understand what motivates your girls because I was one of them. I can keep them in check. I can make sure this case never gets to trial."

Bunny crossed her legs and leisurely settled back into the soft leather sofa. She was quite pleased with herself at the moment. She had managed to get all that out and sound convincing in the process.

Vince turned his back to her again—a classic nonverbal indication of disdain for someone speaking an unwanted truth. He stared at the monitors mounted on his wall. At the moment, the array of screens displayed a full view of the club, upstairs and down; their feed supplied by his hidden cameras.

Had he been in the room with anyone else, the display would have been switched back to its usual presentation—a live feed of the dancers performing on the main stage. But the display had not been changed, which alone spoke volumes. Even in silence, the message he intended to convey was clear. He had been watching.

Vince's focus seemed to settle on the one screen displaying the dancers in their dressing room preparing to perform. Technological advances aside, they were still his bread and butter. He took a long minute to consider Bunny's proposal.

"I'm not worried about the jury. There are plenty of ways to persuade my so-called peers. But these days, everything that goes on in court is tried first on the fucking television news. That could be bad for business," he conceded. "If there's a way to keep things quiet, it's something I have to consider."

Vince emptied his glass, placed it on the desk beside him and turned back to face Bunny. "Like you say, we go way back. I'll think about your offer. I'm not making any promises, though. I've got a meeting with Sam later tonight. He claims to have a fresh perspective."

An acceptable enough response, Bunny decided. Rising from her seat, she spoke with confidence. "You do that," she advised. "I'm certain you'll come to the right conclusion."

She followed her words with a confident smile. Nothing more was required. Vincent was certain to fully understand the implied threat. Still, she couldn't leave this delicious moment without one parting shot.

"Sam is a pretty good lawyer, Vincent, but as we both know, I'm *awesome.*"

A slight chuckle escaped from Vince as he walked with Bunny toward the door of his office. He leaned over to give her a customary farewell kiss on the cheek, and whispered in her ear.

"Best be careful, Buns, or you might fall prey to your own hype."

CHAPTER 2

Riley mentally processed the afternoon agenda during her elevator ride up to corporate headquarters. There was still a lot of ground to cover, and only a few hours left to do it. By all estimates, only one thing weighed in her favor this afternoon. Sex. Nothing else could grab attention in quite the same way.

Sexual harassment isn't a laughing matter, but when teaching a seminar on what to do and not to do in the workplace, sample scenarios often result in just that. However, if the trainees are laughing then they are paying attention. Something good can come from someone else's bad.

When she searched for real-life examples of inappropriate conduct to use as illustrations, it wasn't a struggle to find material. Fact always trumps fiction, and there was plenty of it to go around. The teachable moments Riley had chosen for today's training session came straight from the headlines, with a few names changed to protect the guilty. The media having done some of the legwork meant most in attendance should be vaguely familiar with the cases she planned to use as examples. That familiarity, in turn, often left seminar participants more than a little interested in hearing the rest of the sordid details.

Much like the use of attention-grabbing examples, holding the training session today–a Tuesday–had also been a tactical decision, intended to promote optimal retention of information. Mondays are not ideal because many employees are still recovering from the weekend, cognitively and in pretty much all other respects. On Wednesdays, most employees are distracted by the harsh reality that they are hopelessly behind on their work for the week. On Thursdays, following a frenzied rush toward the finish line, their attention returns to the weekend, this time the coming one. Come Friday, the exhausted shadow-entities which comprise the majority of the work force are merely filling the space behind their desks until the appointed hour of freedom.

Riley's focus was jolted when the elevator made an abrupt stop on the third floor. The doors opened in front of a lanky, casually dressed young man. He was sipping something from a large Styrofoam cup through an equally large straw before he was stopped mid-slurp by the opening door. Seemingly surprised, the young man released suction-hold of the straw. He repositioned his trendy, thick-rimmed glasses to the proper place on the narrow bridge of his nose—an apparent attempt to examine the scene before him with more precise vision. With a courteous nod and smile in Riley's direction, he joined her in the elevator car. Given his choice of the mostly empty space, the young man veered to his left before turning back to face the closing door.

An attractive, professional-looking woman is something most men find highly intimidating. This one was facing the elevator door, though. That might have been the reason a life-long introvert found sufficient courage to initiate a conversation. Whatever the reason, it was destined to be a fateful encounter.

A slight head tilt in Riley's direction preceded his opening line. "You don't work in this building, do you? I'm pretty sure I would remember if I'd seen you here before."

Riley turned slightly to her right to face the young man and returned his smile. "That's a good observation. I don't work here. I'm conducting a training seminar for a company on the eighth floor."

"Oh, that's the sex seminar, isn't it? A friend works there and told me they were having a sex class today. I thought he was shittin' me."

Dude, you said the word "sex" openly to an attractive woman you just met. Winnitude!

Riley attempted to suppress an amused smile. "He might've exaggerated just a bit. I'm not teaching sex. Rather how to manage that aspect of life in the workplace. It's not nearly as much fun as he led you to believe, I'm sure."

"If you're teaching, it can't be all bad," the young man quickly concluded.

Nice one, he internally assessed. *You're getting better at this schmoozing thing.*

"That's very kind of you to say," Riley responded, offering her hand to greet him. "I'm Riley Morgan. I'm usually in the courtroom, when I'm not teaching folks about sex."

The young man eagerly accepted her hand and offered his own with a hearty introduction.

"Wade Warner. I'm in IT with a company on the fifth floor. I also do freelance computer work, so if you need a wireless network or something for your office, I'd be the guy to call." He pulled a business card from his pocket and offered it to Riley. "That's my cell number. You know, if you needed to call…about your computers, and all."

"Thanks," Riley said. She accepted the card and slipped it into her jacket pocket, before fumbling in the recesses of her purse to find one of her own. "Here's one of mine. Hopefully you won't ever need it, or if you do it'll be for expanding your business."

While they spoke, the elevator had stopped a few times on subsequent floors to introduce new passengers to the ride. With each stop, the open space between them had quickly narrowed, prompting Wade to inch ever closer to continue the conversation. He decided that was the smart thing to do once he realized, too late, he'd missed his floor.

"Attorney-at-law," Wade read aloud from the card. "Sweet. You never know when this might come in handy." He tucked the card into the back pocket of his khakis. "I guess the sex class is taking all day, huh?"

"It is a loaded topic," Riley conceded, with a wry smile. "It usually takes at least a full day just to hit the high points."

"Nice one," Wade added with a nod. He was pretty sure she had been playing along with the word pun. "Looks like this is your floor." he added as the elevator signaled its arrival on the eighth.

"It is indeed," Riley surmised. Before stepping out, she held the elevator doors open with her hand long enough to offer a customary parting, "It was a pleasure to meet you, Wade."

"Likewise," Wade responded with a nod, before the doors closed. When the doors were firmly shut, he resumed the recently interrupted interchange between the straw and his Styrofoam cup. There was a long ride ahead before the car would take him back down where he belonged.

Once past the elevator lobby, Riley headed down a long hallway toward a pair of heavy glass doors that had the company name, S.V. Souvenirs, LLC, etched into the glass. If this morning's encounter with the doors was any indication, they were once again going to present a challenge especially since she was still accompanied by her large leather trial bag filled with seminar materials, handouts and a laptop computer.

When she reached the doors, Riley stopped and shifted her purse to the same side as her trial bag in order to free one hand for the door handle. The receptionist, having witnessed Riley's approach from the other side of the glass, rose to open the door and helped to maneuver Riley's heavy rolling trial bag over the raised threshold.

"Back for the afternoon session," Riley advised before making her way past the reception desk and toward the training room.

The young woman nodded, and then hurriedly retreated to her desk to field the barrage of calls that always seemed to come at the precise moment she left her desk.

On her way to the training room, Riley mulled over something that had dawned on her during the lunch break. She'd never heard of this company before today. If the name was any indication, and she presumed it was, the company was in the business of selling souvenirs.

In the Central Florida area, where a number of world-class attractions are located, the souvenir business was surely a profitable venture and this company appeared to follow suit. By all indications, it was doing well or was, at the very least, well-funded. It occupied almost the entire eighth floor of this newly constructed downtown office tower, which was known to charge the highest rent in town. The office building itself was part of an entire commercial complex built during the recent construction boon, and housed not only the wealthiest business clients, but also afforded access on the lower levels to high-end shopping, restaurants and even a movie theater.

She agreed to take on the training seminar at Sam Stone's request, but it remained to be seen whether getting involved with Sam, on any level, was a good idea. Although Sam was a well-known and successful attorney, the man was nothing but trouble with a capital "T" as far as she was concerned. More importantly, he wasn't the type to easily get over their last encounter, where she had given both him and one of his clients a sound spanking. Most men don't like to lose, especially to a woman. What made the matter worse was the fact Sam wasn't most men. His rank on the man scale included a triple multiplier.

Sam indicated the training seminar was needed for a subsidiary company owned by one of his noteworthy clients that was presently embroiled in a heated sexual harassment lawsuit. Given the short notice, he had offered top dollar for her time. As a solo practitioner, it was hard to turn down that kind of money. It wasn't easy to be the only rainmaker keeping a small office afloat.

Riley also agreed to help because she had more noble causes in mind for the extra money she would earn from teaching the seminar. She and Dani were working with the local women's shelter to create a memorial in the name of Vanessa Buehler, a former client. The community was still abuzz over Vanessa's sensational murder, which

Riley had the misfortune of witnessing firsthand. It had been several months since Vanessa's tragic death, but the memory still played on repeat in Riley's mind. Thankfully, with every passing day, it played less often and with fewer of the gory details.

At some point, Riley knew the harrowing moment would no longer be at the forefront of her mind. When that day came, it would be both a blessing and another loss. She wanted to keep Vanessa's memory alive. What happened to her shouldn't be forgotten, lest it be repeated. Hopefully, creating a memorial fund in Vanessa's name to provide services to abused women would do just that. If occasionally helping out a client for a questionable man like Sam furthered that, then so be it.

Still, even with the benefit to her worthy cause, she might have turned Sam and his client's money away if Dani hadn't also goaded her into accepting. According to Dani, playing along was the only way they would be able to find out what Sam really had up his sleeve, or some other part of his attire.

If Sam was indeed up to something, he hadn't revealed himself thus far. The day's sessions had followed the ordinary course; nothing seemed out of place. The bored workers attending the class were trying to make the best of a wasted day at a training session on a subject in which, aside from the amusement factor, they were not all that interested. They were a captive audience, present solely because they had no choice but to succumb to the whim of those at higher pay grades.

The company appeared to have requested the seminar at the eleventh hour, as many often do, after finally coming to the realization that diversity and harassment training could help reduce, if not stave off, the expense of litigation. This type of enlightenment was long in the making but always seemed to come on suddenly, as if little bulbs over management's heads abruptly illuminated the dark reality that a lost day of work paled in comparison to the expense of attorneys. Then and only then, by virtue of some miracle brought on by intense management pressure, the accounting department was able to find money in the budget to pay for something that should have been done before the proverbial shit hit the fan. It was the age-old story of a sleeping giant that awakens slowly, following a commotion.

Still, despite the ordinary appearance of things, Riley planned to corner Sam after she finished today's session, and ask him a few pointed questions. When dealing with her own clients, she took the time to learn more about the business before she went in to conduct a seminar so she could incorporate issues uniquely relevant to the client into the course. She was brought into this situation at the last minute though, and did not have time for her usual preparations. That circumstance, in and of itself, was odd, but Sam had insisted this was a rush job and there was no time to go over details.

The seminar attendees meandered back into the training room and took their seats while Riley set up the laptop computer and pulled down the retractable screen mounted on the back wall for the upcoming Power Point presentation. Newspaper clippings, pictures and diagrams made excellent visual references, and were a good way to hold audience attention during a lecture. For that reason, she always set them aside for the afternoon session.

Once the setup was complete and the employees filled their seats, Riley summoned her well-rehearsed engaging speaker mode. She managed to smile, laugh and entertain the group for the better part of an hour with a segment she liked to call "Stories from the Road." The segment included excerpts from cases she had tried and litigants she had opposed, as well as the ones taken from current headlines and usually proved to be more effective than coffee to shake off the afternoon funk.

Next came the segment where she outlined things to watch for in the common workplace. The list seemed to get longer every time. There were the usual culprits, like off-color water cooler talk, or inappropriate interview questions. Then there were the more obscure forms of discrimination, usually only evidenced by statistical analysis. Those were usually found in hiring trends, where men were inten-tionally or sometimes unintentionally favored over women, or in promotions, where women were often penalized for their family obligations.

With that, the business end of the seminar was complete. Riley then opened the floor for the part that was often the most challenging–audience questions. In every crowd there was that one person who still needed to laugh the whole thing off. Usually he or she was the first to raise their hand. Today was no different.

A portly, older gentleman with a full head of bright white hair raised his hand and waived it emphatically. "I have a question," he announced, and repeated a few times. His zeal afforded everyone else the cover they were hoping for. They all ducked below it, keeping their hands down and thoughts to themselves.

"I see we've got a question from the back of the room," Riley acknowledged and pointed to the animated gentleman. Her thoughts were concealed by a professional demeanor. Inside, she was cringing.

"So, I get that you probably shouldn't date your co-workers, and I know we have a policy that discourages it. I still have a question about workplace romances," the man asked with all sincerity.

"Okay, ask away," Riley encouraged.

"What I still get stuck on is just how many times can you ask a co-worker out before it becomes harassment? Sure, they might say 'no' at first, but I can usually win them over. So, how many tries do I get?"

While the man was speaking, Riley reached back to tug on the base of the projector screen, encouraging the internal mechanism to retract. With the screen lifted, she briefly leaned against the wall in the front of the room to consider her response. As clowns go, this one wasn't so bad. She'd seen worse.

"I'm not sure I'm an authority on dating advice," she responded, taking a step or two forward as she spoke. "In terms of what may or may not rise to the level of harassment, a good rule of thumb is to always take 'no' as a final answer."

"What if she's really hot and broke up with her boyfriend since the last time I asked?" he continued.

Then it depends on whether she really likes you or is just tolerating you because she has to work with you.

It was Riley's initial thought, and what most women might offer in response to his query. Most women would also admit to being surprised that something so obvious to them was lost on a grown man. Riley had learned to consider behavior from both perspectives, though. She was here to teach that insight to others.

What her initial reaction and the shared feminine perspective usually failed to account for was the fact their masculine counterparts often have no idea whether they are in favor, merely tolerated, or outright despised. The language barriers between Venus and Mars were still firmly intact. To bridge that consistent gap, Riley framed a reply she hoped would clue the inquirer in, and send the right message to the group as a whole at the same time.

"If it's a situation where you are a manager or in any way in charge of decisions affecting her job, then 'no' is still her answer and mine," Riley advised. "If she's a co-worker, I would advise you to use common sense and follow the verbal cues. I know a lot of relationships start in the workplace. That is, after all, where the majority of us spend most of our time. I'm not here to debunk the reality of that. I'm just here to advise you to tread lightly and consider how your actions might be perceived by others."

A twenty-something girl from the front of the room raised her hand, and Riley nodded an acknowledgment.

"So, what about stuff like pin-up calendars or bikini model posters and stuff like that? Should that be on the wall in an office or in our cubicles?"

"No, there really shouldn't be any depictions of nudity or even partial nudity in the workplace."

The girl looked to the wall behind Riley and frowned. "Isn't that a nude woman in the painting behind you?"

Riley's eyebrows shot up. She had noticed framed art on the walls earlier in the day, but had not bothered to look past the frames. She turned to face the large print she had been standing in front of for the entire seminar. It was, in fact, an abstract depiction of a naked woman. There was a first time for everything.

The group erupted in laughter. It had been a long day, and they were past due. The only thing to do at this point was to join them in laughing at the irony. It was funny, sort of.

When the merriment subsided, a voice from the center of the room chimed up, "That's Matisse. I think it's called the 'Blue Lady' or something like that."

"Well, you guys called it correctly. That is indeed a depiction of a nude woman, albeit in the abstract," Riley admitted gamely. "It really shouldn't be in the workplace. I'll have to talk to your facilities manager about that before I go."

"She's just pulling your leg, Miss Morgan. That picture ain't no big deal to us. We work with stuff ten times worse than that all day long," a dark haired woman from the far left side of the room explained.

The class seemed amused although, to Riley, it didn't sound like a laughing matter.

"Wait. You...*what?*" Riley inquired with disbelief.

"Yeah, I mean, that's our business. We sell sex toys and porn videos and stuff on the Internet. The illustrations on the packaging alone would make a Penthouse reader blush," the dark haired woman advised. "You knew that, right? That's what the 'S' part of S.V. Souvenirs, LLC stands for. The full name is 'Sexy Vacation Souvenirs.'"

It took all the composure Riley could muster to quell her surprise. At the moment, her only option was to brush it off. To do otherwise would undermine everything she'd spent the entire day trying to convey.

"Well, if I didn't know before, I certainly do now," Riley responded. "Of course, the nature of the business does make some of what we've talked about today a bit of a challenge for you. I would have to add to the list of advice I've given you a special advisory to take extra care in the way each of you interact with your co-workers. Keep it businesslike, and no offhand jokes about the products."

The blank stares and nods Riley received from the class in response to her advice were conclusive evidence–afternoon lethargy had won them over. Their brains were full and there was no point in trying to force feed additional information they couldn't retain.

"So, that's it for today, folks," Riley concluded. She added a broad smile. "It's been a pleasure, and quite an experience, to work with you."

Most of the attendees made a beeline for the door, but a few stopped by to thank Riley for her time while she packed her computer and seminar materials. She made idle chatter and offered her business card, advising them to call if they had any follow-up questions.

Once the classroom emptied, Riley headed for the lobby and then traversed the long hallway back to the elevator. It didn't show outwardly, but she was more than a little annoyed. Sam had intentionally withheld the fact his client sold sex toys just to set her up for the obvious punch line. It was a sophomoric gag, at best. What was the point? He didn't even get the pleasure of watching it go down, and that wasn't like him at all. Was this his endgame? If so, he hadn't lived up to his reputation.

When the elevator doors opened before her, she stepped inside with steely resolve. Sam had played his cards too soon.

CHAPTER 3

"You're late."

The sardonic admonition cast in Wade's direction the moment he re-entered the IT area originated from a nearby office. Wade chose to ignore it. Instead of responding, he tossed his empty Styrofoam cup into a nearby trash can, plopped down in his OSHA-approved ergonomic chair and logged back onto his computer.

Once he realized he had passed his floor while chatting with Riley on the elevator, Wade decided to ride up to the top floor and take the stairs to the roof. Some of the guys from the office took their smoke breaks up there, and one of them owed him money. Seemed as good a time as any to collect it.

Unfortunately, the dude he was looking for wasn't up there. So instead of padding his wallet, he had hung out five, maybe ten, minutes with some of the guys in accounting before heading back down to work. It wasn't a big deal, no matter what the big voice from the little man in the next room had to say. He held the title of "Director" now. Not having to punch a clock was one of the perks from his recent promotion in which he took some pleasure. There were a few others he enjoyed even more.

"I said, you're late," the admonition was reiterated with slightly more emphasis and in an even deeper baritone, pushing toward a bass. The inquisition didn't stop there, and from the sound of it, the purveyor of said warning was coming ever closer. "I don't suppose you have a good excuse, do you? What kind of example do you think that sets for the other employees?"

David Duong, a middle-aged Asian gentleman with graying hair that displayed more salt than pepper, stood in the doorway of his office while continuing to chastise Wade. He was wearing his favorite combination of colors: black. Today's ensemble consisted of a black dress shirt that melded perfectly into the waist band of his black dress slacks. The getup was not surprisingly paired with a black leather belt and black leather dress shoes. It was a look Wade liked to refer to as Duong's "Jackie Cash" look. The humor in tying a martial arts expert and a musician known for wearing all black together by reference was lost on Duong. Then again, most humor was lost on Duong.

"Whatever, Duong," Wade retorted, sarcastically. "I've put in tons of extra hours just this week integrating the new server and updating the SQL databases. We're still having crashes on some of the desktop units. I've been out on the floor all morning, and probably will be out there again for most of the afternoon."

"Are you complaining about workload, again? You know we don't pay you for overtime. I can work you 24 hours a day and not pay you a penny more. That's the beauty of American capitalism. If you work hard, and do good work, we promote you so we can work you more and pay you less for it," Duong chided with an eerily gleeful look in his eyes.

"Yeah, yeah," Wade retorted quickly. "You're just pissy because you're short, Duong. Jacking me isn't gonna make you any taller, now is it?"

That was a sore spot for Duong, and Wade knew it. He only played the height card when he really wanted Duong to mind his own business. A few muffled snickers rose from the other cubicles, their precise origins uncertain since the inhabitants had ducked for cover like frightened meerkats to avoid getting drawn into the friendly fire.

"I may be short, *Wormer*," Duong responded, using one of the many nicknames he randomly derived from Wade's last name, "but I'm still your boss. I get to decide your bonus."

The invocation of the bonus was Duong's predictable fallback position when verbally sparring with Wade. He was well-aware Wade lived from paycheck to paycheck and counted on that extra money to feed his techno-fetish. The new virtual reality gaming system by GigaVerse didn't come cheap, and Wade had made it known he wanted it badly.

"All right, all right, don't pop a vein, old man. I'm back now. Stop blowing hot air at me. You might overheat the servers," Wade conceded. "Next time, I'll bring you back a brownie, how's that?"

The thought of food, especially brownies, usually distracted Duong from his occasional intemperate mood. As bosses go, Duong wasn't the worst. He didn't give Wade too much grief and sometimes he was even a pretty good guy. Today's grousing was probably the result of pressure from corporate regarding the time it had taken to integrate the new system. Nothing was ever fast enough or cheap enough for the suits who resided in the ivory towers at corporate headquarters.

"That's what I like to hear. Make it two and I'll consider letting you keep your job," Duong added before retreating back into his office.

Wade heard the loud creaking of Duong's chair, which meant the boss had settled back behind his desk and was probably resuming a computerized game of solitaire that would likely consume what was left of the day. Fortunately, because Wade's cubicle was directly across from Duong's office, Wade could hear the chair creaking when Duong sat down or got up from his desk.

He learned over time that different creaks meant different things. Slow ones meant Duong was getting up to stretch and take a smoke break. Fast ones meant Duong had been given a directive from corporate and was about to pass it off to his minions. Or it could mean that someone's computer had crashed in the executive suite and hell's heat was about to rise in the IT department. Anything in between meant Duong was probably bored and about to launch into an awkward conversation with anyone who didn't appear too busy.

In spite of its proximity to the boss, Wade's cubicle had been expertly configured for gaming and web surfing. His multiple monitors were intentionally located so that whatever was displayed on the screens wasn't visible from Duong's office. When on the computer, Wade sat facing Duong's office door which meant his array of monitors faced the opposite direction. Whenever Wade heard or saw Duong coming out of his office, he could quickly switch the display to something work related just in case Duong stopped by to complain about some absurd new level of corporate bureaucracy mandated by Mahogany Row. The subject was a recurring frustration for all of IT.

Hiding what he might be working on wasn't as much a necessary endeavor as it was a prophylactic one. For the most part, where Duong was concerned, if Wade chose to take a mental break now and again, he had probably earned it. Wade was good at his job and his boss knew it. Plus, Duong didn't have much room to talk. Everyone in IT knew he spent the better part of his days goofing around on his work computer whenever they weren't in system upgrade crisis mode. Heck, anyone in IT might be caught doing the same thing on any given day.

Yet, unlike his departmental counterparts, the challenge Wade faced and the one that prompted him to remain hypervigilant to the comings and goings of his boss was a little different. Wade wasn't just good at his job; he was too good at it. What Duong didn't know, and would never know if Wade had his way, was Wade's near-genius ability to spread a little work over a long period of time. So when Wade appeared to be dutifully sitting in front of his computer typing away on the keyboard, more often than not whatever he was doing wasn't work related. In some instances, it was possible what he was working on might not be legal, either. For both of those reasons, it was best to keep Duong in the dark.

Most of the employees outside the IT department have no idea how their computers work and have even less of a clue about the workings of the mainframe server or the company intranet. Heck, half of them aren't even sure how to replace the ink cartridges in their printers. The only thing that mattered to the folks on the floor, otherwise known as the business and sales units, was that the expensive electrical boxes on their desks hummed to life when they pressed the magic button. On the rare occasion that didn't happen, or there was some glitch in the overall system, IT's phones ring off the hook and the loser on phone duty is greeted by caller after caller who is certain their entire world will implode if the problem isn't fixed within the next 30 seconds.

Essentially, Wade's job boiled down to dealing out the corporate crack. Increased productivity was the drug of choice, and technology continued to feed that addiction. The affliction had progressed to the point that modern business was completely incapable of functioning if their computers or phone systems went down. Time is money, and money moves at the speed of whoever has the fastest and most reliable technology. All systems were expected to run with complete precision and accuracy and with no downtime. If that didn't happen, the addicts called their dealer, Wade or one of his IT brethren, and they made the rounds.

Having that type of absolute power can go to one's head. Fully aware of the resources available to him, Wade routinely made use of them. Like now, for example. Just for kicks, he was using confidential security access codes to tap into the small ceiling-mounted video cameras installed in the company's reception area.

He had volunteered to be the corporate liaison with the security company responsible for installing the cameras. That ambitious undertaking came with the opportunity to receive hands-on training on the finer points of the system. The training included how to remotely access the video feed or redirect a camera's focus.

Usually, those savvy to the inner-workings of corporate bureaucracy know if you show an interest in something, or foolishly speak up at a meeting about some random subject, you'll soon end up having whatever it was added to your work pile. That can be a good or bad thing, depending on how you play the game. In this case, Wade had played it just right. This time, his atypical display of ambition came with a handsome reward.

As the only person in the company with any knowledge of the security camera hardware, Wade was naturally bestowed the honor of managing the entire security system as well as maintenance of the database where audio and video recordings are stored. In short, he had the extra duty of ensuring the cameras hummed along well enough to provide a false sense of security to the staff. In return for the extra work, he got to listen in on conversations he wasn't supposed to hear and better yet, he had a bird's eye view down the blouses of the hottest girls in the company. All in all, it was a fair exchange.

Halston McKinley, the new receptionist and a favorite target for his voyeuristic endeavors, looked as expensive as her name sounded. It had nothing to do with her attire. But speaking of garments fortunate enough to be acquainted with her exquisite frame, Wade was pleased to note she was wearing a pink bra today. Or at least the lace edges of it that were peeking outside of the neckline of her low-cut blouse appeared pink on his monitor. It might also be lavender, or possibly beige.

It was probably pink though, because her blouse was pink, and fairly sheer. She had coupled that with a fitted grey pencil skirt and a dark grey pair of those ridiculous high heels she always wore. Halston had a thing for shoes. He'd heard her talk about them, incessantly, in the break room with some of the other girls in the office. There was always some big sale on this or that designer at the department stores and the gaggle would be making plans to hit it.

He listened in on those conversations as an outsider, very much like a dorky kid watching the popular ones play ball from across the playground. In his mind, he had joined in their conversations, offering banter and witty retorts; charming the ladies with his sparking wit. Unfortunately, that was all in his head.

He had never actually been invited to hang out with the cool kids, and probably never would be. He had also never summoned the courage to infiltrate them. Whatever. They were never as cool as they imagined, anyway. And things were different now.

He may have once been the stereotypical mop-haired, spectacled computer dork, but that was back in school. A lot had changed since then; some of it was him. For one thing, his sapphire blue eyes could rock the contact lenses, if he remembered to put them in before he rushed out the door in the morning. Plus, those regular workouts at the gym hadn't hurt his image any. He was becoming ripped in some of the right places.

More than a few of the older ladies in the office checked out his butt when they thought he wasn't looking. Sometimes he even added a swagger to his step when he walked past for their viewing pleasure. He had fun toying with them and they, in turn, were always good to him. They made sure he was given a heads-up for the birthday or other celebrations that went down on the floor. If he couldn't join them, they would save him a piece of cake or whatever treats were served.

When he finished school, and was navigating the world of industry in his chosen profession, that's when things really changed for him. In a commerce driven climate, it turned out he had more to offer than many of his more socially-advanced peers. In this world, the names of guys with skills like his were all over Forbes' lists of the richest dudes in the universe. Those who recognized his skills understood he was just an algorithm away from having his name on that list. Of all the changes since his school days, the success of others like him was probably the one that had made the biggest difference.

Empowered by his unexpected but welcome elevation within the corporate food chain, he had recently summoned the courage to speak directly to Halston a few weeks ago when the company's Internet-based phone messaging system went on the fritz. That exchange consisted of five words. He had said, "It's working now," to which she replied, "Okay, thanks."

However brief, the exchange still smoldered in his subconscious; occasionally it bubbled over into his present thoughts. Halston was far too hot to speak to at random, especially for a socially-challenged male such as himself. Nonetheless, having broken the first of the many barriers between them, he now longed for more. Mounting internal pressure to take action had reached the point of complete distraction. The object of his desire was right there, just beneath his fingertips. It was a difficult pull to resist. The time had come for a technology intervention.

Wade's fingers moved purposefully across the keyboard. It only took a few seconds to disconnect Halston's computer from the system, which in turn took down her access to the printers, e-mail, and other shared resources. It would probably take her a minute or two to realize her system was down. Then she would call for help and he would, naturally, be there to save the day.

He watched with pleasure via the security camera while Halston began to randomly hit keys on her keyboard in a futile attempt to send an e-mail. She then turned to one of the secretaries in a nearby cubicle, who smartly advised her to call IT.

"Ask for Wade," the secretary directed matter-of-factly. "He's the best guy we've got."

"Yes. Yes, I am the best," Wade whispered, before a wicked grin took control of his face. "Any time now, my pretty."

A few seconds later, his phone began to buzz. The caller ID register indicated it was none other than his intended prey.

"This is Wade Warner, in corporate IT, how can I assist you today?" Wade intentionally lowered the register of his voice to project a commanding vibe. After listening for a few seconds to Halston's patchy account of the problem, he interjected.

"Sounds like your computer is disconnected from the network. We've had this happen a few times since we've upgraded the system. I'll just pop over and take a look. I can probably have you back up and running in no time."

Wade pulled open a small drawer on the right side of his desk, retrieved a bottle of cologne he stored there for social emergencies, and sprayed it in his general direction. He then grabbed a piece of mint gum from another drawer and a flash drive from a tray that was sitting next to his computer monitor. He popped the gum in his mouth and the flash drive into his pocket. With that, he was ready to perform his civic duty and save the damsel he had just put into distress.

"I've got an issue on the floor," he announced as he passed in front of Duong's office. "Gotta check it out and see what they've messed up now."

It was commonly understood in IT that whatever wasn't working was usually the result of some novice user's unintentional disruption of one of the system's operational files. Humans err far more than machines.

"All right. Make sure you fill out the report when you're done. Corporate needs to know how many times a day we save their asses," Duong replied.

"You got it." Wade's voice echoed in the recycled air as he headed out the door of the secure IT area.

Because they housed and maintained the servers, which in turn held all of the company's proprietary and confidential information, the IT department had the privilege of a separate glass-enclosed work area—a luxury otherwise afforded only to those in the executive suites on Mahogany Row. All the other random schmucks, even some directors and low-level vice presidents, had to work on the floor in open cubicles. In that regard, the IT department was pretty lucky.

The only thing the executive suites had that IT didn't was a window to the outside world. The server room, and consequently the surrounding IT area, was maintained at a preset, de-humidified temperature by a specialized air handling system that operated solely for the benefit of the machinery. As such, he and the rest of the IT department were, for all intents and purposes, working within a

HEPA-filtered bubble in the middle of the office. That was the downside.

Wade breezed past the maze of cubicles on the floor and made a beeline for the reception area at the front of the office. He'd made the same trek from one end of the floor to the other enough times to know he broke his previous time record for this jaunt. That came as no surprise. He was on a mission.

"You called for IT?" Wade inquired as he approached Halston.

"Wow, you're fast," Halston acknowledged, her face brightened by relief. "I barely put down the receiver, and here you are."

"We aim to please," Wade replied. His Cheshire grin somehow managed to widen further. "So what's going on with your computer?"

"I dunno. It just stopped working." Halston sat back down in the task chair behind the reception counter and tapped a few keys on her keyboard. "See, nothing works. I can't send email or print or anything."

"Uh-huh. If you don't mind, let me check out a few things on your system here and maybe we can get you back up and running pronto."

Wade purposefully stood behind Halston so that he could lean over her shoulders to reach the computer keyboard. His face was mere inches from her long, flowing hair.

Cherries. Oh God, her hair smells like ripe summer cherries.

Wade fiddled around with her keyboard, opening and closing a few basic system folders for show. He moved from file to file quickly so that, in the unlikely chance she actually knew anything about computers, she wouldn't be able to follow his actions. Just for fun, he also checked her browser cache.

Few people realized every website they visit is stored in various places on their computer. This was something he was frequently called upon to check for the HR department when they suspected an employee was browsing the Internet instead of working. Sure enough, Halston had been on the Internet, browsing websites that were clearly not work related. One of them was a website selling discount designer shoes. That figured. Others were basic sites for travel or weather information.

Whoa, what's this?

A numerical URL was nestled among the other ordinary domain addresses in her web cache. This most likely meant Halston had been using the Internet to remotely log onto a computer on another network.

Jackpot!

"I'm going to need to get a snapshot of your system and then do some reconfiguring on the mainframe," Wade improvised.

Not really, he mused to himself. *Really, I'm going to download a key logging virus on your hard drive so that I can gain access to your passwords and private information.*

He pulled out the USB flash drive from his pocket and plugged it into a port on the side of the CPU. He could've just as easily uploaded the file to her computer remotely from the IT department, but that would leave a trail that some genius, not unlike himself, could trace back to his computer. For that reason, his well-laid plan included the additional safety measure of installing the program locally. If the program were later discovered, its point of origin would be virtually untraceable, and everyone would just assume Halston had downloaded it by clicking on a link in one of those emails employees were repeatedly reminded not to open.

"It'll just take just a few minutes to load the files," he advised. "After that, I need to go back to IT to reconfigure things."

"Can you have this fixed before the end of the day?" Halston inquired. "I'm not allowed overtime without getting prior approval, and the admin supervisor isn't here today."

"Sure. No problem. I'll have you purring along within the hour." He so intended the pun.

The blinking light on the flash drive indicated the files had finished downloading. That was the first stage of his ingenious endeavor. Now, all he had to do was access her hard drive from the mainframe, reboot her system, and the key logging program would install and begin feeding information to him.

Wade pulled the flash drive out of the CPU and tucked it safely into his pocket. He was pretty sure he had a gold mine on that shiny little piece of 8 GB hardware. The program it stored, one of many he had written in his spare time, was essentially a master key to every piece of information stored on a computer. This wasn't the first time he'd used it, but it would assuredly be the most memorable one.

"I'll buzz you once I've filtered through the files and found the culprit," he advised. "Shouldn't take long."

Halston fluttered her long lashes and flashed a smile that would unnerve any man with heterosexual tendencies. "I really appreciate it. I can't get anything done without my email or phone system. You're a lifesaver!"

Wade surmised the two features, in combination, had likely proven useful for securing whatever she wanted more often than not, although it wasn't as if she needed any help in the wooing department. Halston could walk into a room and stand there without saying a word. Most guys would still stumble over themselves to do what they imagined to be her bidding.

She was beyond pretty, up close. Like those women you see in the magazines, except most of them are airbrushed to perfection. She didn't need any of that. Her skin was nicely bronzed. It could be from the sun or could be the spray-on variety; it was hard for a guy to tell. Her smile was pearl-white perfection, and was expertly complimented by rosy pink lip gloss that looked like it might taste delicious.

There was no way the warm, golden-blonde color of her hair came from a bottle. If it did, her stylist was a master. Sometimes she pulled it away from her face, but today she wore it down, allowing it to fall loosely around her face and shoulders. On top of all that, she had the kind of figure most girls despised–top heavy, with a tiny waist and long legs. She was pretty much, on a dude rating scale, a perfect ten-and-a-half.

It had occurred to Wade, more than once, that someone who looked like Halston working as a receptionist in a boring place like this was more than a little unusual. She could easily make a lot more money working at one of those restaurants or bars that feature hot, scantily-clad waitresses. What stroke of luck had brought her to his door? He marveled at the powers of fate on his short jaunt across the floor back to the IT bubble.

Back at his desk, Wade accessed the hard drive on Halston's desktop computer using his administrative privileges to locate the files he had downloaded. Before things went any further, he needed to ensure the files were downloaded in the proper sector and wouldn't interfere with normal operation. After confirming that minor detail, he initiated the installation of the key logger program by simply rebooting her system.

Once the system restarted, he scanned Halston's hard drive again to locate and confirm installation. He found the program where he expected it to be, and where no one else would find it—neatly disguised as a standard operating file.

All that was left now was to type in the command to restore her email and other peripheral services. For good measure, and to make it seem as if his job were far more complicated than it was, he waited a few more minutes before calling to let her know her system was back in operation. Her apparent gratitude warmed him in all the right ways.

"My pleasure. It's all in a day's work. If you have any other problems with your system, just call my direct line and I'll make sure you get super-fast turnaround," Wade offered, again invoking whatever depth his still developing voice would allow.

Wade leaned back in his chair and reveled in the success of his covert operation. "God, I love this job."

"Glad to hear it," a familiar voice responded.

Apparently, Duong had his ears on high alert, waiting for Wade's return. He could somehow manage to sleep through the roar of

Amtrak trains that sped by the building in the late afternoon, but still hear it when any of the guys in IT grumble, even in hushed tones.

"Guess that means you won't whine if you're on call after hours tonight will you, *Wormer*?"

Wade sat upright and prepared to volley.

"Hey Duong, did I mention they're having pizza in the executive break room?"

CHAPTER 4

Dani had been watching the clock and the door all day, waiting for one of them to blink. According to the local news a hurricane was brewing in the Atlantic. That storm was of lesser concern to her than the nearer one on her horizon. That yet-to-be-named storm had been stirred up when Sam Stone's low-level warm front moved too quickly into a region dominated by Riley's upper-level cool.

With equal opposing forces of their magnitude circling in the same atmosphere, the likelihood of a severe outburst was imminent. If Dani's expert radar was on target, landfall was to occur right... about...now.

Boom!

The door closed hard behind Riley, causing the chimes to sound more like breaking glass than ethereal bliss.

Yep. Thar' she blows. Dani's forecast was on the money. If the loud entrance wasn't enough to confirm it, Riley's expression was.

"I'd say our buddy Sam Stone is in for it," Dani surmised, anticipating Riley's first clap of thunder.

"*In for it* doesn't begin to describe the kind of hailstorm that man has coming," Riley fumed.

"Funny you should use that term."

"What term?" Riley was only half-listening while she briskly filtered through the day's mail she had retrieved from the mailbox in the lobby on her way up.

"Never mind. So, we knew he was up to something. What did Ladykiller do this time?"

Riley handed the relevant mail to Dani before tossing the rest of it–primarily junk mail and catalogs–into the trash. "I don't even know where to start. Do you want the part about the priceless art depicting nudity, or the part about vibrators and nipple clamps?"

"Holy poodle droppings!" Dani's huge blue eyes somehow managed to expand. "This is better than I imagined. It's been a long, dull day here. Start with the vibrator."

Riley did a quick double take before responding. "Holy what? When did you start talking like the Caped Crusader's sidekick?"

"When Jack heard the boys repeating a few of my favorite four-letter words. Kids are a lot like large, very expensive parrots."

Riley shook her head. "Sometimes, you don't make parenthood sound all that appealing. Good thing they're cute."

Riley settled into one of the chairs in front of Dani's desk and launched into a summary of the day's events, starting with the nature of S.V. Souvenirs' business and ending with the anecdotal tidbit about having lectured on sexual harassment in the workplace while standing in front of a vivid blue depiction of a naked woman. At various points during the tale, and upon the story's conclusion, Dani's hysterical laughter filled the room. It was a solid five minutes, maybe more, before she was even able to speak.

"Okay, seriously, you gotta give Sam props," Dani remarked, wiping away the tears of laughter from her eyes. "That is priceless."

Riley wasn't nearly as amused. "Are you really taking his side?"

"C'mon, Riley. He sent you to do a sex seminar at a business that sells dildos. Sam gets the win this round."

"Fine. If that's how you want to call it, so be it. Just keep the scorecard handy. I plan to return fire."

"I'm counting on it," Dani added. "While we're on the subject of men...."

"I don't count Sam Stone in that category."

"Well, you should. He's definitely *all* man. So, like I was saying, while on the subject, I haven't heard you talk about Evan lately, and you haven't flown out there in a few weeks. What's up with that?"

"You're on fire today with the touchy subjects, aren't you?"

"It's like ripping off a bandage. Gotta do it in a single tug."

"Right," Riley retorted, shaking her head to indicate the opposite. "Well, to answer your question, I don't think L.A. is for me. All of the women out there are perfect replications of the female form somehow miniaturized into a size zero. I like cheeseburgers too much to ever be that small again."

"Puh-lease, because you're so fat," Dani said. "You know you aren't fooling me with that cheeseburger nonsense. He failed one of your tests, didn't he?"

Riley gave her friend a knowing look. "Don't they all?"

"So, which test was it? My guess is the one where he was supposed to follow your instructions precisely even though you're giving him the wrong information. Or maybe the one where he's supposed to pick up on your telepathic messages and know what it is you want before you tell him? That one's my favorite."

Dani pursed her lips and raised a brow to end the query, an expression she often adopted when she was being, as she liked to say, "Ironical."

"Pfft. That's advanced stuff. He never made it to that level. Not that anyone has in a long time," Riley said.

"Someday someone will. You'll see. I'm not giving up," Dani advised. "Have you told Evan he's out, or are you just going to leave him guessing?"

"You know me. I don't like open-endings. We talked about it, and we've decided to take a break. It wasn't ugly or anything."

"How did he take it?" Dani asked.

Riley paused. The difficult conversation with her former client and more recent boyfriend, Evan Cole, wasn't far enough in the past to be a comfortable memory. "He wasn't pleased, I guess. He said he understood. He's too busy making music right now to spend much time mulling it over."

"The door's still open, then. That's good. Who knows, things could change for one or both of you someday."

"Maybe, but I'm not standing in the doorway waiting for it swing back this way and smack me in the face. I'm pretty busy myself, you know, teaching Dildo, Inc. how to act right in public," Riley quipped.

"Somebody's gotta do it," Dani replied, smartly. "By the way, you've got no meetings for the rest of the day. Maybe you should make it an early one and go get supplies for the hurricane that's coming our way."

"Storm, schmorm," Riley mocked. "It's only supposed to be a Level 2 by the time it gets here, if it gets here at all. You know we have summer rainstorms fiercer than that. Besides, I'm filing a summary judgment motion next week in that construction defect case we've been working on. I'll be in my office with my nose in a book if you need me."

"Have it your way. Hopefully, those books will provide you shelter and sustenance when the storm hits," Dani said.

Riley rolled her eyes and curled her lip into a smirk before heading down the hall to her office. Dani didn't bother to look up while she jotted a quick reminder to buy extra candles and batteries for Riley.

"Your face is so gonna get stuck like that."

After a few fits of spontaneous giggling over Sam's antics, Dani's attention returned to the *pro-se* pleading she had spent the past two hours trying to decipher. She had barely reviewed a complete paragraph before the business line lit up with a call. If the caller ID was any indication, this was the one she'd been waiting for.

"Morgan Law Firm, can I help you?"

"Yes, you can," a deep, elegant voice directed. "I'd like to speak to Riley."

This was, in fact, *the* call. The voice and articulate manner of speech were unmistakable, as was the occasional lilt in enunciation that leaned toward a British accent—a likely holdover from time at Oxford.

Sam Stone was on the phone, making yet another call consistent with his recent pattern of behavior. He'd turned himself into quite the pest over the past few weeks, calling or stopping by randomly. He usually gave patently bogus reasons for his calls or visits, like he needed to consult with Riley on a contract or he just happened to be in the building. Realistically, those excuses wouldn't hold a drop of water.

It was widely known Sam didn't even consult or strategize with the partners in his own firm. In that case, there was no reason to believe he would come all the way over to Riley's office to consult with her. As to his other convenient excuse, the only other tenants in their small, renovated historic office building were a podiatrist, a real estate listing agency and a counseling center for pregnant teens. Of course with Sam, it was remotely possible he could have some business at the latter, although one hoped otherwise.

Unlike most of his recent overtures, Sam did have a valid reason to call today since Riley was conducting the seminar for his client. For that reason, at least for today, the only real question had been *when* he would call or come by, not whether he would. Surprisingly, it hadn't taken long at all. He'd barely contained himself twenty minutes from the end of the seminar before making the call.

Oddly enough, that twenty minutes correlated precisely with the amount of time it took to traverse the distance between the seminar location and Riley's office. Anyone making such an exceptionally precise estimation could only do so if they knew the route, took the time to do the math, and were willing to gamble heavily on the presumption Riley wouldn't stop anywhere else before returning to the office.

If Sam was that good at calling the odds, it was difficult to discern why he had not, at the very least, waited a few minutes longer before making the call in order to avoid the obvious appearance. Dani speculated eagerness to goad Riley about teaching a seminar at a sex toy sales center had finally gotten the better of him. That, in turn, meant Riley had already gotten under his thick, and undeniably sexy, skin. Perhaps the man wasn't completely impervious to the things that felled other humans.

"Am I just supposed to know who you are?" Dani chided.

"It's Sam, Dani. Sam Stone. We've spoken so frequently as of late I have your lovely voice committed to memory. Of course, it was unwarranted to presume you would recall mine."

Dani suppressed a chuckle. She enjoyed being Riley's gatekeeper when it came to Sam. Adulation flowed from him as naturally as molten lava when he wanted something.

"Sam…that does ring a bell. Wait, Sam Stone, right? Sure, I remember you," Dani joked. "Hey, by the way, people talk you know. So I was wondering, how'd that sheep paternity test go?"

Dani covered her mouth with her hand to choke down a laugh. She cracked herself up sometimes. This time, she wasn't the only one laughing. Sam's genuine mirth filled her earpiece and ran a full course before he responded. Dani decided he deserved a point, maybe two, for having a sense of humor. She considered throwing in another point for having a nice laugh.

"Tell me, Dani, do you talk to all of Riley's colleagues like this? I would hate to think others are missing out on your special treatment," Sam eventually replied.

"A lucky few get all the same, and more," Dani replied matter-of-factly. "If they're on the wrong side of the fence, Riley even pays me extra for it. Trash talk is free for you, though. It's my small, earnest contribution to society."

"Somehow, I am left with the impression I should be honored," Sam said. "Getting back to the business at hand, I expected to hear from Riley after the seminar."

"Under the circumstances, that would be what you'd expect, wouldn't it? Then again, when it comes to Riley, she's never going to do things the way you expect them," Dani advised.

"There's little I enjoy more than a good challenge," Sam taunted. "So, is she in?"

Dani sighed and conceded. "Yes, it so happens she is. Hold, please."

She put the call on hold and pressed the intercom button. Dani announced Sam's call with a voice dripping with sarcasm. "Dash Riprock is on Line 1 for you."

"Dash...who? Isn't that a cartoon character?" Riley inquired before making the connection. "Oh, wait. I get it. It's Sam, isn't it?"

"Dash Riprock. Sam Stone. Whatever. They're both cavemen," Dani concluded.

Dani heard Riley's snicker on the other end of the line.

"All right, tell Mr. Riprock I need to see him in person. He knows where to find me. When he gets here, send him back to my office," Riley directed.

"Wait, you mean I don't get to hear you berate him for his insolence? Not fair," Dani complained, "I always miss the good stuff."

"I'll fill you in when I'm done with him. You'll get all the details."

"Fine," Dani concluded. "But I do want *all* the details when you're *done* with him," she added, with amusement.

She cut the internal call and picked up Line 1 to speak with Sam again. "Mr. Stone, it appears Riley is busy at the moment. She will be available to meet with you in person later. You can stop by any time this evening before 6 p.m."

"Brilliant! I'm at a meeting just down the street from your office. I'll be right there."

"That's a shocker," Dani responded sarcastically. "Don't come empty-handed, though. You need to bring a peace offering if you plan to leave intact."

"I do?" Sam responded with a slight chuckle. "I take it Riley has filled you in on her day."

"That she has," Dani quipped.

"Ah. Very well, then. It will be my pleasure to heed your fair warning," Sam concluded.

Within less than ten minutes, the door chimes sounded and Dani looked up to find Sam in the office lobby. He looked, as he so often did, unbelievably handsome. His attire–a European-cut dark blue and black mélange silk sport coat worn over a French blue dress shirt left casually open just far enough at the neck to reveal a dash of tanned skin and dark chest hair–had only a small part to do with it. The rest of it was all him. If, in the vernacular of her teenage son, anything worth a whit is "stupid," then Sam Stone was just that–completely and utterly stupid.

Although her boss still scoffed at the notion, Dani was certain the reason for Sam's recent attentiveness toward Riley was nothing more than simple biology. Nature rules when an alpha male meets his female counterpart. By now, Dani was positive the persistent attentiveness of this particular alpha male was chaffing against Riley's internal struggle to maintain objectivity and distance. If he wasn't already, Sam would soon be under Riley's skin, just as she was under his.

It was against Riley's moral fiber to be predisposed for or against anyone. For that reason, Riley would never admit it to herself, but she had a type. Dani had been along for the ride during Riley's formative dating years and had witnessed the makings of a pattern. Sam met all the criteria–tall, lean but muscular, dark hair, highly intelligent and overly confident. Even if he wasn't Riley's type, no one would blame her for losing perspective around him. It was virtually impossible to spend much time in the same room with the man without being drawn in by his well-honed charms.

For Dani, the struggle was less dire. Her heart wasn't at stake. In her case, the challenge was reigning in her razor sharp tongue against a worthy adversary. Sam Stone wasn't a mindless playboy, no matter how strongly his reputation suggested otherwise. He had an edge to him that she enjoyed. Unfortunately, he also had a business relationship with Riley's firm at the moment, which meant Dani couldn't challenge him with verbal combat to the extent she might prefer, no matter how much fun it might prove to be. The most she could get away with was the occasional barb, like the one she stuck him with today.

In Dani's mind, the overly confident–men or women for that matter–are asking to be tested, and consequently put in their place if they didn't measure up to their hype. Fortunately, she happened to be blessed with the skill to do it. On first impression, Sam seemed no different from the rest, and at the time that was reason enough to unleash her sharp tongue on him. Lately, she was starting to think that might not have been warranted.

Although Sam certainly met the cocky part of her zing-worthy criteria, there was something else going on with him. Something she had, thus far, been unable to define. Whatever it was, her instincts assured her it wasn't something she needed to fear. Call it intuition or just another reading from her finely-tuned radar. She didn't think Sam was much of a threat to anything other than Riley's boring personal life. Then again, she could be wrong. Ted Bundy was known to be a real charmer.

As promised, Sam had come bearing a gift. Dani decided how he managed to procure his offering, and arrive in such a short amount of time, wasn't nearly as important as what was in the box he was holding. Sam walked casually over to Dani's desk and held the box open, allowing her to survey the contents.

"I wasn't sure which type you lovely ladies might prefer, so I got one of each," he offered with a devilish smile.

Dani stared directly into Sam's eyes with a void expression and held her poker face for as long as she could bear before snatching the box from his hands, and selecting her favorite strawberry cream cheese croissant from the mix of its lesser counterparts.

Before subtracting a huge bite she inquired, "You're trying to bribe me, so you can get close to Riley, aren't you?"

"Perhaps," Sam offered with a beguiling grin. "Is it working?"

"A little," Dani conceded. "It won't always be this easy, though. To get to the next level you're gonna need to bring a lot more than pastries."

She swallowed the last of the croissant and considered tasting another. While calculating the caloric content of the remaining options, she eyed Sam suspiciously. He had chosen the perfect bribe, almost as if he had known she was utterly famished. There was barely time for a piece of toast before she had to get the boys off to camp this morning. Then, with Riley gone all day for the seminar, she was unable to leave the office long enough for lunch.

Sam nodded. "I would expect nothing less. I'll see your boss now, if she's in."

Dani pointed toward Riley's office while she sampled a piece of a guava twist. It wasn't quite as good as the strawberry one, but it came close.

"I'll let her know you're here," Dani mumbled, between hearty bites.

She picked up the telephone receiver, pressed the intercom button with her pinky–the only finger that didn't have guava jelly on it–and advised, "Sam's here. He brought food like a good boy so I let him in, against my better judgment."

Dani gave Sam a long look from head to toe before she continued. "You did invite him, though. Remember that when you see him. And don't blame me if he manages to annoy you even more than usual."

Dani expected Riley would understand the indirect advisory. Sam brought his "A" game and was looking as good as the pastries he'd used to curry favor. When Dani set the receiver back on the cradle, Sam assumed the unspoken verdict by starting in the direction of Riley's office. Her mouth now completely full, Dani confirmed the assumption with a quick tilt of her head.

When Sam popped his head inside the open door of her office, Riley spoke first. She wanted him to know she would be leading the conversation to follow. "You'll want to close the door behind you."

Sam quietly closed the door behind him before reveling in what was intended to be foreboding. "A private, closed-door conference with the lovely Miss Morgan? Today is my lucky day."

"You may not feel lucky when I'm done with you," Riley retorted. She was still fuming. His deception was uncalled for, even if it did involve a somewhat humorous situation.

"Bollocks, Miss Morgan. Any fellow would be lucky to get a round or two with you, even if a bit worse for the wear after."

"I'm not sure how to take that, Mr. Stone," Riley responded with an air of disapproval. "Have a seat and we'll test your theory. Let's start the conversation with why you sent me to do a sexual harassment seminar for the employees of a sex toy distributor."

Sam considered a number of different angles before choosing to make his plea with feigned indignation. He took a seat in one of the chairs in front of her desk and adopted an earnest expression. "Everyone deserves legal representation, Miss Morgan. You of all people know that. That's precisely why you became a lawyer in the first place, isn't it?"

"Don't mock me, Sam. This isn't funny. The point is that you should've given me the choice of whether or not to take on the seminar and more importantly, the ability to tailor it for the audience. The type of business is relevant to the way the class is taught." Riley backed her words with a laser sharp glare.

She did have a point. Sam decided his best option might be to try an alternative strategy. This time he would go with the obvious. "I take it you don't find any humor in my client's dilemma. Honestly, Riley. Have a laugh; it's really quite funny if you think about it. How do you teach employees of a sex toy business not to talk about sex at work?"

The irony of the situation wasn't lost on Riley. Irony, however, didn't translate to amusement for her as easily as it did for Sam. He wasn't getting off the hook that easily. She responded to his inquiry with the same stern look of disapproval.

Why is this monumental jerk bothering me instead of one of his ready admirers? she questioned, while deepening the intensity of her silent stare.

The man did have a bevy of admirers. Even now, with his ridiculous puppy-dog look of contrived innocence, he could have melted most any woman into submission. His head slightly lowered, he looked up at her with deep blue-grey eyes filled with ardent professions of innocence while his strong jaw held firm to imply honorable intent.

The only thing saving Riley from the fate that befell the rest of her gender when it came to Sam was her innate distrust for handsome men. The more strikingly handsome the man, the less regard Riley held for him. She couldn't recall where or when that distrust originated. Perhaps it was a form of reverse psychology, or perhaps it was a learned response from something that happened during her formative years.

Whatever the origin, her distrust had been bolstered by real-world examples more than once. The pattern started early. Cute boys in school were always picked first for teams in gym class. Teachers let them off the hook for bad behavior, no matter how egregious. In college and law school, female professors doted on the attractive male students, while male professors tried to be their cigar-smoking buddies and female classmates took notes for them. It didn't stop there.

In the legal profession, the favoritism was even worse. Attractive men easily land clients, curry favor with judges and cajole the support staff into covering for a multitude of transgressions. From beginning to end, handsome men were given every advantage in life, and Riley had never met one who didn't exploit that advantage for everything it was worth. Sam Stone was no exception to that rule. If anything, he was the *prima facie* example of it.

It had become evident Sam wasn't going to cave to her stare down any time soon. She might as well call him out. Candor was likely not prescribed for him often enough.

"You teach them knowing the actual challenges they face. There was no reason for the deception, except that you were trying to embarrass me, Sam. It was really quite juvenile of you," Riley instructed.

Sam surmised Riley's anger to be genuine and decided to alter his approach yet again. His expression changed from one of innocence to one of regret, albeit still feigned.

"No need to be insulting, Miss Morgan. I can see you aren't able to appreciate my taking a little fun at your expense. Do let me make it up to you. Come with me to dinner tonight."

Although surprised by the request, Riley continued to stare at Sam with steely resolve. She crossed her arms in front of her body to convey she wasn't remotely receptive to the shit he was trying to shovel. "I'm not going on a date with you."

A genuine smile covered Sam's face and he laughed heartily. Riley wasn't going to be easy. That was one of the things he liked the most about her. The challenge only made the chase more interesting.

"You are exceptionally lovely, Miss Morgan, but I'm afraid you've misunderstood my intent," Sam replied. "This would be a business dinner. I'm meeting with a client tonight to discuss pending litigation. I could very much use your expertise."

"Let me guess, another one of your questionable business clients?" Riley inquired with a smirk.

"That depends on your perspective," Sam added, reflectively nodding while considering the drawbacks of affirmation. "This gentleman does own the business where you taught the seminar today, as well as other similar ones all over the world. He has amassed quite a fortune and made...an interesting name for himself, if not an entirely honorable one."

I'll bet he has. "Why couldn't you just spell it out like that before you sent me in to do the seminar? Was that really so hard?" Riley inquired, still giving no physical indication she might yield her position on the matter. She would, however, hear him out. "I'm going to give you the benefit of the doubt and presume you're being straightforward with me now. Go on."

Sam shook his head in response to the rhetorical query. He then settled back in his seat, pleased Riley was still participating in the dialogue. Others had been won over with far less in his favor.

"As you know, or have figured out by now, my client is very much in a bind given the nature of his business. It's a complicated case that requires an expert touch. No pun intended, of course."

Sam paused to confirm Riley was still on his line. It appeared she was, so he added some bait to it.

"The company pays top dollar for my firm's representation. They would pay the same for yours. I realize that money doesn't motivate you in the same way it might an attorney at a large firm. Bear in mind, the fees you could get for a case like this would go a long way toward financing a few of those pro bono cases you seem to prefer."

Sam's practical assessment was precisely what Riley had been thinking when she accepted his request to provide the training seminar. She sure as hell hadn't shared her reasons with him, which made his keen assessment all the more irritating. Who did he think he was? No one had given him permission to figure her out. She took a moment to mull over the offer while her ire subsided.

"I don't suppose there would be any harm in meeting your client. I don't have dinner plans at the moment," Riley concluded. "I need to be home before too late, though. Mason will be expecting me."

"Mason? Have you already traded in the musician for a newer model?" Sam inquired, smugly. He knew Riley was referring to her dog. Something about her stoked his schoolboy urges.

"Yes, he is definitely my *boy*," Riley affirmed. "Mason and I are quite fond of each other. I don't think he would appreciate you taking up too much of my time."

"I wouldn't dream of trifling with such an important fellow," Sam chided as he rose from his seat. "I'll have you home at a proper hour, Miss Morgan. I have a few things to attend to at the office before we go. If it suits your schedule, I'll pick you up in about an hour?"

"That would be fine," Riley responded, while surveying the mountain of books and papers on her desk. "I should be able to find my way out from under this pile by then."

Sam headed toward the door, stopping just short to sum things up. "Excellent. "It's a da–," he started, before correcting himself. "I'll see you shortly."

Within seconds of the door chimes announcing Sam's departure, Dani was in the doorway of Riley's office. Her inordinately giddy expression approximated the look one might see on the supremely intoxicated.

"Sam and Riley, sitting in a tree; they said it's not a date, but it is, real-leee," Dani crooned.

CHAPTER 5

The feeling someone is watching you through the television is not uncommon. Probably more people than not have wondered, at one time or another, if they were somehow being monitored through their boob-tube courtesy of government-sponsored reverse engineering. Most people dismiss the notion as nothing more than abject paranoia. Most people, however, are wrong.

Truth is, with modern technology, you are being watched and have been for years–not so much by the government but by those who have far greater reach. Namely, the television networks. If you think about it, it makes sense. Advertisers choose which television networks to buy air time from based on the number of viewers. That's where the money comes from, so that's where the motive lies.

To sell products during those annoying commercial breaks, networks and advertisers have to know which shows you're watching or recording, as well as which commercials you actually see and which ones you happily zoom past with modern wizardry known as "DVR." But the transmission of your viewing preferences, via the very same cables that bring you the nightly news, is only the tip of the iceberg. There's a lot more information–the kind most people expect to remain private–that can travel to and from the devices and through the wires people absently welcome into their homes.

The prophetic introspective on privacy in the digital age, or the lack thereof, running in the background of Wade Warner's fertile mind was quickly abandoned upon the start of the evening's featured presentation. Wade stared with glazed eyes into his 32-inch LED-backlit LCD computer monitor at two of the roundest and rosiest cheeks he'd ever seen. The rose-colored part of his view wasn't the afterglow of a day in the sun, and it wasn't from a chill in the air. Rose, or pink, or whatever she liked to call it, was apparently one of Halston McKinley's favorite colors. It was obviously a girl thing.

She had worn a similar color earlier today, on top and underneath. This time, unlike the typical shirt-n-skirt office attire she'd selected that morning, there was far less of it. This time, the French-cut legs of her bright pink leotard rode high and fell taut across the muscular curves of the finest ass in town. Wade paused to re-evaluate his assessment. He tilted his head to follow Halston's movement. Correction. Probably the finest ass in the state of Florida.

When Halston commenced "downward facing dog," one of the first positions in the yoga and fitness game presently running in her GigaVerse video gaming system, she turned her back toward the system's natural-user interface. That clever, wildly popular device had the enviable task of reading the movement of her body and then projecting it to the television screen. She then stretched out on the floor, face down in a prone position, before pulling her feet and hands underneath her body.

The best part came next. She thrust her rump toward the ceiling and held the pose for the required count. In that stance, her perfect ass was directly in front of the small camera lens inside the gaming system's movement-sensing device. The result, from where Wade was sitting–in his technology-laden one bedroom apartment clear across town–was breathtaking.

Wade, and a few other highly skilled hackers like him, had only recently found their way into the webcam-based peripherals that were all the rage in modern gaming systems. The hack had been made easier by the recent tendency of gamers to connect their game systems to computers instead of directly to the television. It didn't mean there wasn't a way in if the system was being used in the more traditional manner. The system could still be accessed if it was connected to a wireless network sans computer, either through the gaming device or through something as seemingly benign as an Internet-ready television. That was the electronic threshold he'd crossed tonight to spend quality time with his favorite girl.

It's commonly known, or it should be by now, that if a device is attached to the Internet, whether by wire or wireless router, there's a way in. You just have to have some basic information about the system and the owner; the latter being helpful if you encounter a password-protected gateway. You could try to brute force the password, and there is a lot of software out there to help with that challenge. Even with the right software, though, forcing a password can take a while. Whittling down the millions of possible combinations takes less time if you know where to start. Social engineering to get inside information can make password cracking a breeze. In this case, no engineering was required. The inside information had been sitting there, waiting to be taken.

Working in the same office as Halston, and having the privileges afforded to an IT professional of his caliber, had given Wade access to every piece of personal information she foolishly input into her work computer. A few transgressions against the policy prohibiting personal use of work computers had opened his first window into her world. He was now using another window, of the virtual sort, to get an even closer look.

It helped that she'd been naive enough to actually access her home computer system while at work. From one seemingly benign act on her part he'd been able to obtain her router's IP address and her remote access password. He could've gotten the same information through other sources. Fate offered him an easy in. It would have been rude not to take it.

The information fate had generously provided, along with some other juicy tidbits he surreptitiously filtered from her work computer, gave him access to pretty much every private detail of her life. From now on, he could see who she emailed or chatted with online, where she shopped, and even how much money she had in the bank. Better still, with the information he now had and a few tricks of the trade, he could actually see *her*.

I can seeeeeee you.

The horror-flick taunt echoed in Wade's ears, but it seemed more ominous when it was the catch-phrase in a movie and accompanied by a discordant soundtrack. What he was doing was harmless, for the most part. He wasn't a bad guy.

During the day, he used his skills to protect corporate America from data interlopers and digital thieves. That wasn't uncommon in the field. Many hackers just like him wore white hats to work. So what if he occasionally donned a darker chapeau after hours? That could easily be justified as continuing education. It takes one to know one.

He had stumbled on a tutorial that outlined the procedure for this particular hack while browsing online forums. The video providing step-by-step instruction had been posted online following the live presentation of "How to Hack Game Peripherals" at a recent DEFCON convention. It was a novel concept and just what he needed to up his game; in this case to games, literally.

Heh. The play on words amused him.

He had been into and come back out of almost every other type of computerized system there was without the slightest hint of detection. The thrill of being somewhere he wasn't supposed to be, and having access to things he wasn't supposed to see—the impetus that compelled most like him—had all but gone. He had considered giving it up altogether. That was a difficult bridge to cross.

Hacking was the super-power his imaginary alter ego—the one that replaced his other mild-mannered identity—used to protect himself and others from the darkness of the world beyond his computer-centric microcosm. Whenever the scales of justice needed recalibration, he could digitally invade the evildoer's lair and come out with an extracted truth to right the wrong.

Hacking had been the silent companion that entertained him during the eons of time spent alone in his room waiting for the awkward acne-prone, dental-headgear-wearing teenage years to pass. It was the friend who never left him to hang out with some vacuous sorority girl during his somewhat less dorky, although still socially-awkward, college years.

More recently, unlike many of his colleagues from work, it sat with him in the back of the bar at happy hour rather than chatting up some tipsy, improperly-attired bar wench. Metaphorically, he might even consider his preferred pastime a familiar but still-fond mistress that, in what was intended to be their parting interlude, had taken him to a dark place before leading him into the light—that light being the ceiling-mounted one presently beaming down on Halston's perfect ass.

Damn, she's fine. Too fine for someone like him. He wouldn't even be in the running if the competition to share her time had taken place in the real world. Thankfully, that wasn't the case. This was a virtual world and he "pwned" it. In this world, he had Halston to himself and they were spending an intimate evening at home, alone.

Until her phone bleeped. *No, don't get up. Nooooooo! Damn it.*

Halston rose from the floor at the command of her cell. She reached over to retrieve the phone from its resting place on the coffee table next to the sofa. She had displaced the coffee table from its normal spot when clearing the floor to make room for her yoga mat.

Despite her change in position, Halston was still within the range of the small webcam inside the gaming system interface. Wade watched her reaction as she read the incoming text. Whatever the message, it seemed to be unexpected.

After reading the message, Halston walked toward the television, pressed a button to eject the game disc from the gaming system, and then pressed another on a remote to turn off the television. Everything went black. The show was over. Or was it?

Earlier, when he'd queried Halston's IP address and then used the corresponding information to gain access to her wireless router, the system indicated she had a computer with peripherals somewhere else in the apartment. She had probably left the living room area where her game system was located and headed into another room. It was possible the computer was in the room where she had gone. It was worth a try. He wasn't ready for their evening to be over.

Tonight was their first date. Sort of. It wasn't the garden-variety "take your girl to dinner and a movie" kind of thing. Still, if you discounted the fact she wasn't aware of his presence, it was totally a date. They were spending private time together in the same place. That alone made the evening, thus far, as good as any date he'd been on lately. Yes, that's what it was—a date. Anyway, it sounded better in his head if he called it that, even if law enforcement and the general public might call it something else.

Wade typed a new command into the remote terminal he'd been using as a proxy. He often used a virtual terminal to cover his tracks when crossing into forbidden terrain. The new command took him to a domain that facilitated various hacking endeavors. From there, he used a standard exploit command to access the computer connected to Halston's wireless router.

A few seconds of poking around in the operating system was all he needed to discover the computer was a laptop. Next step, find peripherals she might have attached to it. If she had peripherals like a printer, speaker or webcam attached to the laptop they would be the weakest links in the digital chain and the easiest for him to exploit.

Wade scowled briefly at the results of his search. The only attached peripheral was a printer. No way to get a visual from there. Still, there might be another way. From the information stored on the hard drive, Wade determined the computer was a late-model laptop. That made the odds more than fair it had a built-in webcam. Wade tittered when his suspicion was confirmed. Tonight really was his lucky night.

Unlike a nanny cam or similar device that is usually stuffed up the wazoo of a fluffy teddy bear, a computer webcam was capable of a lot more than just recording static video for replay or facilitating video chats. With remote access, a peripheral webcam or even an integrated one like Halston's could be used to observe a location in real time.

It annoyed Wade, more than a little, when over-hyped television crime dramas tried to make it appear hacking a computer webcam was cutting-edge. In truth, it wasn't a new phenomenon and any ten-year-old with half-a-brain could do it. Doing it well–going in and remaining undetected–was a different story. That was part of the story not often told.

Wade located the camera's device drivers in the operating system and copied the code into the mirrored driver folder he'd created on his own virtual terminal. He then changed the settings for sharing of peripherals in her computer operating system to allow remote operation of the webcam through external drivers.

Before engaging the webcam remotely, he patched the firmware for the webcam's indicator light, the one that comes on whenever the camera is active, and then flashed it. All that meant, if put into layman's terms instead of geek-speak, was the camera indicator light had been deactivated. It couldn't signal his presence or anything else, even if it wanted to. Failing to take that extra precaution is what gets most webcam hackers in hot water. If the light isn't on, most people assume the camera isn't on. That might be a fair assumption in most cases. It wasn't universally true. It certainly wasn't going to be true a few seconds from now for Halston.

Once the drivers for the indicator light were reprogrammed, Wade engaged the webcam in Halston's laptop remotely. A few pixel adjustments later, he had a clear view of what appeared to be Halston's bedroom. He peered into her private world as if staring through a looking glass. With the exception of small areas to the far left and far right, he could see most of the room. He could see enough to know she wasn't in there right now.

Wade leaned back in his chair to consider his options. Abort or explore? He looked at his watch. It was still early and he was already there. Might as well take the time to get to know what made his new secret girlfriend tick. He changed the terminal to display the image of Halston's room full-screen. From the angle of his view, the computer appeared to be on a table of average height located beside her bed.

"Not exactly a neatnik, are you?" Wade surmised from the tousled sheets and bed cover. "No time to make the bed today?"

Pushed to one side were an abundance of those nonsensical throw pillows women love to use to clutter their beds. The pillows were various shapes and sizes, each one a different shade of her favorite color. There were enough of them to completely occupy one side of her bed; something Wade deemed to be a pretty good indicator Halston slept alone. The insight bolstered his hopes considerably.

Those hopes were marginally deflated when he noticed a photo frame on the nightstand beside the bed. There had to be some significance to the fact that the moment Halston chose to capture for all of time and display prominently within the confines of an ornate wood frame was one in which she sat comfortably on the lap of some follicly-challenged dude.

It looked like a vacation picture because the dude was wearing a bright colored polo shirt, khaki Bermuda shorts and deck shoes. His pampered skin seemed to glow in the way a sun tan lotion poster boy's might after spending too many weekends on a yacht getting rub downs from young ingénues.

It could be her father. Or he might be a sugar daddy. *Yeah, an old guy with money*, Wade reasoned. *That figures.*

Wade's momentary twinge of self-pity was doused by a wave of internal justification. He calculated the odds in his favor. One thing old dude doesn't have, and never will again, is youth. Can't buy that. It's also unlikely he's shattered the top scores on any standardized tests lately. So there's that. And old dudes need blue pills to keep up with young guys like me. Halston could get tired of waiting for the pills to get a rise out of grandpa.

Since Halston was nowhere to be seen at the moment, Wade decided to turn his focus inward. Not inward in the sense of examining his motives and present actions, but rather in the sense of looking at what was stored on the hard drive of her laptop. From the remote access terminal Wade could see Halston's computer desktop screen, and could search the contents of her hard drive as easily as he might if he were in the room with the computer.

His first thought was to conduct a quick search for any stored pictures. Sexting had replaced its antiquated predecessor, phone sex, a long time ago. Hot girls like Halston always have pics of themselves wearing lingerie or even less as part of their courting arsenal. Any guy lucky enough to get Halston's digits would surely hit her up for some private photos. Of course, the dude would swear with scout's honor to keep them private.

Yeah, right. That shit never stays private.

Bingo.

"Nice," Wade whispered appreciatively while he examined the photos from Halston's most recent vacation in Palm Beach.

There were pool and beachside shots, as well as some taken in restaurants and bars. Also in the mix were a limited number of candid photos that appeared to have been taken by someone intimately familiar. In one shot, Halston lay languidly across the bed with nothing more than a sheet covering her, and scarcely. In another she was wearing a sheer t-shirt and panties.

Most of the pictures were just of Halston. There were a couple of the restaurant and bar shots that showed her sitting quite close and comfortably with the same older dude from the picture on her nightstand. In a few of the other pictures, it looked like Halston was at a party or some fancy event with a lot of other well-heeled dudes like her sugar daddy who, in turn, were accompanied by other hot girls like Halston.

"Damn, girl! I hope that's your dad. Seriously, you can't be into geriatrics, can you?" Wade commented under his breath with mild annoyance. "I need to find out who that 'Larry King' is and why you're with him."

Wade was inclined to dismiss the old guy as a serious boyfriend. He had seen pictures of Halston's most recent boy-toy on her desk at work and had even seen the guy in real life once or twice when he came by to visit her at the office. That guy was way younger than her sugar daddy and, based on the snippet of one of their conversations Wade overheard, seemed to talk with some kind of hokey accent.

Was she still seeing that hokey-sounding guy? Maybe not. The guy certainly wasn't with her tonight, and hadn't been there for a while if the pillows on her bed were any indication. There had been murmurings between the office secretaries about a breakup. Still, a girl like Halston rebounding with a dude who looked like he was mayor of The Villages didn't make sense.

Wade copied and saved the pictures from Halston's hard drive to his computer for later viewing before moving on to stored email. Nothing too exciting there. A ton of them were snoring emails from her mother detailing the latest drama taking place behind the scenes at choir practice. Way too many others were the inspirational drivel variety, or as he liked to call them, modern-day chain mail. "SEND THIS TO FIVE FRIENDS AND YOU WILL HAVE A BLESSED DAY."

Wade exhaled briskly and shook his head with exasperation. *Why the hell hadn't she deleted those, or at least sent them to the "Spam" folder?*

Wade changed a few settings on Halston's spam filters before continuing his review of her inbox. The remaining saved emails were either from girlfriends or random dudes who were obviously hoping to be more than random.

Her email was stored by date order and, with the exception of one personal subfolder, wasn't otherwise indexed. The lone subfolder bore the vague title of "Work."

"Work? What type of work does a receptionist take home?" Wade queried skeptically.

He double-clicked on the folder, and was greeted by a standard email password request. His mouth puckered with a silent whistle that morphed into a nervous whisper.

"Got it locked up, huh? This must be the good stuff."

Wade's one-sided conversation was cut short by Halston's sudden and unexpected entrance into the bedroom. She crossed the room, picked up a remote control from the nightstand beside the bed and pointed it toward the wall directly across from the foot of the bed. A few seconds later the large flat-screen television mounted on the wall sprung to life.

Wade engaged the laptop's internal microphone so he could enjoy the show along with his date. The strident sound of reality show contestants arguing filled Halston's room, and consequently Wade's too, their braying enhanced by ceiling mounted speakers over Halston's bed.

"Nice setup," Wade concluded. "I know you can't afford a television and sound system like that on your receptionist's salary 'cause I have access to those records in HR. What else are you selling?"

Wade's testosterone-charged brain could only reach one conclusion. "Skin?"

Halston opened a door on the far side of the room across from the bed and disappeared through the threshold into what appeared to be a master bathroom. The sound of running water diluted the mordant sound of fake-reality spewing from her television. A few moments later, she returned to stand just inside the bathroom doorway facing the television as she began to undress. The form-fitting leotard she was wearing seemed unwilling to relinquish its grip on her flesh. Halston twisted from side to side to free herself from the spandex vise.

"Then again, my dear," Wade muttered, "your skin is worth whatever they're paying."

He adjusted the camera's settings to offer maximum resolution, and then appreciatively stared at the most exquisite example of the female form he'd ever seen, short of the touched-up, airbrushed versions in men's magazines. This was different, though. Halston was real and at the moment, really naked. And really, really perfect. No tan lines, no cellulite and from what he could tell, no hair...there, where his eyes were glued.

Transfixed by his virtual-world goddess, Wade failed to notice they were no longer alone. Had he been paying attention his suspicions might have been raised by the fact the intruder entering Halston's bedroom was wearing an oversized black rain slicker, in spite of the heat and absence of rain, along with black pants, similarly black rain boots, and a black ski mask.

Unfortunately, the dark figure didn't enter Wade's field of vision until it passed through the doorway where Halston had been standing. Startle shook Wade from distraction when the intruder entered the master bathroom mere seconds after Halston stepped into the shower on the far left side of the room.

"Whaaa...wait a minute!" Wade's brow furrowed heavily as his mind tried to process what he had just seen. "I know I'm not supposed to be here, but I'm pretty sure he's not supposed to be there, either."

Wade continued to stare at his screen in a state of shock, unsure whether he should continue to watch or attempt to call for help. From the location of the computer's webcam, all he could see was the hideous pink floral shower curtain that hung from a metal bar pressure fixed to the wall. Halston was somewhere behind the curtain, unaware of her ominous-looking visitor.

It was unlikely, but he had to try. Wade checked the system drivers to see if there was a way to further manipulate the camera angle so he could see the full interior of the bathroom. There wasn't.

"Worst time ever to have a fixed-focus webcam, Halston!"

The tall, darkly-clad intruder stood motionless just outside the shower curtain for what seemed like an eternity. Suddenly, with a cobra-like strike the intruder lunged forward to take hold of Halston with both arms, enshrouding her within the shower curtain. Halston appeared to have been caught off guard, her arms and legs flailing wildly as she attempted to struggle against her unknown assailant.

The intruder then pulled Halston, along with the curtain, from the shower and took her to the floor in a wrestling chokehold. With the shower curtain now pulled tightly across her face, Halston's resistance was short-lived. The intruder pinned her against the floor with a masterful grip until she stopped moving.

Now able to lessen his hold, the intruder's gloved hand disappeared into the pocket of his dark jacket and re-emerged with a hypodermic needle. The intruder plunged the sharp needle into Halston's neck and deftly emptied its contents. Halston's perfect body, the one Wade had just been so appreciatively admiring, fell limp against the floor.

The intruder left Halston, still wrapped in the shower curtain, on the floor and returned his attention to the shower long enough to turn off the water and dry the surrounding area with a bath towel. The intruder then meticulously folded the bath towel and hung it on the towel rack next to the shower.

"Oh, God! That did not look good," Wade muttered, his breath leaving him quickly. "Was that for real?"

His internal voice chose to argue for the defense.

Maybe it was some sort of kinky sex game she plays with one of her boyfriends. Or maybe they were practicing for some acting gig. Wasn't that beefcake boyfriend of hers some kind of actor wannabe?

Not wanting to sink further into the quagmire the night had become, Wade hurriedly disconnected from Halston's computer and then from the virtual gateway that had connected them. The muddled instinct of self-preservation compelled him to undo what he knew couldn't be undone. There was no way to erase the vision. He could, however, erase the data. In a bleep, the photos and email were gone.

He debated whether or not to call the police. What would he tell them?

"Sure, officer, here's what happened. I was illegally hacking into this hot chick's computer system and I saw some masked dude grab her while she was naked in the shower," Wade mocked.

His internal voice defined the fear masked by his sarcasm.

Right, you do that, and what will it get you? I'd say five to ten years in a federal prison, if you're lucky.

"It's not like I really know anything. It could've all been fake," Wade reasoned. The lie was feeble consolation. He chose to run with it.

Tomorrow. Tomorrow when Halston shows up at work and is no worse for the wear, tonight will be nothing more than a bad memory. Wade turned off his computer and settled back into his chair. After a few deep breaths, an absent nod confirmed the conclusion of his inner-struggle.

Tomorrow, it will all be fine.

CHAPTER 6

After sharing a laugh at Sam's expense, Riley let Dani take off from work early–partly because Dani had already worked more than a full eight-hour day anyway and partly because Riley wanted to touch up her makeup prior to having dinner with Sam without having to justify her reasons. Vanity played a lesser role than necessity. This was a client meeting, and Sam would be completely in his element and in perfect form, as always. Something about sharing space with that man rattled Riley's usually unshakable confidence sufficiently to warrant a bit of varnish to her façade.

With her game face perfected, Riley headed down to the parking lot to wait for Sam's return. Given the oppressive humidity, she hoped the wait wouldn't be long. Otherwise, the earlier effort would prove a waste of time and she would be greeting her nemesis with molten makeup and heat-curled hair.

Thankfully, Sam was as prompt as he was perfect. His elegant, gleaming black Bentley turned into the parking lot just as Riley stepped outside her office building. Sam pulled the coupe to a precise stop with the passenger side of the car facing Riley. He started out of the car, as a gentleman might, to open her door.

"Stay put," Riley advised. She pulled open the sleek door and slid into the soft leather bucket seat. "Since this isn't a date, you can dispense with the formalities."

"A gentleman's duties aren't tied to the occasion, Miss Morgan. I would open the door for any lady accompanying me," Sam advised. He continued with a mischievous smile. "Even if the aforementioned lady happens to be you."

"That's good to know. I really hate it when people change their behavior based on who they're with. You are who you are, regardless of the company you keep," Riley said.

The remark genuinely intrigued Sam. "Really? The notion of judging a man by his company doesn't ring for you?"

"Yes, and no," Riley replied. "You can tell a lot about someone by what or who they tend to attract. Like does tend to attract like. Who a person is, however, doesn't change as easily as friends or companions do. The company you keep is merely an example of some part of you, much the way a sniffle is a symptom of a cold. A cold is still a cold, whether or not you have the sniffles," she explained.

Sam raised a single brow while considering Riley's analysis. "Miss Morgan, are you always this complex?"

"I just told you I don't like people who change for others. So, what do you think?"

Between the time of his query, and Riley's anticipated pithy retort, he had pulled out of the parking lot and onto a side street that fed traffic onto busy Orange Avenue. Within minutes they were headed south, away from the tall downtown high-rises and toward the more industrial part of town.

Sam had expected their conversation to begin with some comment on his car—effusive or otherwise. That's how most conversations with anyone in his passenger seat usually started. Unlike her predecessors, however, Riley had launched into a complex philosophy on interpersonal associations. He quickly realized the fact that everyone else would be compelled to appreciate his car was precisely the reason Riley wouldn't. Expect the unexpected. He'd have to thank Dani for that insight.

"Touché," Sam acknowledged. "I'm very pleased to hear you don't judge a fellow by the company he keeps, given who we are about to meet."

"Sounds ominous. Who are we about to meet?"

"Vincent Mikles. He's a Florida businessman with a colorful past. You might've heard of him. If so, you'd still only have a fraction of the story."

"The name sounds familiar." Riley paused to search her memory. She snapped her fingers upon making the connection.

"I recall my father mentioning something about a very heated legal challenge to an election. I wasn't old enough to follow the specifics at the time. I think Mikles was also a named party in a seminal obscenity law case we picked apart during Con Law class."

"Ah, yes," Sam recounted, "I think most law students will remember that case long after they've forgotten everything else they encountered in school. My favorite part of the opinion is where the justices disagree on how to define the word 'nipple.' Some of my colleagues refer to the winning side of that debate as the 'too much of a good thing' defense."

A broad smile spread across Sam's face while he reflected on the humorous anecdote. Law could be fun, sometimes. "It would appear you have some notion of what Mikles is about, then?"

"I have a pretty good idea. That leads me to an important question."

"And that is?" Sam queried.

"In what degenerate underworld do you find these clients?" Riley inquired. "First, it was Giordano, now this guy. I've had my shingle out for a while. Thankfully, no one like that has come through my door."

Sam was duly impressed, in spite of the veiled insult. Riley went directly to the point, in record time. Not many people do that. Lawyers, who practically charge by the word, almost never do.

"That's a good question," he gamely acknowledged. "If it isn't my dazzling personality then I imagine it's my peerless reputation for solving complex problems. I have managed to get more than a few clients out of impossible spots, you know."

"That you have. Your reputation as being top-notch most certainly precedes you," Riley mocked.

A wicked smile crossed Sam's face. "If I didn't know better I'd say you're referring to an entirely different subject, Miss Morgan."

He then lost the smile to reflect a serious turn in the conversation. "All kidding aside, Mikles runs an international business with gross proceeds nearing a billion dollars annually. My firm is in the business of making money and to do that, you need clients who can afford to pay."

"Right, money. A necessary evil. It so often gets in the way of real justice, though, and that bothers me," Riley said.

"I've become acutely aware of that, Miss Morgan. Since we're going to be working together, it occurs to me there are likely other things I should know about you."

"I'm not sure I like where you're going with that question," Riley remarked. "What would you like to know?"

"Everything. However, we can start small," Sam offered with a sly half-smile. "Let's start with a general question. What do you do when you are not working?"

"That's an easy one. Nothing. I am almost never *not working*."

"Surely you take time off for the occasional holiday?" Sam inquired.

"I did when my father was alive," Riley offered in a diminished tone. She turned her face away and paused briefly to suppress painful emotions. "These days, I choose to keep a more practical schedule. It's easy to lose focus if you step away and fill your time with frivolity."

"Frivolity? You think taking time to enjoy life is frivolous?" Sam's affront to the notion of repressing pleasure was apparent, but not condemning. It occurred to him the sentiment had likely spilled over into her other impressions. "I suppose that explains why you seem to think so poorly of me. I do take delight in occasional frivolity."

"No surprise there. Some of the women you've been reported to accompany are ready confirmation of that," Riley quipped.

"Miss Morgan is keeping tabs on me? I'm honored," Sam teased.

"Don't flatter yourself. It's hard to miss the publicity that surrounds your 'frivolity.' The legal community isn't that large here, and you know our kind loves to talk."

Sam sent a knowing sideways glance toward Riley. "Certainly, lawyers talk, perhaps more than others. How much of what they say about anyone else do you remember?"

Riley refused to honor his apt query with a reply. As far as Sam was concerned, her silence was tantamount to confirmation.

"I think the lady doth protest too much," he concluded. "I'm growing on you. Before long you'll end up liking me."

"Fat chance," Riley shot back. "I believe it's my turn to ask a question, now."

"I'm an open book," Sam offered, knowing that to be anything but true. "What would you like to know?"

"If that's true, then be forewarned. I usually skip to the end of my books," Riley replied. She took a moment to consider her options. Framing a question of Sam's magnitude wasn't easy. So many questions surrounded him that no one seemed able to answer.

There was a plausible explanation for the lack of information, although it too wasn't widely known. Only a handful of folks, anywhere, knew Sam well. Aside from those chosen few, all anyone else would ever know of him was what they were allowed to see. The limited view most were afforded was of his carefully manufactured persona.

It had always been known, or more aptly expected, that he would follow his father into a career devoted to the protection of government interests. For most of his life, the only suppositions to his impending fate had been when, where and how. The answers, as it turned out, were then, here, and whatever it took.

His career, along with its synthetic persona, was of his own design. He'd always had an affinity for the law, and excelled in debate.

He also excelled in the more refined art of persuasion, which had proven to be mostly a blessing and only rarely a curse. When considering how to combine those unique talents into a suitable career in government service, he had factored into the equation other compelling interests which included minimal oversight and maximum opportunity for illicit encounters with the opposite sex. Add all of it up, and the sum is what he had become—a resourceful, occasionally rule-bending playboy attorney representing high-profile, immensely wealthy clients.

FBI, CIA, NSA—the acronym didn't matter. His work aided them all but was claimed by none. In practice, it went like this: clients come to him, of their own volition or because they've been steered in his direction, to confess all of the seedy, illegal and villainous things they've done. They then pay handsomely for the expectation he will save them from themselves. If the client's desired outcome corresponded with national interests, Sam assisted them by using his wide array of professional contacts, private and governmental, to resolve whatever challenge or roadblock they might face. Naturally, that type of result came with an additional cost. Clients miraculously relieved of major tax burdens, contentious consumer lawsuits or prison time were obligated, gratuitously or otherwise, to be ready assets for Sam should he need them to further the government's interest in some other matter.

Occasionally, when the government adopted a different agenda, Sam's divided loyalty required him to turn the shield of justice into a sword. In those instances, his part in the dark comedy that had become his way of life called for him to obtain physical evidence of whatever transgressions his well-heeled client would prefer remain undiscovered, and deliver said evidence to the appropriate government source, all for the greater good.

To his mind, it made perfect sense to use the widely misunderstood notion of attorney-client privilege to further national interests. The end result of that objective occasionally roused a few suspicions; none were quantifiable. He was careful.

All in all, it was a brilliant cover, and Sam enjoyed it for all it was worth, until recently. He had been trained to analyze behavior by some of the best profilers the United States government had to offer. That intense training only served to sharpen the sixth sense he had always had when it came to reading people. No one could keep a secret from him for long.

Riley, however, was one of those rare people, indeed one of only a few he had ever met, who seemingly held no secrets at all. She looked everyone straight in the eye when she spoke, hid no emotion and said exactly what she was thinking, every time. Well, almost every time. There was the small question of her purported disdain for him, which he had already determined was not an honest account of her feelings. She wasn't hiding her feelings, she simply wasn't aware of them, yet.

Sam intended to fix that. Fixing things was what he did for a living—most often for the government, occasionally for clients when it served a greater interest, and unfailingly for the few people he came to care for.

It had taken a few minutes for Riley to decide which grenade she wanted to launch first. When the choice was made, she pulled the pin and tossed it.

"All right. Do tell, Samuel Stone. Why do you keep getting married?" Riley inquired. "I know it might seem romantic at first. After you've done it once or twice, why bother?"

That wasn't the first question Sam had expected her to ask. He was quickly coming to realize Dani had spoken a great truth. Riley wasn't going to do things as might be expected.

"You're not a fan of marriage, I take it? I might've guessed. You're an over-achiever. If you wanted a husband, you'd have one by now," Sam opined, with a nod to confirm his own assessment. "Not everyone is a cynic, though. I could be a hopeless romantic who believes each time that I've found my soul mate. Or maybe I just enjoy the company of women."

"Bull. On both accounts," Riley protested. "You're about as romantic as my dog. Of course, you enjoy the company of women. You don't have to marry them for it. This isn't the 1950s. There's got to be another reason."

Sam couldn't genuinely deny the accuracy of Riley's assessment. Unfortunately, what kept him from telling her the truth wasn't going to change any time soon.

"Your objection is overruled," he teased, knowing it would only fuel the fire. "You asked a question, so now it's my turn again."

"No, I gave you a straight answer, and I expect to get one in return. Otherwise, I'm not playing your silly game anymore."

"It's like that, is it?" Sam goaded.

"Oh yes, it's like that," Riley declared. She added a talk-to-the-hand gesture for emphasis. "You know, if everything you do is one-sided, you're only going to get what you give thrown back at you."

"Now who's being one-sided?"

"Me one-sided? That makes exactly no sense at all," Riley challenged.

"It seems pretty one-sided to choose not to participate in something simply because things didn't go to your liking. Is that any way to be a team player?" Sam inquired.

Sparring with her was turning out to be even more fun than he had expected. That was a pretty good indicator everything else would be likewise.

"It is, if I'm not on your team," Riley shot back.

She had a point. "Fine," Sam conceded, "we can play with each other another time."

Riley was cognitively fuming. Sam Stone was officially the most infuriating specimen of his gender she had ever encountered. She turned her frustration toward the passenger window and stared out into the darkness.

Traffic was light now that the evening rush had subsided and they were in a more remote part of town. For a few miles, the only visible signs of civilization they encountered were scant street lights that faintly pierced the darkness along the side of the road. In the absence of conversation, the eerie quiet and sense of isolation that settled in were almost as uncomfortable for Riley as the company was insufferable.

A sly smile crossed her face almost as quickly as Sam had brought a frown to it. If she couldn't escape it, she might as well join the effort to annoy.

"Are we there yet?" she inquired, in a droll voice.

"Not just yet," Sam advised.

Riley allowed a few minutes to pass, before starting the next round. "How about now?"

Sam chuckled. "You think you're funny, don't you?"

"Maybe. Or maybe I just want to be rid of you as soon as possible," Riley said.

"Does this mean we're talking now?"

"No."

"All right. Even so, perhaps you'll allow me to offer a compliment on the beautiful watch you're wearing," Sam said, completely ignoring her rebuke. He was drawing her back in, whether she wanted to be back in or not.

Riley glanced down at the vintage art deco style watch adorning her left wrist. The small, intricate face was cased in pink-toned gold, and surrounded by small round diamonds. The band, made of black silk, was wound through openings on each end of the case and secured at various stations by pink gold clamps that matched the case and delicate folding clasp. It was, by any measure, her favorite timepiece and she wore it often, even though it rarely kept accurate time—a forgivable flaw largely due to the fact she seldom remembered to wind it.

An unknown reflex caused Riley to cover her wrist. "What does my watch have to do with whether or not we're talking?"

"Nothing. I just noticed it when you were waiving your hand in my face a minute ago," Sam answered. "It's very elegant and old-fashioned. Not something I see every day."

Riley turned the watch around on her wrist to view the face. As usual, the hands were still. She spun the dial a couple of times to resuscitate the movement and then reset the time. She spent a few more seconds toying with the clasp, without cause, before responding.

"It's from the late '40s. It was a wedding gift from my grandfather to my grandmother. I used to sneak into her jewelry box when I was little just to get a look at it," Riley recalled fondly. "She gave it to me when I went off to law school as a reminder of the value of my time."

Sam smiled, reflecting on his achievement. He had gotten her to open up, and on something quite personal, with little more than a wisely-placed compliment.

Riley, in stark contrast, was none too pleased Sam had managed to pry something so private out of her. Sticking to lighthearted banter seemed the safer choice until she could figure out what angle he was playing. She raised her wrist high and toward the faint light coming in from the street lights while continuing to fidget with her watch.

"Unfortunately, I can feel the value of my time slipping away tonight with every mile," she added. "I suppose that brings us full circle."

"That circle being...where?" Sam inquired.

"You tell me. You're driving," Riley taunted, hoping to daze him with a quick jab, before landing her next punch.

"I'm not the one making obtuse spherical references," Sam fired back.

"Is that so? Seems to me you've driven in nothing but circles tonight, in both direction and reasoning. So, let me finish this one for you," Riley offered. "You never answered my question."

"We're returning to that, are we?" Sam said. "I absolutely did answer, just not in the way you wanted."

"I'm not talking about the marriage question, Sam."

"Very well, then. Seems I've become lost in your maze of derision," Sam conceded, still enjoying whatever game it was they were playing. "Ask me again. Maybe I'll answer correctly this time."

Riley stared at him through slivers, her arms crossed in front of her like an insolent child. The look suited the moment. "Fine. I'll refresh your recollection and speak slowly, so you can follow along. Are. . .we. . .there. . .yet?"

Sam nodded in affirmation. "As a matter of fact, petal, we are."

CHAPTER 7

Sam turned his Bentley coupe into a sprawling parking lot in front of a two-story, stucco-faced building and pulled into one of the few spaces still open. He quieted the engine and started out of the car while Riley briefly scanned the crowd.

By the look of it, wherever it was Sam had chosen for tonight's meeting, most of Orlando's male populace planned to join them there. The line of male patrons standing behind a rope hoping for permission to enter the building stretched around the front and down the far side of it. Given the proximity to the dinner hour, it was possible they were simply there to break bread. Unless they all intended to dine without dates, however, Riley deemed it unlikely. Something far more enticing than steak was to be served at this location tonight.

Riley leaned forward and strained her neck to peer out of the front windshield at the flashing neon signs on the building before them. The signs were mounted against a tall black panel that extended the full height of the two story building and then some. The dark background was a perfect milieu for the illuminated art, allowing it to shine even in the extended daylight of a summer night.

The most prominent of the signs was an animated version of a scantily clad female straddling a flag pole. The sequencing of the lights made it appear she was moving up and down the pole—or as

Dani might say, "humping" it. At the top of the pole, red, white and blue lights patterned after a United States flag intermittently twinkled and faded, which made the electronic pennant appear to be waiving valiantly. Another sign intermittently flashed the words "Super Tuesday" and "Extended Dinner Show."

"Oh, good Lord," Riley whispered, "what have I gotten myself into?"

Sam, having made it around to her side of the car, was ready with both a response and an open door. "You were in such a hurry before. Now you don't seem to want to come along," he teased. "Don't worry, they won't ask you to dance."

Sam was standing beside the open car door and directly in front of Riley, with his right arm extended to hold the door open. As she rose from the car seat, Riley shot a stern look up at Sam to advise his feeble attempt at humor had failed. Once standing, with her feet firmly planted on the ground, she faced him.

She had expected him to take a step back as she rose from the car. Quite intentionally, he did not. As a result, Riley found herself standing dangerously close to someone she had not welcomed to join her personal space. Both held their ground, face-to-face and dead-locked, neither intending to blink.

Riley was aware Sam was trying to unnerve her with the maneuver. She found his resort to something as trite and overplayed as the "hover" surprising. Did he really think close proximity would cause her heart to flutter?

Sam was at least six inches taller than Riley, despite her heels. That gave him the height advantage, not the overall advantage. If his latest move, or more aptly refusal to move, was indicative of his hand, he didn't have the winning one. Calling his bluff by raising the stakes would be easy enough.

First step, turn up the heat. She moved in slightly closer, reached up to straighten his collar, and then tugged on it to pull his face down to hers.

Second step, light a fire. "Are we going to stand out here all night, or are we going to get on with this?" Riley whispered, moving her lips ever closer to his as she spoke.

Third step, pour a bucket of ice on it.

Once it was clear she had drawn and held Sam's full attention, Riley released his collar and gave a soft push against his shoulders. Her unexpected advance took him by surprise. He was engaged by her vexing just long enough to be set off balance, sufficiently so that he had to take a step backwards to regain sure footing.

When Sam stepped back, Riley moved forward into his space before brushing past him, allowing her chest to brush against his. She paused in her brisk pace toward the door only long enough to verbalize a taunt. "You coming?"

Sam, now grinning broadly, responded in the forced tone of a hen-pecked husband. "Yes, dear, I'm right behind you."

Although already a few steps ahead, Riley heard the car door close and the car's expensive alarm system engage. The sound of Sam's quick footsteps followed as he hastened to shorten her lead. He caught up with her in a few strides and then kept pace as she walked; something that might have annoyed her had it not turned out to be fortunate.

Like most parking lots in the area this one was paved with black tar, but not the smooth sort. Small rocks had been blended into the tar to improve traction and reduce wear. There were also a few not-so-small rocks that had somehow managed to make it into the blend, one of which caused Riley to turn her ankle.

Riley's thoughts coincided with her knee, following her ankle's lead, starting to buckle. *What the hell? These are my sensible shoes.*

The abrupt change in Riley's pace caused Sam's quick instincts to trigger. He deftly circled his arm around Riley's waist to balance her. "Already tipsy and we've not even made it to the bar. I like that in a date."

"This isn't a date," Riley said. "And the fact you prefer your women off-balance goes without saying."

Riley regained her posture and pushed away from Sam to get a look at the heel of her shoe. She was wearing a new pair of Tod's dark grey patent pumps. They had cost a small fortune, but were of the style and quality assured to last a lifetime. She wouldn't have splurged on them otherwise. Thankfully, the shoe was unscathed, even if her ego wasn't.

"I believe what you meant to say was 'thank you,'" Sam offered with a chuckle. "I know how important your shoes are to you."

They walked in silence a few paces before he continued speaking his thoughts. "While we're conversing on your attire—,"

"Excuse me? There was no conversing going on, and most certainly not about my attire," Riley shot back.

"I'm certain there was. Here's the thing. You look exceptionally lovely, as always. I expect that will be to our advantage when we tell Mikles another attorney has been added to his bill. To ensure he's adequately distracted, however, you might consider loosening a few buttons."

Riley stopped and looked down at her charcoal and copper tweed jacket. It was a go-to piece, mostly because it was fitted at the waist and had short cap-style sleeves. The former being more flattering for a girl with curves, like herself, than the boxy style of most professional suit jackets; the latter necessary to retain some measure of comfort in the heat. The sleeves and soft middle-weight fabric made it perfect for long days of vacillating between the outdoor heat of a Florida summer and the hyper-cooled air of most business offices.

The jacket had paired nicely with the matching off-black fitted skirt that had just enough Lycra in the lightweight wool weave to allow for ease of movement. She had chosen to wear the jacket for today's seminar session because it was a softer style than many of her business suits. The last thing you need when trying to get a buy-in from bored seminar attendees is to come across as stiff.

Beneath her jacket, she wore a soft, black silk tank with buttons extending halfway down the front. The tank had a long scarf-like tie at the nape she'd chosen to wear loosely knotted just below the collarbone. She preferred tying the scarf just tightly enough for it to fall below the last button she had chosen to fasten. Unbuttoning even one more button would expose a lot more cleavage than she would consider appropriate for any ordinary client meeting. That alone was reason enough not to comply with Sam's request. The far greater reason was the fact it was *Sam's* request.

Riley hastened her walk toward the building with determination. "Not going to happen. Feel free to unbutton your shirt, if you'd like."

Sam shook his head. "Can't do that, here. I wouldn't want to be responsible for you getting trampled by the dancers and waitresses. If you ask later, when we're alone, I might."

"I'll take that under advisement," Riley mocked.

Sam quickened his pace and stepped before Riley as they approached the entrance of the building. There were no windows or openings of any kind at the front of the bar, with the exception of two heavy, solid-wood double doors. The entryway was lit only by the red, white and blue neon signs that were affixed to the exterior wall adjacent to the door, and a single flush-mount overhead light mounted to the ceiling over the door.

Sam moved to the right to open one of the doors, and held it open for Riley to enter. "Ladies first, as always."

Riley gave him a wary sideways glance as she passed him on the way into the building. Sam returned her gaze, winked, and then followed closely behind her. She might have surprised him with her earlier advance, but as far as he was concerned, tonight's game was far from over.

They were greeted inside the entryway by a hostess standing behind an ornate carved-wood hostess station crowned with a translucent golden onyx countertop. The mixture of natural gold, ivory and green swirls in the countertop was enhanced by intense white backlighting. Although the hostess was partially shielded behind the high counter, her waist and shoulders were visible. The silvery sequined tank top she wore reflected the radiant golden light from the counter onto her face and highly-exposed bosom. The reflection of light surrounded her with an otherworldly aura that was complimentary to her olive complexion and luminescent blonde hair.

Riley surmised the intent of the lighting was to provide the customer, upon first impression, the vision of an ethereal young angel who just happened to be moonlighting on the dark side. The notion was likely borrowed from those oddly-timed television commercials where scantily clad models traipse around in underwear pretending to be heavenly creatures who've decided, since heaven apparently provides limited career choices, to hawk panties.

Enveloped by the darkness a few feet behind the unnaturally illuminated hostess was a man wearing dark clothing. Because the light emanating from the counter drew all attention toward the hostess, the man standing in her shadow was barely visible. He would scarcely be noticed by anyone entering the bar if they were not paying close attention to their surroundings. It appeared both his location and dark clothing might have been chosen for just that reason.

Occasionally, when the hostess moved to the left or right, a hint of light refracted from the man's muscular arms, exposed by the short sleeves of his dark, polo-style shirt. The light didn't travel far enough north to illuminate more than the outline of his face. Where it found him elsewhere, the colorful tattoos decorating his arms left it little room to play.

Riley might not have noticed the man at all, if a sudden movement of his right arm hadn't caught her eye. She strained her eyes to gain focus. From the whispers of light that intermittently escaped, she could tell the man was of average height; possibly just less than six feet tall if Sam's six-foot-three frame were any measure. He appeared to have little or no hair, or possibly it was shaved, as there was nothing to obstruct the lines of his angular jaw and prominent nose.

The man stood fixed in place and nearly motionless, far longer than customary, with a formal bearing seemingly misplaced for the venue. Riley surmised his rigid posture might be a remnant of the past, instilled during military service or a stint in law enforcement.

She couldn't be certain in the darkness but from the angle of his jaw, it appeared the man was looking directly at Sam.

"Sam Stone," Sam announced with authority to the hostess. His deep voice rose slightly to overcome the loud music reverberating from somewhere deeper inside the building. "This is my plus-one. We've got a table reserved. Tell Vince we're here."

The hostess looked welcomingly at Sam, as women often did, and nodded her assent to his command. "Of course, Mr. Stone. Welcome back. It's nice to see you, again. Follow me."

She motioned for them to come along as she turned and walked into the main seating area. The silvery sequins of her short mini-skirt matched those on her top, and somehow managed to pull a dazzling reflection of light from the dimly lit room when she moved. Riley dealt a glimpse to Sam and discovered, as expected, his eyes trained on the hostess specifically to an area just below her waist.

"Come here often?" Riley quipped, while they weaved through a maze of tables. *Of course he does,* her inner voice responded.

Sam's smile was cryptic. He was enjoying the fact Riley was more than a little annoyed by what she perceived of him. Her unwitting bias, undoubtedly a defense mechanism, was a humanizing revelation. She was one to talk. She intentionally played upon her attributes to distract her opponents, and had done so quite successfully against his client when they sat on opposing sides of the table.

"As duty calls, my dear," Sam responded. "Does that alarm you?"

"Not really, nor does it surprise me."

"I don't know why you have such disdain for this place," he chided. "It's got really great food. It makes the 'Best of Orlando' list regularly."

"I'm sure it's on a lot of lists, none of which I consult," Riley retorted.

The hostess led them to a U-shaped booth in the back of the venue partly divided from the main seating area by floor-to-ceiling partitions. Thick hides of dark red, hand-tooled leather adorned the center panels of the tall shoji-style dividers. The filigree swirls carved into the leather upholstery were randomly filled with burnished gold paint. The metallic paint eased the otherwise heavy appearance of the partitions by adding colorful reflections of the surrounding ambient light.

The booth reserved for Riley and Sam had deep cushions upholstered in dark red diamond-shaped, button-tucked velvet; its smooth leather seats a shade lighter. Similar U-shaped booths were behind the other two or three groups of partitions in the area, all with two sides joining high backs that sat flush against the wall facing the center stage. The upholstery for each booth and its corresponding leather partitions varied between deep-hued jewel tones of red, blue and green.

The dense screens provided a healthy measure of sound proofing for the area. When behind the partitions, Riley noticed the music was barely audible, relegated to vibrations of bass. Those enjoying the show from this vantage point were not observable to other patrons, although the main stage and performers were still visible to them. The area was clearly designed for conversations, or as in this case, business meetings.

"You've got one of the best seats in the house," the hostess advised, with a glowing smile intended only for Sam. "Your drinks have been ordered, and the voting proctor for your precinct will be by to take your ballot momentarily."

She left menus, not surprisingly entitled "Sample Ballots" on the table in front of them before departing to attend to other guests.

Riley shot a heated look at Sam. "What drinks? I didn't order anything. Even if I had, why would we need a 'proctor' for them?"

"Are you sure? Maybe you did order and don't recall. You've had a challenging day," Sam taunted.

Sam sat down on one side of the U-shaped booth and slid along the leather seat until he reached the center section that allowed him to sit with his back against the wall. From this position, he had cover as well as a view of the room, the stage and most of the first floor exits.

"I guess we'll see when the drinks come," he continued. "While we're waiting, why don't you budge up over here and sit next to me?"

"I'm not budging at all, when it comes to you," Riley retorted hotly as she took a seat on the left side of the booth.

In this spot, she was facing the right partition, and had limited view into the club or of her surroundings. Normally, she would have preferred to sit exactly where Sam was sitting. There was a tactical advantage to having all areas of approach in your line of sight and Riley preferred to have that advantage. In her present location, however, she was able to find solace in the fact the essentially naked dancers on the stage weren't clouding her vision.

"Have it your way. Although, it will be hard for you to talk to our client from there. It might also be perceived as impolite for you not to face him," Sam said.

"Here's a novel idea," Riley responded dryly, "and one I'm sure you haven't considered. What if you budged up and sat where I chose?"

"If you insist, Miss Morgan," Sam replied.

He slid to the side just enough to approach Riley's location on the left return of the booth before rising halfway and then planting himself uncomfortably close to her. Once settled in, he reached over to collect the menu that had been sitting in front of him and turned to face Riley to make an assessment.

"This is cozy," Sam said. "Still, we both know this isn't really where you want to sit."

Riley met Sam's arrogant gaze and held it. Her inner voice spoke loudly to be heard above the music; so much so she feared it might have been audible. *I hate you, Sam Stone.*

Before she could turn those thoughts into slightly less dramatic words, a clothing-challenged proctor arrived with a tray of drinks.

"Here you go, folks," the young girl advised, her attention directed exclusively to Sam.

Sam's focus, in turn, appeared to be happily set upon her getup, which consisted of a black push-up bra and a matching miniscule pair of silk tap pants over black fishnet stockings. The girl smiled know-ingly at Sam and carefully bent over the table in front of him, baring the ample swells of her breasts dangerously close to his face when she placed a drink before Riley.

"This is for yewwww, ma'am," she drawled.

Riley looked up at her with inquiring eyes. "What is it?"

"It's a Stone Sour. We fixed it special using fresh ingredients in-stead of a mix. The apricot brandy in it is super-expensive, but only the best for Sam. And his friends, of course," the proctor advised, her tone cooling with each word wasted on Riley.

The proctor's disposition improved when she brushed past Sam again to return her attention to the tray of drinks. She retrieved a shot glass and a highball glass both bearing some form of clear liquid, and placed both before him.

"This one's for yeewww, handsome. When you're ready for another, just give me a tweak," she teased.

The proctor a.k.a. waitress finished attending to Sam and made her way back toward the bar. Once the proctor was out of range, Riley carefully lifted her glass and took a sip. She had waited out of respect. It wasn't fair to the server for it to appear she had somehow made a mistake by bringing a beverage her customer did not seem to enjoy. That fault was Sam's alone.

"So, *ma'am*," Sam taunted, "how is it?"

"It doesn't suck," Riley retorted. "And don't call me *ma'am*."

Her words did not reflect her thoughts. The drink was actually quite good and probably exactly what she would have ordered, if she had known such a thing existed. She was fairly certain she was annoyed, or perturbed, or something. The precise level of her aggra-vation was unclear mostly because while Sam wasn't wrong about her preferences, his effrontery was starting to get on her nerves. She wanted to slap him, but decided he might enjoy that too much.

Her internal fire still stoked, she looked over at Sam and nodded in the direction of the beverages sitting before him. "What are you drinking?"

A broad smile spread across Sam's face. One of his many off-campus pursuits while attending Oxford was the art of mixology. It remained a favorite pastime.

"This is a combination of my own conception," Sam said. He pointed to the shot glass first. "On this side, we have a shot of tequila, Patrón to be precise. The other part is a straight mix of vodka and lime soda. It's a clever little pairing I like to call a Mexican Pole Dancer."

Riley's eyes moved upward to follow the curl of her upper lip. "Naturally. Who wouldn't call it that?"

Sam grinned wickedly. "Bear in mind where we are, my dear. When it Rome. Normally, I would pour bourbon at the end of a busy day. Since this is business, I thought it best to keep things light."

Sam picked up the shot glass and tapped it against Riley's glass. "Here's to new colleagues and friends."

He turned to Riley and held a purposeful stare directly into her eyes before he pressed the shot glass to his lips and drew in the contents. He held the tequila in his mouth only long enough to fully comprehend its flavor. It was strong-willed, full-bodied, and filled with richly complicated undertones. It also carried a distinct burn, but not enough to deter his focus. At the moment, two of his senses were sharing in a similar experience.

His eyes left Riley's and moved downward toward a point of interest slightly to the south. He fixed on her full lips before swallowing the intoxicating elixir, hard. When the last of the liquid's burn left him, he looked back up to meet Riley's eyes with a smoldering gaze.

None of what he was thinking required words. Riley felt her cheeks warm and instinctively turned away from the source of the heat. She grabbed her purse and rustled nervously through the contents as if searching for something relevant. The ruse did nothing to diminish the burn. She could still feel Sam's gaze bearing down on her which caused the flush to spread beyond her cheeks. As if by divine intervention, the silent heat between them was redirected when Sam's sport coat started to buzz.

Sam pulled his cell phone from his pocket and stared intently at the display. A slight scowl crossed his face.

"I'd better take this. I'll be right back," he commented with a hint of apology. He pressed a button on the phone and barked into it, "Hold on, I'm in the middle of something."

Sam rose from his seat and headed in the direction of the entrance. He stepped outside of the building and looked around cautiously before he responded to the caller. Kent Donovan, his longtime friend and current partner in fighting crime, had a knack for calling at the most inopportune moments.

"Special Agent Donovan. Got to hand it to you. You landed one helluva cushy gig this go-round. Are you still hiding behind that cute hostess?"

"No, jackass. I'm on my break. Told one of the cleaning girls I needed to make a private call. Got her to let me into an office in the back," Kent advised. "Word is Mikles keeps some kind of files locked up back here like gold in Fort Knox. Thought I'd check it out while I checked on your lame ass. They call that multitasking, I believe. You should try it, sometime."

"I invented multitasking and trained the guy that taught you, Donovan," Sam quipped.

"The only thing I've learned from you is what not to do on an assignment," Kent shot back.

"Someone who hasn't mastered the art might think that the lesson," Sam replied. "What type of files are we talking about? I wasn't directed to bring in anything specific."

"If I knew that, I'd know where to look. That would be waaaay too easy," Kent chided. "By the way, your screwing around with Riley in there is pretty damn obvious."

"Right. What I'm doing is obvious. As if you can see everything that's going on in the back of the club while you're tossing inebriated customers out the front of it," Sam countered.

Instinctively, as a bird might to misdirect another giving chase, Sam changed course. "How long have you been inside on this one? I didn't see you the last time I was here."

Kent didn't miss the breakneck turn. "Long enough to know you're going to fuck this up if you aren't careful. This isn't somewhere Riley should be. These people wouldn't think twice about putting a pretty girl like her on a boat chartered to a place where she'd never be found."

"Yeah, well, I've been on this one a while. I know what we're up against and I know what I'm doing. Riley's safe with me. I need her on the case."

"Bullshit! You're hoping she'll distract Mikles long enough for you to seduce one of his girls into switching sides to do your job for you. I know you, Sam. Riley's anything *but* safe when it comes to you. I've got the inside covered. Would it kill you to let me work the female angle for once?"

"Yes, it would. Women like me better," Sam contended. "You're too uptight."

"*Girls* like you better," Kent readily shot back. "You've never had a woman."

"How long of a break do you get, anyway? Don't you have work to do?"

"I'm only going to say it once more: Keep Riley out of this. We don't need high-profile collateral damage," Kent warned.

CHAPTER 8

S am stood in the parking lot to check a few messages on his phone before heading back into the club. By the time Sam re-entered the building, Kent had returned to his nearly invisible post behind the hostess. Sam tapped on the counter and waived at the hostess as he passed by.

"Headed back to my table," Sam advised, after considering and then abandoning the temptation, while still in Kent's audible range, to say something about the bouncer having let in some riff-raff.

Sam reached the booth where he and Riley had been seated just behind Vincent Mikles, who had already started to unleash his rough-hewn brand of charm on Sam's companion.

"What kinda idiot leaves a lovely lady like this unattended?" Vince inquired, in a louder-than-necessary tone that benefitted from his unique accent—a remnant from his misspent youth on the streets of Chicago. He didn't wait for an answer, but instead followed the greeting with a hand extended in Riley's direction. The question was rhetorical, since he had seen Sam's approach from behind through the reflections in mirrors mounted on the wall above the booth.

"That's a fair question," Riley surmised, with a welcoming smile. She rose to greet Vince and shook his extended hand. "Riley Morgan. It's a pleasure to meet you. The answer to your question is Sam Stone. I believe you two know each other well."

Riley returned to her seat and invited Vince to join her with a nod toward the opposing side of the booth. Vince moved into the seat facing Riley to continue their conversation.

"The business has had its share of setbacks lately. Sam has managed to turn 'em around for us, so far," Vince admitted. "Doubt I've seen all our boy's tricks, though. He's obviously got a few he's using to keep company with the likes of you."

Riley was surprised to find Vincent Mikles somewhat affable, both in appearance and demeanor. She had expected him to be smarmy and imposing, given his reputation and line of work. He was decidedly neither.

His dark brown hair had started to recede. Where it still held ground, it was thick, and full of unruly curls. The long, dense sideburns he wore bore a bit of nostalgia, reminiscent of a look that might be worn by a man's man from the 1970s. Still, aside from the facial-hair flashback, the impression he left was modern.

Vince was tall, like Sam; that being the only real similarity between the two. Mikles had a much thicker build. Where Sam had an athletic, lean frame, Vince was built more like a mastiff. His imposing size wasn't the only thing he had going for him. He also had the air and confidence of someone who had managed to be successful at turning whatever shit life offered into something more marketable. That air was further supported by his impeccable and expensive-looking outfit, most likely an upgrade from the usual in honor of the evening's special event.

With a sense of style and panache similar to Sam's business-casual look, Vince had paired the elegant dark grey herringbone tweed sport jacket he wore with grey dress pants. The collar of his luxurious pale green silk shirt was left open at the neck, allowing the thick yellow gold Figaro link chain he wore to announce itself when he moved. In this garb, he could easily have been mistaken for any of the trendy, upbeat sales professionals Riley often encountered at local chamber of commerce meetings.

Experience, or perhaps instinct, had stopped Riley's assessment from ending there. It took her a minute or two of close and insightful observation to find the hint of trouble presently dormant behind Mikles' calm, inviting persona. Behind the engaging, fern green eyes, currently twinkling with boyish mischief, was a man completely in the know. Vincent Mikles was a hunter, never the hunted. Not much escaped his sharp appraisal.

Mikles was the kind of person who could easily say in your presence what you wanted to hear, and do so in such a way that left no reasonable doubt of his conviction, only to turn and strike viciously the moment he was safely behind you. He was not a man to be taken lightly. Those who made that mistake made it once, and were probably not around to warn others of their oversight. On that account, Riley made a mental note.

During the exchange of pleasantries, Sam casually slipped into the seat next to Riley. His confidence was bolstered considerably by what he observed thus far. Vince's eyes had scarcely moved from Riley, and he had only vaguely acknowledged Sam's presence. This could work.

"You're right. I was foolishly putting my clients first. I've come to my senses now," Sam quipped. "Good to see you, Vince. From the looks of things, business is good."

"Excellent. Even in this dog-piss economy. The colder the markets get on the outside, the hotter it gets in here," Vince responded. Upon the recollection he was in mixed company, Vince attempted to self-edit. "Pardon the French, of course. It's a good business, though, giving the people what they want."

"You certainly excel at gearing the product to your market. The food is excellent and your entertainers are…," Sam paused to give additional emphasis to his word choice, *"well-qualified."*

The men both smiled broadly and nodded in unison at Sam's assessment. Riley looked away so her companions, both of whom were presently demonstrating high levels of cultural regression, wouldn't witness a frustrated eye roll. *Men.*

"As you might expect, the lawyering business, at least for litigators, also improves when the economy is tough," Sam said, following the men's shared guffaw. "More people choose to fight over what little profit there is to go around. That's one of the reasons we've got a loaded trial calendar this summer at the firm. Fortunately, Riley has graciously agreed to help us out on a few matters. I'm sure you'll be pleased that one of them is yours."

Sam gestured at Riley as he continued the introduction. "Riley's the attorney I told you about when we spoke the other day. She's got a great deal of experience in employment law, specifically in sexual harassment cases, and was kind enough to assist us with today's training for the staff at one of your online, um…marketplaces. I think she'll be an excellent addition to the trial team, as well."

Mikles sucked in his cheeks and pursed his lips; a look that implied disapproval. "Yeah, I heard about that. The crew said you were good and they learned a bunch. They also said something about you not liking the way things are decorated over there."

His expression changed again aided by a taunting half-smile that mirrored the amusement in his eyes. "Say it ain't so. Surely a guy can't go wrong hanging a masterpiece on the wall."

Sam felt the heat rise under his collar. There was a high probability Riley was still sensitive about the humor he'd taken at her expense. If she were, this would be an opportune moment for her to get even, and that would undoubtedly damage his position with Mikles. Perhaps Kent was right and he had carried the novelty of the situation a bit too far this time. Hoping to implore Riley's continued goodwill, Sam reached under the table and gently grasped her arm. Riley quickly brushed him away.

"I'm not going to lie to you, Mr. Mikles," Riley started in the calm, professional tone she often used when advising clients in routine matters, although this was anything but routine. "That type of painting isn't something you could get away with in most workplaces. Of course, I realize your business is somewhat different. Still, it probably wouldn't hurt your bottom-line to keep such works of beauty tucked away somewhere for your own enjoyment. Like Sam said, the economy is tough and that means people are looking to fill in spaces where their paychecks no longer fit."

Riley met Mikles' surprised eyes dead on and held her gaze steady. To convey the friendly intent of her advice, she added a pleasant smile. The man wasn't used to women speaking to him as a peer. While trying to decide whether or not he liked being spoken to in that way, Mikles stared blankly back at Riley. The conclusion that he didn't mind, at least this once, was made evident by the wide grin that subsequently crossed his face.

"I like this one, Stone. She's smart and she's got brass."

"I tend to agree," Sam chimed. "Why don't you join us for a drink to welcome her to the team?"

"I'd love to but I got some things to attend to in the back," Vince replied. "They don't make it easy to run a business in this country. I've gotta file reports about the reports I filed on my reports, and pay a fee to file the lot of 'em. Someone oughta sue the damn government for that kinda bullshit."

"I suspect someone has," Riley answered. "Probably not successfully, though. The government plays by its own rules most of the time. Sam's firm does have a corporate division. Perhaps they could save some of your valuable time by preparing your reports for you."

Vince surveyed Riley with genuine regard. "Ah, nah, these we gotta do in house. But hey," he added tapping Sam on the shoulder as he rose from the booth, "the little lady's already working on more business for you. How'd that fancy firm of yours miss out on her?"

Sam laughed. "She won't have us. I'm lucky to have her on this project. Miss Morgan's a bit of a maverick. Likes to drive her own car, so to speak."

Sam rose to shake hands with Vince. "We've got depositions starting next week. I'll get Riley up to speed and let you know the schedule once it's solid."

"You do that," Vince added, pointing an index finger toward Sam in affirmation before turning to face Riley. "Pleasure meetin' you, Miss Morgan. I'll stick around and chat next time."

"Thank you, Mr. Mikles. It was a pleasure meeting you, as well." Riley said.

"Oh, and dinner's on me," Vince directed to Sam. "You two should stay for tonight's show. It's a doozy."

Vince stopped his departure briefly to speak with their waitress who had just returned to check on them. After that, he disappeared behind the curtains surrounding the back side of the center stage.

Anticipating the question their waitress would ask upon reaching the table, Sam slid back into his seat and turned to Riley to inquire, "You hungry?"

Riley glanced down at her watch. "Not yet. I don't usually get away from the office this early in the evening."

"Take a look at the menu, anyway," Sam requested. "Making sure you're well-fed is the least I can do for pulling you out into the night."

"For the record, your client said dinner was on him. That means you aren't buying it or feeding me in any way," Riley corrected.

"I wouldn't dream of it," Sam said. "So, we're ordering?"

"Any other time, accepting a gift from someone like Mikles might concern me. After the day I've had, I think you both owe me," Riley advised. "If we can get it to go, I'm game."

"Have you decided what you'd like?" the waitress inquired when she reached the table, her timing impeccable.

She picked up their menus from the table as she spoke, assuming they were no longer required. Riley wasn't sure if the act was an unconscious reflection of the young woman's familiarity with Sam's preferences, or a nonverbal indication of disinterest in taking the order if Riley was to share it with him.

"Yes," Sam was quick to respond.

"No," Riley corrected. "I've not seen the menu yet."

"No need. I know what you like," Sam said.

"Seriously, Sam. We've only recently met, and we've never eaten in the same room together, much less at the same table. You don't know me."

Sam could rebut her presumption, but the truth would only anger her more. He knew her. He knew her well. Just not in the way he would like to know her. Yet.

Covert surveillance was part of the job, and happened to be one Sam excelled in. It also didn't hurt to have his innate talent for observation augmented by access to whatever cutting-edge tool he desired. That wasn't an advantage he was above using, especially on Riley.

Following her daily routine to become familiar with her habits and preferences had been no challenge at all. The basic stuff like where she lived, what car she drove, and which fast-food restaurant she frequented, was easy. He knew more.

He knew where she shopped for groceries and what items were routinely on her grocery list, on the rare occasions she bought groceries. He knew where she boarded Mason on the days she expected to be home late from work, and what time of night she let the dog out before going to bed. He knew she liked to sleep in on the weekends and then take hours to prepare a huge breakfast to share with no one but the dog.

"It's a hobby of mine," Sam answered, openly accepting the challenge. "I try to discern people's likes and dislikes. It comes in handy when picking jurors. Perhaps you'll indulge me this once?"

"Fine. Don't be insulted if I don't like what you order. I'm very picky."

"I've noticed," Sam commented as he quickly perused the menu. Pointing to his selections, he advised the waitress, "I'll have this, medium rare, and the lady will have this one, medium, and this on the side."

"You got it. Should take about 20 minutes. I'll box it up for y'all to go," the waitress concluded before walking away.

During the wait for their food and on the ride back to her office, Sam filled Riley in on a few of the details of Mikles' case and on the schedule for upcoming discovery. Depositions of primary witnesses were starting next week, which left Riley little time to prepare. Sam decided it would be best if they focused on the discovery and deposition prep for the remainder of the week and possibly over the weekend.

Riley had handled enough cases at similar stages of litigation to find Sam's assessment hard to reconcile. From what he'd told her thus far, the case didn't sound sufficiently complex to warrant that amount of preparation, especially since she was only coming on as co-counsel. She decided not to object, though. The billable hours, and more importantly, the money Mikles would pay for them would find its way to more noble causes when placed in her hands.

"I'll give you a call tomorrow to set up a schedule for witness preparation and for meeting with the other litigation counsel working with us on the case," he advised as they pulled into the parking lot behind Riley's office building.

"All right. I'll keep some time open," Riley said. She scooted to the edge of the deep leather bucket seat and then stood up. "Thanks for dinner, I guess. I'm not really sure I should thank you for anything else, yet."

"This case will be good experience for you. You'll see," Sam said.

Riley closed the car door behind her and headed back into the office to grab a few files and to leave her boxed dinner in the break room fridge. Although the setting sun's half-light left the impression it was still relatively early, it was after 8:00 p.m.–about the time she usually made it home for dinner.

The long, unusually eventful day had left her disinterested in a heavy meal tonight. She was, however, more than ready to get home and veg on the sofa with Mason while watching something mindless on television. It was Mason's night to pick the show, which meant they would probably be enjoying something on The Animal Channel.

It occurred to Riley, as she traversed the single flight of stairs up to her office, that Dani would enjoy sharing the expensive meal tomorrow for lunch while they reflected on every minute detail of the prior evening. Truth be told, she would enjoy that as much as Dani would. Although much of their past was shared, their few points of divergence had given Dani a perspective on life Riley didn't have. Between the two of them, most of life could be fully analyzed, dissected and put into proper perspective on any given day within the time it took to enjoy lunch. Tomorrow would be a good day to do just that.

Pride kept Riley from opening the box to see what Sam had ordered until she was safely within the confines of her own territory. On the ride home, she found it somewhat surprising Sam hadn't bothered to ask whether his selections were acceptable. Pride was likely responsible for that as well. She didn't want to give Sam the pleasure of her surprise if he had somehow correctly guessed her preferences, and it would never occur to Sam that his selections were anything but accurate.

Riley carefully placed the box on a shelf in the fridge, and then opened the lid to survey the contents. As she opened the box, an appetizing smoky fragrance from a perfectly cooked piece of aged beef wafted toward her. She peered inside to find a salt-crusted eight ounce filet, still warm and succulent, accompanied by a side of grilled broccoli, zucchini and butternut squash that must have been brushed lightly with virgin olive oil and a hint of rosemary, if her sense of smell were to be trusted at this late hour. It was exactly what she would've ordered.

I really, really hate you, Sam Stone. I guess.

CHAPTER 9

"It's that time again, folks. Time to vote your candidate into office!"

The speaker's tone made a gradual crescendo as he moved toward the conclusion of his announcement. It was one of many mechanisms that would be utilized over the course of the evening to heighten anticipation, and thereby lower inhibition. The audience was already captive, in a manner of speaking, but they still had dominion over their wallets—at least for the moment. This evening the objective of every employee on duty at The Polling Place was to pry open the annoying leather folds that stood between the audience's money and the club's coffers, and relieve said wallets of their contents.

Many of the club's "registered voters" had come to vote in person; others had given friends or business clients the privilege of placing their vote by proxy. Additionally, unlike public elections, the voters not able to make tonight's election weren't limited to sending in absentee ballots via snail-mail, but could actively participate in voting through The Polling Place's recent addition of virtual gateways. The club's broad-based approach to "get out the vote" was designed to do something public elections had yet to achieve—easy and equal voting access for all. By all indications, that extra effort had been well-received. Super Tuesdays, of any kind, draw big crowds in Florida, and this one was no exception.

Vincent Mikles was widely known to be a shrewd businessman with an uncanny ability to recognize and seize opportunities before his peers. He owned several similar clubs in the United States and abroad, many of which held "elections" and other politically-themed events. The clubs, however, were merely the keystone of his success.

In recent years, he had come to the realization there was greater potential for income from sources that didn't require a brick and mortar establishment. The ingenious offspring of his epiphany was the idea to combine his existing clubs with the omnipresence of the Internet, thereby giving those who didn't live within the geographic area a similar experience to those attending the live show.

The Polling Place stood alone among its skin-peddling competitors not only for its use of sarcasm toward the obviously flawed national election process, but also for using cutting-edge technology to vastly expand its consumer base. The initial price tag for the high-definition video cameras, computer mainframes, custom mobile apps, and flashy, professionally-designed websites necessary to make Mikles' vision a reality had been steep. They had paid off handsomely, as had the effort to obtain licenses to broadcast the shows internationally. The end result was the removal of standard impediments such as the weather, the local economy, or even geography from the income potential generated by the club's regular shows and special events.

The global expansion of his enterprise was something Mikles took great pride in. From the few dollars he had left after a disastrous and short-lived political career, he had built a worldwide adult entertainment conglomerate. He had reached the top of his chosen mountain, and had no intention of stopping there. A few more summits in the world of business and finance, many of them virtual, remained to be conquered. Mikles' potential to plant one of his flags on each of those peaks rose exponentially with each registered voter.

The voting process for club-sponsored elections was a pivotal part of Mikles' success, and among the more creative aspects of his business plan. There were many ways the registered voters in attendance at tonight's election, and the off-site voters viewing the event via the live globally broadcast, could fund their favorite candidate's campaign.

Voters and patrons in attendance at the club could hold fundraising events for a candidate at their table by purchasing exorbitantly priced dinner plates, typically costing anywhere from $100 to $1000 dollars per plate. Naturally, events falling on the higher end of that scale weren't expected to take place without the participants receiving a proper return on their investment. Those sponsoring dinners or fund-raising events that pulled in over $10,000 in donations would get a personal appearance at their table from their candidate, with the term "personal" not used lightly in this context.

Online participants in the election process had the choice of sending lump-sum donations to their candidate's campaign via withdrawal from a bank account or credit card, or they could take part in the election by casting an unlimited number of votes purchased online for $1.00 apiece. In addition to purchasing votes, online participants could earn them in various denominations by visiting the websites of The Polling Place's paid sponsors.

Votes, whether purchased or earned online, could be cast in the Super Tuesday election by clicking the "Vote" button under each candidate's photograph on The Polling Place's election page. If an online voter accumulated a very high pre-established level of votes, the websites also provided a means by which those votes, rather than being cast individually, could be combined into a voting bloc and traded for tokens. Tokens, which could be earned by trading or uncovered through stealth deduction during online participation, carried privileges that if used at pivotal points during the election had the potential to sway the electorate.

Similar to those attending events in person, online voters making large enough contributions, or casting a sufficient number of votes in an election, were also awarded with the option of various forms of digital interaction with their candidate. Those options included things like a personalized prerecorded video message from a candidate or even a one-on-one live video chat.

Among the most sought-after privileges for online voters was a private virtual meeting with the candidate in the club's specially designed "office" using a prototype human interface device Mikles was reportedly developing especially for his clubs. That particular privilege for online voters wasn't yet among the official list posted on Polling Place websites, but that minute technicality did nothing to diminish the buzz. Another buzz-worthy rumor circulating in cyber-space was that there was a token hidden somewhere online that, if found, could be exchanged for the privilege of testing the new interface device before it went public.

Nothing, aside from the club's unrobed candidates, held the rapt attention of the male voters, many of whom were also avid gamers, more strongly than a hint of new technology. For that reason it was entirely possible that the rumors, which had been met with vague denials, may have originated from inside the club as part of a pre-release marketing strategy. If so, that alleged error could have been yet another example of Mikles' uncanny business acumen. It could also have been nothing more than a loose-lip hoping to sink Mikles' ship. The murky waters Mikles swam in were filled with more than a few razor-toothed hazards.

At the end of the night if online voters didn't use all of the votes they accumulated during this election they had the option of saving them for the next election, selling or trading them to other voters, or even cashing them out. When cashing out, the votes could be exchanged for the player's currency of choice using standard exchange rates through an affiliated financial conduit that only exacted a five percent transaction fee off the top.

Last, but not remotely least, for devoted patrons there was an online process by which a single voter or a group of voters could form and fund a "SuperPAC." Similar to recent changes in U.S. campaign finance laws, SuperPACs participating in Polling Place elections could offer an unlimited amount of financial support. In contrast to their public counterparts, the Polling Place's SuperPACs were allowed to directly support their candidate of choice, thereby casting aside the thin separation between cause and candidate that has cast a long shadow of irony over the financing of campaigns for public office in the United States.

One other minor distinction between these SuperPACs and their real-world counterparts was the meaning behind the acronym. While "PAC" in the original version stands for "political action committee," the same combination of letters in this context stands for "Pussy Access Control." This particular distinction was largely seen to be one without a difference by most voters.

"Voters...let's meet the candidates!"

The announcer's voice was amplified over the cheers of the crowd while the lights dimmed and several colorful spotlights moved their beams from other locations to direct the light, and everyone's attention, to a circular stage that jutted into the center of the room.

"Representing Florida's Blue Ray District we have...Raven Byrd. Raven has previously held office here in Florida and is seeking re-election for another term."

A brilliant blue spotlight moved to the back of the stage where it met an attractive, athletic-looking, raven-haired young woman dressed in a dark blue, fitted suit jacket and a matching pencil skirt. The light followed her as she worked the stage and the audience on her way to a tall rectangular booth on the far left of the stage. She blew a kiss to the audience before she ducked behind the heavy blue velvet curtain that covered the front of the booth.

A moment later, the audience erupted into a renewed cheer as Raven's jacket and skirt were tossed into the crowd. For the time being, her unique qualifications to hold office weren't going to be released to the public. They, along with the rest of her, would remain behind the blue curtain unless or until her constituents adequately funded her campaign. Just like any candidate in a real political election, she needed money to get airtime.

The stage lights shifted location and color drawing attention away from Raven and back to the announcer.

"And representing the Red Light District of Florida...." The announcer paused briefly to allow the inevitable chortles to subside. When the room quieted again, he continued. "We have Honey Duex. She's a rising young star new to the campaign trail. Will she unseat Raven when all the votes are counted? It's up to you, voters!"

A deep red spotlight met Honey, a nubile, leggy, darkly tanned twenty-something with platinum blonde hair, at the side of the stage and followed her to her designated voting booth on the far right. The red spotlight seemed to dance happily over the clear rhinestone studs on her form-fitting white sheath dress, the reflection from her dress and platinum hair assuming various shades of red and pink in the process.

Honey quickly ducked behind the deep red velvet curtain that shielded the interior of her voting booth from the audience's view. The sounds of Velcro releasing preceded the re-emergence of at least a small portion of her from the booth. In her slight hand, Honey held the two sections of her dress that were previously one before their deft separation. She teased the audience by twirling the scant pieces of cloth in circles before launching them into the air in the direction of the crowd. Nearby voters scrambled to retrieve a scrap of the coveted cloth.

"Last, but not least, representing the Swinging Electorate Party, we have Ginger Fahn. She's the dark horse in tonight's race, who appears to be sponsored by deep pockets. Can Ginger buy her way into office? We'll know shortly."

A bright white spotlight met a curvy, well-endowed redhead at the back of the stage. Her glossy coppery-red hair and pale skin were radiant under the intense stage lighting—the color of both further accentuated by the deep purple shade of her silky blouse. She had paired said blouse with a skin-tight spandex skirt in a matching color of purple, and completed the look with sky-high black patent platform pumps. Both Ginger, and her well-chosen attire, worked her enviable physique like a pair of pros, while she made her way toward a booth centrally located between those of Raven and Honey.

Before entering her booth, she stepped over to the right side of the stage and struck a fashion-model pose for the crowd; she repeated the same for the crowd sitting on the opposite side of the stage. As an independent candidate, she needed to steal votes away from the mainstream candidates on either side. She undoubtedly pried a few dollars from the hands of undecided voters before ducking behind the dark green curtain of her booth. A few more likely joined her camp when she tossed not only her blouse and skirt out, but a tiny black thong as well.

"All right, voters! The number of appearances your candidates can make during tonight's campaign, as well as the outcome of the election, are in your hands. Make sure you give your favorite gal every advantage. You can make donations and hold fundraisers at your table, and those of you at the bar can participate in the events and voting through the in-counter touch-screen terminals. Votes can be cast with cash or credit. But remember, you have to be registered to vote. So, if you haven't registered, please see your proctor or bartender, and we'll get you signed up."

The announcer looked up toward the club's balcony level as video screens mounted along the outside of the circular opening in the middle of the second level floor surged to life. Each of the three screens displayed various pictures of the candidates, along with a running total of the funds contributed to their campaign thus far, and a real-time calculation of the votes received.

The first candidate to receive enough funds to buy airtime was Honey Duex. Her ceiling-mounted video screen sprung to life with a prerecorded segment that gave the voters a behind the scenes look at their candidate. In the segment, Honey was at her apartment taking a bubble bath while she spoke about growing up on a farm in Kansas. The segment then switched to show her walking into a classroom distracting both her male classmates and the male instructor with a super-short skirt and her super-long legs. She ended the recorded segment with her campaign slogan and a wink.

"I'm Honey Duex, and I believe a girl can *do* anything or anyone she puts her mind to. Oh, and I totally approved this message."

Cheers erupted from the crowd when Honey emerged from her booth wearing only a small pair of red silk panties. After acknowledging the crowd, she made her way to a pole that had miraculously appeared in the center of the stage. The pole stood above the rest of the stage positioned prominently on a raised circular platform that housed a neon sign. Two words, "Candidate Platform," scrolled continuously around the base of the platform, visible to the audience on any side of the circular stage.

Honey took hold of the pole with one hand and walked around it once before she mounted it with a twirling leap which left her straddling the pole, one long leg wrapping around it and the other extended toward the ceiling. She clearly intended to make her case as a newcomer in the field with a pair of undeniably long assets. From the immediate surge in both donations and votes displayed on Honey's video monitor, her platform was especially popular among tonight's voters. When the music stopped, Honey slid down the pole and danced her way back into her booth, not to reappear until her coffers were once again filled with the necessary funds.

The next candidate to get airtime was Raven, who emerged from her booth to an uproar of approval from the crowd. She wasn't new to this political arena and had developed quite a few supporters and fans among voters. She had chosen to wear only a small blue and black lace g-string under the business-like suit she had tossed into the crowd earlier.

Raven's video biography was short and sweet. In it, she was sitting behind a desk in what appeared to be a simulation of the Oval Office. She was wearing a jacket buttoned only at the lowest point, easily revealing that there was nothing between it and her smooth, taut skin underneath. She leaned back in the chair, thus causing the lapels of her jacket to open further, and propped her athletic, shapely legs on the desk revealing the red underside of her insanely high-heeled designer pumps to the camera. Her slogan was as direct as her presentation.

"I'm Raven. Y'all know me. Let's get this party started."

The music that accompanied Raven's "platform" presentation was hip and heavy with electric guitar. She worked the music and the stage with the skill of a formally trained gymnast, adding a quick round-off and back handspring into her short jaunt over to the pole; no small feat while wearing stilettos. When she reached the center of the stage, Raven did a half-flip, grabbing the pole with both hands mid-rotation.

Still heels-over-head, Raven released one hand from the pole while she wrapped her left leg around it. She then removed her other hand and slid down toward the stage in a circular motion using only her left leg to support and guide her movement. To accentuate the rotation of her descent, she strategically placed one arm in front and one arm behind her torso. It was an inspiring feat of athletic prowess, and very well-received by the audience.

Raven had barely returned to an upright position when the crowd caught wind that Ginger was on tap—the last to be released from oblivion through the generosity of her constituents. Ever fickle in pursuit of prurient interests, the crowd's attention turned from Raven to the center voting booth.

Ginger's platform music was as exotic as its muse, with pentatonic tones akin to that of a snake charmer. Ginger displayed the same hypnotic appeal. At first, all the audience could see as the green velvet curtain lifted was the delicious view of her leg, from ankle to shapely upper thigh. Once the music began to build, the entrancing vision of Ginger's leg was accompanied by the sound of tinkling bells.

Ginger slowly pulled back the curtain just enough to extend her full leg, along with a hint of her curvaceous derriere, outside of the booth and press a tiny, henna-embellished foot toward the floor. The rest of her enviable figure remained behind the curtain while she toyed with the audience, the sound of handbells continuing to herald each slight movement of her exposed hip. She obviously had no intention of giving anything more away until the voters were fully primed by reviewing the content of her video.

In the video, she was naked and suggestively reclined on her stomach in a blue-tiled Turkish bath. Her pale skin was covered with oil and slight beads of moisture from the steam which, in the light of the camera, gave the appearance she was covered in small diamonds. Ginger's voice, as she delivered her personal message to the crowd, was throaty and seductive.

"Hello, boys. I'm the one and only candidate for you in tonight's election because I have unparalleled skills in both domestic and foreign affairs. Don't you think it's time to unite our nations?"

Ginger had skillfully played the crowd, allowing their curiosity to grow while they called the odds, fueled by the suggestion in her video that she was to be the only candidate intending to provide complete "transparency" for voters. When the curtain was finally drawn, it was clear. Ginger was worth the wait.

Her tiny undergarment, which could easily serve double duty as an implement for masochistic torture, was completely transparent. It had been cleverly crafted of a transparent latex fabric that looked like heavy duty Saran Wrap. Attached to the innovative panty in very strategic locations in the front and along a center seam in the back were small jingle bells that enjoyed heralding even the slightest movement of her hips. Ginger made expert use of those bells during her exotic, harem-style dance toward the pole, beguiling the crowd with each playful syncopated movement of her creamy thighs cleverly paired with the transfixing sound.

When Ginger reached the pole, she danced around it suggestively, leaving the men in the room to imagine themselves in its place. The implication was almost as clear as her undergarment. If the voters wanted that vision of her to become their reality, they would have to sponsor her at their table.

Whoever the strategist was for Ginger's campaign, they were obviously wise. The private contribution tally on her video monitor soared with every move she made. The early returns already indicated she would be performing more than a few private dances tonight. The contributors in line to receive that tantalizing treat would have to wait, though. Right now, Ginger had the stage and platform to herself.

Facing the crowd from behind the pole, Ginger reached over her head, grabbed the pole firmly and lifted herself a few feet off the ground before straddling the pole in a half-pike position. She held the pose easily, with elegant posture and pointed toes, while using sheer strength to pull herself up a few feet higher on the pole. When she reached a suitable height, she gracefully wrapped one leg around the pole, released both hands, and slowly rode the pole down to the platform. Having made the strength of her position quite clear, she returned to the center booth amid the vocal protestations of admirers.

As the evening progressed, the candidates appeared several more times to present additional platforms to the voters, sometimes one at a time and sometimes two or all three of them at once. They all also made special trips to the tables that had held successful fundraisers on their behalf, to mingle and take photos with their supporters. In the span of just a few hours, each candidate had accumulated hundreds of thousands of dollars in both contributions to their campaigns and purchased votes. Finally, at the stroke of midnight, the announcer took the stage once more.

"Voting is now closed in all precincts, including online. Looks like it's time to tally 'em up and declare our winner."

All eyes turned upward to the video monitors. The three screens had pictures of the candidates and a scrolling stream of numbers by their names, a final contrived effort to prolong the suspense.

"Tonight's winner will hold office until next month's election, voters. That means she'll be available in our not-so-public office upstairs for meetings with special interests and high paying donors, just like your local Congressman!" The announcer paused while the patrons guffawed; the pun was sublimely humorous in its manifest truth.

"I know. I know. That's how it works, right?" The announcer nodded, joining the collective in appreciation of an irony. "Okay everyone! Let's see who'll be making your 'pole-*icy*' this week." The crowd looked up as the scrolling numbers on the screens started to slow.

In a hemisphere far, far away, a young man who'd been staring at his monitor for the past two hours enjoying the show hit the "Enter" key with emphasis. He'd been waiting for the vote count to begin so he could use the token he'd earned by securing more votes than almost all other online players. It wasn't *the* token he and many others were hoping to hold this evening. It wasn't without its own value, either. Being the first to engage in live-action cybersex was not the only prize of the night. An equally compelling one, in the mind of this particular interloper, was the ability to create chaos.

The numbers scrolling on the screens above the club's stage stopped and the boxes went blank. The announcer, with an equally empty look, received information via his ear piece from the producers. He began to provide the totals intended to fill the blank screens above the stage.

"Congratulations, voters! We've set new records tonight for all candidates. Let's start with incumbent Raven Byrd. Our dark-haired beauty has secured a total of 123,000 votes!"

The audience erupted in applause while Raven, standing on stage next to her worthy competition, took a bow.

"Honey Duex, our fresh new face in this political arena, has a total of 122,907 votes. That's awfully close, folks. We might be looking at a runoff!"

The crowd acknowledged the close score with equal zeal, and Honey took her bow.

"Finally, we get the total for our homegrown sprinkle of spice. Our ravishing redhead, Ginger, has been endowed in more ways than one! Let's see if we're gonna have a three-way."

The announcer once again paused to revel in his own humor. A moment later, his reserve collected, he continued the announcement.

"Ginger's votes tonight total…122,999! Looks like tonight's winner will be—," the announcer paused, a confused look replacing his practiced smile.

He looked to the left and then right of the stage, hoping to get confirmation from someone with authority. No answer in sight, he directed his query and focus to the electrical control booth in the balcony.

"Is this right? We've never had this before." He received a verbal response through his headset and nodded in affirmation.

"Well, folks, it's Florida, so this might not come as a surprise. Our online voting system has left us with none other than a hanging chad."

The audience looked bewildered before resigning themselves to fate by uttering a collective "Awwwww."

Someone in the crowd vocalized the question most were thinking, in a voice loud enough to rise above the vocalized disappointment surrounding it.

"What happens now?"

"Good question," the announcer acknowledged. "It means we're gonna have a recount, unless someone else has enough tokens to buy a judge."

The crowd erupted in laughter. Scandal seemed a fitting end for the night especially since, in this case, everyone had already won.

CHAPTER 10

Wade was early. Any other day, he would have skated into the office in the final second of the last minute before 9:00 a.m.; that early to bed, early to rise gig not being his style. Today, he was parked, in the building and riding the elevator with the annoying early birds that somehow always managed to be in their seats by 8:00 a.m.

The whole bed thing, in general, hadn't worked like it was supposed to last night. He might've gotten a minute or two of good sleep, if he was lucky. He wasn't feeling lucky right now. A forceful yawn rose in his throat and commanded him to oblige its escape. He acquiesced and covered his mouth with a hand, hoping the insurrection wouldn't be contagious.

Wade had tried to access Halston's laptop computer and camera again during the wee hours of the morning, intentionally defying the internal voices that fervently counseled a different course. After tossing and turning for hours, he silenced the subconscious debate by concluding the chance for peace of mind outweighed the risk of getting caught.

This time, in spite of numerous attempts using different approaches, he wasn't able to gain access. That alone wasn't telling, as it could mean any number of things. It could mean the computer and Internet-ready television that bridged the distance between them last night were simply turned off. It was also possible that, if the apparent attacker was really just a common thief, neither device was in Halston's apartment any longer.

Ultimately, the lack of another solution was the cause. Its corresponding effect was the force that motivated him to abandon an extra hour of sleep, or anything else he usually enjoyed in the morning, and hasten the slog in to work. Halston, as the receptionist, had to be at her desk before most of the other staff arrived. That's what Wade had observed on the rare occasions he had to come in early to test the servers.

On one of those days, he had recorded her morning ritual intending to inject himself into it, quite randomly of course, on some future date. He attempted to do just that on a few subsequent mornings when his job required an early start, but never quite raised the nerve. He did, however, walk away from those failed attempts with some useful information—the girl kept to an eerily precise schedule.

Halston's days started with a stop for coffee at the shop in the lobby at 7:49. By 7:54, she would be in the elevator lobby waiting for the next elevator car, and by 7:58 at her desk. Hopefully, this morning had gone down just like all the others. He was counting on it like his life depended on it; maybe because it did.

If fate had decided to spare him, he would find Halston in the office this morning sitting behind that stupid piece of office furniture that maddeningly hid her exquisite legs from view. Then it would be confirmed. Everything he had witnessed last night was some kind of messed up hoax.

Wade's impatience grew while the elevator took longer than usual to make its rounds. Everyone riding with him appeared to be lost in a morning fog. Some missed their floors. Many pushed the wrong buttons. Wade's face echoed the frustration that filled his thoughts.

Great, I'm stuck on an elevator with day-walking zombies, he internally surmised. *Just what I need.*

Ding. They were on the third floor now. More people entered. Ding, ding. Door closed and they moved on to the fourth floor.

The building staff apparently had the air conditioning off overnight, as they often did to cut expenses. The elevator was warm, and getting hotter by the minute. Wade felt a bead of sweat trickle down the side of his face. His color might've deepened from the heat around him, or perhaps from his internal engines now running at full throttle while burning the fuel of despair.

Ding. Fourth floor.

Some zombies departed, a few more got on. Ding, ding. Doors closed. They had now stopped at every floor between the lobby and the fifth floor where he was headed. If this damn elevator took two more seconds to get there, Wade was fairly sure his head would explode.

Ding. Fifth floor.

Wade made his way to the front of the elevator before the doors opened. When the doors parted, he galloped through them like a thoroughbred leaving the gate. His company occupied most of the fifth floor and the reception desk wasn't far from the elevator. Just a short hallway and a left turn to go.

Wade rounded the corner and nervously eyed the reception lobby which was visible behind the heavy glass wall and glass double-door entry to the office. There was no sign of her.

He pushed open one of the heavy glass doors and made his way inside. He stopped by Halston's desk in the reception area hoping to see an indication that she had made it in this morning. He found nothing to ease his conscience. No unattended cup of hot coffee. No expensive leather purse tucked under the desk. No new messages in the outbox waiting to be picked up. Nothing. No, worse than nothing; her computer wasn't on.

Wade hurried past mostly empty cubicles on the way to his own desk in the IT department, ignoring customary morning salutations offered to him from behind the few cubicles that were occupied. Right now, he was more concerned with checking the morning boot log than with social custom.

The company's time-management system uses a number of software programs to record each time an employee logs on or off their computer. Those programs were useful in collecting information necessary for human resources to keep track of non-exempt employee time, and to make decisions regarding scheduling or the need for additional hires. The programs were equally useful for developing metrics that enabled management and IT to calculate the need for and timing of hardware upgrades. Another version of the same type of software was used to prompt employees doing heavy data-entry work to take regular breaks.

The latter program, and the one he intended to make a completely different use of this morning, was recently installed due to a memo from the legal department about heightened requirements in some random federal law. As far as he could tell, folks who spent their days sitting around and typing up stuff apparently didn't enjoy their jobs very much, so they decided to make an issue of it and get a bunch of rules passed that regulated how long employees should be required to sit and type stuff. The geniuses that passed said rules then decided to have some federal agency impose the burden of monitoring all that nonsense on employers.

Once apprised of yet another work-related standard, employers and the marketplaces that serve their interests decided the best way to track the time employees spent in front of their computers was, naturally, through the IT department. Until now, Wade had lamented IT's role in meeting those compliance standards as a tad more than bothersome. Today the information it afforded on the comings and goings of his co-workers could prove to be priceless.

He chose to access the program in question because it was one IT routinely monitored and it had the easiest search parameters. With this program, he could find what he needed quickly, and the information provided would be up to the minute. It was possible Halston had signed on and then stepped away from her desk to go to the ladies room. If she had been gone for more than a few minutes after logging in, her computer would go into power-save mode, thus appearing from outward observation to be dormant. The program would tell him whether or not that appearance was deceiving. The fleeting thought of an affirmative sign-on report offered some hope.

At his desk, a few keystrokes later, Wade was once again met with disappointment. Halston hadn't logged onto the system from her work station or even remotely from home to check her email. Checking the morning's incoming email didn't yield uplifting results, either. There were no emails from Halston to anyone stating she would be coming in late. The phone logs also didn't show any incoming calls from her phone number. This was not looking good at all.

The only thing left to do now was wait—for a little while anyway. Wade sat rigid in his seat while his mind continued to race. He internally debated each alternative and its likely conclusion. Maybe Halston was on the way in and just got stuck in traffic. She could have left at her usual time and therefore had no need to call from home before leaving the apartment. Of course, she wouldn't use her cell to call while driving, especially if she was navigating heavy traffic. If for some reason she had tried to answer her cell phone while driving, it was possible she had gotten into a fender-bender or something. Although, his internal recollection countered, there wasn't much in the way of traffic on the way in this morning, and there were no reports of accidents. Okay, so then maybe Halston was planning to take the day off and had forgotten to call in for some reason. Or not. She knew the policy for taking leave, and he didn't recall hearing about her taking any previously without following protocol.

The rush of heat Wade felt in the elevator returned and intensified. The button-down collar of his dress shirt tightened around his neck like a noose. He tugged at it nervously, hoping that might ease the deepening clutch that was beginning to threaten his airway. It didn't. Beads of sweat began to congregate on his forehead.

What if it was real? What if she doesn't come through the door in a few minutes? Then I'm screwed.

He would have to tell someone then. There would be questions. People would start looking for her. They wouldn't be looking at him though. He hadn't done anything wrong. Not that wrong, anyway. Plus, he had covered his tracks well. It wasn't like there would be any obvious indication of his remote surveillance.

Still, the authorities would come to his boss, Duong, and request him to search for anything useful that might be stored in the files on Halston's work computer. They would want access to the company emails and web archives. Duong would, inevitably, pass that buck on to him. How likely was it he could interact with law enforcement without giving something away? Not likely. He was a tech-geek, not a spy. He only played one as a kid, on Nintendo.

Another frantic twenty minutes passed before the panic of not knowing was replaced by clear affirmation. Wade's worst fears were his new reality. Halston had not come into work and no one had heard from her, or so said the office manager in a curt email sent two minutes ago to the girl who regularly covered the reception desk whenever Halston was away. He had opened the portal that gave him direct access to the office manager's email hoping there might be an email from or to Halston, but no such luck. There was just the one email from the office manager sent to Halston's fill-in, directing her to cover the reception desk while the office manager made a few calls to investigate.

The first of those calls had been to Halston's home number. Wade knew that because the company used an Internet based telecommunications system that made it easy to tap into the line, see the number dialed, and listen to the call from his computer. He listened nervously while the line rang, five times; it then went to voicemail.

Hi, it's Halston. I'm doing something fabulous. Leave a message. Beep.

The office manager left a brief message stating concern for Halston's well-being and noting her departure from standard procedure by not calling in before her absence. She advised Halston to call back right away.

"That's not gonna happen," Wade muttered after severing the digital connection. "Great. Now what?"

Duong would be in soon and would surely notice not only that Wade had made it in before him, an almost historical non-occurrence, but also his nervous and erratic demeanor. Duong tended to pick up on shit like that, and today would be no exception if Wade couldn't find a way to hide it. Focusing on mundane programming work wasn't going to be an option until he knew where Halston was. He could barely stay in his seat at the moment, much less focus on searching for random errors in the operating system's universal code.

"Do I wait? Do I say something? Who would I tell? Maybe human resources?" Wade asked himself.

Wade considered the latter option. Human resources would oversee whatever type of investigation took place. They have people on staff that interact with the cops when computers or inventory occasionally went missing. They even have their own investigators that function much like internal private eyes. Damn Nazi-like militants, some of those guys.

"I'm toast if I go to them," Wade concluded. He reached in his pocket and pulled out his cell phone. "I've gotta do something. I've gotta tell someone who can talk to the authorities without getting me into trouble."

He pulled open the small drawer in the center of his desk to filter through the disarray of business cards and handwritten notes he routinely tossed inside. He found the one he wanted near the top of the pile.

This wasn't the way he'd hoped things would go down. Any previous thoughts he'd entertained of a salacious nature were sequestered to an unknown place. His fingers shook as he attempted to press the tiny numbers on the touch-screen of his phone, so much so that he had to re-enter the numbers a couple of times before getting them right. The third time was the charm. His call connected and the line began to ring.

CHAPTER 11

She didn't often have the luxury of a quiet early morning drive to work but on this particular morning, Dani was blessed with just that—the uncommon splendor afforded by virtue of her husband's brief and soon-to-be-ending stint of shore duty. During the routine three to six month periods Jack was out to sea or on some covert assignment, she had to manage the home front alone. Alone meant really, really alone.

For all practical purposes during those times, she was a single mother. When her husband, a Navy SEAL, was out on assignment there was no way to contact him. Dani, like most military wives, understood that the complete separation was necessary. Her man was risking his life for democracy in a faraway land, and couldn't be distracted by the tedious details of his family's civilian life. The Navy also couldn't risk anyone outside the chain of command knowing Jack's whereabouts at any given time, as that would reveal details of government interests to those who would happily turn them into headlines for the evening news.

So, while Jack executed plots to foil dictators, Dani was driving the boys to school or orthodontist's appointments or camp before putting in a full day at work, and then picking them up after evening practice for whatever sport was in season. She would then somehow manage to find time and energy to pull together something for them to eat before they completed homework or chores and were off to bed.

With two growing boys—one in the early throws of puberty—being a pseudo-single parent was becoming more and more difficult. She never complained about the challenge, though. It wasn't her nature to complain, and she had always found humor to be a more effective outlet, anyway. Plus, the Navy had been good to them in ways that outweighed the bad. There were health benefits, housing and tuition assistance, and the intense camaraderie she shared with those who were also members of the elite group of families with firsthand knowledge of what it means to serve and support the country at the highest level.

Jackson, otherwise known as "Jack" to pretty much anyone with remote familiarity, was on shore duty for only a few more days, and then he'd be off again on another clandestine adventure. Today, as one of those last precious days of freedom from the full weight of family obligations, was one Dani planned to make the most of. Jack was taking the boys to their summer day camp and then to their oldest son's baseball game tonight. His assistance gave her the chance to enjoy a quiet morning, a long lunch, and possibly a stop by her favorite vintage clothing store on her way home from work.

Riley would probably let her off a little early. Flexible scheduling was one of the many perks of working for her best friend. Not having to hide her effusive personality under a cloak of false propriety was another. Still, not one to take advantage, she had come in an hour early to offset the hour or two she might take off this afternoon. That way she could put in a full day's worth of work, even if she did knock off before 5 or 6 p.m.

Despite rush-hour traffic on I-4, she managed to make it to the office in record time. By 7:30—an hour earlier than usual—she was in the office, with the alarm system disengaged, and making her way to the small conference room that doubled as their break room. The first order of business was a hot cup of coffee. Riley had gotten one of those single-cup machines that dispensed a preselected portion of whatever brew the recipient preferred. Starting the morning with a machine that had so many bells and whistles was a lot more fun than messing around with a regular old coffee pot.

Dani spun the spindle of the countertop dispenser that held the various prepacked beverage choices. Riley kept it stocked with quality coffees, teas and cocoa. Today's cup would need to be a strong one. Even with Jack's assistance, the unusually hectic work schedule was doing a number on her. Over the past week or two, something that could only be described as a mortal fatigue had come over her, starting almost from the moment she got out of bed and lasting far longer than the ordinary late-afternoon fugue. The worst part of it was that no amount of sleep had compelled the fatigue to release its persistent hold.

Hawaiian Kona coffee was today's winner. Starting the day as one might in paradise couldn't hurt. Dani pulled the small cartridge from the dispenser, her face already displaying pleasure she anticipated from the coming treat.

Riley had that after-hours client meeting with Sam last night which meant she probably wouldn't be in before 9:00 today. That left Dani time to casually enjoy her coffee and watch the morning news while she filtered through a pile of intake paperwork from potential new clients. The intake pile was getting larger every day, most likely the result of media coverage following the tragic murder of Riley's client Vanessa Buehler.

While most of the viewing public saw a tragic tale of a fractured family, others saw only Riley, the champion of Vanessa's cause in spite of the odds. By the number of calls they'd received lately, it appeared the world was in desperate need of a champion for lost causes. Thankfully, Dani was tasked with filtering through the details of potential cases before they made it to her boss. Riley had a hard time turning away someone in need. Dani, however, was more practical in her approach to rendering aid. With two boys and an alpha-male husband, she was highly skilled at reading between the lines, filtering through a minefield of persuasive jargon and wielding the word "no" whenever practical or necessary.

Dani pointed a remote at the wall-mounted flat screen television on the far side of the room. On cue, the device sprang to life. She checked to ensure the sound was on a low setting, thereby making whatever she chose to watch inaudible from the office reception area. Not everyone–that everyone including her boss–shared her taste in programming.

She opened the small refrigerator located below the counter of the built-in serving area expecting to find a carton of cream, or at least some half-and-half. Coffee, the good kind, was better when accompanied by a splash of real cream or some close approximation thereof. Riley, on the rare occasions she drank coffee, took a splash in hers as well, so there was usually a container in the fridge. Today, said container was not in its ordinary spot on the center shelf. In its place, front and center, was a large plastic takeout carton.

"Oooo, this must be from last night," Dani mused as she took a peek inside the container. "Filet and grilled veggies. Yumble!"

A container like that in the fridge meant Riley was planning to eat-in for lunch today. It also meant there was one hell of a story to tell from last night.

"You are too delicious not to come with a backstory," Dani advised the plate of food. She wasn't above conversations with inanimate objects, especially when those objects were edible. "Riley better dish on your details when she gets here, my culinary friend."

Dani grabbed the cream from the fridge door and finished mixing her morning brew. Nestled into one of the cushiony leather conference chairs, she commenced her review of the new client paperwork. Before draining the last drop of coffee from her mug, she had managed to sift and sort the pile. A few lost souls who had recently darkened their doorstep were singled out for meetings with Riley, a majority of the others were placed in a pile for referral to other attorneys, and the few remaining ones were tossed in the rejection pile. There simply wasn't enough time to help everyone, and absolutely no time to help those who hadn't even tried to help themselves.

She had just returned to her desk in the reception area of the office when the phone announced the day's first call.

"Wow, it's barely past 8:30. Someone either has the wrong number or is in real trouble." She picked up the receiver and answered with her usual salutation. "Morgan Law Office. Can we help you?"

"Um . . . yeah . . . I hope so," came a halting reply. "Is this Riley Morgan?"

"This is Miss Morgan's office, and I'm her assistant. What can I do for you?"

"Okay, good. I was wondering if I could see her today. It's urgent."

"It usually is. We're pretty well booked for the rest of the week, though. Could you come in next week?"

"This really is life or death," the caller advised with thinly disguised desperation. "I think someone I know is missing."

Dani sighed. So much for today's early departure.

"All right, let's do this. Stop by this afternoon at the end of the day, around five o'clock, maybe, and I'll get the details of your troubles from you. We usually do that before scheduling an attorney meeting, anyway."

"Five o'clock. That's like the whole day from now." The caller paused to reflect momentarily. "Okay, I'll be there."

"Great," Dani concluded. "So, who shall I be meeting with?"

"The name's Wade, Wade Warner. I met Miss Morgan yesterday when she was teaching that seminar. I'm really glad you can work me in. I'm in a real mess."

"Do you know where we are located?"

"Yeah. I think so. The address is on the card."

"All right. We'll see you at 5:00. In the meantime, write down anything you want to discuss so you won't forget to bring it up in the meeting," Dani added before ending the call.

"Great," Dani whispered as she returned the receiver to its cradle, "someone from the sexual harassment seminar. Just what Riley and I need at the end of a long day—a horn-dog in a pickle."

Dani printed out copies of emails received overnight and started to organize, by priority, any phone messages left over from yesterday. She then pulled the case files for the matters with the most immediate deadlines and had them ready to hand over to Riley as well. A few minutes later the door chimes sounded and Dani, now fully prepared to start the day, looked up to greet Riley.

"Good morning, Boss. You look tired. Late night?" Dani ended her query with a slight giggle. It was pretty obvious from the darkened recesses under Riley's eyes that she had been on edge the entire time she was with Sam, and that tension had carried over into a fitful sleep.

Riley was like that—overly analytical sometimes. She couldn't see Sam for the amusing trifle he was, and she wasn't willing to overlook his skirt-chasing reputation long enough for a good giggle at his expense. Dani wasn't burdened with the same solemn nature.

Dani chuckled at her inner thoughts. Men always think they're the cat's meow, when they are more often like what the cat brings in after a long night out in the rain. A girl was damned if she couldn't love them for just that. Men, just like the wet, rodent-toting feline, usually mean well. Sam didn't appear to be any different.

"Ha! Very funny," Riley replied as she headed down the hall toward her office. "It wasn't as bad as I expected, but there are some details I think you'll enjoy."

"Yes!" That was what Dani wanted to hear. She grabbed the messages and new client paperwork and followed Riley back to her office. Riley stopped their forward progress before they reached the door.

"Hey, make me a cup of that new Kona coffee and let's meet in the conference room. You'll need the extra space to roll on the floor laughing."

"Aye, aye!" Dani made a swift turn into the conference room.

After booting up her computer and sending off a few quick emails, Riley joined Dani in their conference-slash-break-room. They settled into seats on opposite sides of the conference table, Riley with her coffee in hand. After Riley filled Dani in on a few of the finer moments of the prior evening, Dani leaned back in her seat to mull it all over.

"He took you to a frikken strip club to apologize for the sex toy stunt? That man has balls of steel. "

"I'm not sure if it's balls, or balderdash. Either way, it was one of the more memorable client meetings I've had in a long time," Riley said.

"So, what now? Are you gonna try the case with him?"

"I guess so. We're meeting to go over the details sometime today. He's supposed to call to set up a time, so I'll leave that up to you "

"You said there was another attorney working on the case with Sam, right? Who is it?"

"Sam hasn't told me yet," Riley advised. "We should get copies of the pleadings from him today. The names of all counsel of record will be listed there. Once you set up the file, go ahead and pull information on the other trial attorney and the plaintiff's attorney. We need to know who we're dealing with."

"Standard procedure," Dani added with a nod. "I know this is good for business and stuff, but does Sam know you're not going to sleep with him while you're working with him?"

Riley nearly choked on her coffee. She grabbed a napkin to avoid a nasty spill. "Gimme a break. I'm not going to sleep with him, before, during or after the case."

"Why not? He's handsome, apparently single or will be as soon as that third or fourth or whatever number divorce goes through. And he totally has the hots for you."

"Sam has the hots for all women. You're the one who calls him 'Ladykiller,' remember?"

"True, but there's nothing wrong with that, in the right context. I'm just saying, not every dude has to be Mr. Right. Besides, I think he'd be fun to toy with for a while."

"Easy for you to say. You're happily married to a guy who's the rare combination of Prince Charming and Rambo. Besides, comparing Sam to Mr. Right would be like comparing a diaper to a daisy."

Dani let out a hearty laugh at Riley's exaggeration. "More like I'm married to Rambo than the Prince these days. He's in mission-mode almost all of the time now. The other day, he told our youngest to drop and give him 20 when he refused to stop playing video games. Besides, my boring, settled life is not what we're talking about now, is it?"

"Sam is nothing but trouble," Riley concluded, in an end-of-conversation tone.

Riley swiveled her chair to face the television to emphasize the point—the subject of Sam was tabled for a number of reasons, none of which she was ready or able to articulate. She hadn't even decided how to feel about working with him yet, much less entertained the notion of anything more intimate. To make matters worse, despite her valiant efforts to keep him at bay, Sam had managed to get under her skin in ways other men had never been capable of doing. That was no small feat. Many before him had tried and failed.

"When did you decide to be on Sam's team anyway? I thought you didn't trust him any more than I do," Riley added as an aside.

"I'm not on his team. I've just seen a different side to him lately. I think there's more to him than you give him credit for. I might be wrong. But, you know, I'm not usually wrong about people."

"There's always a first time. I'm not sure I'd want your first error to be made on a wager as high as Sam." Riley motioned to Dani for the remote. "Turn the sound up. Looks like they're talking about Calvin's trial on the news."

Dani pressed the remote to raise the television sound a few notches. They both listened intently as the reporter outlined details of the case.

Our sources say jury selection was expected to start next week but was postponed due to bitter pretrial wrangling between the prosecution and defense that has already put three evidentiary issues before the court of appeal on the first degree murder trial of Calvin Buehler, the local man accused of gunning down his wife at this very spot in the courthouse parking lot.

Riley winced at the painful memory resurrected by the female reporter, who was standing in the exact spot where Vanessa stood when she was shot and killed by her husband.

Prosecutors have already indicated their intent to seek the death penalty in this case. The court-appointed defense counsel has challenged the death penalty as a violation of his client's religious beliefs and has threatened to take the issue before the Florida Supreme Court if the Fifth District Court of Appeal doesn't rule in his favor. According to the defense, Buehler believes only God, through his ordained disciples, can take the life of another. In a number of letters Buehler has sent to the media from his prison cell, he claims he is innocent because God authorized the killing of his wife, Vanessa, through the scriptures of the Old Testament.

Viewers may recall that Buehler, who remained at large for weeks after his wife's murder, was arrested when authorities spotted him stalking his children at a local concert. We'll be covering the trial live and via Twitter, and will be the first to bring viewers updates on the proceedings. That's all we have for now. Back to you, Bob.

The station then went to a commercial and Dani muted the sound.

"I can't believe we were in the same building, watching Evan's concert, when Calvin was caught. How did Calvin know his kids were there?"

"He must've been tailing them or their foster family somehow," Riley considered, openly. "Or maybe he knew his kids were fans of the show and would want to go to the concert. Anyway, it gives me chills to think of how close he came to taking, or worse yet, hurting them. They've had enough tragedy for one lifetime."

Dani shook her head in frustration at Riley's failure to consider her own well-being. "Have you thought about how close he might've come to harming you that night? You told me he was seconds away from shooting you at the courthouse, and might have if someone hadn't pulled you back."

"I haven't forgotten about that. Staring down the muzzle of a madman's gun isn't a vision that easily fades," Riley replied.

"I haven't seen a subpoena or anything from the prosecutor," Dani inquired. "Are you gonna be called as a witness at Calvin's trial?"

"They haven't decided yet. It poses a bit of a conflict because I was Vanessa's attorney. They have a number of other eye witnesses from the parking lot that day. I'm hoping they don't need me. I'll be there if they do."

Dani realized it was time to turn the conversation elsewhere. Riley didn't need to relive that moment any more than was necessary. Fortunately, the newscast had progressed to the weather segment, affording the perfect segue. The future weather maps had the local area covered with precipitation indicators in the most severe colors of red and purple. Dani turned up the sound.

A new update is in from the National Hurricane Center. It looks like Tropical Storm Adonis is nearing hurricane strength and headed for Florida. From the current projected path, it will likely come ashore somewhere just below the Satellite Beach area early in the morning on Friday as a Category 2 or 3 storm, possibly even a Category 4 if conditions cause it to strengthen more than expected over the next few days. That means the Orlando area will be getting hurricane force winds and rain as the storm continues on a north-westerly track across the state and toward the Gulf of Mexico.

"Speaking of thunder," Dani surmised. "Guess we're in for some. You know, I thought they'd stop naming storms after gods or other historical religious figures when Hurricane Delilah took out that hair clinic in Boca Raton last year."

"Can't imagine how that obvious lesson was missed," Riley added with a hint of amusement. "I guess there is something more ominous about a storm's potential when its name has a history. We've been through big storms before. I'm not too worried."

"Hell yeah, it's ominous," Dani shot back. Dani's deadpan facial expression only served to emphasize the humor of the coming irony. "All I know is if I even hear mention of a breeze named Moses, I'm outta here."

"Duly noted. I'll make sure to count that as religious leave," Riley said.

"Sounds like you're getting your sense of humor back."

"I don't have much choice about that with you around," Riley teased. "So, what's next on the agenda for today?"

"I've got a few potential new clients to go over with you, and a meeting set up with some guy named Wade Warner this afternoon about a new matter. He called this morning. Said he met you at the seminar."

"I don't remember a Wade on the list of attendees." Riley paused to recall the events of the seminar yesterday, much of which had been overshadowed by her experience with Sam last night. "That could be the guy I met in the elevator after lunch. He's in IT or something at another company in the same building."

"Could be, he didn't say. He is, however, apparently in a lot of trouble. I told him I'd work him in today at 5:00."

"I'll meet with him. Why don't you take off early since Jack is still in town? You don't get to do that often."

Dani internally sighed with relief. She had only mentioned in passing that Jack was on shore duty, but Riley hadn't forgotten. She'd even remembered the dates. Not having to beg for time off was another perk of working with her best friend.

"You sure? I don't mind staying."

"Well, I mind. Besides, we're gonna have some late nights coming up with the depositions in Sam's case. Go do something fun this afternoon, for the both of us."

"All right, I will. And, since you're meeting with Sam later, why don't you do something fun with him for the both of us?"

Riley looked down at her note pad and began to write as she spoke. "Note to self: Send paralegal to sexual harassment training seminar."

CHAPTER 12

Riley had barely closed the car door before Sam started to peel out of the parking lot, the eight cylinders of the Bentley's turbo-injected engine firing in unison.

"Let's go to Crawdaddy's," he said.

"What? Wait, I thought we were going to your office to go over the files?"

"We can do that after we eat. You haven't eaten yet, right?"

"No, I haven't. But Crawdaddy's is over in Cocoa Beach. That's a thirty-five to forty minute drive, even in light traffic."

Sam turned to face Riley, his eyes beaming with mischief and confidence. He bore down on the gas pedal for emphasis. "Not for me."

"Of course. How silly of me. Time and space are your puppets. You have the wheel. No point arguing about it. I have a client meeting at 5:00, though. I have to be back before then," Riley conceded.

"Understood," Sam advised, with a single nod of assurance. "The reason I chose the restaurant is because the owner, Sean Crawford, is also a client of mine. He's a former professional hockey player from Canada. He retired down here a few years back, opened the restaurant shortly afterward. It's been a huge success, so he's ready to franchise now. He asked me to handle the details of that for him, and I asked him to open up a chef's table for us."

"You didn't have to do that," Riley responded cautiously. Sam was confusing her with not only what he was doing, but why he might be doing it. "Hold on. If you already reserved a table, then you counted on me agreeing to go to lunch with you, didn't you?"

"Some things are a given," Sam gloated. "Anyway, Sean wanted me to tell you, whatever you want, he's got it."

"That's good to know," Riley acknowledged, still unsure where all of this was going.

"I don't think he meant it quite the way it sounded," Sam advised. "Like most professional athletes, Sean's highly competitive by nature. I imagine he plans to spend the afternoon trying to steal you away when I'm not looking. Which leads me to ask, for my ego's sake, can you put on a smile and pretend you like me just a little?"

"Don't push it," Riley retorted. "I wouldn't know how to fake something like that, even if I wanted to."

"Fair enough. I'll just have to take you as you are," Sam added, appearing to accept the minor setback to his strategy. His mind had already wandered elsewhere.

"What is that look for?"

"What look?" Sam inquired, consciously removing any trace of expression that might have reflected his less than noble thoughts.

"It's gone now. Never mind."

"Works for me. Minding is not my nature."

Sam decided contemplating something most assuredly not on to-day's lunch menu was too much of a distraction, anyway. He took on a more serious tone to reflect the impending change in topic.

"While we're en route let me give you some background infor-mation on our case."

"Sounds like a plan," Riley affirmed.

"All right. To start with, we'll be working with Bunny Keiler. Do you know her?"

"Can't say I do. Is she opposing counsel?"

"No, she's on our side, as co-counsel."

"Okay, that's a little odd. Why does your firm have another out-side attorney on the case?"

"She was an associate at my firm when the case came in. Apparently, she had some ties to Mikles. When he came to me about the case—,"

"Mikles came to you with the case? Just out of the blue, he chose you?"

"I think you know the answer to that. It's not as if last night was the first time I've been to one of his clubs."

Riley shook her head and sighed. "Naturally. Please continue."

"As I was saying, Mikles asked me to put Bunny on the defense team as a favor to her. At least that's what he called it. Since then, he hasn't seemed particularly beholden to her in any way beyond that simple request. The case was still in the pre-suit administrative stages before the EEOC when Bunny left my firm to go into solo practice. At that time, I didn't think the case would go anywhere, so I let Bunny stay on as co-counsel."

"Now that the case has gone somewhere what will Bunny's role be?"

"That remains to be seen," Sam said. "I believe it won't be as pivotal as she imagines. This is a high-profile case. As I said last night, Mikles is a very wealthy businessman with a colorful past who has made his fortune in . . . colorful ways."

"So, what you're saying is that your firm wants the lead in order to get all the free publicity on this one? I get it. You can't really buy the kind of advertising a case like this brings. I imagine Bunny is thinking the same thing."

Sam nodded in agreement, his eyes fixed on the road. "From what I recall of her, I'm sure that's true."

"I expect she's also very familiar with the pleadings and evidence by now, which is a benefit for the client. That still leaves me wondering why you need me."

"Bunny doesn't have any real experience in employment law. Since she's been out on her own, most of what she handles are quickie divorces or small-time cases in traffic court. And, as you know, I've litigated just about every type of case out there, except one like this. That's why we need your input. You're the specialist."

"No need to pile on the flattery, Sam. I'm already on board and now captive in your car, no less."

Sam smiled broadly. "Captivating women is one of my talents."

"I've noticed. Back to the case. You said we've got depositions coming up. Who's first?" Riley asked.

"We were lucky enough to set the plaintiff, Audra Weyland, first. She goes on Monday. Mikles is next. We set him for Wednesday, leaving a day open just in case Audra's testimony takes longer than anticipated."

"Good strategy. It's best to get the plaintiff's position on the record before you have to settle on defenses," Riley said.

"I thought so. Right now, Bunny is intent on doing the questioning. I'm not so sure that's the best idea."

Riley furrowed her brow in apparent disapproval. "You think you'd be better at questioning a woman about being harassed? Is that because she's just a stripper and you know how to charm girls like that?"

Sam bit his lip, pulled his right hand off of the steering wheel and placed it over his heart. "I'm crushed that you think so little of my litigation skills."

Returning his hand to the wheel, he added in a more serious tone, "If you had given me the chance to finish, you would have discovered that I want you to lead on Audra's deposition."

Riley's face accurately reflected her genuine surprise. "Me? Why me?"

"Because I think you would be able to get behind her defenses without agitating her. Bunny is not the most subtle of creatures, nor is she one to sympathize with other women. You'll see when we meet with her tomorrow."

"Fair enough. I have been known to turn parties around during depositions." Riley hoped Sam wouldn't miss the slight jab in his direction.

"Yes, I recall. That has been taken into account. It's good to have you on my side, this time."

"So, what are the claims? What did Mikles do? Allegedly, of course," Riley asked.

"The pleadings are pretty bare-bones so far. There are basic allegations of improper touching, some off-color comments and requests for favors."

"*Quid pro quo*, then?"

"I recall that term being tossed in the mix," Sam replied.

"The touching part could be troublesome. Courts don't tolerate that in this country," Riley said. She followed with a directed question. "Are specific dates given for any of the incidents? I ask because, in most cases, that kind of detail in the pleadings indicates they've got something more than just Audra's recollection of events."

"Not so far. You know plaintiffs' lawyers never show you their cards until well into discovery. Even then, they hold a few for trial," Sam answered.

"You're in federal court, right?"

"Yes. We pulled Judge Kimble."

"Ouch. Toughest female jurist in the state."

Sam nodded in agreement. "She's also one of the few female jurists who does not seem to appreciate my many charms."

"How dare she?" Riley teased.

Riley raised her hand to shield the sun from her eyes. They were headed due east, which placed the hot summer sun directly overhead. She pulled her purse from its resting spot on the floorboard in front of her and rummaged through it. "Damn it! I don't have my sunglasses."

Sam abruptly reached over toward Riley with his right hand, triggering a reflex withdrawal in Riley.

"Hey, you, I'm not the touchy-feely type."

Sam laughed heartily. "I am aware of that. However, you are the sun-sensitive type. Which is why I was about to offer you some protection."

He pulled his arm back and returned his focus to the road before them. "If you check the glove compartment in front of you, you should find a pair of sunglasses."

Riley pressed the button on the small leather-clad compartment in front of her and the door gently opened. Inside among the manuals, tire gauge and various parking receipts was a small bronze embossed leather case that bore the Gucci imprint. She reached in the compartment, pulled the case out and opened it. Inside was a pair of tortoiseshell framed sunglasses with mirrored, polarized lenses.

"They're very nice. Although, I'm not sure whichever of your conquests left these would appreciate me wearing them," she said.

"Cute. They belong to me," Sam advised. "I keep them there for my conquests to wear, when I spirit them off for impromptu rendezvous on the coast."

Riley didn't miss the obvious innuendo. "The day I become your conquest, Sam, will be the day you become domesticated."

Sam paused to consider the notion. It wasn't one he found entirely unpleasant. "You never know. I might enjoy being your pet."

"Right. Well, I expect my pets to be well trained and come when I call."

"Still enjoying it. You're gonna have to do a lot more than that to get the vision I have of you feeding me by hand out of my head."

Damn him! "Are we there yet?"

"Almost. Have you been to Crawdaddy's before?"

"No. I've heard of the place, though. It's the only restaurant that serves Calabash-style seafood in the area. That is one of the few things I miss about the Carolinas."

Sam inwardly beamed at the acknowledgment. He hadn't chosen the restaurant without forethought. His training and inherent analytical skill gave him the edge when it came to dissecting even the most minor nuances of personality. Many years studying the perplexing ways of women had also afforded him a keen sense of when such knowledge could be used for the greatest return.

Riley was still a Southern girl, even if she had long since been transplanted into the Florida sun. The southernmost point in the States might be found in Florida. That was just geography. The real South—the Deep South—has a flavor all its own, but very little of that flavor had trickled down into the Sunshine State. There were splashes of it to be found in or around North Florida, but Riley had come from where it originated. It still showed in the way she dressed, her gentle manners, and occasionally in her dialect.

The impending storm had pulled all the clouds away from the area and taken them out to the staging area at sea. The clouds would soon return, with newly-acquired reinforcements, but for now the sky was clear and, appropriately, Carolina blue. There was a slight breeze that had taken away most of the overbearing humidity. At the beach, that breeze would also carry the fragrance of the ocean.

The very detailed dossier he had compiled on Riley indicated she had grown up on the Carolina coast, spending most of her summers at the beach. In that case, the smells and sounds of a summer day by the ocean could only invoke fond memories. The accompaniment of those memories with the familiarity of comfort food should be enough to seal the deal. The perfect day, the perfect plan, and all was going accordingly.

"I thought I noticed a hint of a drawl," Sam coaxed. "Good to see you haven't lost all Southern charm."

"Are you implying that I'm not charming?" Riley asked.

"Heavens, no! Why would I imply that?" Sam said. "It's not as if you've been the slightest bit defensive or uncomplimentary to me."

Sarcasm. So that was his ploy. Unfortunately, it was a good one. He had a point. Riley paused to consider it. Maybe she was being too hard on him. Dani seemed to think he wasn't all rotten, and was even starting to enjoy his scheduled and impromptu visits to their office. Of course, that was also because he usually brought her something to eat, or a book, or just chatted with her about the latest all-too-real daytime drama at the courthouse.

Even today, when Sam called to schedule the lunchtime meeting with Riley, she heard Dani laughing uproariously at something he had said. Whatever it was, it seemed to have improved Dani's spirits, which had been uncharacteristically low as of late. Maybe it wouldn't hurt to ease up on Sam. They were going to have to work together for a while, anyway. She might as well make the best of it.

Sam wasn't sure what he'd said to prompt the spin of the wheels now churning in Riley's complex mind. Hopefully, she wasn't reconsidering joining him in the case.

"Am I to get the silent treatment for the rest of our trip? Or would you like to share your thoughts on whatever evil it is you're calculating?"

"I doubt you'll hear this from me ever again but, you're right," Riley admitted.

Sam's eyes left the road momentarily for a double take. "Of course I am. It's entirely not like you to concede, though. What game are we playing now?"

"No, I'm serious. I haven't been treating you the same as I might treat other attorneys I work with. And I think I have been a little defensive around you."

"I won't argue with that. As long as you're confessing, would you care to tell me why?"

"You have a reputation, Sam. It's not all that good when it comes to women. As you might have noticed, I'm a woman."

"That had come to my attention."

"So, color me protective of myself, of my gender, or just in general," Riley said. "I'm not the average girl that you can wrap around your finger. I understand why you have an effect on women. You're not entirely unappealing. I even understand why you use the advantage that gives you."

"So far so good," Sam added, while Riley paused to choose her words. "Although, I'm pretty sure there's a 'but' coming now."

Riley coyly dropped her chin. "There is. The 'but' is . . . I don't like playing games. I don't want to be on-guard all the time with people close to me. I'm not the type of person who works angles. I do that for a living, occasionally, and only when I have to. Aside from that, it's just not who I am. I get the impression it is who you are."

"Ouch. That hurt. I think," Sam replied. "Although, unless my ears deceived me, there was a hint of a compliment hidden in that first part somewhere."

Riley couldn't suppress a chuckle. "I guess I should be relieved you didn't take all of it as a compliment."

"I didn't and I probably deserve the parts that weren't. Now it's my turn to share." Sam slowed the car as they turned into the parking lot at Crawdaddy's.

"I like you, Riley. That's not a game. As a colleague, you fascinate me with your unwavering conviction. I also like you as a person, especially just now, when you told me exactly how you feel. And, if I'm really being honest, I have to say I like you for less honorable reasons, one of them being the way those silk blouses you love to wear pull against your breasts when you breathe."

Riley stared back at him, eyes fixed and lips slightly agape, likely parted by the gasp that followed his unexpected turn from propriety. It appeared his words had made their mark. She was shocked, of course, but it would fade. Some things needed to be said.

"I'm a man, Riley. I hope you won't continue to hold it against me," Sam concluded before deftly pulling into an open spot next to the front door of the small oceanfront restaurant. Once the engine quieted, he turned to face Riley. "I'm also famished. Care to join me inside?"

Riley blinked herself back to the present. *Damn you, Sam Stone. What the hell am I supposed to say to all of that?*

ono ono ono

Dani wolfed down the last bite of the takeout Riley had left in the fridge when she heard the door chimes sound. "Aaaand that would be the delivery of the documents from Sam's office," she announced to herself.

She wiped her hands on a napkin, tossed the plate in the trash and headed toward the front of the office. Sure enough, the courier had arrived with four large banker boxes of records. More than enough to fill her afternoon with sorting, collating and reorganizing. After signing for the delivery, she opened the box labeled "Pleadings." There she would likely find the info she needed on the parties and counsel of record to begin the background reviews Riley requested.

"Alrighty then. Who's got the balls to sue a strip club owner for sexual harassment?" Dani mused while parsing through the documents.

Fortunately, Sam's office had organized the documents perfectly. The pleadings, discovery requests and correspondence were all in separate files, each with their own chronological index—a vast divergence from the morass of disorganized documents he'd sent over when they were on opposing sides in Evan Cole's case.

"Guess it's better to work with Sam than against him," she mused. "Can't say I mind being on the same team. The food's good, anyway. Now, what else is in here?"

It occurred to Dani some people might consider it odd for her to talk openly to herself while alone in an empty room. She didn't give a grit what people might think. Someone had to keep her company on the long days when Riley was in meetings or in court, and on the long nights when her husband was out to sea. Talking to herself, and answering back on occasion, helped her keep hold of her sanity. It wasn't a heady price for something that important, and had fewer side effects than pharmaceutical remedies.

"Oh my God!" That came out louder than she had anticipated. She covered her mouth with her hand, partly to quell another outburst, and partly because it had fallen open and wasn't willing to close just yet.

"Elson Ortiz-Donatti is opposing counsel! Riley is going to flip when she hears this."

Elson was a fairly successful plaintiff's lawyer in the area. He was an interesting mix of transplanted Florida cultures. His father had defected from Cuba, and had brought with him a strong appreciation for hard work and community service. He had apparently managed to instill at least a smidge of that appreciation in Elson. An aeolist, who enjoyed the sound of his voice amplified through a microphone, Elson routinely spoke at schools and political events on issues of local concern, or at least on issues that held the public's attention long enough for some of it to flow in his direction. He also regularly extolled the virtues of working to pay one's way through secondary and graduate school, that accomplishment being one of the many he managed to bring into almost every conversation.

The more flamboyant side of his persona was apparently garnered from his mother, a well-known fixture in Tampa's Italian-American community. That side of his heritage was most evident by outward appearances. On most days, Elson dressed the part of a transplanted Mafioso. His heavily gelled and styled coiffure stood erect at least two inches from his head. All of his suits were expensive, perfectly tailored, and made from imported Italian fabrics with special refractory threads woven into the wool. In the direct sun, his attire always appeared to sparkle, much like literary depictions of the undead.

Dani surmised the over-the-top attire and overly complicated pompadour were intended to detract attention from the fact he was a little more than challenged vertically. On a good day, and with heavily-soled shoes, he stood a mere 5' 2" tall. Imagining Elson going toe-to-toe with six-foot-something Sam was a humorous notion, and one she would hopefully get to witness firsthand.

Elson and Riley had twice been on opposing sides of the fence. The first time was the case of the receptionist who sued her employer because she had been asked to wear something other than flip-flops to work. The receptionist claimed the flip-flops were required due to a disability that caused her to suffer pain when she wore women's dress shoes.

Riley easily dispensed of that case by taking one deposition–the plaintiff's podiatrist. Turned out the lady ran marathons on her time off, so it was no wonder her feet hurt. Her podiatrist had treated her regularly for foot and ankle injuries suffered as a result of the physically demanding activity. That fact alone had made it pretty clear the woman's claims of bias had little to do with the moderately conservative shoes she'd been asked to wear for work, and more to do with her own self-interest. The corresponding defense was also bolstered by the fact Riley knew the ins and outs of women's dress shoes. One other well-placed question regarding the propriety of available shoe designs to the podiatrist had knocked the ball out of the park for their client.

The next time Riley and Elson butted heads was a case involving an inmate's right to religious freedom. Donatti brought suit on behalf of a Florida inmate on claims that correction officials were violating his client's constitutional right to practice his religion of choice, that religion being Vodun. The inmate claimed that in order to fully participate in the tenets of his voodoo-derivative faith, he must let his hair grow naturally and wear it in dreads. He also claimed it was necessary for him to wear the customary decorations of those sharing his belief system–nipple rings.

Riley, as counsel for the Florida Attorney General, easily defended the claim on the ground that even constitutional guarantees are not absolute. They can be abrogated in the name of more compelling interests. For those whose conduct has placed them in prison, the concern of safety–theirs and that of others–can and does trump religion on occasion. This happened to be one such occasion. With an argument directed to that end, Riley got the case dismissed on the face of the pleadings without having to appear in court.

So, to date, if one were keeping score, Riley was up two to zero when it came to matchups with Elson Ortiz-Donatti. Dani wasn't sure if coming into this case at a later stage would upset Riley's perfect record in that matchup, but that was the only real disadvantage she could see at the moment. The case itself appeared to be yet another example of the publicity-driven activism that could only originate from the guileful mind of Donatti.

Dani finished filtering through the boxes of files and placed the majority of them in the filing cabinet drawer she had cleared just for them. A large stack of folders from closed cases sat piled in the corner, waiting to be transported to an off-site record storage facility. Finding space to keep case files was becoming more of a challenge now than finding clients.

The primary pleading file Sam had sent over was not placed in the filing cabinet along with the others. Rather, Dani kept it out and in a prominent spot on her desk. The rest of the afternoon would be spent summarizing its contents and researching the parties and their attorneys; those summaries intended to assist Riley in quickly getting up to speed on the case.

First up was co-counsel Bunny Keiler. Dani settled into her desk chair and woke the computer.

"Let's see what the all-knowing interwebs know about you, Madame Keiler."

CHAPTER 13

Dani was so engrossed with her work she didn't realize several hours slipped past without her moving, even slightly, from her well-warmed, slightly uncomfortable spot in front of the computer. It took the door chimes to break the spell. She looked up to find Riley in the doorway.

"Hey, Boss. How was your *meeeeeting?*" The exaggerated emphasis on the last part was more than intentional. A man like Sam wouldn't have spent that much time with anyone of the female persuasion without some mischief involved.

"The *meeeeeeeting* was fine," Riley retorted, mimicking her friends exaggerated drawl. "We actually drove over to the coast and had lunch while we went over the case. Well, I should say, Sam drove to the coast for lunch. I was unfortunately captive in his car at the time."

"You don't look too upset about having been his prisoner," Dani mused.

Riley felt her cheeks warm. "I was. I am . . .maybe." The amused expression on Dani's face didn't help. "I don't know what I am right now. That man confuses me."

Dani let out a deep sigh of recognition. She'd been married a long time, but still recognized the early stages of it all. "The best ones usually do."

Riley didn't respond, and the fact she didn't dispute Dani's evaluation said more than any words could convey.

"You know, you might've met your match in that one. You're not always going to have the upper hand with him like you do with other men."

"Oh, so now you're not only a member, but the president of the Sam Stone Fan Club?" Riley chided, defensively, while she made a hasty retreat to her office down the hall. "Don't you have work to do?"

"I sure do," Dani added with a salute and a chuckle.

"Great. Then talk to the file, and see what it says about Sam."

"So far, I've not seen too much to complain about in terms of what Sam's firm has done on the case. Turns out, Sam may be the easy one to deal with among your legal peers on this one."

Riley stopped midway down the hall and returned to Dani's desk in the reception area. "What does that mean?"

"Well, for starters, you're gonna get another go at your pal, Elson Ortiz-Donatti. He's plaintiff's counsel."

"That's not so bad. I've got his number. I'll just wear my four-inch heels when we meet with him. He hates having to look up to women. So, if it's not Sam or Elson, who's the troublemaker?"

"Trouble appears to start with the letter 'B' in this one. B as in Bunny, your illustrious co-counsel," Dani said.

"I knew there was more to that story than Sam told me at lunch. He said she had ties to Vince Mikles who, as you know, is primarily in the adult entertainment business these days."

"The story doesn't end there. It seems Ms. Keiler is as enigmatic in her new profession as she might've been in a former one, which I'll get to in a moment. Check this out."

Dani scooted her chair to the right so Riley could join her in front of the computer. She typed a URL into the browser and her computer began to slowly load a website.

"Is the Internet usually this slow on your computer?" Riley asked.

"No, not at all. It's the content that's loading. Bunny's got a lot of cabbage in her garden."

When the website finally loaded it launched into a high-def video with full audio starring none other than Miss Bunny Keiler.

Hello, I'm Attorney Bunny Keiler. I've developed an exclusive practice here in Central Florida for clients just like you. I represent businesses and individuals in all types of law suits in state and federal courts. Does the SEC think you had insider information? I can prove them wrong. Do you need to sue your neighbors for not cutting their lawn? When I'm done with them they'll ask you when they can mow and how low to go. Do your employees think they can join a union? Let's remind them who's boss.

You've found my website, which means you have great taste. You can read all about my education and experience in the Biography section. And don't forget to read about my latest cases in the News and Updates section. Before you leave, you'll want to stop by and read the client testimonials. My clients agree and so will you . . .I'm awesome.

Riley stared blankly at the screen, brows furrowed and eyes blinking with disbelief. Dani twisted in her chair to face Riley. She stared at her boss, waiting for something. Anything. Riley always had an opinion.

Dani reached toward the mouse. "You want me to play it again?"

"No, definitely not." Riley's tone was matter-of-fact. "I'm fairly certain that's something I hope never to see again. How did the Bar even sanction that? They are extremely picky on lawyer advertising. Self-aggrandizement is usually a big no-no."

"That's the fun part." Dani sifted through a pile of papers sitting on the output tray of her desk printer. She pulled out several pages, stapled them and handed the assembled document to Riley. "It's a published Bar opinion from an administrative case Bunny filed challenging the Bar's denial of her catchphrase, 'I'm awesome.' She somehow managed to get the Bar to concede that the phrase was premised on actual client testimonials, and therefore not in violation of the rules."

"Great. Just when I thought dealing with Sam was going to make me insane. This is going to be the best case ever, isn't it?"

"It gets better," Dani said eagerly.

"Is that possible?"

"Oh, yes. I found out the connection between Bunny and the client, Vince Mikles. She used to work for him. First, as a stripper, then as a manager at one of his clubs."

Riley nodded a slow affirmation while she assessed the relevance of the information. Bunny was bottle-blonde, and although the bright red lipstick she wore in the video on her website did nothing for her skin tone, she was still relatively attractive. She was probably a lot more so as a young lawyer, when she started out at Sam's firm. She had been perfectly comfortable in the past disrobing for strange men, so naturally, Sam would find her fascinating. It was all starting to fall into place.

"I guess that explains how she came to work with Sam, too," Riley said. "It makes perfect sense, now that I've seen her. I have to admit, I can also see Mikles' strategy for asking Sam to put Bunny on the case. She knows the business. That could come in handy when we start talking to witnesses."

"I hope you'll let me sit in on some of the witness interviews. If not, you better take video," Dani said. "There's nothing good on television during the summer. I've got lots of time at night and nothing interesting to do with it, especially with Jack going back out on assignment."

Riley took a step back, picked up the pleadings file from Dani's desk, and turned to head down the hall to her office.

"That's right, he's leaving in a few days, which is precisely why you are supposed to be making an early day of it," Riley said. "Pack this up and get on with your bad self. I'll need you to be bright-eyed and all that jazz over the next few weeks."

"Don't have to ask me twice." Dani started to organize the papers and folders on her desk into neat piles. There was nothing worse first thing in the morning than returning to a cluttered desk.

"Oh, and since I don't say it enough, great work today. This is exactly what I needed," Riley advised.

"Of course, Boss. As my clients will tell you, I'm awe—,"

Riley, who had started toward the hall, turned and popped her head back into the reception area before Dani could finish. "Don't you start with that."

ᏬᎧ ᏬᎧ ᏬᎧ

Riley finished skimming over the pleadings from the Mikles case and looked down at her watch. She had a few minutes before her late afternoon meeting with Wade, the young IT technician she met yesterday. She stood, stretched her arms over her head, and tried to clear her thoughts.

The Mikles case pleadings were fairly straightforward, as Sam had said. Still, there was every indication, given the unusual nature of the case, what came next would be anything but simple. The parties would be colorful enough in their own right. When attorneys like Bunny, Sam and Elson were added to the mix, the case had all the makings of a three-ring circus.

A sigh escaped when Riley raised her arms over her head again to stretch her muscles. She took a deep breath and then exhaled slowly as she lowered her arms. Good thing she had started doing yoga again. The one certainty in this case so far was that it would require all the zen she could muster.

She absentmindedly tapped her pen on her desk while contemplating the upcoming deposition schedule. The rhythmic sound helped her to stay focused on the case, rather than thoughts of Sam and the mind games he was playing. Per the deposition notices on file, the Plaintiff, Audra Weyland, would be deposed first. That deposition would be led by Sam or Bunny, or she might be the one given that honor, if Sam had his way. Then their client, Vince Mikles, would be deposed by Elson.

After that, it appeared Elson had requested Sam set aside dates for Elson to take the depositions of some yet-to-be-identified witnesses who were, purportedly, either current or former employees. Elson setting depositions without naming the witnesses he sought to depose was more than a little unusual. Sam agreeing to something like that was pure insanity.

Another unusual aspect of the deposition schedule was that the depositions would commence before the deadline for document disclosures. Elson had hit Sam with a request for production listing nearly 350 categories of documents to be produced. Among the documents to be provided were detailed lists of all of Mikles' employees, including ones employed outside the United States, and information from the personnel records of the dancers at all of Mikles' clubs.

It was a blatant fishing expedition, which meant they might be able to get the court to limit some of the requests as over-reaching. There was no doubt, however, that they would have to turn over the records pertaining to dancers who had direct interaction with Mikles. Those girls would be considered similarly situated to Audra by the court, and that made their records discoverable.

Since the document requests had not been served on Sam's firm far enough in advance, the records weren't due until after the date of Audra's deposition. That was the odd part of it. Most attorneys ask for records well in advance of depositions in order to frame their questions on facts supported by the evidence. But Elson was Elson, and timeliness had never been one of his strong suits. His tendency had always been to wait to the last minute and if things didn't go his way, fast-talk himself out of whatever hole his temporal deficiencies had dug for him.

The primary concern for Sam and the defense team was whether any of the information requested by Elson would lead to the discovery of other dancers who could corroborate Audra's claims of sexual harassment. Corroboration would compound the impact of Audra's expected testimony if the case went to a jury. Surprise witness corroboration would be deadly to the defense.

The defense team could allay some of those inherent concerns by meeting with and taking the statements of employees in advance. According to Sam, Vince had offered them access to his employee files, which made the job easier. Sam also said Bunny had interviewed some of the club's female employees already. Unfortunately, even with access to the club's records, former employees would be hard to locate. And, if found, they would be far less amenable to intrusive questioning. No longer being on the payroll was usually a huge disincentive to witness cooperation.

Riley had encountered that type of uncooperative attitude in the past when dealing with former employees, and had a few tricks that might help to compel cooperation. Even with that small strategic advantage to fall back on, the defense was behind the eight ball. Their quandary returned full circle to the unusual circumstance of Elson not providing the names of his intended witnesses in advance. Even with three attorneys on the defense team, there was no way for them to interview all the potential witnesses before the dates Elson set for depositions.

Elson's excuse for not naming the deponents was that he hadn't fully determined who he intended to depose prior to scheduling. He had used that type of vague excuse on Riley before. She didn't buy it then any more than she did now. While it was remotely possible Elson genuinely didn't know who he intended to call—especially since the documents he had requested had not been produced yet—there was still no way he would be able to get through the number of documents he had requested before the depositions. That, in and of itself, led to one conclusion: Elson was up to something.

The only way any of Elson's actions made sense was if Elson didn't really need the documents he had requested. It was possible the witnesses Elson intended to depose weren't included in or identified by the document requests at all. Elson might have found other girls who aren't employees that claim Mikles harassed them.

If Elson already knew the names of witnesses who could corroborate Audra's claims—witnesses who in all likelihood would not be found in the employee records—Elson could pull those names out of his hat at the last possible moment before the scheduled "Jane Doe" depositions without ever reviewing the requested documents. Or, worse yet, Elson wouldn't depose those witnesses at all. Instead, he could depose random employees next week, and use them to lay the groundwork for the yet-to-be-named witnesses he knows will corroborate Audra's testimony. He would then call those witnesses for surprise rebuttal testimony at trial.

That had to be it. Elson made the expansive document request and set the "Jane Doe" depositions to keep the defense team busy looking in the wrong place for something that amounted to nothing.

Riley's deep concentration was broken by the sound of a primate mating call. It was her cell phone, playing the MP3 she had downloaded and assigned to Sam's number. He was nothing more than a business acquaintance, despite his obvious attempts to move up the food chain. That status wouldn't ordinarily warrant a special ringtone, but Sam had left enough of an impression to deserve some form of identifier.

A slight smile uncontrollably spread across Riley's face before she answered. "You again? I just can't get away from you, can I?"

Sam cleared his throat. "Not easily, of course. Thought I'd check on you to see if you had any questions on the files I sent over."

"So far, so good. I am concerned about Elson's mystery witnesses, though. Have you or Bunny done any more legwork on that front?"

"Funny that you should mention Bunny and 'legwork' in the same sentence. I'm fairly certain you are aware of her past by now."

"I presume you are referring to the fact she worked a pole before she worked you . . . I mean, worked *with* you? Sure, I know all about that. Dani does a hell of a background check. I'm not sure why you didn't just tell me this at lunch."

"I didn't want to deprive Dani the pleasure of that discovery. I knew she would eventually come across that intriguing detail," Sam said. "Perhaps you could brief me on whatever else Dani discovered over coffee? You could come a little early for our meeting with Bunny tomorrow morning."

"Funny you should mention yourself and the word 'brief' in the same sentence," Riley said.

"Walked right into that one, didn't I? Does that mean we are back to idle barbs?"

Riley could no longer suppress an all-out grin. Sam really was a worthy opponent. He had his own objective to accomplish, and was fully aware that exchanging insults wouldn't get him there. For that reason, he had chosen another tactic–mild humility coupled with a hint of remorse. Understanding how to misdirect your prey and gain their trust was an important skill for a hunter. Recognizing that your opponent was utilizing that tactic could be a lifesaver for the hunted.

"You did, actually," Riley teased. "To be honest, I'm not sure how early I can be tomorrow. I'm not a morning person. I guess if I have to start my day early *and* with you, I'd prefer tea."

"Really? No coffee? Afraid I'll be hard to resist after you've had too much caffeine?"

"Sure, that's it."

Sam laughed amiably. "I'll concede to your better judgment, this once. I'll make sure we have tea on hand for you tomorrow. Name your preference."

"That's very thoughtful of you," Riley said. "My favorite is jasmine blended with green tea. It's not easy to find."

"Not for me. I'll have it, hot and awaiting your arrival."

Riley felt her cheeks warm. "Sam, do you say things like that on purpose, or do they just come out that way?"

Her inquiry was met with a slight chuckle. "That's a great question. See, I knew you'd be the right person to take the depositions in this case," Sam acknowledged. "To answer your inquiry, I can't say I'm entirely in control of my thoughts or words lately, especially when it comes to you."

"That sounds like an admission. Are you sure that's the statement you want to put on record?"

"It's my only defense. I'll have to rest my case on it," Sam conceded.

Silence filled a brief lapse in the conversation while they both considered the changing dynamic between them.

"I'll see you tomorrow, Sam."

"Tomorrow it is. Good night, Riley."

CHAPTER 14

"Let me get this straight," Riley interjected as she settled back into her desk chair. Deep in thought, she started to rub her chin while reflecting on the information she had just received. "You downloaded an unauthorized program on a computer at your workplace, misappropriated information through the use of that program, then used the personal information you obtained to invade the privacy of a female co-worker in her own home and, in the process of all this, you might've become the only witness to a murder?"

Wade paused to consider Riley's summation and crinkled his brow. It sounded worse when she put it that way.

"I guess you could say that. In my defense, Halston wasn't supposed to be using her work computer to goof off on the Internet anyway. And the key logger program I used is a version that our human resources folks had asked the IT department to test."

Wrong answer. Riley scooted forward in her seat and stared solemnly at Wade. "Let's get this part out of the way right now. I'm the one who decides whether something is valid to your defense. Got that?"

"Yes, ma'am," Wade responded, sheepishly

"Good. Now, while what you are saying may be true, Halston is the victim here and you'll get nowhere trying to vilify her for a few minor work policy transgressions."

Riley paused to review the random notes she had jotted down while Wade was spilling the details of the extensive mess he was in. "So, you haven't reported anything to the authorities yet, correct?"

"Not yet," Wade replied. "I wasn't sure until today that what I had seen was even real. When Halston didn't show up for work or call in, that's when I knew it had to be real. Then, I didn't know what to do without getting myself into a mountain of trouble."

"You're right on that last part—you are likely in a heap of trouble," Riley said. "You were smart to secure counsel before approaching the authorities. You're definitely going to need some help navigating this minefield."

Wade heaved a heavy sigh of relief. "This means you're gonna help me, right?"

Riley weighed her options while she observed Wade's reaction. There it was—the look. The one she'd seen many times before, most often after whoever was sitting across from her in that very chair unloaded their burden and placed it squarely on her shoulders.

If she had to describe the look, its verbal depiction would include words like "despair" and "frustration," mixed with "hope" and "relief." Giving clients the sense that they could still have some measure of control over their life, in spite of whatever madness might be going on around them, was the nature of the relationship between client and counsel. She had long since accepted it.

Good attorneys are natural problem solvers and that was usually the hallmark of their success. It was a skill that Riley took particular pride in. Over the years, a few clients had even referred to her ability to solve complex problems as something of a gift. Their gratitude was always rewarding, but often she felt more like a comic book superhero; one who considers herself as equally burdened by her unique skills as she is blessed by them.

Enough with the retrospection. It was time to give him an answer.

"Yes, I'm going to *try* to help you. Note my emphasis on the word 'try.' This is new ground for me, as well. I don't usually take on criminal matters. In this instance though, your activity is or should be of lesser concern to the authorities than the fact a murder appears to have been committed."

"Thank, God," Wade responded, his entire body seeming to heave with his subsequent sigh of relief. "What happens now?"

"We need to contact the authorities and let them know what you know. I will approach them first to see if I can't get an agreement not to prosecute or charge you in exchange for the information you have to offer. However, no matter what, they will want to speak with you and it would be my advice to cooperate with them."

"Will that be tonight, or sometime later?" Wade asked.

"I don't suggest waiting any longer than necessary. The longer you wait to come forward, the more questions they will have for you about your involvement. It's important we make it clear that you were merely a passive observer in all of this," Riley advised.

"What does that mean? It sounds like you think they might believe I am . . . that I was involved or something."

"Law enforcement is required to consider all reasonable possibilities. So, yes, they will look at you as a possible suspect until they can verify your version of events. It's important that you not give them any reason to disbelieve what you are saying, or any reason to think you have any ulterior motives. You don't, do you?"

"I don't what?" Wade asked.

"Have any other motives for being here? You've told me everything, right?"

"Yes, I told you everything I did, and everything I know. I had no reason to hurt Halston. I'm crazy about her." Wade stopped himself when the reality of what he'd witnessed hit hard. "I mean . . .I *was* . . .crazy about her."

"While I vastly disapprove of your actions, I do believe you, Wade. I believe you didn't intend to do anything to hurt Halston, although you have to know that invading a woman's privacy is far more hurtful to her than you might realize. I'm sure you know that crazy people often do crazy things. For that reason, I'd suggest you not use that word in describing your actions to anyone else."

"Right. No more crazy talk. What next?"

"There are a few administrative details we have to take care of before we proceed. I've had my assistant prepare a formal representation letter for you that details the nature of my work and my fee. You'll need to review and sign that. Then I can begin working on your problem," Riley said. "While I figure out how to approach law enforcement with this, I need you to write down everything you remember from the time you downloaded the program on Halston's computer until now. You should include anything you noticed or witnessed when you went into work today."

Wade nodded to convey his understanding while Riley handed him the folder with the papers Dani had prepared earlier in the day.

"I have a contact in the FDLE computer forensics department. I doubt I can reach her tonight, but I will leave a message for her. She probably won't get back to me until tomorrow. When she does, be ready to jump when I say jump."

"I understand. I'll be ready," Wade agreed.

"Good. I'll be in a meeting most of tomorrow morning. I'll check in for messages when I can," Riley said. "If you have any questions, just leave a message on my voicemail or with Dani, my paralegal. We'll get back to you as soon as we know something or hear from my contact."

"Okay. Thank you. You have no idea how much I appreciate your help." Wade rose from his chair and moved toward the door of Riley's office. He paused before heading to the reception area to review the documents she had given him. "Ms. Morgan?"

"Please, call me Riley. Is there something else?"

"I'm really worried about Halston. What if what I saw was real? She could be hurt or something. She might even be . . . she could be dead, couldn't she?"

Riley looked up from the Mikles employee list she had started to review, and paused to consider her response. Wade was seeking comfort and an assurance that everything would be okay, but she couldn't give him either.

Comforting him could impart a sense of approval of his behavior, and that would send the wrong message. Wade's conduct was illegal and he needed to understand there would be consequences for it. Also, he was going to need to grow a serious backbone to make it through the difficult days ahead. Law enforcement wasn't going to be easy on him. He needed to be ready to face what had happened and, worse yet, relive and repeat it over and over until the authorities were satisfied they had every ounce of information he had to give. More to the point, giving assurances, of any kind, to a remorseful client, especially in a criminal matter, was a mistake usually reserved for a rookie attorney. Riley bit her lip while she calculated her response. When she found the right words, she spoke carefully.

"I hope that is not the case, but yes, what you saw could be real. Halston could be dead," Riley said. "You will need to be prepared for that possibility. If that is the case, your coming forward could help the authorities find out who is responsible for what happened to her. It won't change what happened, but it could give her family some peace."

Wade winced at Riley's words. It wasn't what he was hoping to hear. "How am I supposed to go back in to work tomorrow? I'm not gonna be able to think about anything else while I'm waiting to find out how this is going down."

"That's a good question. You probably shouldn't go to work while we work through this. Do you have some leave time coming?" Riley asked.

"Yeah, I've got a few PTO days," Wade said.

"Then I suggest you take one tomorrow. You may need to take more, and I have to advise you that once we give your statement to the police, your employer will have to be notified of the investigation. After that, you could have plenty of time to consider your actions, because you will probably be suspended, or even fired. It is not likely an employer would keep you on under these circumstances."

Wade's head sunk further into his chest. "Oh, man. I didn't even think about that."

"That's the least of your worries right now. Jobs will come and go," Riley advised. "You'll have better odds of getting another decent one if we can keep your record clean. Let's just focus on that."

Wade nodded and turned to leave, his head still hung low. Riley couldn't help but feel sorry for him. Tonight was going to feel like one of the longest and darkest he would ever know.

Riley took a brief break from reviewing the Mikles files long enough to see Wade out after he completed the forms. She locked the entry door behind him and headed back toward her office. It was probably going to be a late night, the downtown area around her office was deserted, and she was working alone. She was usually fairly attentive to safety and security matters, but after hearing Wade's story, she was even more acutely aware of her vulnerability. Dani had suggested they put an alarm system in the office and she was glad she decided to bite that bullet and install one.

Back in her office Riley opened the calendar application on her computer and typed in a quick task-list reminder to have Dani look into some of the questions she had encountered regarding the Mikles case. She could direct some of her questions to Sam before their meeting with Bunny tomorrow. Dani's role would be finding information to confirm or dispute the parts of the story Riley anticipated Sam couldn't aptly explain. She then filtered through her electronic contact list.

"Kristina . . . Kris . . . why can't I remember your last name?" Riley mused before she stopped other cognition to perform a full-scale mental scan. The most reliable databanks weren't always of the electronic variety. It had been about a year since she'd last seen Kristina. It had been far longer since she had referred to Kristina on anything other than a first-name basis, and a shortened one at that.

"It starts with a 'v' I think. Veniable. That's it."

Riley typed the name into the search box and the contact card popped up. She dialed the work number listed and after a few rings, as expected at this hour, she was forwarded to voice mail. It occurred to Riley, after leaving her message requesting a return call, that her initial encounter with Kristina had been one of those life experiences that leave an indelible mark. From the very beginning, it felt as if fate had intended for them to cross paths. That was the impression they both were left with after the first case they were assigned to as young professionals.

After graduating from law school and completing her term as a federal law clerk, Riley had taken a position with the Florida Attorney General's office. It was a great way for a young lawyer to get first chair litigation experience in high-profile matters. When she took the job, she had no idea just how much experience she would be getting. While most baby lawyers with just a few years under their belt are relegated to writing research memos for lazy partners in the big firms, Riley was handling depositions, arguing dispositive motions, and even acting as lead counsel in major litigation.

One of her first assigned cases involved a high-ranking member of the Governor's cabinet, clandestine meetings with campaign contributors vying for lucrative government contracts and the destruction of documents related to the bidding process. The documents in question were supposed to be available to the public via the generous provisions of Florida's Sunshine Law. Kristina, freshly appointed to an entry-level position with the Florida Department of Law Enforcement as a computer forensic analyst, was the State's lead investigator assigned to the case.

At the time it had escaped Riley's notice. Some years and a great deal of political experience later, it dawned on her that the case had been assigned to them, a fledgling litigator and a brand new investigator, because no one expected them to be able to unravel the intricate trail of deception and lies. None of the naysayers had bothered to tell the newbies. So, with the same perseverance the two young professionals had used to tackle every other obstacle tossed into their path, they found a way to do what wasn't supposed to be done.

It took a whole year to filter through the data and to work around the bureaucratic maze that had been set up to sidetrack them. Working together to navigate that labyrinth, they managed to build a strong case. Kristina seemed to have a sixth sense about where information might be hidden or stored on computers or mainframe systems. She had been nothing short of amazing when it came to locating and retrieving the deleted information. Once they had that, the "who," the "how" and even the "why" came together easily.

In the end, due to the long-reaching political implications, a deal to avoid prosecution in favor of quiet and timely resignations was struck among parties at far higher pay-grades than she or Kristina had held. Still, as far as she and Kristina were concerned, it was a win for the people of Florida. Misuse of public funds and the abuse of public trust were serious offenses and those in power needed to be reminded that the people were watching.

With the dilemma Wade was now facing, it appeared there could be something else in store for the powerhouse Riley/Kris pairing. Sometimes, people cross paths long before the true purpose of their encounter is revealed. This was likely one of those times.

For Wade, the importance of having an attorney with a good friend at FDLE in the very division that would be investigating his conduct was probably a God-send. The innocuous way he had made that fortuitous connection was one of life's true ironies. It really is possible for a person to stumble, completely by chance, into the right place at the right time or in this case into the right elevator car at the right time, to meet the one other person who could literally change their entire future. Such is the game of life.

CHAPTER 15

With eerily precise timing Sam's prim and proper assistant, Mona, appeared from behind a heavy birch wood and satin-finished steel framed door in the reception lobby at the exact moment Riley entered the firm's offices from the elevator lobby.

"Good morning, Miss Morgan. Mr. Stone is expecting you. Please follow me," Mona directed.

Riley followed Mona's wool-clad form through the doorway from which she had just appeared and down a long narrow corridor that ran the length of the floor. On the right side of the open passageway were fields of five-tiered metal filing cabinets and on the other side, a string of small windowless offices. Glancing into a few of the offices, Riley concluded the occupants were low-level associates or paralegals, who would necessarily be stationed near the documents and files that comprised the bulk of their billable days.

Following her stint with the attorney general's office, Riley had worked as an associate attorney with some of the area's largest firms and was quite familiar with the hollow-eyed, expressionless appearances on the faces of those who inhabited the small, dark offices. In order to prove worthy of partnership in the privileged, high-finance world of the legal elite, young attorneys have to all but trade their souls for the few choice case assignments tossed down into their pit of despair. If they are lucky enough to secure a spot on a trial team for one of those cases, there would be no rest until the final argument made on appeal.

After a few turns in various directions and a maze of similar corridors, the hint of natural light appeared in the distance. They were now approaching the high-rent area of the office where the partners, at least the ones who inhabited this upper floor, would be found. At a firm like this, a partner's place in the pecking order is reflected by the size of his or her office and its location. Relevance in that hierarchy is further defined, of course, by the window count. According to the natural order in a mega-firm, the partner with the most windows wins.

In the jungle-like social order of most law firms, it stood to reason that those inhabiting the expansive corner offices were the leaders of their given pack. Riley fully expected that Sam would be found among those leaders. Unsurprisingly, Mona continued down what appeared to be partners' row to the very end and stopped before a double door entryway that, given the distance between the remotely neighboring entryways, appeared to be large enough to be a small conference room. It was not. Riley had been ushered directly to the "jungle king's" inner chamber.

Mona opened both doors and stood in front of one while she gestured for Riley to enter.

"Miss Morgan is here and she's early as you requested, Mr. Stone. I will have your coffee prepared and it will be served in the conference room," Mona advised after Riley stepped past her into the office. "I have the tea you requested, Miss Morgan. Do you take that with sugar and cream?"

"Oh, um . . . no cream," Riley responded haltingly, her mental faculties momentarily taxed by the survey of her opulent surroundings. Sam didn't have the most windows in the firm—he appeared to have all the windows in the firm. Wall-to-wall glass extended from the ceiling down to the floor in any direction she turned. The visually unencumbered transition between interior and exterior offered the most impressive view of the "City Beautiful" that Riley had ever seen.

It occurred to Riley, primarily because Mona was standing there staring at her with a blank expression, that she hadn't fully answered the pending question. "I prefer Splenda, if you have it."

"As you wish," Mona acknowledged. When Riley turned to thank her, she was met with only the cautious click of a softly-closed door. Mona's exit was effected as deftly as her entrance.

A slight rustling sound from across the room preceded Sam's approach. It was followed by the scent of an expensive men's fragrance. Riley generally favored natural fragrances and this one did not disappoint. It hailed some combination of sandalwood, ginger and lime; it's aroma pure masculinity.

"What is that smell?" Riley wrinkled her nose as she turned to face Sam who, for some odd reason, was smiling from ear to ear.

"You don't like it?"

"Did I say that? No, I don't think I did," Riley retorted. "I just asked what it was."

"Ah, I see. There is more to language than meets the ear, my dear. Haven't you said that? Am I misreading the message conveyed by the harsh wrinkling of your adorable little nose?"

"Oh, stop fretting, Sam. I'm just messing with you," Riley confessed. "You don't strike me as the type of man who puts on cologne for this type of thing. We're just meeting with Bunny today, remember?"

"Really? I don't strike you as a man who would want heightened appeal when in the presence of beautiful women?"

"Good point. That would totally be your game. I stand corrected," Riley said.

"No need to stand. I can easily dispel your notions while offering you a more comfortable arrangement. You are my guest today," Sam offered generously. "As such, I am yours for the messing."

He motioned toward one of the overstuffed black leather chairs that were perfectly stationed in front of a large, glass-topped piece of contemporary-style wood framed furniture that must be what he considered a desk. Others of a less indulgent nature might consider it to be a place to dine for a party of eight. Riley followed him across the room and took a seat in front of the desk, while Sam returned to his seat behind it.

"You know, it unnerves me when you are being nice, Sam. It seems contrary to your nature. What are you up to?"

Sam's smile remained and was joined by a brief flash of mischief in his steel-blue eyes. He looked every bit the schoolboy about to launch a classroom prank. "Nothing much. Just expecting to have a little fun with our co-counsel. You'll see."

"Can't wait," Riley responded, drolly. "So, was there something other than a hot beverage that warranted my early arrival? Did you want to go over something in particular? If not, I have a few questions of my own."

"I do have some thoughts I'd like to share on opposing counsel's mystery witnesses. I also wanted to strategize with you before we meet with Bunny. As you know, my firm's objective is to retain the position of sole lead counsel in this case. However, we still need some of Bunny's insight before we transition her out."

"Sounds as if you plan to use her and then cast her aside. Is that the sum of your intent?"

Sam's eyes narrowed at the rebuke, which undoubtedly stung only because it wasn't off the mark. "Not exactly. Besides, she has been and will be well compensated for all of her input."

"I suppose for someone like Bunny, if all I've read and seen of her is true, money would lessen the burn of your betrayal. Just for the record, though, that wouldn't work for me. You should know that before you make any similar plans to do away with me."

"I have no such plans, Miss Morgan. Indeed, my greater concern when it comes to you is where or when you might be reminded of something you already know."

"Which is?" Riley asked.

"That I am far more in need of you and your expertise than you are of any of mine at the moment."

"Oh, there must have been some mistake, then. I've not forgotten that at all." Riley emphasized her conclusion with a slight tilt of her head.

"And yet, here you are."

"And yet, here I am," Riley echoed. "It does boggle the mind. Since I am here and we've still got time, please enlighten me on how you plan to extract the information you want from Bunny without her becoming wise to your plan."

"Another great question from my favorite inquisitor," Sam offered. "The plan is based on simple human nature. Or really, if I'm to be exact, the nature of women."

Riley shook her head. *That figures.* "Obviously. Smart of you to play to your strengths. Exactly what of the nature of my gender have you surmised to be universal?"

"A great deal, of course. This being just one of many insights. In my experience, there's a certain cattiness women exhibit when faced with another woman they deem to be. . . ." Sam paused to choose his words carefully. "How shall I put this? A woman they feel is . . . a threat."

Riley's face registered genuine confusion. "I don't disagree with you on the premise. But why would Bunny see me as a threat?"

"Do I really have to count the ways?"

"Yes, you do."

"Fine. You're younger, prettier, more accomplished, have a better social and professional background, and simply put, you're a better attorney. That's the short-list of the reasons her fur will bristle when she joins us in the conference room a few minutes from now. I can recite from the longer list if you'd like."

At the moment, it was Riley's fur that bristled. Sam may have meant all of that as a compliment. It didn't sound like one to Riley. She wasn't taken in by the barrage of flowery words intended to mask his intent.

"How am I supposed to take that? I don't like being placed as the pawn in your power play with Bunny. I thought you brought me into this case for my legal expertise."

Sam rose from the black Nappa leather executive chair behind his desk, walked around the desk and positioned himself directly in front of Riley. He leaned back casually against the desk, crossing his arms in front of his chest. He intended to uncross them as a nonverbal signal that he was being completely open, when the time came. That move was only a small supplement to the other forms of subliminal persuasion he routinely employed at times like this. His physical proximity to her was intended to signify solidarity or, if she were even remotely as attracted to him as he was to her, it could also distract her. Either would suit his purpose, although he couldn't deny the latter was his preference.

"I did. And your expertise has already proven useful. However, as a litigator, and one with experience, you know this game is played on many levels. We've got a case involving a rich, powerful businessman who makes most of his money from the wiles of beautiful women. If Elson plays his hand as I would, he will parade before the jury a bevy of beautiful women, all cleaned-up and styled for the show. He will present them as sympathetically as possible, showing them to be not unlike the female jurors, or the mothers, sisters or daughters of any male member of the jury. Elson's next play will be to portray our client as the big bad wolf, preying on these lovely, innocent victims."

Sam uncrossed his arms and let them fall naturally to his sides. He also stared down at Riley with an earnest expression, clearly indicating he was open to her reply, regardless of what it might be.

Riley nodded. "None of that is news, Sam. I don't disagree with you on that being the strategy Elson will likely employ. There's nothing in that equation, however, which adds up to me taking Bunny's place in the show."

"You are correct on the latter point. What I'm illustrating now is just one of the many reasons you are here. We need to show beautiful women such as you have nothing to fear from Vince, and are ready and able to defend him and his businesses. It's not just about getting Bunny off the case. It's entirely possible you won't be needed for that purpose at all."

"If it's just a pretty face you need at your table, why wouldn't Bunny's suffice?" Riley asked.

Sam pursed his lips as if he'd bitten into a lemon. "Bunny might have some pleasant attributes. Still, I don't think she will compare to the young women we're likely to be opposing. She also isn't likely to connect with the jury. Whatever appeal Bunny might initially carry will be lost the second she opens her mouth."

"I don't follow."

"I think it's best to let you experience that for yourself," Sam added with confidence. He relinquished all outward reflection of the bitter aftertaste brought on by the mere thought of Bunny, and replaced the expression with its predecessor.

"As I mentioned, it may be that your presence won't be the catalyst to our securing Bunny's removal from the case in any event. It's very possible that she might encounter a conflict from her past that cannot be removed."

"That sounds like you know something you're not telling me. I don't work that way, Sam. You are going to have to be completely upfront with me or I'm out."

A broad smile spread across Sam's chiseled face. Deeming Riley's tension sufficiently diffused, in spite of her outward attempt to show otherwise, Sam returned to his comfortable leather perch behind his enormous desk.

"Keeping me honest. I fully expected that of you," Sam acknowledged. "I think it's fair to say that I've been very open with you so far, haven't I?"

"Yes, Sam. You have certainly given me insight into your scheme I didn't expect you to give," Riley said.

"I intend to continue to do that. Though, I can't tell you what I don't yet know. Right now, the last part is more of an educated guess."

Riley feigned disappointment at Sam's failure to oblige her with the details of his so-called "guess." The reasons Bunny might find herself in conflict with representation of Vincent Mikles in this case, including her former employment with him at a managerial level, were somewhat apparent. She could just as easily be called as a witness as any former employee might be. Still, it seemed Sam was not speaking of something quite so obvious. His tone had an ominous sense about it.

"You know, I think you enjoy the whole man-of-mystery air you put on just a little too much."

"There may be some truth to that," Sam concurred. "But only to the extent it helps me hold your interest. And I am, aren't I?"

"You are what?" Riley asked.

"Holding your interest?"

"I guess. I haven't felt the urge to yawn, yet. The day is still young, though. You could easily bore me at any moment." Riley looked down at her watch to bolster her retort.

"I seem to recall you yawned at me when we first met. Were you bored then?"

"Did I? I'm surprised you would remember something so insignificant. I couldn't honestly tell you if I was bored or not. I don't recall our first meeting that well."

That was a lie. Sam wasn't the only one with a lasting impression of their first encounter. Mostly, the impression Riley carried away from the exchange was one of annoyance, premised on the fact the rumors of Sam's arrogance had not been greatly exaggerated. There had also been the lingering recognition of the fact that, in many ways, his self-assurance wasn't entirely unwarranted. He was handsome, obviously. And by all indications, he was intelligent, well-educated, highly successful and generally respected among his peers.

Sam moved, spoke and acted purposefully, as if the world had assured him of his prominence and import. Come to think of it, the world probably had done just that in a memo to the universe heralding his birth. Riley might have been impressed had she witnessed the same innate sense of self-worth in a prize-winning thoroughbred race horse. For some reason, display of that hubris in a human male seemed far less appealing.

Sam was the personification of a "ladykiller," which Dani had so aptly dubbed him in the past. By all accounts, women fell at his feet, often waiting with bated breath for a crumb of his attention, or if they were truly charmed, a night in his bed. As would any red-blooded mammal in a fairly high position on the food chain, he was known to have enjoyed the fruits of his wiles on many occasions, only to cast aside the vanquished once they no longer piqued his interest or served his needs. His current plan for ridding himself of Bunny only served to reinforce that perception. While that sort of self-serving prowess might be the norm in the animal kingdom, humans seemed to view it somewhat differently, particularly the humans whose gender placed them among his prey.

Riley stared back at Sam with a droll expression she'd borrowed from Dani's repertoire. When it came to the appearance of disinterest, Dani held the patent. Sam tried to call the bluff with his best poker face. He lost that guise when an internal, apparently off-topic cognition caused a broad smile to cross his face. Riley found the change almost as annoying as his ever-apparent overconfidence. Who sits across from someone wearing a grin like that and doesn't share the thought?

"I'm pretty sure I don't want to know what has caused that goofy expression you're now wearing."

"I am enjoying the company, that's all. Would you rather I grimace during our meetings?" He made an exaggerated grimace to emphasize his point. The look was ridiculous, and amusing. Riley could no more suppress genuine laughter than she could have suppressed a real yawn—although the latter was unlikely to be brought on by anything Sam did or said. The man wasn't boring, even if she wanted him to think otherwise.

"Okay, you win. You grin and I'll bear it, for now. But you may want to turn down the wattage on that when we meet with Bunny.

She will surely know you are up to something if you go in there looking like that."

"I am up to something."

"Yes, of course. However, you don't want her to be on to you. At least not in *that* way."

"I'd certainly prefer she not be," Sam said.

"Really? I had heard otherwise."

"That was in the past. The very distant past. Before my last marriage, even."

Riley recoiled slightly at the odd revelation. "You make that sound so nonchalant, as if each marriage is merely a way to account for the passage of time. Is that really how you recall them?"

It was Sam's turn to respond with laughter. He was genuinely amused by Riley's naivety on the subject. His laughter was also intended to divert her attention. Riley wouldn't understand the nature of his past relationships or the fact that, due to the covert nature of his position, almost none of his public persona was what it seemed.

"You've never been married, Riley. Cagamosis is probably among the few concepts beyond your expansive intellectual purview. We can revisit the subject when you've had more experience with it."

"Thanks, but no thanks. I don't plan on having the experience of an unhappy marriage, Sam. I have to say, though, it seems I might've hit a nerve. I don't mean to sound judgmental. It's just I'm not one for casual relationships, of any kind. And marriage would seem to be the least casual relationship of all. It's hard to imagine how that would even work."

"It works, until it doesn't. Simple as that, really. Speaking of relationships, how is that musician of yours?"

Riley fumbled with her purse, intentionally avoiding Sam's gaze. "I thought we weren't going to talk about relationships."

"No, actually, we weren't going to talk about marriage," Sam recounted and then continued with a mischievous grin. "Yet, anyway. Relationships, hook-ups, flings, any of those are fair game."

"So, what about co-workers?"

Sam's eyes widened briefly then narrowed with introspection. Was that a hint, or was she just toying with him again?

"Co-workers? As you and I are, right now? That's an interesting thought." Sam stopped and rubbed his chin for emphasis. "I've heard there are studies that say most people find their mate at the office."

Riley smirked. He had taken the bait. Time to yank the chain.

"No, Sam. I am talking about the case. You know, the part about the mystery witness or witnesses who may be co-workers of Audra's? What are your thoughts on the co-workers?"

Sam nodded, reluctantly. "Right. Of course. The answer to your question is, 'yes.'"

"Meaning, you have thoughts on the subject?"

"Was that your question? I got the distinct impression you were using the inquiry to mask a more personal one."

Riley felt her cheeks warm, and she wasn't at all pleased by her reflexive reaction to Sam's taunt. How does he do it? How does he find so many ways to turn her very precise words into something else entirely? It was fine, though. If Sam wanted to play word games, he could have at it. A few measly words, however, would be all of her he was getting. Might as well get that settled and out of the way, before his less-than-subtle suggestions went any further.

"I'm not sleeping with you, Sam. Not as a co-worker, not as part of a field study on marriage, and not in any other respect during this lifetime, or the next."

There it was again—the annoying grin. It was as if her resistance only engaged him more.

"Duly noted. Although, I don't recall the subject having come up. We can add it to the growing list of the topics to revisit after you've had more experience."

"We can do that. Although, revisiting the issue is not going to alter the conclusion," Riley replied, with a hint of exasperation. "Can we talk about the case now?"

"Indeed, we can and should. Bunny will be here soon. We'll wrap things up here and wait for her in the conference room."

Sam rose from his chair and walked over to a large credenza that stood against the glass wall behind his desk. He picked up a file folder from the top of the credenza and returned to his seat. After briefly glancing inside to confirm the contents, he handed the file to Riley.

"I had Mona filter the personnel records Vince provided into categories, separating them by gender, age, marital status, and the like. We have a pretty good idea of Mikles' type, so I think that's where we start our search. He obviously has a thing for leggy blondes–the younger the better. I've no doubt he's continued to 'audition' them personally, in spite of his marriage to Cayren, one of his former dancers." Sam said. He followed by outlining an action plan. "I think the next step is to break them down by dates of employment and then contact the ones whose last dates of work put them within the statute of limitations for bringing suit."

Although she didn't want to be, Riley was impressed. Sam's approach made perfect sense, given the nature of the case and the known proclivity of their client. Why hadn't she thought of it?

"You're giving me a look I've not seen before. What ungodly thing have I managed to do that warrants a look like that?" Sam queried.

"For once, I can't argue with you. Knowing Elson as I do, he would absolutely look for witnesses to bolster Audra's claims and possibly even ones who might join in the case as plaintiffs. How you wanted to head that off was one of the questions I had for you," Riley said.

Sam was outwardly pleased. "We're on the same page, then. That's good."

"Yes, looks like we are," Riley replied. "Taking that approach makes sense for Elson. From his perspective, having multiple plaintiffs substantially increases the amount and likelihood of a settlement, especially where the case is one of first impression. A judge is going to have a hard time accepting that someone in Audra's line of work was offended by much. Corroboration is almost mandatory."

"Exactly. It's going to take a while to go through these. I'll need your help with that if we're going to finish before the depositions start next week."

"So, basically, you're telling me I should expect to be spending a lot of time with you?"

That thought had crossed Sam's mind, in other respects. "Again, the answer to your question is 'yes.' It seems unavoidable given the tight deadline. Do you have plans for the weekend?"

"Nothing specific. However, I do charge extra on weekends," Riley replied.

That wasn't true. Normally, she charged her clients the same, no matter how many nights or weekends their case might devour. This was an entirely different situation. If she was forced to bear Sam's company after hours, and for a less-than-sympathetic client, someone was going to have to pay.

"Why don't we double your fee for after-hour time? Even at that rate, you'd still be billing below our junior partner fee."

"I wouldn't say that in front of your client, Sam. In this economy, he might take offense to the fact your firm's rates are so high," Riley advised.

Sam's expression implied agreement before he refuted the assumption. "Not Mikles. He knows you get what you pay for in this world, especially when it comes to a service industry. As you know, his business is based on customers paying a premium to indulge their vices. That comes with the understanding a similar premium will be required by those he engages, out of necessity, to aid him in continuing to offer those services. Expect to be well-paid for your time. I've already told Vince you'll be worth every penny."

Now he was just openly goading her, and not on a subject she found amusing. Riley felt the need to nip him for it. "I understand Mikles' view that throwing money at a woman is the way to get what he wants. That being said, I expect you to understand tucking bills into my garter isn't the way to go."

"I am fully aware of that, Miss Morgan." Sam's gaze knowingly followed the length of her, leaving Riley with a sense he knew her intimately. "Besides, you aren't wearing a garter. We'll have to deposit the money in your bank, instead."

Sam rose, picked up the rest of the file folders and documents from his credenza and moved toward the double doors at the front of his office. He opened one of the doors and stood aside to let Riley pass first.

Riley glared at him and stopped briefly as she walked past. "That was out of line. Don't expect to get away with it."

Sam followed her out the door and quickly caught stride beside her. He pointed to a nearby conference room and then opened the door for her to enter. As Riley passed, he offered a hushed reply.

"Getting away isn't part of the plan."

CHAPTER 16

The conference room Sam had chosen for today's meeting was smaller than the ginormous one behind the reception area he used when Riley deposed his client Tony Giordano. Sam's firm had likely learned a few things about staging from some of the local entertainment experts. World-class attractions like Disney or Universal Studios, both major players in Florida's billion-dollar tourism industry, are known for leaving no detail unattended when putting on a show. The art of attraction is not unlike the art of war. The details matter.

Among the most important of details in either form of art is where to make your first stand. Using the firm's expansive glass-enclosed main conference room, wisely located just behind the main lobby, to impress prospective clients or awe the opposition into submission was a smart first move. For prospective clients, the opportunity to be seen taking a meeting in the blinged-out main staging area fostered a sense of privilege and importance. Alternatively, staging a deposition or arbitration in the highly visible conference room could create unease in an opponent merely by playing upon the same fishbowl effect. Once behind the glass curtain, the room's occupants became featured players in a legal drama that played daily for a captive audience in the lobby.

Converse logic set the stage for the show Sam had planned for Bunny. The smaller, less grandiose back-office conference room was intended to convey a specific, albeit entirely different, sentiment. Bunny Keiler had worked with the firm as an associate attorney. She was intimately familiar with the office, as well as the things that go on behind their stage. There was no need to awe or inspire her. Rather, the staging for today was intended to convey a far different message— one resembling the final curtain call of an overextended production at the local playhouse.

Given the proximity to Sam's office and knowing Sam's reputation as a skirt chaser, it occurred to Riley that Bunny might also be familiar with this particular conference room in a different, more biblical sense. That would, of course, have also been among the reasons Sam chose it. He either intended to evoke fond memories in an effort to utilize whatever lingering goodwill remained between them, or if Bunny's memories were not so fond, he hoped having to share the familiar quarters with him again would make her uncomfortable. Either way, the plan was to throw Bunny off her game.

Riley wasn't sure which part of the scenario bothered her more— the fact Sam had surely considered all of the foregoing in setting the stage for today, or the fact she could so easily recognize the logic behind it. His mind seemed a treacherous place, where every thought was carefully tailored to achieve the maximum return for whatever small part of him might be invested. The type of person who could employ that level of strategy on something as simple as this wasn't the type to ever really let down their guard. And, if by some chance they did, it was doubtful anyone had the privilege of sharing the moment. That realization was briefly joined by a pang of sympathy. Someone with Sam's mindset wasn't likely to let anyone get too close. No wonder his relationships all end badly.

His relationship with Bunny, at least the professional one, had seemed to remain cordial to this point. But that, too, was about to turn dark for some reason Sam seemed unwilling to convey. This wasn't the usual tug of war over a wealthy client—at least not for him.

Sam and his firm continued to draw in a plethora of high-profile clients, in spite of the dour economy. Bunny might need the money but they didn't, and certainly not from a questionable character like Vince Mikles. Riley's spidey senses started to tingle. She needed to pay close attention to these two. Something was up. And by all indications that something was about to get interesting–or dangerous.

Sam casually walked to the far side of the room and picked up a remote control. He pointed it toward the window and pressed a button. The dark colored sheer sunshades that covered the expansive window on the far side of the room quietly rose on his command allowing morning light to fill the room. Sam then settled into the traditional power seat at the end of the table and directed Riley to the chair at his right. No sooner had they taken their seats than the receptionist announced Bunny's arrival via speakerphone. A few moments later, Mona escorted Bunny into the room. Before departing, Mona advised she would return shortly with the menu for beverage and pastry service.

Riley was struck by the unusual nature of Mona's advisory. Most firms do not have prepared menus for this type of meeting. Then again, most firms also don't inhabit multiple floors in the most expensive office building in town or have conference rooms with remote controlled window coverings. The thought of how Dani might protest if asked to engage in such a grandiose endeavor quickly replaced the concerns Riley harbored over Sam's methodical staging for today's meeting. It wasn't hard to find humor in the unwarranted formality.

Riley had only seen Bunny in the online video posted on her website. Dani indicated that same video had been running as an advertisement during the news on one local channel. Riley had been fortunate enough to miss viewing it on the larger screen. In person, Bunny appeared much the same as she did online, only taller. She wore her blonde hair in the same sharply cut, shoulder-length bob as she had in her advertisements. Her makeup and eye shadow were applied heavily and in layers, and in the way one might wear them in order not to appear washed-out on stage or camera. In person, that much of an otherwise good thing tended to have the opposite effect.

On the positive side of things, Bunny did have the good fortune of an olive-toned complexion. This, along with the platinum blonde highlights in her hair, accentuated her blue eyes. Overall, if Riley had only one criticism to make of Bunny's appearance, it would likely be the outdated navy power jacket that she had paired with a slightly too-small navy and white plaid pencil skirt. The broad-shouldered jacket, paired with her intense hair color and makeup, conveyed the harshness of someone who could be expected to screw the world before it got the chance to return the favor.

Riley self-consciously smoothed her own softly-fitted, teal jacket. She had never favored harsh shoulder pads, even in the decade they were mandated by fashion's elite. Riley's disdain for the foam-filled enhancers had been set long before she ever donned a jacket or imagined joining a profession that required one. That was her Aunt Mary's fault. Her unflinching observations on the necessary elements of style found fertile ground in Riley's impressionable young ears.

When evaluating the attire of the other ladies at church on Sundays, Aunt Mary frequently advised Riley on what to wear and what not to wear. A central theme in her fashion philosophy was to dress softly and like a lady, so they won't know what you're armed with until they're within range. It made sense at the time. It still did on some level.

Riley's assessment of Bunny and her grand entrance ended when Sam rose from his chair to greet Bunny. Riley decided to join him in that act of courtesy. Bunny immediately shrugged them off.

"An unnecessary formality," Bunny advised in a raspy, first-of-the morning tone that wasn't at all softened by her lingering drawl—the origins of which Riley's learned ear placed somewhere near Atlanta. "We've been here and done that, Sam. And I've seen the lovely Miss Morgan on the news more times than I can recall. You do stay in the thick of things, don't you, Hon?"

Riley blinked a few times as she processed Bunny's awkward salutation. Perhaps Bunny's jacket wasn't false armor at all. It was possible she cast out on every voyage with her cannons loaded and ready to fire. Perhaps Sam's concern over her demeanor wasn't misplaced. A jury comprised mostly of women, as many often were, would not take favorably to that type of brash manner, especially when coupled with Bunny's sharp-edged appearance.

Their profession fostered many age-old double standards, and gender bias was still among them. While male litigators could easily be brash and aggressive—in fact the more the merrier—their female counterparts would be vilified for doing precisely the same thing. It wasn't fair, but it wasn't anyone's fault. Juries are comprised of everyday people, all of whom bring their social biases along for the ride. For the time being, and the foreseeable future, those biases still bent toward the patriarchal in this part of the state.

"Charming as always, Ms. Keiler," Sam advised, his casual tone hinting at sarcasm. "It's nice to see you again. We haven't had the chance to talk in a while. How have you been?"

"I'm good, Sam. Then again, I'm always good," Bunny replied. "Exceptionally inundated, though. You know how it is. Doesn't matter if the economy is good or bad, people like to sue and people like our boy Vincent get sued." Bunny followed her abridged version of the litigation process with a throaty laugh and broad smile, obviously unconfined by the notion that laughing at their client's misfortune might not be the height of political correctness.

"Splendid. Good to hear you are doing well," Sam replied politely. "Please take a seat and we'll get down to business. We've got a lot of ground to cover."

Sam directed Bunny toward the chair on his left—the seat traditionally reserved for the opposition. Bunny paused for a moment to assess the scene. A single eyebrow rose as she reached some conclusion.

"That we do, Sam. The first of which is what brings Miss Morgan to our table today? I know you mentioned she was doing some harassment training for the business units to set up defenses for trial. I didn't postulate her presence as part of our strategy sessions."

Sam was ready with a reply, almost as if he had anticipated the objection. It appeared Bunny was falling into the trap he had carefully planned for her. The first indicator of success was the fact she had resorted to the imprecise use of multisyllabic words.

"As you may or may not know, Riley has an extensive background in the area of employment discrimination, and specifically with sexual harassment claims. Since neither you nor I have that type of experience, I've decided it would be good for the client to have Riley join the litigation team on this one."

Bunny stared at Riley with a tilted eye. Apparently getting riled up was all it took for her to revert to a full Southern drawl, as well.

"Mm hmm. And I reckon Vincent was all in favor of you having this little three-way, wudn't he?"

Riley's eyes flew open. The gasp that escaped might've been audible. She couldn't tell for sure because the rush of blood to her face eclipsed all sound. Sam, however, didn't appear remotely surprised by Bunny's brashness and responded with ease.

"Vince was quite pleased to have someone with Riley's expertise sitting on his side of the table. Both he and I think she can turn the odds in our favor."

"You boys. You sure stick together. Of course, neither of you contemplated the propriety of collaborating with me before making the decision," Bunny concluded while shaking her head with apparent annoyance. "I reckon what's *fait accompli* is done. Presumptively best to move to other topics."

Bunny placed her briefcase on the table and took the seat Sam had offered. There obviously wasn't any point in arguing with him right now. The new girl was sitting in what used to be her chair, and Sam had relegated Bunny to the less favorable position facing the window. And because he had, no doubt intentionally, opened the blinds that normally shielded the room from the intense Florida sun, she would have to either come off as a diva by objecting to the glare or spend the entire meeting staring into the sun. It was a no-win, either way. Nothing Sam Stone did was unscripted.

Rather than listen to Sam's introductory blabber about the procedural history of Audra's case, which he was only offering for Riley's benefit, Bunny reflected on her options. Sam's intent was for her to feel unwelcome and as a result, off balance. He could try to unnerve her if he wanted. It wouldn't change the course of things to come. He wasn't the only one with a plan to oust the other from the case. He might've brought a well-groomed, young co-counsel as the sacrificial offering to Mikles, but what Bunny had would trump that card any day.

The groundwork was set during her recent meeting with Vincent, which was really less about the meeting and more about planting a seed. Documenting the inner workings and behind-the-scenes debauchery at his flagship club was a small part of the plan—an ace she intended to hold until later in the game. She wasn't fool enough to expect a win with a single high card, though. Obviously, a few more hands would be dealt in this game.

When it was time for the players to call, she would not only lay her ace-in-hand on the table, but the other ones she planned to pull from her sleeve. The choice of whether to use or not to use Vincent's own information against him would be contingent on the choice he made. There were only two options: make her sole litigation counsel and send all future business to her, or have authorities at all levels raid his businesses and seize his assets for apparent racketeering. Actually, when it was laid out in that manner, using the word choice seemed overly generous. There really wasn't much of a choice for Vincent in the matter. It was her way or straight to hell. That was the beauty of it.

That might not seem fair to the casual observer. As far as Bunny was concerned, it was. Unlike most of his vast fortune, Vincent had earned what she was about to give him. The success and extravagant lifestyle he boasted of were gained by exploiting the girls that worked for him, and those exploits included herself as well as Cayren, her long-time friend who was now Vincent's long-suffering wife. Most of the girls working at his clubs seemed okay with an arrangement that returned the majority of the money they brought in to Vincent—the one person who had done the least to earn it. Bunny wasn't of like mind, and never had been.

Unlike the brainless bimbos who once shared the stage with her at night, Bunny was capable of more. She could make things happen. While they spent their daylight hours lounging by the pool dreaming of landing a sugar-daddy who might share his mansion, yacht or Porsche with them, Bunny spent hers planning and preparing to own all of those things herself. Why should she have to suffer the whims of boorish men to live the life she deserved? Short answer: she shouldn't. And soon, she wouldn't.

Her plan was well in the works, so she could easily bide her time and hold her tongue today. Better to let Sam think he had won this round. Truth be told, it wouldn't matter if he did.

A sinfully sweet smile spread across Bunny's face as she imagined the extent of Sam's surprise and fury when Vincent called to advise she would be taking over the case along with all the other legal work for his business empire. It was too bad that Sam's new little plaything would be caught in the crossfire between them. She had never met Riley and had nothing against her, personally. Riley seemed like a nice-enough girl which, now that Bunny thought about it, made her association with Sam unusual at best. Maybe, just to annoy Sam, she would keep Riley on as second chair in this case. That would really frost Sam's crotch.

Mona's silent re-entry to the room had gone unnoticed. She startled Riley from deep thought when she suddenly appeared beside her with the printed menus in hand. For a millisecond, Riley considered asking where Mona had learned her near-creepy brand of stealth, but decided the day was already off to an odd-enough start. Instead, she chose to mask her startle with a warm smile and accepted the menu from Mona with a nod of gratitude.

Mona then slipped away to the other side of the room, took a tray from the built-in serving station and returned to the table to serve beverages. After placing a steeping cup of jasmine-scented green tea before Riley, she turned away to serve Sam.

"Let me know what type of pastry you would like with your tea," Mona advised Riley while she poured Sam's coffee into the deep ceramic mug that mysteriously appeared before him. Turning to Bunny, she added, "Will you have your usual?"

Bunny smiled sweetly and replied with a nod. "Absolewtly! I take mine black, as you know. I'm curious, though. Why aren't we using those mugs I gave y'all last year for Christmas? You do still have them, don't you, Say-um?" Her Southern-fried enunciation of his name seemed to encompass a full turn of the clock's second hand.

"We do," Mona replied without hesitation, knowing her boss couldn't be bothered with the knowledge of who had given them what for which occasion, much less where any of it was kept. It was her job to attend to those details. "I took the liberty of bringing one in for you," she added, before placing a cheap-looking, mass-production style white mug in front of Bunny.

"I'm just thrilled with how these turned out," Bunny mused, turning the mug around so Riley could get a full view.

The mug bore the advisory "I'm Awesome" just below a large picture of Bunny standing confidently before a bookcase filled with leather-bound law books.

"I've found having a slogan to be a highly effective form of marketing. People tend to identify you with it, which is why I make a real effort to propagate it. You're a solo practitioner, too, right Riley? You comprehend the allusion. I doubt Sam does. He hadn't had to hunt for his kill like we do."

Riley wasn't exactly sure what Bunny had intended to say. She took a stab at it, anyway. "That's right, I am in a solo practice. I've worked with larger firms, but I prefer being my own boss. Even if I do have to hunt once in a while."

"I'm with you there. Not that it wasn't fun to work with you, Samuel. There were some good times." Bunny capped her comment by reaching out to run her fingers along Sam's sleeve in a knowing manner.

Well, that answers that question, Riley supposed. *They've made use of this room before.*

Sam chose the perfect moment to reach for his coffee, thus extracting himself from Bunny's gesture of affection before she could burrow her fingers under his French-cuffed sleeve. Bunny wasn't fazed. She continued to smile at Sam with a wicked gleam in her eye. Toying with him was fun in its own right. It was even better if it came with the chance to goad his *new* girl, Riley, into at least a minor twinge of jealousy.

Riley wasn't nearly as concerned with the display of affection as she was impressed by the practicum on offensive strategy. Both Sam and Bunny were pros, and this master class in manipulation was far beyond anything taught in law school. It was like watching a formerly married couple, long after their bitter divorce. They still knew just enough about each other to press the right buttons.

Sam wasn't pleased his valuable time was being spent handling the "Bunny" matter. Bunny's feelings on the situation were obviously mutual. And as good as the show was, Riley had other things on her agenda—a new client who was the sole witness to a murder being at the top of that list. Concerned she might be joining Wade in the witness-to-murder club, Riley decided it was time to intervene in the escalating firefight between Sam and Bunny.

"I do a bit of my own marketing, but I don't have a slogan. Perhaps I should come up with something," Riley interjected in a friendly tone, hoping to draw Bunny into a less contentious conversation.

"Mine is taken!" Bunny barked, sharply returning her focus to Riley and her hand to her own side of the table. "It's trademarked."

That brought a chuckle from Sam. "Really? You sold the PTO on registering the word 'awesome'?"

"It wasn't rocket surgery, Sam. I filed it as a service mark. You know, because it depicts the level of services I facilitate."

"Ah. How did I miss that obvious attribute?" Sam chided, before taking the conversation on a sharp turn. "Now that we're settled in and have our coffee, let's get back to business, shall we?"

"About time, Sam. We're all tenanted people," Bunny complained as she might have if she really cared.

She didn't care because none of what Sam had on today's schedule mattered in the long run. But the current audience didn't know that. She'd been summoned on stage as the jester for today's episode of the "Sam Stone Show." He had all the lines scripted. That would do little, however, to keep her from stealing a scene or two.

She needed to stand in his spotlight. Sam wouldn't go for her directing the conversation, especially since he'd already assumed the lead. As far as Bunny was concerned, that alone was reason enough to do it.

"I think the first detail we should attend is the stratagem for the Plaintiff's deposition. I've prepared the outline. If you would like to add something, just let me know." Bunny rifled around in her soft-frame leather briefcase pretending to look for copies of her outline while she waited for Sam to pull back on the reigns. *Five, four, three, two . . . .*

"I agree that we should start with Audra," Sam noted in a dismissive tone. Bunny was still being vainglorious, which was a good sign. She was on edge. Treating her as irrelevant should stoke that fire. "We can dispense with that order of business quickly. Riley should take the deposition. And I don't think we need to tell her how to do it."

That suggestion got a genuine rise out of Bunny; one she quickly quelled. It was taking a lot out of her, but she wasn't going to let Sam actually get to her. Still, he'd be suspicious if she didn't put up a fight at all. She had to play this just right. A little cattiness should do the trick. Men expect that from women they presume to be jealous.

"Oh good gawd, Sam! We're not picking prom dates here. This is serious business. What, aside from Riley's classic good looks and your erectile organ, led you to that conclusion?"

"It has nothing to do with Riley's appearance. It has to do with the fact she knows the law and knows just how far to take an inquiry of this nature with a plaintiff like Audra."

"Oh, so you think she has something I don't have, then. Is that it?" Bunny gave him her best pissy face, while she internally congratulated herself for the award-winning performance.

Sam chuckled. He seemed pleased Bunny was taking the bait. "As you so aptly noted, Bunny, this isn't a beauty contest. It's about getting the best result for the client."

"Exactly, which is just another reason your belated change in plans doesn't make a modicum of sense. 'Little Miss Thing' here couldn't possibly be up to speed on the case yet."

"Her name is 'Riley,' and she has started to review the files already," Sam defended. "I plan to make sure she's fully briefed by Monday."

"Oh, I've no doubt of that," Bunny huffed. "I reckon she'll get more 'n her fill of your briefs by then."

"That was uncalled for!" Riley warned. She had no idea where this venom was coming from, but she wasn't going to politely ignore it any longer.

Bunny was actually starting to enjoy playing the part of the angry, jilted feline. Fighting is easier when you really don't care. What she had surmised from the outset of the meeting was patently clear now— Sam was planning to do to her exactly what she had planned to do to him. This was as good a time as any to cap off her performance, and call it a day.

Bunny shot out of her chair and began to gather her things. "You're right, Riley, at least where you're concerned. It's not your fault Sam has chosen you as his flavor this month."

For emphasis, Bunny all but stuffed the few papers she had pulled from her briefcase back from whence they came while delivering her monologue. "I've been working on this case since the early stages before the EEOC. I've spent hundreds of hours preparing to take Audra's deposition. Now all of that work was for nuthin'. You two obviously have it covered. Go ahead with your little concilliabule endeavor. I'm going to attend to my other clients!"

Bunny didn't wait for a reply. A hasty departure suited her purpose quite well. She turned and stomped out of the room, briefcase and trademarked coffee cup in tow, before Sam or Riley had a chance to respond. With her back turned to them, neither saw the wide smile she wore on her way out.

CHAPTER 17

Riley slowly eased back into her seat before looking to Sam for direction. His brows were drawn. He seemed surprised by Bunny's hasty departure.

"Was that not part of the master plan?"

"Not exactly." Sam rubbed his forehead while he reflected. "Bunny never gives up that easily. I expected more of a fight."

"I'm not sure how well you'd fare in that fight. It might be a good thing she let you win this one."

"I can handle Bunny, any day."

"Any day, except today, you mean? You didn't get the information you wanted from her before she stomped out of here."

"Any day, including today. This isn't over. She retreated to regroup. We'd better do the same."

"Retreat or regroup?" Riley asked.

"Regroup. Are you going to respond to everything I say with another question?"

"That depends. Are you going to continue to say ambiguous things?"

Sam's furrowed brow softened, and one corner of his mouth bent slightly upward. He looked away from Riley and intentionally placed his focus on shuffling the files in front of him. Riley was taunting him to lighten his mood, a sure sign she was starting to care. She was even watching him closely now to gauge whether her banter had made its mark. It had, but he wasn't going to give that away just yet. He wanted to savor the small token of her affection. A long moment passed before he responded.

"Maybe. I like to keep my options open."

"Is that what you call it?"

"Sure, that's how it is. For example, I haven't made plans for lunch yet and by doing so, I've kept all options open. See how that works?"

"You are an inspiration, Mr. Stone."

"I try. That brings me to my next question."

"I wait with bated breath. What might the illustrious Sam Stone not already know?"

Sam responded with a smirk. "What would you like for lunch?"

Riley stared back at him, expressionless. The man was relentless. He didn't bother to ask her to join him, he just decided she would. He deserved bonus points for chutzpah. But something Bunny had said struck a thinly-veiled nerve that was still throbbing.

"I haven't thought about that yet. I do know what you won't be having."

"Really? Okay, I'll bite. What will my lunch *not* be?" Sam asked.

"It won't be something that tastes like your flavor of the month."

Sam turned to face Riley with a genuine look of concern. "That's just Bunny prattling. Don't let her get to you."

"I'm not worried about Bunny at the moment. This is about you, or more accurately you and me, and this arrangement or whatever it is we have going on at the moment. We managed to cover your thoughts on relationships this morning, or more specifically your thoughts on how to measure the multitude of them you've already had. It often seems that you've sampled the entire spectrum of flavors, save one. I'm not keen on being that one. I'm only interested in the professional side of our arrangement."

Sam shook his head to negate the presumption. "Since you've chosen to stick with Bunny's ill-fitting comparison, so will I. The thing about having tried all the flavors is that once you have, you can be certain of the one you want."

"Maybe you are certain, for the given moment. As Sophocles aptly noted, 'Man is not constituted to take pleasure in the same things always.' No one always wants the same flavor, every time."

"That's pure bollocks, and I can count the ways. First of all, Sortaclueless, or whatever his name was, apparently never had a single malt Scotch. And given that he's been dead for centuries, I'm pretty sure he didn't know your father, did he?"

Riley bristled as the mention of her father. "That's a stupid question and you know it. Where are you going with this?"

"I knew your father, Riley. I was in his court and chambers arguing cases many times. I knew him and his reputation well enough to ask you this: When he took you out for ice cream, what did he order?"

Riley paused to reflect. Ice cream was her father's thing. He preferred the kind that was homemade and hand scooped at old-fashioned soda shops. It had been their shared Saturday afternoon ritual for most of her childhood. When he became ill and was unable to leave the house, she kept his favorite flavor in the fridge for the rare occasion when he felt well enough to eat.

"He ordered vanilla. Every time. How did you know that?"

"A good litigator makes a point of knowing everything there is to know about the judges they appear before. Your father was known to be one of the most consistent jurists in the state. His reputation for that consistency was said to be evident in everything he did."

"It was," Riley affirmed.

"I know," Sam offered with a smile.

"That was a low blow. Besides, you are nothing like my father."

"How do you know? You haven't sampled my flavor," he added, pairing his taunt with a sly half-smile. "Anyway, I certainly don't want you to see me as a father figure. I was just pointing out the error in your logic. Your point isn't universally true. You'll have to give me the benefit of reasonable doubt."

Riley had to admit it. Once again, the man had made a valid point. "You have an answer for everything, don't you?" she replied.

The irony of Riley offering that as an insult brought a hearty laugh from Sam. "I do. I guess that means you and I have something in common as well."

"You know, if you're not careful, Sam, you're gonna have two women in the span of an hour telling you to talk to their backside."

"Wouldn't be the first time," Sam quickly parried, still delighting in Riley's ire. "You do both honor me with the view, so I'll not complain."

Grrrrrrr. That was the only response that came to Riley's now genuinely frustrated mind. Sam was turning everything she said into something entirely different. Who does that?

Lawyers, Riley's little voice reminded.

Rather than respond to Sam's goading, Riley started packing her things. Sam watched her with a look of pure mischief. His usually steel-blue eyes had suddenly taken on sparkling hints of green and turquoise in a combination that rivaled shallow pools in the Caribbean when struck by the morning sun. Only in this case, assuming a shallow depth would have been a mistake. Something stirred in Sam's waters that didn't normally swim there.

While the look Sam wore might have been outwardly appealing, whatever was going on behind it wasn't, at least not to Riley. She couldn't help wondering what he was enjoying. And why so much? Curious as she was, she still deemed it unworthy of investigation.

"As it turns out, I've lost my appetite," Riley advised, once she finished collecting her things. "I don't think I'll be having lunch anytime soon. Anyway, I've got to return calls and put out a few fires this afternoon."

Both were true. Spending the past few days in the presence of or referring to women who spend most of their time naked had made Riley a little too aware of her own body and all of its flaws, real or imagined. And then there was the Wade matter.

"That's too bad. My appetite seems to have increased as the morning has progressed," Sam responded with a hint of disappointment. "I'm sure I can find something to whet it."

"I'm sure you will," Riley responded coolly as she moved toward the door. "It's of no concern to me, however. I'm your co-counsel, not your second course."

"Very well, then. Why don't we start fresh tomorrow? Clear your calendar for the next few days. It's going to be a long weekend for the both of us," Sam advised.

Mona appeared at the conference room door as if summoned by the gods. Only this time, Riley found her uncanny timing to be something of a blessing.

"Can you help me navigate back to the front, Mona? I have somewhere else I need to be."

Mona nodded and then directed her quiet response to Sam before following Riley out of the conference room.

"Don't we all?"

०४० ०४० ०४०

"Hello, Adonis. Now send in the clowns."

"Who are you talking to?" Riley inquired. It was good to be back on her turf, talking to someone who usually made sense.

"The television, of course," Dani mocked. "It's my new best friend, now that Sam has stolen you away."

"Sam hasn't stolen anything other than Bunny's client," Riley stated.

Dani fiddled with the remote. "Sounds like you've had an interesting morning."

"It was. Sort of. It was also very tiring. There are so many games being played between the two of them, and on so many levels. I feel like I've already been through a storm."

"Better keep your rain gear out. The storm trackers all agree. We're soon to be ravaged by a Greek god, and not in a good way."

"So, that's what your commentary was about?" Riley asked.

"Yep. That and the certain barrage of yellow-rain-slicker-wearing weather goons who are about to head on down to gleefully gawk at our misery."

"Shit! I really can't deal with a storm right now. That's not going to fit into my schedule," Riley complained. "Sam wants me to work most of the weekend to prepare for the depositions next week. I'm supposed to take the lead on Audra's."

"I hate to be the first to break this to you, but Mother Nature's not gonna check your calendar before she decides to blow hot air up your skirt," Dani snarked. "Speaking of hot air and a skirt, I'm surprised Sam made his move on Bunny so quickly. That's ballsy. I'll bet she hit the roof."

Riley stopped in her tracks. "Wasn't as explosive as you might expect, which leads me to think Bunny's holding out on Sam. He seems to think so, too."

"Could be. Since the depos are next week, she can't hold on to whatever it is for much longer, can she?" Dani asked.

"Nope. Which means we should expect a few hurricane-strength wind gusts coming this way over the next few days."

Dani rolled her eyes at her friend's attempt at humor. "Weird storm analogies are my shtick. You're far too stiff to pull that off."

"I'm going to take that as a compliment. Stiff is just one of my many charms," Riley retorted before traversing the final few steps between the break room and her office.

"Your messages are on the desk," Dani called after her, with just enough inflection to bridge the sound gap between them.

"Got 'em. Thanks," Riley advised. When she reached her desk, she grabbed the pile of phone message notes Dani had left on the corner of her desk, and quickly reviewed them. The one she was looking for wasn't there.

"Are these all of the messages?"

"Mm hmmph," Dani replied, through a full mouth. She appeared in Riley's doorway to confirm her response after swallowing the last bite of the sandwich she had brought for lunch. "Yep, that's all she wrote. And by she, I mean me, of course."

Riley rifled through the notes and messages a second time, hoping she might've missed one the first go-round. She hadn't. There was still no call from Kristina. Given the approaching storm, that wasn't entirely unexpected, though it was a cause for concern. Kristina was responsible for gathering and storing computerized forensic evidence for FDLE. With the approaching storm, she was likely overwhelmed with hurricane preparations. Time was of the essence in storm prep. It was also weighing heavily against Wade right now.

The more time that elapsed between the incident and the report, the less likely law enforcement would look favorably on the mere act of reporting. If all that Wade had told her was true, he wasn't the worst villain in the scenario by any means. That didn't leave him in the clear, either. He had a lot of explaining to do.

Riley picked up the phone and dialed Kristina's number again. This time her friend picked up on the second ring. After a brief detail of the facts from Riley, which included Wade's account of what happened but not the source of that information, Kristina agreed to have a couple of officers check on Halston.

"If there's anything that looks off, I'll give you a call," Kristina offered.

"Thanks, I really appreciate it."

"If we do find something, you know you are going to have to identify your client, right? He or she is going to have to come forward."

"That's understood. My client intends to do the right thing. The circumstances, of course, are highly unusual," Riley said. "I knew you would handle this with discretion. I really appreciate that."

"Hope you don't mind if I change the subject, while I've got you on the phone."

"Not at all," Riley offered. "What's up? Have you got a new boyfriend I haven't heard about, yet?"

"Nah, I'm too busy for anything like that. I am still working with the Foundation for Cystic Fibrosis, however."

Though they were in different locations, Riley nodded with her reply just as she would've had they been in the same room. The cause was important to Kristina because the disease ran in her family. After losing her younger sister to it at only nineteen years of age, Kris had made the difficult choice not to have children of her own at an age and time when most young women aren't challenged with life choices of that magnitude.

Although she had been fortunate enough not to be born with the full-blown illness, Kris did carry the genetic markers for it, which meant her children could suffer just as her sister had. The risk of having to helplessly watch another child endure and eventually succumb to the disease was too great to bear. The choice Kris had made was selfless and courageous, and something Riley believed warranted a great deal of respect.

Following her sister's death, Kristina diligently sought to raise money for research, and to aid those who suffered from the disease as well as their families. She and her family knew all too well how the necessary medical treatment of a terminally ill loved one could bankrupt those left behind to grieve. Despite the overwhelming odds, Kristina still held out hope for a cure.

Miracles aren't cheap, and with the world in such financial turmoil, all charitable organizations were scrambling to attract the attention of the few large-scale donors still out there. Kristina had attacked that challenge just as she had all others in her life—with tireless resolve and lasting optimism. There wasn't a mountain Kristina couldn't move, if she wanted it out of the way.

"Yes, I saw something in the paper about that. You're chairing the committee on fundraising, right?"

"I am, and we're close to reaching our goal again this year. Our next event is a black-tie fundraiser at the Casa Verde Resort."

"That's a gorgeous location. When is it?"

"Next Saturday, actually. I was going to give you a call to talk about it, before I got your message yesterday. There's going to be a live band and a silent auction, and we have some other great stuff planned for the night."

Riley's face lit up. She was due an elegant evening out and what better way than to spend it helping a friend. She had a gorgeous lavender gown in her closet that would be perfect for the event. Her enlightened expression turned darker when her mind's eye interposed Sam into the lovely vision of a glamorous night.

She was puzzled, at first, why she would picture Sam in that context. It didn't take long for the reason to find her. Sam would look amazing in a tux. Which, she reminded her rambling neurons, was exactly why she preferred not to think of him that way. While her mind was taking a fast flight to places she'd rather it not go, Riley's present reaction was short and to the point.

"That sounds like fun."

"I hope you can make it," Kris replied. "Everyone had such a great time last year. I'll give you more details later. Let's see what happens with your client first."

"I'll keep the date open," Riley said. "Hopefully, we'll have this other stuff wrapped up by then."

"Stay near your phone. I'll call you when I have an update. I'm putting the call in to dispatch now."

"Thanks, Kris."

Riley hated that she couldn't offer a donation for the event right away, even though she knew Kristina would never ask. That was Kristina, business first. In this case, there were additional reasons supporting Kristina's reserve. Anyone holding a public office, especially one responsible for investigating potentially unlawful activity, didn't need the intense circumspection that would follow the mere suggestion that someone bought a favor. Kristina was by the book, and that's what made her a great cop and an even better investigator. Wade's fate was in excellent hands.

Riley spent the next hour with her nose buried in The Polling Place's employee files. It was standard procedure for counsel to review their client's documents thoroughly before turning copies over to the opposing side. When she finally realized what was missing from the pile, she was a little disappointed in herself. It should not have taken her that long to catch the glaring omission. She also should not have been the first to notice.

There were mountains of files for current and past bartenders, bouncers, waitresses and clerical staff for Mikles' clubs. There were even files for employees of some of his other businesses. Thus far, however, she had not come across a personnel file for even one of the dancers. Come to think of it, she also hadn't seen Audra's complete personnel file.

The file Sam sent over had a few email communications between Audra and the club manager in which they discussed scheduling, hours and additional bonuses for work in the VIP rooms. There were also copies of company checks made payable to Audra. There were, however, none of the standard employment documents most businesses are required by law to keep.

"That's weird. There has to be more than this. Why didn't Vince send Sam everything? Or was it Sam who didn't send me everything?" Riley openly mused.

Her internal query was interrupted by the speakerphone.

"Kris is on Line 1. It sounds important." Dani announced.

"Thanks," Riley responded. She disengaged the speaker function to take the call. "That was fast, Kris. What've you got?"

"I'm with our forensics people at the address you gave me. There are definite signs that something's not right here. The shower curtain is missing and there are a couple of curtain rings on the floor behind the commode. It looks like the curtain might have been pulled from the shower bar just like your client said. Also, there is a power cord for a computer in the bedroom, but no computer. In my experience, no one takes their computer without the power cord," Kris reported.

Riley released a silent expletive for Wade's sake. So far, it did not sound like this was going to turn out as she had hoped for him. "It sounds like what my client saw was real," she assessed.

"Unfortunately, yes," Kris replied. "We've confirmed that no one has seen or heard from Halston since Tuesday, just like your client reported. Got that from the emergency contacts listed on her rental application. Apparently, it's not entirely unheard of for her to travel on a whim. She usually stays connected either by phone or computer, though. I'm told she responds instantly to her email and routinely posts updates on social networks. She hasn't done either for almost 48 hours."

"Have they found blood or anything that might indicate something violent occurred in the apartment?" Riley inquired. "My client only saw the abduction, nothing after."

"I can't give out too many specifics now that this is an open investigation. I can only confirm or deny what your client has reported. We are going to continue a forensic review of the apartment and also list Halston as officially missing so we can commence electronic monitoring protocols," Kris advised.

"I understand. Is there anything else you need from me or my client?" Riley asked.

"Yeah. You're going to have to bring your client to the scene. Once forensics is done gathering evidence, we need a walk-through of everything the witness saw. You can come along as counsel, but we'll expect full cooperation."

"You know my first obligation is to protect my client's interests. As long as we're all heading in the same direction, we'll be there."

"Hold on." Kris interjected. Riley heard a voice in the background giving Kris an update on some new discovery. "Gotta go, Riley. There's a lot going on here. Get back to me about bringing in your client, and soon, okay?"

CHAPTER 18

"Fuck me," Wade whispered, as he passed the slim wisp of air that remained in his lungs through nervously clenched teeth. "I'm fucked, aren't I?"

"I would tell you to watch your language, though I don't see the point of correcting you when you're right. You are in a heap of shit," Riley advised, ignoring her own admonition. "Still, we don't know the whole story yet, so try to keep it together."

Thankfully, she had insisted on driving. It was pretty clear when she broke the news to Wade he was in no shape to navigate the perils of afternoon traffic on I-4.

Wade's chant continued, internally. His mind was reeling. He felt as pallid as he was certain he looked. There was no blood left for his face following its forced evacuation to more pertinent organs. He fumbled briefly with the buttons on the passenger's side door, trying to find the one that would release him from the vortex that controlled his oxygen-starved atmosphere.

Riley peripherally caught the motion and pressed the master button on the driver's side to create a narrow opening in Wade's window. Wade gratefully sucked at the incoming air like a troubled swimmer pulled from the grip of a fierce undertow. When he finally managed to secure enough oxygen to have a little to spare, he was able to release the words piercing him from the inside.

"Are they. . . ." Wade lowered his voice to a whisper, subconsciously hoping that saying what he was about to say quietly might change the answer. "Are they gonna arrest me?"

There was no good way to cushion the blow. "Kris will tell me if that's what they intend. She will give me the option of bringing you in," Riley replied.

"Isn't that what you're doing now?" Wade asked.

"Yes, in a way, although not for the same purpose. Right now, they need to know what you know. Right now, I am still advising you to cooperate. If at any time I sense a change in their focus, I will tell you otherwise. Understand? Just listen and follow my lead, okay?"

Wade could only nod. He had spent what little emotional energy he had left making the inquiry and was now drowning in shallow channels of fear. Conversation had become an endurance sport he could no longer endure. The rest of their journey would be made in silence.

Riley took an exit ramp off of I-4 that fed into one of the city's main thoroughfares. They would only travel that road a short distance before reaching Halston's apartment complex. As soon as they turned into the divided two-lane entrance of the complex, they were stopped by a deputy whose patrol car blocked the opposing lane to ensure control of all ingress and egress. He bent down and examined them both at eye level through Riley's open window. Once advised of the reason for their visit and having radio confirmation of the same, he allowed them to pull into the parking lot that was already crowded with police and forensic vehicles.

Luckily, the news media had not yet caught wind of the matter. That allowed Riley to usher Wade into the building where Halston's apartment was located without notice. It was doubtful they would be able to make an exit with the same ease. Even if not allowed on site, the press would be hovering over and making use of their long-range lenses the second they got wind that this many of FDLE's and Orlando's finest were congregated in one location.

Each stand-alone apartment building had at least five floors, with each floor labeled in succession on signs posted by the stairs as a "Level." There were four apartment units on each level with two units, one left and one right, facing the parking lot and two units, similarly situated, facing the other direction. In typical Florida fashion, the two back-facing apartment units on all levels fronted a drainage ditch with a fountain-like aerator that supposedly dressed the ditch up enough for the complex to tout those apartments as "lakefront."

When Wade and Riley reached the top of the third-level stairs, they were greeted by an officer who appeared to be the final gatekeeper assigned to secure the crime scene. The officer had been apprised of their impending arrival and radioed a message to someone that the witness was on site. He then directed Riley toward the left-side, ditch-facing apartment, and advised her to wait for Kristina at the door.

Riley directed Wade to stand behind her while she peered into the doorway. There were a few officers inside taking pictures and another that appeared to be writing information on small plastic evidence bags. A few moments later, Kristina appeared in the apartment living area and motioned for them to join her.

"Is this the witness?" Kristina inquired, while studying Wade carefully.

"Yes, this is Wade Warner. He's the witness who provided the information I gave you on Halston's disappearance. Wade, this is Kristina. She's an agent with FDLE and is the internal contact we talked about."

Wade nodded at Kristina and remained silent as Riley had directed. He had no plans to utter a sound until Riley indicated he could speak.

"Our guys have finished the forensic sweep of the apartment so we can go over what Wade saw. We wanted to make sure that we didn't contaminate the scene before we swept for prints or other bio-identifiers that might've been left behind," Kris advised. "Before we commence, I need to ask your client whether or not he's been here before."

Riley turned to Wade and nodded. "You can answer that."

Wade started to speak. Unfortunately, his throat had become so tight he could barely make a sound. He cleared his airways by coughing a few times and tried again.

"No, I've never been here before, in person, anyway," he managed to eke out. "I only saw the place through the webcam on the computer."

"So, your prints or DNA won't be in any of the evidence we've collected thus far, is that right?" Kris inquired.

Wade's eyes widened with fear. The entire universe had just gone surreal. This was like watching an intense crime drama on television, which was something he usually enjoyed. Only this drama wasn't playing on a television screen. It was playing out in front of him and he was the idiot witness the police had in the hot seat. From this side of things, crime drama wasn't nearly as much fun.

"No, ma'am. You shouldn't find any prints or anything of mine here," Wade responded resolutely.

"I shouldn't or I won't?" Kristina countered dryly.

This was police business, not a casual conversation. All the details mattered right now because they were looking for a missing person, who everyone hoped might still be alive. It was widely known that the first few days following abduction were critical for finding evidence that could lead to recovery. Beyond that time, it became far too easy for the perpetrators to have moved, either with or without their victim, to a safe house or untraceable location. Although her interrogations usually took the form of database code queries and the witnesses were most often inanimate technological devices, Kris still knew better than to leave an ambiguous statement like that hanging.

Wade winced at the pointed inquiry and looked to Riley for direction. Thankfully, she had some, and supplied it generously.

"I believe Wade is just trying to be cautious, Kris. He knows you have to consider everyone a suspect, including and especially him since, so far, he's the only witness to Halston's disappearance. Wade worked with Halston, so it is possible that he was close enough to her at any given time for hair or prints to have been on some item or clothing she wore at the workplace, but it's not likely. Is that a fair clarification of your response, Wade?"

Wade nodded slowly.

"You need to answer her audibly," Riley directed.

Wade nodded again and turned to Kristina to confirm. "Yes, that is what I was trying to say. I haven't been here. I did see her at work on the day she disappeared. What Miss Morgan said is what I meant."

Kristina studied Wade closely for any outward signs of deception. Appearing satisfied with his response, she jotted a few notes in a notebook and then directed Wade to follow her across the room and toward the bedrooms. The unit appeared to be a two bedroom unit with at least one full bathroom down the hallway just past the small kitchen and living area.

"Now, if I understand correctly, you hacked into the victim's laptop that was in her bedroom. Is that accurate?"

"Um, the computer I accessed—,"

"You mean hacked, don't you?" Kristina corrected. "You didn't have authority to access her computer?"

Wade swallowed hard. This bitter pill wasn't going down easy. Riley interjected on his behalf.

"I believe you're more interested in developing the sequence of events than the means right now, Kris. Is that accurate?" Riley asked.

Kris nodded and then jotted down a few more notes.

"Wade, why don't you tell Kris what you saw from your end," Riley directed.

"Okay. I . . . um . . . my viewpoint was through the webcam on a computer that appeared to be in a bedroom," Wade conveyed.

"Is this the room you saw?" Kristina directed him to the first bedroom that was on the right side of the apartment just across from the kitchen area. Wade stuck his head into the doorway to get a better view.

"No, this one is smaller and there's no adjoining bath. The room I saw had a bathroom."

"All right, let's take a look at the other bedroom." Kristina led them a little further down the hallway, just past the full hall bath, and stopped before the last door on the left. The door was closed and standard yellow police tape was strewn across the frame. Kris opened the door and let Wade peer inside.

Wade recognized the room configuration immediately.

"This is the room I saw," he affirmed, recollection now rushing over him. "It looks the same."

"In what way?" Kris probed.

"Well, I mean, the sheets and bed linens are still mussed up, like they were that night. I remember that. And the bathroom door was open, just like it is now." Wade's eyes darted back and forth as he drew from mental notes. "Can I go in? I can show you the angle that I viewed it from."

"Yes, I will need you to go in," Kristina advised as she lifted the crime scene barrier tape to allow them to pass under it.

Wade stood at the foot of the bed for a moment to get his bearings and then moved toward the window on the far side of the room. The desk where Halston's computer had been sitting was facing the window.

Wade stood behind the desk with his back to the window and pointed toward the bed. "This looks like where the computer had to be, because this is the view I had. The computer was facing away from the window and toward the bed. She must've sat at this desk and faced the window when she used it."

Wade turned toward the window and then back to face the bed. "But the computer's not here, now."

"That's right, it's not," Kris replied. "We do believe that desk is where the computer was previously located."

"Wait, so you guys didn't take that into evidence?" Wade asked.

"I can't reveal information on the investigation," Kris directed her response more to Riley than Wade, then shifted her eyes back to Wade. "Is there something about the computer we should know?"

"Well . . . I guess you already know I accessed it, so I can tell you some stuff about it if you need me to," Wade said.

"That would be helpful," Kris advised.

"I was on my Mac, and I had to switch to the bifurcated drive because Halston had a Windows operating system. I think it was a HardTec laptop, or it might've been a Shikomi. I got that from examining the hardware configuration when I disabled the webcam notification process by deleting that code in the driver. I had to look online to get the source file names so I could access the drivers in the operating system. I remember the computer had an Intel 5 dual-core processor, and the camera was integrated," Wade recounted.

"What about software or other data files?" Kris asked.

"There weren't many aftermarket programs loaded on it, just a couple of video games," Wade recalled. "I recall there being a lot of pictures though, and some other saved files. And she had downloaded email, too. I remember that because she used a basic program to access and organize email from different accounts. I read some of her email, but not all of it."

"What did you do next?" Kris nudged. She needed specifics. It was imperative they follow every step from the night in question.

"You mean after I accessed the computer?"

"Yes, after that. Did you download or copy anything?"

"I downloaded most of her pictures," Wade said. "I deleted them later, though."

Kristina hardened her gaze fairly certain this line of questioning was going to get them somewhere. "Why did you delete them?"

"I had to. I mean, I thought I had to," Wade said. "I was scared, so I wasn't really thinking clearly. I just didn't want to leave any kind of trace that I had been there. Virtually, that is."

"And when you say you deleted them do you mean completely, in the technical sense? You know what I'm asking, right?"

"Yeah, I think so. You mean did I scrub the drive?"

Kristina nodded. Anyone with even moderate knowledge knew data was never really gone from a hard drive unless extraordinary measures were taken to remove it.

"I didn't get a chance to do that. I was a little preoccupied by being scared shitless," Wade replied.

"Funny how murder can kill a mood," Kristina commented under her breath as she jotted down some notes.

Riley, who had been listening intently and taking her own notes stopped to inquire. "You two are doing the geek-speak stuff, again. What does it mean that it wasn't scrubbed?"

Kristina started to explain and Wade joined in the simultaneous reply. "It means the information could still be accessible."

"Okay," Riley acknowledged, "that's good news. Where would the files be?"

Kristina looked at Wade and let him offer the response this time. She was hoping he would reach the conclusion she wanted without coercion.

"Um, well . . . they would be on my computer's hard drive." Wade turned to Kristina with a defeated look when he recognized the full weight of his response. "I guess you'll need to examine my computer, won't you?"

"Yes, we'll need to get that from you. We can do that one of two ways. I can let you give it to Riley to bring in, or I can have an officer go to your place to pick it up. If I let you bring it in, you will have to submit an affidavit affirming the chain of custody and that you haven't changed anything on it since the time in question. I'll leave that for you and Riley to decide when we're done here."

Wade looked at Riley with concern. "I think I need to discuss that with my attorney. I have some work stuff and a lot of personal stuff on my Mac."

"I'll discuss it with Wade. We'll give you everything we can," Riley advised Kristina.

"I don't have to remind you that I can subpoena the computer if I need to," Kris added, more for Wade's sake than Riley's.

"Of course not. I am aware of that, and Wade wants to cooperate," Riley said. "But there may be proprietary information involved that I need to examine, especially if it belongs to a third party such as his employer."

"Okay, I'll give you two until the end of the day to work that out. Let's move on with what you saw, Wade. Did you get a good look around the room that night?"

"I did, sort of. I wasn't watching too long before Halston came in, though."

"Okay, look around the room now, and tell me whether everything is exactly as you saw it that night?" Kris asked.

Wade scanned the room in the same sequence he had a few nights ago. The bed was unmade, the same as it had been. Check. All the stupid pillows were just as they had been. Check. The television on the wall across from the bed was there. Check. The clock on the nightstand was there and . . . wait.

"The picture is gone."

"What picture?" Kristina asked.

Wade walked over to the nightstand and pointed to the location where it had been.

"There was a picture, right here. It was in one of those fancy silver frames with jewels or sparkly things around it."

"Do you recall who or what was in the picture?" Kris inquired.

"It was Halston and some dude–some old dude. She was sitting in his lap. It was from her vacation to Palm Beach."

"How do you know that?" Riley voiced the obvious follow-up query before Kristina had the chance.

"Because it was the same as one of the pictures I saw on her computer. They were in a subfolder called 'Palm Beach.'"

Kristina and Riley looked at each other with surprise and then back at Wade. Both were aware Wade might've just given the investigators a big break in the case. Kris hadn't confirmed the computer was taken by the intruder. Riley deemed that a given from her cautious response. It was not a coincidence that whoever had kidnapped Halston apparently made a special effort to remove only two things: the computer and that picture frame. Both possessed similar information.

"You're talking about the same photos that you downloaded from her computer?" Kristina looked directly into Wade's eyes for confirmation of his almost certain response.

"Well, yeah. I mean I downloaded all of the pictures. This one was in the more recent ones that I looked at, so I remember it pretty well. I was kinda surprised that she would be hanging with a relic like that. That's why I remember it."

Kristina followed with what sounded a typical police show question. "Would you recognize the man in the picture if you saw him?"

"Uh, I dunno. I was mostly looking at Halston. I would remember the photo if I saw it again." Wade turned to Riley seeking direction in a slightly hushed tone, though still in earshot of the agent. "Glorked! They're seriously gonna need my computer now, aren't they?"

Riley nodded. "Unfortunately, this does make their request more compelling, as if it weren't already."

"Yes, we will need to examine it," Kris confirmed. "I'm not sure I can wait until later today, now that we know our most likely suspect is hiding somewhere on your hard drive, Wade. Time really matters right now. If we're going to find Halston, and hopefully find her alive, we've got to act fast."

Kristina emphasized her conclusion by closing her note pad and pulling out her radio. She rattled off a command to one of the officers stationed outside. "I need a uniform to escort my witness out and a CSI unit dispatched to secure evidence offsite."

"Do you need anything else from Wade before we go?" Riley inquired.

"I need you to go over what you saw take place in the bathroom for the record. We'll do that now, and then you can discuss your options regarding the computer on your way back to Wade's. A CSI officer is going to meet you there to take the computer into evidence. If we need a warrant, let me know and I'll have it by the time the officer gets there."

Riley nodded and pulled her phone out to make a quick call to Dani. This was going to take a lot longer than she had expected, which meant everything else for today would have to be pushed back.

After Wade finished giving the details on Halston's attack and abduction, Riley pulled him aside for a quick conference.

"I need to know who owns the computer you used that night, and what's on it that you're worried about other than those pictures."

Wade scanned his memory to account for the multitude of things on his computer he would rather wind up in the hands of a fellow hacker than with the police. Most of the serious stuff was heavily encrypted so maybe they wouldn't be able to access it. But there was a lot of web history stored on his browser he'd rather they not know about. Unfortunately, it was far too late to grow a conscience now.

"I was using my personal computer that night. I don't use my work laptop when I'm off duty. I may have a few things from work stored on my computer's hard drive. That's marginal, though."

Riley considered the information and the interests of the relevant parties. "Okay. I think we're probably okay in not demanding a subpoena for your computer," she concluded. "You can agree to turn it over if you want. If it had been your work computer, you would be doubly screwed because we'd have to notify your employer for permission and a release or have them served with a subpoena. So, what else is on there?"

"Just a lot of code I've written, some could be considered malicious."

Riley's eyes widened. "In what way?"

"Hacking is. . .it's kind of an art," Wade said. "It takes a certain level of skill, but there's also an element of style. There's a real sense of community and competition among the guys that've got both. I've met a lot of other coders online by posting in group forums and one of the things we do is go on scavenger hunts where we're given a list of sites we gotta break to find code that's been hidden there. It gets pretty heated sometimes, but most of it's just for lulz. We don't mess with anything or steal stuff. It's more about testing security measures than actually doing any harm."

"Okay, first of all, I have no idea what constitutes a 'lulz' or why that would compel one to commit a crime. Secondly, and more importantly, are you telling me you've hacked other computers or websites?" Riley said.

"Well, yeah, I do it all the time. It's pretty easy, unless you're going into some of the high level defense sites or tailing a ghost in Russia. Those wizards have got code. Their SpyEye shit is insane. It dominates the other bots."

"You're not making it easy for me to keep you out of trouble here, Wade." Riley didn't want him to see her frustration so she took a step back and turned away while she considered their limited options. When she had some semblance of a plan, she turned back to advise him.

"Okay, this code of yours and anything else that might indicate your extracurricular activities, would that be in the same place on your hard drive as the deleted pictures of Halston?"

"Not exactly. Everything is on the hard drive. The deleted stuff is in a different place, though, and the search is different than if you were looking for data that's still archived," Wade stated.

"That might give me something to work with," Riley replied. "I can request that we, or at least you, be present when your computer is examined and that the search be limited to the location where the deleted files might be. I'll need you to give me the specifics on that location, from a technical perspective."

Wade's faced reflected a momentary sign of relief, before it was once again covered with clouds of concern. "Oh, shit. There's something else I hadn't thought of that's worse than the police getting their hands on my code."

"What's that?"

"If the bad guy, or bad guys if there is more than one, have Halston's computer and they know anything at all about computers, they could probably tell it was accessed remotely and that the drivers and stuff were altered." Wade wiped his now sweaty palms on his jeans and then instinctively drew one hand up to cover his mouth, hoping to stop himself from breathing life into more of his secret fears.

This just keeps getting better. Riley exhaled in exasperation. "And what, if anything, would that tell them?"

Wade had to fight the instinct of self-preservation that foolishly implied a truth, if unspoken, would somehow become less true. He withdrew his hand from his mouth and accepted defeat. "They could trace it back to my IP address, which would basically take them to my apartment."

"Wow. You were right earlier. You're really fucked," Riley responded.

Riley rubbed her forehead while in thought. The external sensory stimulation ceased once the internal process ended. "You can't go back there alone, or stay there for any length of time. I'm going to have to discuss protection options with Kris. I presume you will be safe enough at the computer forensics lab while they work on your computer. After that, things could get complicated."

CHAPTER 19

For the moment, Wade was safely tucked away at FDLE's Computer Forensics Lab working with Kristina to cull whatever information might still remain on the hard drive of his computer. That could take just an hour or all night. There was no way to know.

Riley glanced at the sky before heading into her office building. Thanks to the usually dreaded Daylight Savings Time, the late hour wasn't apparent. The sun was still hanging around to blast weary Earth-dwellers with its death rays. The sky was clear, and would stay that way as long as the storm hovered offshore and continued to absorb all upper-level moisture.

After she and Wade left Halston's apartment, Riley made the trek to Wade's apartment to shepherd the turnover of his computer to law enforcement, accompanied Wade and the investigators to the FDLE lab, and negotiated the parameters of the search with Kris. Kris agreed to limit the search to the drive space that would house deleted files, for now. She had rightfully made no guarantees to constrain the investigation if the deleted pictures weren't found.

There could be other information on the computer that might help them find Halston. If the investigators needed it they wouldn't give a second thought about Wade's delicate sensibilities or his questionable pursuits. Nor should they. Riley had left Wade with a few words of eternal wisdom: The Fifth Amendment is your new best friend.

It had already been a long day; it was going to get longer. Riley still had to pick up the Mikles files from the office and then close things down for the night. That wasn't where the day would end, though. Once she got home, changed clothes and let Mason out for his nightly jaunt, she faced the daunting task of reviewing pile upon pile of documents from the Mikles case to prepare for tomorrow's meeting with Sam.

There was no way in hell she was going into a meeting with that man unprepared, especially not after their recent spat or whatever it was that took place at his office this morning. His unseemly familiarity with every aspect of her life was as unnerving as his perfect smile. Sam was the type of man who would use whatever was within reach to his advantage, without hesitation or consideration of the resulting cost. She would have to keep her guard up, despite what Dani or anyone else thought about him.

Riley fully expected, as she entered the office, that Dani would be long gone. Her expectations were quickly confirmed. Dani's chair was empty and most of the lights had been dimmed. She had likely waited for Riley to return as long as she could before heading out– well past her scheduled quitting time–to pick up the boys from their summer soccer camp and fight the crowds for whatever few storm supplies might still be on the store shelves. She had emphatically encouraged Riley to do the same when they spoke on the phone earlier. Riley had agreed in order to avoid a prolonged lecture.

Dani was as persistent as Riley could be stubborn, which is why they made a formidable team when they turned their focus to the same cause. On the rare occasions they stood in separate corners, a stalemate was often the best either could hope for. In this case, however, Riley might have to concede. Dani was right. She needed to prepare for the storm, but she didn't have the luxury of time to make the admission much less for the task itself. Whoever was responsible for deciding how many hours there were in the day made their decision with the absence of foresight. No one she knew, if asked, would request fewer.

Maybe, if she were lucky, she could steal a few hours from tomorrow's allotment for her own self-preservation. Right. Who was she kidding? Too many of the factors that could influence tomorrow's luck lay in the hands of others. She decided to abandon foolish optimism in favor of the pragmatic. There was work to be done.

As was her custom before leaving at the end of the day, Dani left behind a small pile of notes and messages on Riley's desk for review. She had also left a Post-It note stuck to the computer monitor in Riley's office. Riley pulled the note from its post and held it under her desk lamp to see the hastily scrambled message more clearly.

Beware! Geeks are watching you.

Riley chuckled and then crumpled the small yellow slip and tossed it in the trash before outwardly ruminating. "You have no idea, my friend."

Normally, Riley welcomed the chance to peer inside the lives of others without having to carry the full burden of their reality. It was one of the perks of her profession. In Wade's case, the view was a virtual one and even with that level of disconnect, it wasn't safe. The whole thing was one colossal booby-trap.

Ignorance of that reality had been bliss. Technology had always fascinated her almost as much as the risks that came with it frightened her. Today she had been given a crash course in online privacy and information security and the underworld of computer hacking. She now knew more about both than she ever really cared to. The takeaway wasn't pretty.

Rare was the conversation in which she couldn't participate. This afternoon, she stood by helplessly, as might a foreigner in a foreign land, while Kristina and Wade traded theories on ways they might segregate the hard drive on Wade's computer to scan for file remnants or use a MAC number to trace Halston's computer to its current location.

Riley felt confident that, even in the absence of personal under-standing, the two of them knew what they were doing. She was little more than a third wheel in their two-wheeled race against time. As the odd one out, it made sense to redirect her attention to a task where her wheel could spin more productively. That decision led her back here to put an end to a tumultuous day whose auspicious beginning had promised far more than it could possibly deliver before its deadline.

She filtered through the Mikles case files Dani had already re-viewed and set aside for her, and piled the majority of them into a banker's style cardboard box. The boxes, along with their matching cardboard lids, were kept on hand because they were the most convenient way to transport a large number of files from one place to another and then back again. Even with the files she intended to review this evening, there would be more boxes to fill and move between now and the depositions on Monday. If the storm hit, which was by all accounts a certainty now, she and Sam would be working from some other location this weekend. If she had a say in the matter, and she had already decided she would, that location would be one of her choosing, not his.

Streaming consciousness led Riley's thoughts back to the office, and particularly, what needed to be done to protect the electronic equipment and client files in the event of a roof leak or broken window. Ignoring her own safety was one thing; ignoring the interests of her clients was something else entirely. The former was tolerable, to her mind; the latter was unacceptable. If she acted now, there was still time to remedy that oversight. She picked up her cell and hit the "Call" button. By default, it dialed the number she called the most.

ojo ojo ojo

Dani was directing her boys through the MassiveMart with the skill and precision of a drill sergeant. Each had a list of items to locate, procure, and bring to the extraction point, otherwise known as the checkout, within the next fifteen minutes. If they managed to complete the drill, with unfailing accuracy and speed, they got to go back into the field and procure something for themselves.

The militant style of management was second nature to her husband, who had successfully employed it with their boys as soon as they were old enough to walk. She wasn't above borrowing from Jack's parenting playbook. It was a good exercise in discipline and focus, and worked like a charm. It also gave her time to do a little shopping herself, a luxury any working mother could easily cherish.

She was closely examining the ingredients of an expensive salon-quality shampoo when her cell rang. The hour and timing of the call prompted her to answer it, rather than let it go to voicemail. Ninety-nine out of a hundred were the odds Riley was on the line. She pulled her phone from the front pocket of her leather shopping tote and answered.

"Hey, Riley. Guess you finally made it back?"

"How did you know I was in the office?"

"I played the odds," Dani joked. "Looks like I won. Maybe I should get a lotto ticket while I'm out."

"Oh, good. You are still at the store, then?"

"Yep. I'm with the boys and we're stocking up. Need me to get you anything?" Dani asked.

"Now that you mention it, I do," Riley said. "But not for me. We need a few things for the office. Can I text you the list?"

"Sure, I'll grab 'em while I'm here and bring 'em to work in the morning," Dani said.

"Great. Hey, while I've got you on the phone, I wanted to talk to you about Kristina's charity gala. They're doing it again, this year. It's the Saturday after next. You wanna go?"

Dani cackled. "Do I wanna get dolled up and go to a party? That's a dumb question. I'll need to arrange for a sitter, but I think I've got someone I can call."

"Cool. I'll get our tickets online," Riley confirmed.

"Wait, why are you asking me to the dance?"

"It's not really a dance, Dani."

"You know what I mean. I'm your backup plan, aren't I? You want to go with Sam. You just don't want to ask him," Dani chided.

"No, I don't. I don't want to go anywhere with that man, ever again."

"Mm hmm. Sure. So what am I supposed to wear to this shindig? Is it a swanky affair, like it was last year? You know my closet's not as deep as yours."

"I think so. Probably a cocktail dress or just something black would be fine."

Dani pshawed. "Black? That's for sissies who don't have the balls to wear a real color."

"We all know that wouldn't be you," Riley responded with a chuckle. "If you need a dress, pick something up when you get a chance. I have it on good authority that you'll be getting a mid-year bonus due to all the extra hours you've been putting in."

"That's music to my ears. I'm definitely in the mood to dance now."

"It's not a dance, damn it!"

"Everything's a dance if there's music and I'm in the mood."

"Fine. You can dance, then," Riley concluded. "Don't expect me to join you unless it's a song I like."

"I'll make friends with the DJ and put in a request for you."

"Gee, thanks. Not to change the subject, but I've still got a ton to do tonight. I'm taking most of the Mikles files home with me. If they're not here when you get in tomorrow, don't freak out. That's where they'll be."

"Listen, don't stay up too late just because Sam brought you into this at the last minute. You're good enough to wing it at Audra's deposition if you have to."

"I appreciate your confidence. I'll get through what I can tonight. I don't plan to pull an all-nighter, though. I've managed to get this far in life without ever having to. I don't intend to start now."

"That's the spirit," Dani coached. While still on the call, she switched the screen of her phone to determine how much time she had left before the boys returned from their mission. There was still time. "Go ahead and send me the list of items you want. I can have the boys pick them up while I shop for a dress."

Riley smiled. "Smart use of resources. The next mission for your recruits is headed your way. Thanks."

Tasking her boys with Riley's list bought Dani another fifteen or maybe even twenty minutes to shop. This wasn't the first place she would have chosen to find the type of dress one would wear to a gala. Once in a while, she could find cute, basic dresses on a clearance rack here. They also had great accessories. With the right accompaniments, she could make just about anything work.

Dani meandered over to the clothing section and scanned the racks. There were a few dresses that might work in what appeared to be her size, or a near approximation thereof. One was a rich color of peridot green she expected would nicely compliment her strawberry blonde hair and pale ivory skin. It was a fairly simple, faux-wrap style knee-length dress fashioned from a silky stretch Lycra-infused fabric. There was another navy cotton-knit dress that showed promise, although the color didn't really excite her. She pulled both from the rack and headed back to the dressing room.

In keeping with her standard protocol, she tried on the blue one first. It was best to get confirmation on the presumed rejects right out of the box. She then lifted the green dress from the hanger and examined it to determine the points of access. There did not appear to be a zipper, so presumably this one was a pullover. Not weighing the dress down with a metal zipper made sense, given the stretchy nature of the fabric.

She pulled the dress over her head and started to wriggle into it. She had it about halfway down her torso, with one arm in and one arm out, when her progress was halted by an unexpected sensation. She turned around to face the dressing room mirror to survey the culprit—her left breast.

"Witch. Why the hell are you sore? It's not that time of the month," Dani murmured.

Dani pulled her arm out from inside the dress and tugged the rest of the stretchy fabric down over her hips and thighs. She was right about one thing: the color was perfect. Unfortunately, the size was all wrong, and the fabric didn't help any. The dress clung to her real-woman curves in all the wrong places.

Dani advised her reflection of the unavoidable conclusion. "Girl, you look like a sausage in this. Definitely not the look you were going for."

She pulled the dress back over her head and returned it to the hanger. Before putting her top back on, Dani pressed her breast a few times to determine the source of sensitivity. At her age, and after two babies, it could be nothing more than hormones. Or it could be something else.

"I swear to God, Jack. If you knocked me up before you left town, I'm going to find whatever God-forsaken dung-hole the Navy assigned you to and kick your ass."

CHAPTER 20

Special Agent Kent Donovan stood in front of The Polling Place's blocky, stucco-faced building while checking his phone for messages. A few more minutes in his own skin felt good, since he would soon don that of another. It was a ritual he repeated almost every day since he'd been on assignment at the club.

"One text, no calls. Good. Don't have time to yap," he muttered.

The text was from Sam, sent on a spoofed number he often used for covert communications. Officially, they didn't run in the same circles.

Having dinner @ the club. U working?

Kent texted back a short affirmation. *I'm here.*

This part of Florida is filled with tourist attractions. In Kent's mind, this wasn't one of them. Places like this were called "strip clubs" for more than the obvious reasons. They strip you of your money and your good sense. He'd seen colleagues in the Secret Service get sucked into the so-called high life these places touted. More than a few good men had destroyed their marriages, lost their careers, and faced financial ruin before awakening from the strobe-light-induced delirium a place like this could provoke.

In spite of the inherent pitfalls, his current assignment—undercover monitoring of agency targets at a notorious gentleman's club—had been highly coveted among the area's field agents. A number of them had gone so far as to call in favors from high ranking members of the Department of Defense and Homeland Security in an effort to land the gig. Kent hadn't even bothered to throw his hat into the ring. If he had to wager a guess, that was probably why he'd been chosen.

The unknown powers who make such decisions likely read his lack of interest as an indication that he wasn't the type to be easily distracted by the assignment's trappings, as compelling as they might be. That, in turn, increased the odds of a favorable outcome. In that regard, he couldn't argue with their logic. They were correct in their assessment. His blood was as red as any other guy's, but spending his evenings pulling inebriated assholes off of attractive, naked women wasn't on his bucket list. Or it wouldn't be, if he had one.

There were only a few lone wolves like him left in the agency, and even fewer with experience in deep-cover operations. Those reasons might also be among the ones that compelled the agency to choose him over the other candidates. Protocol mandated a solid cover on an assignment like this. Once inside, everyone on the outside had to buy the ticket at face value. It was an easy enough sell in his case. No one would be calling his supervisor to complain about the late nights or the bare-breasted company he was keeping.

Kent pressed a button at the top of his cell phone and it replied with a standard bleep before switching to silent mode. He slid it into his pant pocket, and exhaled slowly before resigning himself to his plight. Like it or not, it was time for the sheepdog to dissolve into the flock for another night's watch. Kent reminded himself as he opened the door and crossed the threshold that it would all be over soon enough.

The club was as sparsely populated as the parking lot, which was highly unusual for almost any evening, and especially one leading into the weekend. On any given Thursday or Friday, the regulars would arrive at 4:00 p.m. for happy hour and when that ended, their over-indulgence in half-price, top-shelf beverages, and the fear of getting caught intoxicated behind the wheel, was reason enough to stick around and order from the dinner menu. If they could get away with it, and most of them could, they would then extend dinner into an excuse to stay for after-dinner drinks. But none of that creative scheduling was taking place tonight. Apparently, the looming prospect of a major hurricane was enough to turn even the least-likely contenders into homebodies.

If asked, Kent would say he came in on his day off to help with storm preparations. There were only a few men on staff at the club, and even fewer who might be capable of actually lifting something heavier than an ice bucket. In reality, he planned to use this opportunity to explore parts of the club to which he didn't usually have access. The excuse that he needed to secure the windows, and move necessary equipment elsewhere to protect it from water damage should be sufficient to give him access to pretty much any part of the facility today, including the back offices.

Tamara, the evening hostess, was entranced by a paperback book she only halfheartedly tried to conceal behind the lip of the front counter. It was probably one of those steamy romances she usually brought with her when she worked evenings. He'd seen her reading them on a few of the late night shifts they shared. Nothing like a skillfully narrated daydream to ward off sleep on a slow night.

Tamara reluctantly pulled away from her literary lover to greet the most recent interloper. Once she recognized Kent she smiled appreciatively, her eyes following the length of him with the type of ardor only a skillful romance novelist can generate.

Since today would be less about escorting inebriated guests from the facility and more about preparing the place for the impending storm, he had dressed more casually than he might on any other night. His dark grey, screen printed t-shirt and khaki, cotton cargo pants would enable him to move about more freely while moving equipment and securing windows. Given the overbearing humidity that had settled in ahead of the storm, he had welcomed the chance to wear something with a lighter weight and feel than the dark, collared golf-style shirts he had to wear when on duty. He hadn't considered there might be other benefits to his chosen attire.

Tonight's fitted t-shirt firmly hugged his muscular torso and its short sleeves ended at just the right spot to lend deserving emphasis to his well-honed biceps. He possessed neither by chance or for show. Rather, they and whatever else of his physique Tamara might be admiring resulted from the discipline of daily workouts–something he firmly believed came with its own rewards. Appreciation from the opposite gender was among those rewards, although it wasn't the motivating factor that drove him to the gym at 5:00 a.m. every morning. Still, it didn't hurt to have someone applaud the effort, now and then.

His t-shirt also revealed tats on both his shoulders that extended down his arm to end just below the short sleeves. Further down on his left forearm was another tat he'd been forced to get a few years back after losing a bet with Sam. The design incorporated a colorful snake that wrapped around his forearm, along with a sword and something Sam had referred to as an "idiom." Or maybe Sam had said "idiot." The latter would more aptly describe how the tat made Kent feel.

The ink looked imposing enough, and came in handy on assignments such as this where Kent needed to establish himself as part of the city's subculture. So, he'd kept it long after both he and Sam had forgotten the "what" or "why" of their bet. Every now and then, he considered asking Sam what the symbols meant, but then thought better of it. Knowing Sam, it probably identified him as a headless chicken destined for soup. Some things are just better left alone, especially when time reveals them to be a mixed blessing.

Recent events afforded him a much greater appreciation for the permanent penance Sam had imposed. A still-healing scar on his forearm just below the tat was made far less noticeable by the colorful snake. Kent rubbed the area self-consciously. It still smarted sometimes, but what bothered him most about it was the constant reminder he'd let that bastard Calvin Buehler get the jump on him.

Fortunately, the young woman staring at it and him at the moment didn't seem to care about Sam's idiotic symbols or the scar. She was simply taking it all in, and clearly appreciating the view. If he'd been the blushing type, Kent might've felt the heat of her gaze. He wasn't, so he didn't. Instead he felt the cool reassurance of logic, and stored a mental note. Tamara might prove to be an asset, should he need to deepen his cover.

Kent stopped by the counter, flashed a quick smile and looked down at Tamara's book. He turned the pages back to view the cover. "Must be a slow night. Did you finish that one you were reading the other day? How'd it turn out?"

"The same way they always do. The hero and heroine have a mind-blowing romp between the sheets," she responded. "I hope my story ends like that someday."

"I'd rather my story end with what happens after the sheets are washed. That's when it gets real. All relationships start with heat. The really good stuff is the part that comes later."

Tamara pondered the notion for a moment before discarding it.

"No, not for me. I'm pretty sure I just want the hot stuff. The rest is for mommy-types," she concluded. "But how do you know? You said you don't have a girlfriend and haven't for a while."

She continued to stare at Kent with the look a famished dieter might give a plate of fried chicken. Or the look Kent might give a medium rare ribeye steak right about now. Fine steaks, the kind that weren't often in the budget of a government employee, were one of the club's biggest draws.

"I don't. Can't say I'm the mommy-type, either," Kent added. "I like to savor my kills, and ya can't do that with a quickie. So, what's on the menu tonight? It's pretty slow. Think we'll get leftovers?"

"I hope so," Tamara admitted. "The Dimpled Ballot on the new dessert menu looks good. It's a seven-layer white chocolate cake covered with toffee sprinkles. I think it's my new favorite."

"I'm in to do storm prep tonight, so I should be in the kitchen at some point." Kent advised. "I'll see if I can swipe a piece for you."

Tamara looked as if she might leap over the counter and devour him whole. "Oh my God, that would be aaaaamaaazing. You are the best! Bruce never did anything nice for me."

"Bruce sounds like a moron. Whatever happened to him, anyway?" Kent asked, nonchalantly.

It was a rhetorical question. Bruce had suddenly, and conveniently, found himself in hot water over his questionable immigration status. Finding a vulnerable employee and exploiting that vulnerability, thereby creating an employment opportunity, was just one of the many tactics used to get an agent inside a targeted enterprise. In this case, that tactic resulted in the prior third-shift bouncer earning a long engagement in a far less desirable place, courtesy of some of Kent's friends at the INS.

There were a number of ways to get eyes and ears inside a business. The old-fashioned way, which was rarely used in these days of high technology, was to break in. Now, the use of heat sensors and sonar-enhanced listening devices, Wi-Fi scanners, Bluetooth sniffing and snarfing, and other similar technology made the job much easier and less likely to result in detection. But there are still some things technology can't do, one of which is testify.

Whatever they found via electronic or other means would still need to be authenticated by a reliable source. For that, a real live person was required. An agent infiltrating the business could provide the testimony to some degree. In this case, Kent might end up being that person. A far better scenario would be to find and flip a person on the inside that had long-term, in-depth experience with the organization. Preferably, someone articulate enough to engage a jury.

Technology wasn't going to find that person for them or gain their trust. And the trust part was crucial in this case. Whoever they found that could or would turn on Mikles, if such a person even existed, would be giving up life as they knew it. Mikles' type of wealth had a long reach. Prison wasn't likely to hamper that.

What all of that meant, in this situation, was that both a few old-fashioned and some new-fangled spy games were required. The

Service needed a man on the inside and the best way to do that was to create a job opening. That part had been easy enough to do. There were far more illegal workers in Florida than the general public really wanted to know. If that tactic hadn't worked, the agency had other avenues. No one ever correctly files their tax returns, and some don't even bother to file returns at all. If the Bruce card hadn't worked out, the agency had identified a number of other employees they could target for tax evasion.

Creating an opening was just the first step. The next was making sure their agent got the job. Borrowing a trick from the hackers they often targeted, the agency's tech branch cleverly attached a Trojan virus to the email Kent sent with his résumé to the club's email address. Once activated by the download of Kent's résumé, the planted bug enabled the agency to divert all other applicants' résumés to an unrelated email address. The agency then replaced those applications with fake ones from nonexistent persons, none of whom were remotely qualified for the position.

The bug also contained a key logging virus, which would be used to monitor activity on the infected computer. All in all, it was a clever and nasty little insect they had crafted from the code an analyst uncovered while investigating a Nigerian banking scam. It was high-tech, conveniently camouflaged within the computer's operating system, and virtually undetectable by most commercial antivirus software programs.

Tamara had returned her attention to her book long enough to dog-ear the corner of the last page she had read. She wasn't as intrigued by the fictional romance now that a real one might be playing out in front of her. She looked back up at Kent with renewed interest.

"Oh, Bruce? I heard he found a better opportunity. I dunno where in this economy, 'cause the pay here is pretty good. But he was a jerk. Always grabbing my ass, and stuff. I don't mind the upgrade at all," she added, brightly.

"His loss, my gain," Kent concurred, plying her with a smile that appeared equally enthusiastic. "I better get in there and see what needs to be done. I'll check back on my way out."

Kent stopped by the main bar on the first floor to cement today's cover. He leaned onto one of the barstools and grabbed a few beer nuts from a nearby bowl.

"What brings you to The Polling Place today, my friend? Are you registered to vote?"

The gruff voice came from a burly guy behind a large black granite-topped bar, before he looked up and realized he wasn't greeting a guest.

"With my record, I'm not allowed to vote," Kent responded with a wink.

"Danny Boy! Why are you here on your day off? Hooking up with one of the dancers, already?"

The bartender wouldn't be the first person today to refer to Kent by the only name he had allowed them to know. Kent laughed off the suggestion.

"You and I don't make enough money for those girls, Charlie."

"That so? The way I hear it, any one of them would spot you an after-hours show. You do know they call you 'Dan the Man,' don't you?"

"Dan the Man? Great. Sounds like a character from Dr. Seuss." Kent embellished the remark with a smirk.

No matter how long the undercover assignment, it doesn't get easier to be referred to by someone else's name. A dude with any other name just isn't the same. For weeks now, he'd been otherwise known as Daniel Pearson, a former marine and ex-cop from Boston, who moved to Florida to help care for his ailing mother. His cover had been carefully crafted to ensure he was a shoe-in for the job, which meant his résumé touted him as an expert in weapons, martial arts, and gently showing inebriated assholes to the door; all the necessary skills for a bouncer at a high-end bar.

No one here knew him as Kentucky, the unfortunate name in-flicted on him at birth, or even Kent as he was known to his friends. The upside of his new name meant he didn't have to suffer the dim-witted "Special K" jokes often lodged by fellow agents in the Secret Service. The downside was that there were many equally as banal bastardizations of "Daniel."

"Figured you guys would need some help getting ready for the storm. Has anyone started securing the place?" Kent asked.

"Don't think so," Charlie responded. "The big guy was here earli-er. His wife and some guy in an expensive suit came in with him. Looked like they was taking care of some kind of business or some-thing. He may still be here, but you probably should check with the bar manager about what needs to be done for the storm. He'd know more about that."

"Good idea. Is he around?" Kent asked.

"He's in the kitchen going over inventory with the chef. I'll let him know you're here."

"Actually, don't bother. I'm heading back there. Told Tamara I'd sneak her one of the new desserts, if I got the chance."

Charlie laughed. "I knew it. I knew you were courting one of our ladies."

"Maybe," Kent responded with a sheepish smile, "but like I said not one of the dancers. Can't buy their attention with something as simple as dessert."

He shifted from the barstool and headed for the kitchen. From there, he could easily slip into the back offices unnoticed, and hopefully be able to remain there undetected long enough to search the computers and file cabinets for anything the government could use to expand its investigation.

As he passed by one of the bar's many "performance" areas, his gaze settled on the young girl doing acrobatic turns on a thin metal pole that spanned from floor to ceiling. She was tall, largely due to a pair of ungodly long legs. She was also quite thin yet surprisingly, and most likely artificially, filled out in all the right places.

Despite her obviously attractive features, the only thought that crossed Kent's mind was that she was someone's little girl. Probably half of the middle-aged men who regularly came to the club to ogle her had daughters around her age. Ironically, girls like her had made Mikles a multimillionaire, but all he had made them was slightly infamous for being naked before a crowd. That unbalanced exchange was just one of the many questionable transactions Mikles was engaged in. Unfortunately, it wasn't one Kent had any authority to remedy.

Although the U.S. is far more puritanical than many countries when it comes to selling sex, the government was more concerned about controlling the flow of commerce than protecting young women. The feds had only come inside Mikles' den of iniquity to follow the money. Whatever human casualties they might encounter there were considered someone else's problem.

Mikles presently ran a wide range of adult-entertainment businesses, some of which were clubs similar to this one. His other high-end brick-and-mortar establishments were located in Miami, Las Vegas, the Bahamas, and Dubai. While his clubs were plenty profitable, an even greater majority of his income came from a number of online adult-oriented businesses. Mikles had also cleverly expanded his empire by using those sex-themed websites to cross-market goods he referred to as "souvenirs," which he distributed via a local company. That was the company where Sam had sent an unsuspecting Riley Morgan to lecture on sexual harassment.

What made Mikles' businesses distinct from other run-of-the-mill Internet porn providers was that his websites utilized a virtual bank, owned and operated under a foreign charter for all online transactions. Because the bank was Internet based, it could be run from anywhere in the world and therefore didn't have to meet any specific nation's banking requirements, much less the heightened ones imposed on U.S. banks. It was either an unlikely coincidence or a great misfortune that Mikles used a bank that appeared to be chartered in Dubai—a country known for its financial institutions catering to wealthy international clientele no matter their source of income. That was apparently the first red flag that brought his empire to the attention of the Secret Service.

The web-based banking portal Mikles utilized allowed accounts to be opened by anyone, anywhere, at any time, without verification of the name, address or other identifying information that was generally required under the Patriot Act, and a number of other laws, for all banks operating with U.S. currency. Once an account was opened, funds would be deposited, withdrawn, transferred, and exchanged without any record of the source of the transaction. The absence of any real oversight created a perfect setup for laundering illegal funds, and for allowing transactions by potential terrorists or terrorist organizations that have been subjected to financial sanctions by the Treasury Department's Office of Foreign Assets Control (OFAC).

As the agency with direct responsibility for enforcing U.S. imposed financial sanctions, OFAC created a list of Specially Designated Nationals (SDNs) that included persons, corporations, entities, organizations and countries subject to asset-blocking orders or other types of economic sanctions. OFAC then charged U.S. financial institutions of all types with heightened responsibility to monitor and screen financial transactions for any connection to the SDNs.

By all outward appearances, Mikles was attempting to circumvent the additional transaction monitoring cost imposed on U.S. banks by using an innovative banking alternative. Whether or not his solution proved to be wise or even legal remained to be seen. The relevant law and regulations were complex and full of holes courtesy of the banking industry's powerful lobbyists. Thankfully, putting together a case that stood up to the rigors of prosecution was someone else's job. Kent's part was simply to find pieces of the puzzle and turn them over to the bookish types.

If any pieces of that puzzle were to be found at Mikles' flagship club, they would most likely be in the back offices. Kent rattled the seals and locks of the windows along the back wall of the club, giving tenor to his cover, before making his way toward the corridor just outside of the kitchen that led to the business offices.

The sound of a single set of footsteps prompted a quick change in plan. Even with a decent cover, it was best he not be seen prowling around the offices. He ducked into one of the restrooms at the front of the hallway.

"This better be the men's room," Kent muttered while he manually expedited the sweep of the closing door behind him. The click-clack sound faded as the person passed further down the hall. By the sound of things, it was obviously a woman with a long-legged stride, wearing heels.

"What if it isn't?" a familiar voice inquired.

"Fuck you, Sam."

CHAPTER 21

B unny glanced down at her watch for the hundredth time. Finally. It was 9:15 p.m. on the dot. As if on cue, the first round of kitchen crew on the evening shift stepped out to take their smoke break. Few things in life were as consistent as a chemical dependency.

The Polling Place staff were required to take breaks on the quarter-hour so the time away from their stations fell in-between the reserved half-hour table seatings of guests. They were permitted two fifteen-minute breaks, in addition to a meal break, per shift. Employee breaks were also to be staggered so that only three or four workers on any given shift would be on break at a time. The detailed break-time policy was one Bunny had suggested and then implemented when she was one of Vincent's managers. Her policy was obviously still being utilized by the current manager. Bunny gleamed with pride. The remnants of her colorful past had once again proved beneficial. In this instance, it gave her the advantage of knowing the staff's recurring cycle well.

The distraction caused by the growing need to feed their nicotine habit usually caused the employees who smoke, which was about half of the overall staff and ninety percent of the kitchen staff, to stop doing anything productive in favor of clock-gazing for at least two to three minutes prior to their scheduled break. They utilized the stolen work time to stage their impending exit and correspondingly maximize the benefit of their personal time. The staff on schedule for the first break of the evening had likely been standing by the rear exit door, cigarettes and lighters in hand, for the past few minutes counting the seconds just as she had—although the fix she was seeking was of an entirely different variety.

Florida's Clean Indoor Air Act prohibits practically all smoking indoors so, like many employers, Vincent had created an outdoor smoking section behind the club complete with table and chairs for the staff smokers. The table was located on a small brick-paved patio partially closed in with stucco half-walls that blended with the club's exterior. The patio was a good twenty feet away and to the left of the kitchen exit doorway. It had been strategically placed there to keep the cigarette smoke from filtering back into the kitchen and impacting the flavor or aroma of the food. It was an intelligent design and, as it turned out for Bunny, a convenient one.

She was barely visible standing near the dumpsters to the far right of the exit doorway, and if she timed it right, her entrance from that location would be shielded from the smokers' view by the slow-moving industrial door. The moment the smokers turned their backs to her and headed toward the patio, Bunny tiptoed toward the still-open door, her steps masked by the creaks and groans of the door's heavy joints as it slowly pulled itself shut. It took only a few seconds for her to reach the door and dart inside.

This wasn't an official visit, and unlike Tuesday night, the plan was not to be seen coming or going. With a little luck, and a lot of smarts, it was possible she wouldn't be seen by Vincent, his cameras or any of his management people who sometimes worked late in the back offices. She quickly glanced around the kitchen to ensure her entrance had, in fact, been unobserved. So far, so good.

At the moment, she was alone in the back part of the kitchen because the entire cooking staff and dishwashing crew had chosen to take their smoke break at the same time. They were only permitted to do that when it was a slow night for the restaurant section of the club. Fate had once again chosen to twist in her favor. This particular twist meant she could pass through the kitchen and into the back offices without encountering a soul.

All she had to do now was crouch low enough at a certain point on her route through the kitchen to avoid the lens of the single camera Vincent had installed there, although it was of lesser concern to her than the staff. The cameras he installed in employee areas weren't recording their feed, and were rarely monitored. Vincent wasn't really interested in what his employees were doing, so long as they kept the customers happy. He had bigger fish to fry.

She had spent most of the day, following her morning tantrum at Sam's office, plotting her next move. There was no way to avoid it now—she was going to have to secure the heavy artillery to quell Sam's impending occupation of her territory. Since Vincent lived in the area, and this was his largest club, he very likely still kept his important documents where he had back in the day. She would start here and then broaden her search if necessary.

The management and executive offices were all located down a long corridor just outside of the kitchen. Bunny slipped out of the kitchen and into the server prep and food staging area of the club through double swinging doors. This was still a semi-private work area, and was enclosed on all sides to shield the usually frantic comings and goings of the wait staff from public view. There were two open passageways that led from the prep area. The one on the right led into the club. Bunny made a quick turn headed in the other direction toward the dimly-lit corridor. Again, so far, so good. She hadn't run into a single employee or patron.

A set of public bathrooms, reserved for the VIPs seated at the back tables on the first floor, were located at the front of the corridor, with the men's room on one side and the women's on the other. The corridor housed a few other management offices and a storage closet just past the VIP bathrooms, and ended at the entrance to Vincent's expansive office. The location of Vincent's office provided not only a view of a man-made lake behind the club through a set of darkly tinted windows, but an equally compelling view of the main performance area by virtue of two-way mirrors mounted on the wall on the opposite side of the room.

In spite of the prime location and views, Vincent didn't spend much time in his office in the evenings. He was the consummate schmoozer, and preferred to be on the club floor pressing palms with high-brow guests once the sun went down and the music got loud. Bunny was hoping tonight would be no exception. When she reached the closed door of his office, she tapped on it lightly. No reply. She pressed her ear against the door hoping to catch the sound of any occupants. All silent.

She turned the knob and, much to her surprise, it gave way. This discovery was both an advantage and a setback. On the upside, she didn't have to pick the lock. On the downside, she would have to act quickly. Vincent rarely left his office door unlocked. He would only do so if he had stepped away momentarily and was still in the building somewhere. He would never leave it unlocked if he wasn't nearby. Even the most loyal of his employees could be tempted by the types of things they might find behind that heavy steel-reinforced door.

Among those temptations were basic business records along with the nightly cash and credit card receipts, all of which were in a hidden wall safe. An ordinary intruder or foolish employee would go straight for that bounty, if they knew where it was located. Bunny glanced over at a tacky wall painting that was commercially reproduced to look like a stately oil-on-canvas portrait. Vincent had ordered it online.

The painting was of Cayren, his wife, wearing some sort of Jackie-O getup and sitting on an expensive looking wingback chair. She was flanked on both sides by the couple's overly pampered and appropriately named Pomeranians, Fluff and Muff, who were adorned with what appeared to be small tiaras. The sparkling headpieces matched their diamond-crusted dog collars. The portrait, and its prominent placement, was intended to give Vincent the appearance of legitimacy that accompanies a family man.

Bunny's lip curled in disgust. "That's a double dose of shit-zu. Vincent, and you know it," she muttered.

Bunny looked away and then glanced back. Cayren's green eyes seemed to glow in the dim light of Vincent's halogen desk lamp. Were they following her, or was that just her imagination?

"Get a grip," she commanded herself.

She walked over to Vincent's neat-as-a-pin desk, something she had always considered to be another prime example of his controlling nature, and pulled on the bottom drawer on the right-hand side. It didn't give way. That was a good sign. She was looking in the right place. The fact it was locked meant Vincent still kept valuables there.

She tinkered around the expensive pens displayed on Vincent's desk in a Jefferson-style pewter cup, tackily monogrammed with Vincent's initials, until her fingers made their way to the bottom of the cup. She came across paper clips and other assorted knick-knacks lying against the bottom of the cup, most likely tossed inside in one of Vincent's obsessive clearing frenzies, and then touched something that was cool and smooth on one side, yet jagged and toothy on the other. She pinched it between her index and middle fingers before pulling it from the cup. The silver metal key sparkled under the light of Vincent's desk lamp.

"Aren't you a thing of beauty?" Bunny mused. "Let's see if this slipper fits for Cinderella."

The key slid easily into the drawer lock. Bunny turned it and then pulled on the drawer handle. This time the drawer gave way. From all outward appearances, the locked drawer was only protecting a very expensive humidor that was probably filled with contraband cigars. Most people would assume that was the purpose of the lock. But most people didn't know, and certainly not with the same level of assurance, that the possession of a secret stash of Cuban cigars was the least of Mikles' transgressions.

Bunny removed the humidor and set it on the desk. She then felt around the drawer for a lever or catch. Once found, she pressed it and then lifted the drawer's false bottom. Underneath was a steel-framed built-in drawer safe. On the front of the safe were punch buttons with the numbers one through nine printed on them, along with a button on the bottom left marked "Open" and one on the bottom right marked "Lock."

"I bet you use the same code for your private safe as you do for the wall safe, you testosterone-laden buffoon," Bunny whispered.

She punched in the date that Mikles opened his first gentleman's club. "Nope. Guess you're smarter than the average human afflicted with a penis. I would use a different code, too, since your management employees go into your wall safe all the time."

What else would he use? Bunny knew him well. This shouldn't be too hard to figure out. The things that mattered to him had always been fairly constant. Success and power, or at least whatever gave him the appearance thereof. Those two motivations had always been a driving force for Vincent. Still, one thing trumped both of them. Unfortunately for her friend, Cayren, it wasn't in that hideous picture on the wall.

The opposite of success is failure. Vincent had only failed at one thing—the game of politics. His embarrassing removal after three days in political office was a taboo subject and always had been. It was known as the "thing-that-is-not-spoken" around the club. Despite the fact he'd built his whole empire as a thumb-on-the-nose salute to it, it was no laughing matter. In the past, anyone who dared even whisper anything that suggested a reference to it had been escorted from the premises by security.

Nothing burned brighter in Vincent's belly than the fire of revenge. No one who knew him socially would ever guess that about him. On the surface, he was always the amiable, ready-for-anything guy who threw a great party. But that image was as fake as the one of Cayren on his wall. Vincent was actually a tightly-wound control freak who needed to dominate everyone and everything around him. He was the type who could easily greet his opposition with open arms and sit for hours enjoying drinks with them while his special recipe for revenge was marinating. When the seasoning was just right, he would serve it cold, as if pulled directly from a commercial-quality refrigerator.

The recipe for Vincent's special dish started with an ample portion of common stock that included pictures of exposed body parts his targets had easily been cajoled into sexting to one of his girls. He then kicked the brew up a notch with video tapes of politicos having sex-capades with some of his most attractive female employees. The award-winning versions of those films usually featured more than one girl at a time. A few of those videos were made while the politicians were on all-expense-paid junkets Vincent sponsored on his yacht.

Better yet, some recorded escapades had taken place on government property, which included courthouses and even the Governor's Mansion. This ingredient was far more valuable to the revenge recipe than the videos he kept from basic VIP parties or the video short Bunny had made herself during her recent visit. It was one thing to over-indulge in alcohol or to struggle with the challenges of substance abuse. Politicians could easily escape to rehab and claim a disability for those vices. It was an entirely different ballgame to be caught with your pants down while on the job–literally.

Vincent handpicked the girls who interacted with his "special clients" and paid them handsomely. Vincent's use of his girls to obtain leverage over those who might oppose him was well-known among long-term employees who had shown enough loyalty to garner his trust. Bunny had been one of those employees when she worked for him, as had Cayren. At the time, it bothered them both that Vincent didn't ask them to assist him with his *special* customers. But now that she knew more about what he had been up to, she was relieved. It was far better to own the ammunition than to be the ammunition.

The chosen girls were provided bonuses if they got their targets to speak poorly about constituents or contributors while canoodling. Nothing adds flavor to an election like a recording of a butt-naked politician using salty language while referring to the residents in his district as whining losers who expect handouts. A girl's bonus would be doubled if she managed to film her mark speaking poorly of his long-suffering wife or family. Most politicians use their families as pawns to get them into office, so it seemed poetic justice for Vincent to use their families as a means to get them out of office, if he so desired. He liked to call that little irony "Varma," a word which presumably describes his own special brand of karma.

The best return of all was offered to any girl who brought heat to the recipe by getting a confession of criminal conduct on tape. That lucky girl would be pretty well set for life, which was a good thing. It was doubtful she would be able to show her face in public again if the tapes were released or used as leverage.

Vincent's intention had always been to use his tapes as exhibits to the discussion points of conversations he would rather not have. His preference, with regard to clients, is to keep the flow of alcohol heavy and the conversation light. It undoubtedly took great skill and focus to maintain relationships with the very rich and powerful on an even keel, but Vincent had managed to do just that, so far. Still, if one of his unfortunate marks tried to cross him, or exert their power or influence in a way that didn't suit him, Vincent wouldn't hesitate to remind them not only where their bread was buttered, but that he had already toasted it for them.

At first, the reminder would be done quietly and in private. The mere suggestion of embarrassment was usually enough for most of those who live in the public eye. Rare would be the occasion he would actually need to release a tape to the public. That was not to say Vincent wouldn't release the tapes through the cheesiest of tabloids if some fool challenged him on it, but his preference was to deal with matters quietly and behind the scenes.

For as long as she'd known him, Vincent had been preparing a very special version of his cold plate to be served on two high-profile men who had never set foot in his club. This dish included all of his best ingredients, a few others that were homegrown and some that remained unknown, even to those who knew him well. Vincent had personally prepared this dish for the two political movers and shakers who were behind the voting debacle that had resulted in his removal from office. Their names and faces sat squarely in the middle of Vincent's proverbial dartboard. Come to think of it, she'd actually seen their pictures posted on his dartboard in the private den at his house.

Neil Wainwright and August Grayling were big men around Florida's political campus. Wainwright had made billions from a Florida-based business he created that processed and filled medical prescriptions under various Medicare, Medicaid, and workers' compensation programs. Although he was less instrumental in the day-to-day business of his company after he made his initial fortune, he still held controlling stock. At least, he did until the indictments citing him and his business for fraud started coming down. In the face of mounting pressure from investors and shareholders, Wainright cashed out of the business in order to focus his energies on his legal defense.

During the many years of wrangling over the criminal charges lodged against him, and despite what would appear to have been an obvious conflict of interest, Wainright still managed to secure appointments to the board of directors of various Fortune 500 companies. He also became heavily involved in Florida politics, often throwing large sums of money into the campaign coffers of candidates whose political views aligned with his interests. Not coincidentally, it was the candidate Wainwright had backed who took Vincent Mikles' place in office nearly a decade ago following the mysterious discovery of a large number of uncounted absentee ballots on the day after the election. Perhaps even less coincidentally, that same candidate went on to become a one-term governor whose parting gift to the electorate after failing to win re-election was ending the criminal investigation into Wainright and his former company.

August Grayling was a rare breed of Floridian—a native. Most in the state are transplants from somewhere else, but his family had come over with the alligator, or so it seemed. His fortune was in land, which had borne him financial fruit via orange groves in the early years when the crop was a mainstay of Florida's economy. His extensive real estate holdings continued to increase in value even after other countries, like Costa Rica, replaced Florida as the citrus capital of the world. Grayling's most recent successes had been in the development of high-end residential communities. He'd been fortunate to jump into those ventures well before the real estate boom in 2004 and cash out with brimming pockets by 2008, when the bubble started to burst.

Wainright and Grayling had run in the same affluent circles for many years, and were well-known to be thick as thieves. For that reason, it wasn't too surprising, at least not to Mikles, that the uncounted absentee ballots responsible for displacing Mikles from office were largely from newly-registered voters with addresses in Grayling's communities.

Although Grayling had never shown any interest in politics, his son had become quite the promising candidate. Handsome, well-spoken and Ivy League educated, Archer Grayling had handily won his first election to the Florida House of Representatives just three years ago. Now one year into his second two-year term, he was already his party's heir apparent for the gubernatorial race. Vincent had always been highly suspicious of the younger Grayling as well, but never indicated he had any reason other than the familial one.

Both Wainwright and the elder Grayling appeared to have an un-canny ability to stay ahead of the curve, but that was all about to change. If Vincent had his way about it, their days of basking in the limelight as elite businessmen who call the shots in Sunshine State politics were limited, and not by anything as commonplace as a miscalculation of votes. That sort of thing was old news for the State of Florida. No, what those guys had coming would be remembered long after the embarrassment of Mikles' removal from office had faded to a footnote in Florida's storied history of political fiascos.

The means to accomplish that coup, as well as the means to con-trol or take down a few other big names in politics and industry, was rumored to be on a flash drive that resided in the drawer safe Bunny was trying to crack. There was no telling what else might be found there. If the information on that drive was as its legend foretold, whoever possessed it could change the face of Florida's future.

Bunny searched her memory for the exact date. History had never been her forte, but this wasn't a date from an abstract event. This event hit close to home. It was the day that made the man who had in turn made her. She pulled out her smartphone and did a quick search on the Internet. It was a great equalizer when it came to such things. The days of having to clog your memory with abstract trivia were long gone. Now, anything you need to know is available 24/7 at the speed of whatever cell tower you were nearest.

It took a moment to type in the query with the small touch-screen keyboard. Once the query was entered, she hit the search button. A moment later, there it was. The date of Mikles' doom.

She pressed the keys on the front of the safe to correspond with the six digits of the day, month and year, and then pressed the "Open" button. Nothing happened.

"*Mierda*," she muttered quietly.

Wait, maybe he did it backwards to make it harder. She tried the combination in reverse. Nothing.

"*Dos mierdas*," Bunny recounted, making full use of her limited knowledge of Spanish. Bad words sounded smarter if uttered in a foreign tongue.

Now what? On a hunch, she tried one more combination. It included the same day and month as Vincent's doomsday, but a different year. She again pressed the "Open" button. The latch that held the top of the drawer safe in place gave way and the box sprung open, offering her all of its treasures as the reward for her ingenuity.

The combination wasn't the day Vincent suffered his most embarrassing loss; it was the day he planned to serve his enemies theirs. She figured he might have chosen something like that, which was why she started with the current year and then planned to move forward from there. It made sense though, that Vincent would have chosen this as the year for his end game. By all accounts, the world was gonna end in 2012 anyway. Why risk missing his chance to witness his enemies' demise? It's a lot easier to stomach the end of your days if you know your enemy will be going out on an even lower note.

The safe held not only the coveted flash drive, but also a few stacks of 24k gold Krugerrands and an accountant's book filled with letters and numbers combined in no recognizable manner. Bunny figured the coins were Vincent's other form of doomsday insurance, should the world markets maintain their volatile ways. The book, however, told some other story.

She had heard Vincent kept a second set of books that tracked how much money he really pulled in, where it came from and, most importantly, where much of it was hidden. It was Cayren who came across one such book lying out in the open on Vincent's desk one Sunday morning. Vincent often came in on Sunday mornings, the only time the club was closed, to attend to the books and inventory without the interruption of other employees. Although Cayren had never been the sharpest tool in the shed, she was smart enough to glean—mostly from Vincent's hurried effort to shield the book from her view—that the book had to be the key to the vast amount of money she was sure he was hiding.

Bunny didn't really need the book as collateral. She expected the flash drive held more than enough to negotiate the exclusive right to manage Vincent's legal affairs and that of a whole slew of other well-to-do clients. On second thought, she grabbed the book anyway, leaving only the Krugerrands behind. Mikles could keep those. He might need them sooner than he thought.

It wasn't likely Cayren had the skills to crack the code Vincent used for his secret accounts, but you never know. If she could, she probably deserved every penny she could take. But if the codes proved too challenging, Cayren could always use the books to get Vincent to fork over a few million into a private rainy-day fund. Either way, Vincent would come up on the short end of the deal, and at the hand of two former dancers he'd often referred to with a four-letter c-word. She cringed as she recalled how many times he'd called her that. The jackass would learn the hard way; it's not nice to bite the bitches that feed you.

Bunny slipped the flash drive into the pocket of her fitted suit-jacket, and tucked the books into her oversized alligator-embossed leather purse. She had purchased the monstrosity of a bag at one of those I-Drive outlets to serve as an informal briefcase. It had come in especially handy when she travelled or had lunch meetings with clients, or on days like today when she was committing corporate espionage. You could stuff a lot into it and still manage to zip it up tightly—which she did, just now.

She closed and re-locked the safe, and then wiped it and the drawer handle clean with a tissue from the box on Vincent's desk. With the same tissue, she lifted the humidor, placed it back onto the false bottom in the drawer, pushed the drawer shut and locked it. She then wiped the key clean and carefully placed the key back in the cup. The deed was all but done. All she had to do now was slip out the way she'd come in.

She managed to make it out of the office and pull the door shut before she heard Vincent's heavy steps approaching and his heavier voice call out to her.

"Bon Buns, what in the name of Elvis are you doing here again? You didn't tell me you were stopping by. Twice in one week, that's a real surprise."

It was. No reason for her to be back here again so soon. Bunny put on her game face, and started with a white lie. "I didn't want to discuss this over the phone, Vincent. It's too important."

Vince quickly covered the distance between them and stopped a few feet short from where Bunny stood. He looked down at her with suspicious eyes.

"Business? Are you nuts? There's a Cat-4 headed this way, and you wanna talk shop?"

Bunny met his gaze dead-on, her blue eyes filled with false confidence. A smile spread across Vince's face.

"Guess we're two of a kind, you and me. What's got your feathers fluffed tonight?"

"Sam, that's what, or more accurately, who. The 'what' part is what he's doing in your case."

"I figured you might still be pushing that. Sam stopped by to have an early dinner with me and Cay. He said you weren't playing nice."

"I fully expected him to recast his treachery in a favorable light. That's not what happened, at all. Look, do you want to talk about this out in the hallway, or can we go in your office? I figured you were in there, and was just about to knock."

"Sure, I've got a few minutes. Come on in," Vince said as he reached around Bunny and opened the door to his office.

Bunny sidestepped, allowing Vince to enter first. She wanted to watch his body language to see if he tensed when they entered. If he suspected she'd already been in his office, he would clench his jaw and the telltale vein in his neck would pulse. So far he was still relaxed and apparently in a rare, genuinely good mood. Sam must've done some excellent schmoozing over dinner.

Vince sauntered over to his desk, dropped into his plush leather chair and propped his feet on the desk.

"Have a seat. Let's chat," he offered.

The mint he was toying with made a clicking noise as he moved it from one side of his mouth to the other, and then back again with his tongue. Bunny abhorred the sound, especially coming from him. It annoyed her to the point she envisioned smacking him hard enough to knock the mint and a few teeth from his mouth. There was no discounting the possibility she would do just that, someday.

Bunny held her ground and made use of her disdain. "I'm not sure I'll be here long enough to warrant taking a seat, Vincent. Looks like you've already made up your mind about the case."

"What makes you say that?"

"You're in a good mood, for one thing. And you always side with the boys. Even if they're all wrong and you know it," Bunny stated.

"Don't make this personal, Buns. It's business. Sam's got a big firm behind him, and that sends a message to Audra and her no-good weasel of an attorney. Let's 'em know I'm in for the full four quarters."

"Tell me something. Just how did you come to choose Sam's firm out of all the big-name firms in this town?" Bunny expected him to say because he knew she was working there.

"What's that got to do with anything?" Vince asked.

"In my business, it has a lot to do with a lot. Answer the question," she demanded.

"You got me on the stand now, Buns? You know, I like it when you get feisty and on your high-horse. Reminds me of *old* times."

He had intentionally placed emphasis on the word "old." Like he's a rooster in his prime. Bunny was grateful to be reminded of just how much the man was a total bastard. It made what she was doing easier to rationalize.

"Look, I need edification on how Sam's firm got the case, that's all," Bunny stated.

"It wasn't a big deal. He had been a customer for a while. I brought it up over lunch one day after I got those fucking papers from that EEO or whatever-the-hell-it's-called agency in the mail."

"You had no idea that I worked at his firm back then?"

"I had heard something about that. I asked and Sam said you was a pretty good attorney. So I told him it was okay to bring you on the case," Vince explained.

Bunny stomped. "He said I'm just 'pretty good,' huh? I'm exponentially better than good, and he's an asshole."

"Whoa, now, hold up. Seems to me Sam was doin' you a favor."

"You would see it that way," Bunny huffed. "Let's just get to the point. Are you giving me the case, or not?"

Vince stopped his annoying mint-sucking while he considered his reply. "Can't see that working out for me, Buns. I need a big gun on this one, like I said."

"Okay, then, are you gonna make me your exclusive attorney for other legal matters like we discussed?" Bunny inquired.

Vince pulled his legs from the desk and straightened up in his chair. He wasn't accustomed to being put on the spot and his mood, although good, wasn't good enough to withstand the anomaly.

"You know, I don't have anything else going on right now that calls for a hired gun. Most of the time, things around here get resolved without needing to bring your kind in on it. Let's see what happens down the road."

Bunny tightened her stance. "I may not be on that road with you, Vincent. I've got my own path to follow."

"You're thinking small right now, Buns. That's not like you. I've got a lot of say with other businesses here in town. You know that. I can call in a few favors and send some of them your way, if that's all you want."

You mean you "had" a lot of say. Right now that say is in my left pocket, Bunny thought.

He was right, though. There was a bigger prize, if she wanted to take it. Unlike Vincent, she had hoped to get her business on the up and up, sort of. But it was still a man's world. If this was their game, she would beat them all at it as surely as she beat the odds at everything else.

"I don't want your pals tossing a few pathetic crumbs at me. I've earned a place at the table, and I expect to be taken seriously."

Vince stared back at her with a confused expression. "Buns, you're a fine little attorney, I'm sure. Is that what all this is about?"

A fine "little" attorney? Did he really just say that? Oh, hell-to-the-no.

It was time to end this, her second show of the day, and move on to another script—the one she had written with an alternate ending. Knowing Mikles, she had about 24 hours, maybe more if he was distracted by the storm, to shift course.

"Vincent, you're full of bovine excrement, as usual. I've got to go get ready for the storm," Bunny griped.

Bunny clenched her leather bag close to her chest and stomped out of the office, slamming the door behind her. She could leave from the front exit now. There was no need to slink out the back like the ten-dollar whore Vincent and every other man on the face of the Earth had always presumed her to be.

When she approached the front of the club, she saw the new bouncer talking to the hostess, Tamara. He was handing Tamara a dessert plate and she was welcoming it and him with a shit-eating grin.

Bunny concluded him to be the new guy all the girls were talking about. She could see why. He wasn't half bad if you like your men thick and muscular, which she did. If she wasn't storming out with most of the contents of Vincent's secret safe, she might've stopped to chat. She gave him a second assessment as she hurried by.

Good body and better than good butt. He could do a lot better than that dense little man-trolling hostess.

You better get it while you can, Honey. You won't be cute for long, if you keep eating desserts like that, Bunny mused.

When she hit the parking lot, Bunny practically jogged to her car, in spite of the tight skirt and four-inch heels she was wearing. Remote in hand, she unlocked the doors on approach, threw the driver's side door open and tossed her leather bag into the passenger seat. With a single swift move, she was in the driver's seat with the door closed and the key in the ignition. All those years of dancing still came in handy sometimes. She still had the coordination and agility of a cat.

She was about to turn the key, when someone tapped on her window. The tap was followed by an urgent plea.

"Open up. We need to talk. Something's come up."

Bunny looked up to face the person who stood between her and a clean getaway. She pressed a button to scroll down her window and voiced her frustration with an irascible tone.

"What have you done, now?"

CHAPTER 22

Swirling leaves. Apparently, that's all it took to completely transfix Sam Stone today. He'd been staring out the window of his office for a while now, saying nothing. His gaze lowered down toward the street as he watched the wind toy with people's clothes. He looked up at the growing clouds, which seemed to darken under his watchful eye.

"Who was that on the phone?" Riley inquired, hoping to break the trance. She might as well have been talking to the wind. "Did you hear me, Sam? Is something wrong?" Riley was getting a little annoyed at this point. Her time was valuable, too. "Do you have somewhere else you need to be?"

"I'm sorry, what were you saying?" Sam turned to face her momentarily and then turned back to the window.

"It seems you might have something else on your mind today, Sam."

"No, not really." He rubbed his chin for a moment, and then changed his mind. "Actually, yes, I do need to take care of something."

"Obviously."

"Why don't you go over the new files I brought from the club and see if there's anything else you need to prepare for the deposition."

"You're just going to leave me here doing your work?" Riley chided.

Sam managed a half-hearted chuckle with his smirk. "That was obviously the plan. Didn't you get my memo?"

"I must have missed it while I was reviewing everything else you sent over," Riley replied, with no attempt to hide her growing dissatisfaction. She followed with an exasperated headshake. *Whatever. He might was well leave. He wasn't paying attention anyway.*

"Are you sure the deposition is still going forward on Monday? The weather reports all indicate we're getting that storm. We may not even have power." Riley was hoping the blasted weather event might be good for something. She could use more time to prepare.

"They haven't called it off, and I'm not going to be the first to blink," Sam advised. "It took a lot of wrangling to get Elson to let us set Audra's deposition before he deposes Mikles. He'll either insist we go forward, or insist we rearrange the whole schedule."

Riley sighed. "Guess I'm stuck here doing your work then."

"Guess so," Sam responded smugly. "I'll check in on you later."

He grabbed his jacket, keys and cell phone, and stuffed a few files in his briefcase before heading out the door.

Riley sat still for what seemed an eternity, certain he had to be joking. *He was coming back through the door any minute now. Right?*

A few more minutes passed with no sound to compete with the wailing of the wind. Obviously, Sam was not coming back through those doors anytime soon. Riley pulled out her cell phone and dialed her office.

"Wassup, Boss?" Dani quipped.

"Sam just left me sitting here holding the bag. The nerve of that man!"

"Where'd he go?"

"I dunno. He didn't say. Just said he had something to do."

"Well, maybe you should go, too. That storm is getting closer and the winds are starting to pick up. The first squalls are supposed to hit later this afternoon, or tonight. It won't be pretty trying to drive through any of that during rush hour."

"I might just do that. I can work at home by myself, just as well as I can here. Except I'll have to lug all these files with me. How safe do you think this office building will be during the storm?"

"You are not riding out the storm in Sam's office, Riley."

"He's not here. I think that makes it a lot safer."

"Har, har. When did you get a license to sass?"

"I've pretty much had that since birth," Riley replied.

"Okay, well since when did you decide to start using your caustic wit on me? You know that's my shtick."

"Just now, I think."

"Well, stop it. I'm not your problem. He is. And really, it's not even him. It's all you."

"Oh, bull! It's most definitely him. I'm sitting here doing his work while he's doing God-knows-what."

"Sounds to me like he's just smarter than you," Dani surmised.

Riley rolled her eyes, for the sake of it. "Now who's being sarcastic?"

"Okay, fine, I am. But it was my turn, and you started it."

"And…?"

"And what?"

"And is there anything else you might want to say?" Riley prodded.

"Probably, but I think the barometric pressure is interfering with your telepathic signals. You might have to spell it out for me."

"I'm the boss of you. You're not supposed to snark at me."

"Okay, if you say so. But listen, *Boss*, I'm leaving early today. I've got an appointment with my doctor, and then I've got to pick the boys up. Their summer camp will be releasing them early due to the storm."

"That's fine. Just make sure to unplug the equipment and secure the files in the file cabinets. Oh, and were you able to find that plastic sheeting at the store last night?"

"I did. You setting up a kill-room in case the deposition goes badly?"

"Sarcasm, again? Didn't we just go over that?"

"Maybe. It's still a fair question."

"You know what it's for. Drape it over the file cabinets that are near the windows. Just in case."

"Righto. I'm on it. I get the impression you're not in a playful mood today, so I'll behave," Dani conceded. "Will you be coming back by the office?"

"Probably not. I'm going to finish up here and head home. I haven't done any storm prep at all. Mason and I might just have to curl up in the wine cellar and hope for the best."

"Well, you never know. Maybe one of your neighbors will help you."

"Have you met my neighbors?"

"Now that you mention it, I don't think I have."

"That's right. How many times have you been to my house?"

"A ton," Dani quickly answered.

"I rest my case."

"Okay, so the wine cellar it is. At least I'll know where to look for you in the rubble."

"Thanks, that's comforting," Riley said. "You and the boys stay safe. I'll talk to you later."

"Ditto, Boss. And cheer up. I think Sam's okay. He just needs a swift kick in the shin now and again. I don't know a man who doesn't."

"I'm not so sure about that, but I'll make sure to kick him for you next time I see him. I'll tell him you said I could," Riley remarked before cutting the call.

She returned her attention to the files spread out on Sam's enormous desk for a while longer, genuinely expecting he would return at any moment. When the early afternoon rolled around and he still hadn't returned, Riley gave up and started to pack her things. If she left now, there might still be time to pick up a few items from a grocery store before the first serious storm squalls hit making travel nearly impossible.

With Sam pulling her in so many directions, and the time it had taken to deal with the challenges posed by Wade's situation, along with her otherwise hefty case load, she'd barely had time to sleep much less make it into the kitchen for a meal. She hadn't verified it, but it was a safe bet to presume her refrigerator and pantry weren't well-stocked. Mason would be fine. His dog food was delivered by a local pet food provider every four weeks, so he had the provisions he needed. That recognition prompted a sigh of relief from Riley.

"Too bad it's not that easy for humans. I wish someone could deliver what I need," she reflected. She paused for a moment to consider the notion. It had one flaw.

There's little point in wishing on a star if you don't know what to wish for. That might be why she had seldom wasted much time wishing, and obviously now was not the time to start. In addition to storm preparations, there were still quite a few boxes of documents that she needed to review to prepare for the deposition on Monday, assuming the storm didn't pull the plug on it. There was no reason she couldn't take the documents with her and review them while she sat at home waiting for the storm to pass. By all indications, Sam had no plans to work on the case any time soon, so he wasn't going to miss them.

The only real challenge to the plan was getting the boxes to her car. Riley headed to the door to see if Mona was still at her desk just outside of Sam's office. Maybe she could arrange for someone in the mail room to help with the boxes. She opened the door only to be startled by Mona who was standing directly outside.

"I'm sorry. Did I startle you, Miss Morgan?" Mona offered in a fairly robotic tone.

"A little. It was so quiet out here I wasn't sure anyone was still around with the storm coming and all," Riley confessed.

"I've just requested one of our file clerks to bring a dolly and assist you with transferring the documents to your car. He should be here momentarily."

"Excellent. How did you know . . . ?"

Mona interrupted before Riley could finish. It was a pointless question and one she couldn't answer anyway. "Will you require anything else?"

"No, I guess not. That should do it. Thank you."

"Very well, then. I'll advise Mr. Stone of your status."

"Speaking of Mr. Stone," Riley inquired with a hint of annoyance, "where is he?"

"I've been instructed that he is engaged in another matter and cannot be reached. I believe he will be speaking with you later."

"I'm not sure how much he's going to want to hear what I have to say. But sure, tell him we'll talk later."

"Mr. Stone will be very interested in your impressions, Miss Morgan. Not many people speak to him with candor. I believe he is very much in need of it."

Riley turned away from the boxes she had been hurriedly repacking to stare at Mona under wary lids. "Well, I imagine you know him better than anyone. I'll take your word on that."

Riley had returned her attention to the boxes so she wasn't certain, but it sounded like Mona might've said something like "you have no idea." Riley looked back toward the door intending to seek clarification. Mona was already on the other side with the door long-since closed behind her.

"I've never seen anyone leave a room and close the door behind them in less than a second while making absolutely no sound," Riley muttered. "I swear, Sam and everyone he works with is just plain spooky."

It took no time at all for the mail clerk to load the boxes of documents into Riley's car. She was easily halfway home–due to the light traffic on usually jammed thoroughfares–by the time of day she might otherwise be returning to work from a lunch meeting. She pulled into the small, locally-owned supermarket near her house, and dodged intermittent rain blasts to scuttle inside. She'd been through enough tropical storms, and even more hurricanes, to know that an umbrella was generally a waste of time and energy. The wind would have mocked her for even considering it.

There were a few other foolish holdouts, such as herself, who had waited until the last minute to stock-up in anticipation of the storm. They were strolling up and down the mostly barren aisles with empty carts. Riley grabbed one of the few remaining carts at the front of the store and joined the race. This was a competition, of sorts. Getting a piece of whatever was left behind was the challenge each competitor faced. She was going to have to think and act fast to come away with anything she could actually use.

Squewreee. Squer-wreeech. Squereeeeee.

Naturally, she had grabbed the cart with a loose wheel that wouldn't turn properly. It had also apparently already made a few too many trips in and out of the store today. The wheels were wet and the floor was waxed, which meant neither had any interest in cooperating with the other.

Her father's familiar advice rang in her ears as soundly as if he were standing next to her. *Better ditch that thing. A one-legged donkey is worthless in a horse race.* He was an expert at embellishing the obvious.

"Yes, Dad, I'm aware," Riley responded under her breath before pushing the cart back toward its kind at the front of the store and heading off instead with one of the store's plastic shopping baskets. The basket wouldn't hold much, but there wouldn't be much for it to hold, anyway.

She shopped here often, when she bothered to shop, because she preferred to frequent locally-owned businesses. That preference gave her an advantage over many of the others shoppers in this instance because she already knew which aisles might still hold the items she was seeking. On the other hand, it occurred to her that a larger national chain store was more likely to still have something useful on its shelves. There's a give and take to everything.

The bakery section had two loaves of some kind of bread left. She didn't check the label to see what kind. This wasn't the time to be picky. Emergencies and preferences are inherently antithetical concepts. She grabbed one of the loaves, securing it just seconds before it would've been the prize in another shopper's cart. A small internal celebration followed that victory—one she recognized as bittersweet. No one wants to gloat for snatching food out of the hands of another.

There were still plenty of fresh meats in the freezer section, but there was a reason for that. If the power goes out, which it always does–sometimes on purpose while the power companies attempt to limit the danger of downed lines–fresh meat is among the first of the refrigerator casualties. Most storm veterans know that if you are lucky enough to secure the golden commodity otherwise known as ice while waiting for the power to return, it won't last long enough to keep fresh meat from spoiling, nor would it be wise to waste it on that type of luxury.

Riley grabbed a few filets and tossed them in her basket. It was an unchallenged victory, but only because her competition didn't know the game quite as well. If she cooked it all as soon as she got home, it could last for a few days, especially if she froze whatever she didn't eat before the power went out. At least she'd have protein, but she was still without the most precious commodity of all–water.

Water sustains all life, and despite centuries of other inventions, mankind had yet to find a way to survive any length of time without it. By law, water isn't considered as something that can be owned. That didn't stop beverage companies from making fortunes extracting it from ground wells, filtering it and then selling it back to the public, who seemingly have no idea they hold the same right to access it from the local aquifers. If more people knew that, they would probably balk at the exorbitant prices those companies now demanded for a product they obtained from a public source.

When it came to bottled water, some of the best in the business came from nearby natural springs, but Riley deemed it unlikely there would be any of that left on the shelves. She was right. She turned the corner to head down the beverage aisle, only to find the most barren shelves of all. She strolled halfway down to examine the solitary item that remained–children's fruit juice. Not just any fruit juice, but the worst possible–the kind that comes in single-serve boxes which only relinquish their contents when forcefully assaulted with a tiny straw.

Great. Repeating kindergarten is what I get for procrastinating. That'll teach me, Riley mused.

She grabbed a few packages of the juice and then noticed there were a also a few bottles of store-brand ginger ale hiding in the back of a lower shelf. She snatched those and added them to her basket, thereby leaving little room for much else. Not a real setback, since there wouldn't be much else available. A bag of chips, a box of animal crackers, and a can or two of some kind of bean soup rounded out the eclectic mix. The soup didn't sound very appetizing, but it was the kind of thing that could last for years in the back of your pantry and still provide basic sustenance if ever called upon to do so.

Riley surveyed her bounty as she placed it on the counter before the cashier. All in all, it wasn't a bad haul considering the circumstances. The only other thing she might need was likely a pipe dream.

"Any chance you've still got ice?"

The clerk looked at her as if she were speaking Martian. She raised a pierced brow and smirked before returning her attention to the register.

"Guess that was a no," Riley surmised. It didn't hurt to ask–well it didn't hurt much, just a slight bruise to the ego. The clerk probably thought she was a storm-novice with that type of naïve-sounding inquiry. Riley brushed the fleeting concern aside. It wasn't wise to let pride get in the way of survival.

Once everything was checked and bagged, Riley sprinted back to her car with two bags in tow. Aided by the convenience of power locks, she managed to quickly toss the bags into the back seat and slip into the driver's seat without getting completely soaked by scattered torrents of rain.

Only a mile or two stood between her and home, and the ride was an easy one. If the state highway patrol hadn't already advised against venturing out, they soon would. At first it would be an advisory, and then they'd get serious and start to pull people over and issue a stern, more personal warning. It was a necessary and responsible form of precaution, even if seemingly overbearing.

At some point, for their own safety, all law enforcement patrols would be called back to headquarters to ride out the worst of the storm and wouldn't be available to aid stranded motorists. It didn't make sense to allow those who failed to heed the more-than-ample warnings to put the lives of dedicated civil servants at risk. If you were stupid enough to think you could take on Mother Nature at her worst, protected only by a hunk of fiberglass and metal filled with explosive liquid, you were probably in need of the lesson that might follow.

Riley pulled into her driveway, and then slowed on her approach to the garage to assess something she hadn't expected to encounter—a sleek black Bentley coupe. She only knew one person who sported a car like that. Was that his car parked next to the single-car side of her garage? It had to be.

She engaged the garage door opener with a click, and pulled past the coupe into the two-car side of her three-car garage. Once parked in her normal spot nearest to the garage door, she grabbed the grocery bags from the back seat and headed inside. Normally, she would hear Mason barking loudly to herald her return, but the house was silent when she entered.

"Mason? Where are you, pretty boy?"

The resounding sound of nothing in response to her query was weird and more than a little unnerving.

"Sam, are you here? If you are, you have some serious explaining to do."

Again, nothing. Even more unnerving.

She carried the bags of groceries to the kitchen and started to put the perishable items away. The plan was to head back outside to search for Mason and Sam after the provisions were properly stored. The worst of whatever those two were doing was likely already done. It occurred to her that her beloved pet and her less-than-cherished colleague had at least one thing in common. Both could be likened to dogs, although the latter of the two seemed devoid of the unflinching loyalty displayed by the canine variety. That made him more of a "dawg" in the urban sense of the word.

Riley opened the refrigerator and then stepped back in startle. It was already full, with everything she hadn't been able to find during her last-minute grocery dash. She pulled open the freezer section and met the same surprise. It was stocked with several bags of ice.

"What the frick?"

It was like the alternate-universe of Goldilocks, which made sense in a way given that she was brunette and wasn't prone to trespass. Apparently, someone else was the interloper in this version of the story. That someone had brought her porridge, as well as something far more important–bottled water. She made that discovery when she pulled her head out of the freezer and turned to her left. Case after case of bottled water was piled on the floor next to her pantry.

She was awakened from the waking dream by a tapping noise outside–a welcome indication that she wasn't the lone character trapped in this backward fairy tale. She pulled open the French doors leading from the kitchen to the covered lanai; the lanai, in turn, faced a paved deck that surrounded the pool. Passing the pool on her way to the back yard, Riley noticed the water was starting to show white-caps pushed by the building winds.

Once outside she found Mason lying on the ground on the far right, past the lanai and near the living room windows. He was uncharacteristically transfixed by the show. With the exception of the fact he had been trained not to interact with strangers, she could hardly blame him. The scene did have all the makings of a soapy daytime drama.

In this episode, the select set of viewers had the privilege of watching a shirtless man perform various acts while standing on a tall ladder. The star of today's episode wasn't just any shirtless man, but the perfect example of how a man should look when shirtless. He was lean, tan and possessed the most perfectly ripped shoulders and abs humanly possible. Actually, those abs went far beyond those possessed by mere mortals. As did the way his well-worn jeans fit just below his v-line and tapered down a set of ridiculously long legs.

Riley's astonishment was tinged with anger. Who did Sam think he was, coming to her house uninvited and worse yet, hanging out half-naked with her dog?

"What is that man doing here?" It might seem odd to pose such a question to a dog, but Mason wasn't just any dog. He could almost always read her thoughts, and would usually respond by following along, even if her commands were unspoken.

She hadn't intended to speak her thoughts loud enough for human ears, but apparently had as her query was intercepted. Sam stopped what he was doing and turned to face her. He was well soaked from the intermittent rain, which didn't help the matter. It only served to worsen the view by glistening against his tanned skin and adding an annoying boyish curl to his dark hair. He met her astonished face with a wicked smile.

"It's about time you got home. We've been waiting for you for hours, haven't we Mason?"

Mason dutifully rose at the mention of his name by his new-found friend. Having first ignored his master's approach, he now turned to face Riley and sounded his accord.

"Rrroawr."

Riley looked down at Mason with a disapproving look that usually caused him to tuck his tail. This time he just wagged it and returned her stare with an openmouthed, tongue-exposed happy face–a strangely passive, but patently obvious act of defiance.

"*Et tu*, Mason?"

CHAPTER 23

S am deftly stepped down the rungs of the ladder and came over to greet Riley. Mason followed behind him, apparently now part of the he-man pack.

"Since Mason didn't really answer my question, maybe you will. What are you doing?" Riley asked.

"I'm installing your storm panels," Sam replied, as nonchalantly as if it were something he did every day. "It was pretty clever of you to get the clear ones. They seem to be custom cut for your windows, too, so that's made the job easier."

"My father had those made years ago," Riley said.

"Ah. I'm guessing he was the one who also labeled them by room?"

"Yes, he was a stickler for details. Anyway, I already knew *what* you were doing. Perhaps I should rephrase the question. *Why* are you doing it?"

"Someone had to," Sam said, trying his best to avoid her gaze.

"You're avoiding the question."

"I was told I wasn't to tell you. I suppose, now that I've been caught in the act, I can say you tortured it out of me."

"I will most certainly torture you, if you don't answer me."

"The phone call I got earlier was Dani. She read me the riot act for taking up so much of your time with the storm coming and reminded me that you have this big house to deal with now, and no one to help with it. So, I stopped by your office when I left. Dani gave me her key to the house and told me where I'd find your storm covers."

"Which you took as an invitation to just waltz into my house," Riley surmised. "Mason didn't at least try to bite you? What did you do to him?"

"He's a smart dog. He knew I was here to help. Plus, I got him a nice bone when I stopped at the store for your supplies," Sam said.

"I see you brought me a few bribes as well. My pantry is fuller than it's been in years. Did you do my laundry, too, while you waited for me to finish working on your case?"

"Didn't make it that far, yet. I'd be happy to wash your delicates for you, though, provided you're still in them." Sam coupled the taunt with a mischievous half-smile.

I'm pretty sure I hate you again, Sam Stone. Riley's internal fume took a different verbal form. "My delicates are just fine as they are. You're the one who appears to need a good wash."

Sam looked down to note he was not only soaking wet, but had managed to pick up a few nice splashes of mud when moving the ladder between the windows. He wiped his hands on his pants.

"Guess a hot shower would be nice. Not sure if you'll oblige me that. I would appreciate it if you'd lend me a towel before I'm summarily dismissed."

"I'm not going to send you off into the storm, Sam. Geez. I'm not cruel. I'm just not sure what to make of you. You don't have a reputation for charitable endeavors."

"It's never too soon to start," Sam quipped. "Besides, I feel that I owe you. I have been taking up a lot of your time with the Mikles case. This was the least I could do. Dani was right to call me on it."

Riley surveyed Sam's handiwork. "Looks like you're almost finished. Only the kitchen windows are left?"

"Just the large window over your sink and the French doors. I'll have those up in a snap." He alone smiled at the joke. The covers actually snap into the window sills. He would, literally, be done after a snap, or two.

"All right, I guess I can have a towel here for you when you're done," Riley offered in a sardonic tone. She was pretending to still be offended by the intrusion into her privacy. She was actually relieved.

The storm covers had completely slipped her mind. She'd weathered the last few years' storms in her condo. Her father had managed to take care of this place by himself before he became ill. The large trees in the yard could easily lose branches during the storm, and those could become high-powered projectiles if caught up in the winds, easily shattering the windows or glass inserts in her French doors. In this case, an ounce of prevention could be worth a helluva lot of cure.

A few minutes later Sam snapped the last cover over the French doors that led from the kitchen. When finished, he tapped on the covered glass to garner Riley's attention and pointed toward the garage.

"I'll come in that way," he advised, his voice muted by the window coverings and the strong winds.

Riley waved an acknowledgment before heading off to open the garage door. It turned out she didn't need to. Sam was already in the garage when she got there, having entered via the single garage door that opened the side of the garage where her father's vintage car was parked.

"You're just full of tricks, today. How'd you get in here? The key doesn't open the garage doors," Riley inquired with a hint of concern.

"The electronic garage door opener on this side appears to be broken. The door can be opened from the outside. I can probably fix that for you when it stops raining."

"That's odd. It was working fine a few months ago when I took my father's car in for service. I haven't used it since then."

Sam pulled up the car cover to take another look at the vintage Jag. He'd checked the car out earlier when retrieving the storm covers from the garage.

"Your father had a brilliant ride. You should take it out for a spin once in a while."

"Yeah, I should do a lot of things," Riley sighed. "I'm not ready for that yet. That car was his pride and joy. He never let me drive it. Wouldn't feel right to drive it now."

Sam responded with genuine disbelief. "I'm pretty sure if asked, your father would've said you were his pride and joy, Riley. The car is nice, but it's just a car. If the storm covers for the windows are any indication, your father had his priorities in the right place."

"That he did," Riley said.

Sam looked around quizzically and then directed his query to Riley. "So, where's my towel?"

"It's inside, next to the shower in the guest bathroom. I figured you'd want it there when you get out."

"Does that mean I now have your permission to enter your humble abode?"

"Yes. I guess. It's a limited time offer, though. You'd better take advantage of it."

Sam didn't bother to argue or wait for her to change her mind. The tropical warm front didn't feel all that warm or tropical while soaking wet. A hot shower sounded like heaven.

The towel was found where promised. When he emerged from the shower, Sam wrapped it around his waist. He considered taunting Riley by traipsing through her house in that state of undress. Unfortunately, she had already denied him that turn of boyish mischief by placing his T-shirt and jeans neatly on a hanger outside the bathroom door. He pulled his clothes from the hanger, surprised as he did so to find them still warm from the dryer. It was a little thing, but it was something. It brought a smile.

A guy could get accustomed to having someone like Riley around to take care of little things like that for him—if the guy had the kind of life that would afford such a luxury. Sam couldn't deny the burn of his current reality. He didn't feel it often, which made it all the more worthy of notice. There was actually something out there he wanted, but didn't have. Maybe never could.

The last part wasn't something Sam chose to accept. He brushed it aside as easily as he brushed his dark hair back from his face with his hands. He stared into the steam-covered bathroom mirror, his thoughts moving on to more immediate concerns. The medicine cabinet could hold the thing he most needed now. He searched it, unsuccessfully.

Perfectly coiffed, even without the aid of borrowed hair product, Sam strolled back into the kitchen to find Riley putting away some of the groceries he'd bought. "Sorry to leave those sitting there. I wasn't sure where you put things."

"No need to apologize. It would have been more than a little weird if you had known where everything goes."

"Speaking of weird, I found my clothes hanging on the bathroom door when I got out of the shower. They were suddenly dry and neatly placed on a hanger. I'm quite certain I didn't leave them that way."

"No, you didn't," Riley said.

"I didn't take you as the type to spy on a fellow while he's in the shower. Since it appears you are, why didn't you join me? There was room enough for two," Sam teased.

Riley's smile turned upside down and then twisted into a smirk. The smug Sam Stone she knew so well had obviously not been replaced by a clone, after all. He was still in there, somewhere, continuing to operate on the false assumption that all women secretly pined for him.

"I did not spy on you. You left the door half open and your clothes in a pile in the doorway. I just did what any good host might."

"Ah, so I guess you didn't take any of that as a hint?" Sam inquired.

He was obviously teasing her. Surely, she knew that. His humor was met with another stern look. It occurred to Sam he might have misjudged the extent to which she possessed a sense of humor.

"Whatever the reason, your kindness was well-received," he added. "I fully expected you to offer me nothing more than a frilly pink robe while I waited for my clothes to dry."

"Damn. Why didn't I think of that?" Riley cracked.

It was a funny notion. One picture of that spectacle would've easily garnered a month of free overtime from Dani. Sneaking a peek at a handsome dude in the buff wasn't her style. Making a man's man like Sam look silly in a pink robe? That was definitely her style.

"Now that the storm panels are up and your shelves are stocked, there's just one last thing and then I'll be out of your way."

"One last . . .?" Riley stared to inquire. What else was there? He'd already done more than enough.

"I doubt you had time to fill up your car. Did you?"

"I barely had time to stop by the grocery store."

"I trust you've been through enough storms to know that if the power goes out, gas stations won't be open, possibly for days. There's a reason the experts suggest a full tank," Sam advised.

"I know the reasons. Power out, shortages, long lines at any open pump, yada, yada, yada."

"Yada, nothing. I'm not going to leave you an excuse for not making it to the depositions next week. As I said before, I'm pretty sure Elson will insist we go forward, electricity or not. I'm sure there's a station still open somewhere. Give me your keys and, for once, try not to argue."

It was hard to argue with him when he took charge like that. It was almost nice, except for the fact the man was a complete jerk. In keeping with her conflicting emotions, Riley responded by offering Sam the same annoyed teenager look she used to give her father when he displayed similar protective instincts.

"Here are my keys. If you're crazy enough to go back out in that weather, at least try to bring my car back in one piece."

"Just the car?"

"If the car's in one piece, odds are anything in it will be."

Sam had to admit, in a strangely perverted way, her reasoning made sense. "You're a clever one, Miss Morgan. Too clever for me," he quipped.

"I thought that was a given."

"Indeed. Yet you never miss a chance to remind me."

"That's the cleverest part."

Sam laughed. Most women he encountered were far too busy trying to impress him with push-up bras or tight skirts to consider engaging him intellectually. Riley's approach was exactly the opposite, yet easily garnered what the others were seeking. He slid her keys into the pocket of his jeans and headed to the garage. Somewhere in the recesses of his mind, the pleasure he derived from having something of hers in his possession was recorded for future reference.

Riley was also dealing with a few slow-waking realizations. Sam was not the kind of man a woman should develop feelings for. Rather, he's the kind a girl's mother warns her about, provided her mother isn't already under his spell. She knew she would do well to put him out of her mind. If only she could. The man did have her car. He had a few other things going for him as well.

Riley's mother never found the right time to talk to her about men, which made the notion of accepting advice on the subject a foreign one. Not that her mother would've had any advice on a man like Sam, anyway. There had only been one man in her mother's life, and that was her father. They started dating when her mother was barely 19, and were married less than a year later. Advice derived from limited experiences that took place in decades past would hardly prove relevant in this circumstance. Riley was living in the present, harboring random thoughts of what might transpire with a man like Sam in the future, with no one around to guide her. Well, almost no one.

Riley looked down at Mason, fondly. He had settled in by her feet while she sat on a counter stool by the kitchen island. There were a multitude of other places in the house where she could work. More often than not, she ended up here–nowhere else offered as much space to spread out.

At the moment, most of the island's hard-surface countertop was covered by files and papers she had started to review while Sam was in the shower. Work had seemed a necessary distraction at that particular point in time. Riley pushed the mountain of papers into their designated files and stuffed the lot back into the boxes from whence they came. No point in forcing focus. There would be time during the coming weekend to go over the rest of it.

"I don't know about you, Mason, but I'm hungry. How does steak sound?"

Mason likely had no idea what she had said. He wagged his tail appreciatively and barked an accord in any event. "Wwroof, woof."

"I'll take that as a yes. Should we invite your new friend for dinner?"

Mason rose to his feet, studied her quizzically and then looked toward the garage–the last place he'd seen his new friend. Perhaps he knew more about what was going on than she did. He plopped back down at her feet before responding. "Woof, arooroo."

"Okay, I'm not sure about that last part. He's your friend, though, not mine. If he wants to stay for dinner, you'll have to share your steak with him."

Mason's head drooped to the floor, coming to rest between his front paws. He looked up at Riley with a face that would melt even a cat-lover's heart.

"Oh, okay. You don't have to share. Damn you, men, you're all alike. Always finding a way to get what you want."

Riley took the filets she'd picked up at the store out of the refrigerator and spread them out on the cutting board. With some of the vegetables Sam brought, they would make great kabobs. The gas grill in the summer kitchen outside was under the covered lanai. She could easily grill them there, in spite of the rain. Cooking out there would also make cleanup a lot easier.

She pulled a cutting board from under the kitchen island, and laid out the vegetables to slice. After absently reaching for the large butcher's knife usually found in the cutlery block on her counter–a mistake she'd made more than once over the past few weeks–she made the same mental note she had every other time. *Find that dang knife or get a new one.*

She hadn't done any serious cooking in quite a while, so it wasn't likely she'd misplaced it. It was possible Dani borrowed it. With Jack home and two growing boys, Dani was always in the kitchen cooking up something. If not in her own kitchen, then in Riley's, taking charge as if it were her own. That was perfectly fine with Riley. The art of cooking was one of the few creative endeavors she didn't find engaging.

Not that she didn't appreciate a culinary masterpiece; she did, as long as it was prepared by someone else. Riley could cook, if she had to. It was just that, aside from the occasional pancake breakfasts she shared with Mason, there wasn't much point to it. Why spend hours preparing something that takes less than ten minutes to eat when there are people who prepare the same thing for a living? It better served the economy for Riley to do what she did best–practice law–and let other people shine in their element.

According to Dani, that particular logic was the saddest example of an economic theory since someone decided money trickled down. But Dani hadn't cooked for one in a long time. Things are different when you're alone.

Riley's cell phone rang. She wiped her hands on a nearby towel before reaching across the island to retrieve it. Fully expecting to learn that Sam had run into trouble finding an open gas station, she took the call without checking the call register.

"What's taking you so long?"

"Riley?"

"Oh. Hi, Kris. I was expecting another call," Riley explained. "Have you got good news for me?"

"I do have news," Kris advised. "This time it falls more into the indifferent category."

"I'll take it," Riley said. Indifferent could still turn out to go her way. It was a lot harder to reconfigure bad news into something useful.

"We haven't found anything on Wade's computer. Tried a number of different approaches, but we weren't able to isolate the memory where the pictures might've been stored. Looks like we'll have to suspend our efforts for a while because of the storm," Kris advised. "I've got to secure our servers and do standard storm preparedness protocol for securing digital evidence for the Department right now. As soon as the weather clears, we'll try again before we start looking at other options. I'll let you know when that happens."

"I understand. Thanks for the update," Riley said. "Is Wade still there?"

"I sent him home with a uniformed escort. The officer will do a sweep of the place to make sure he's safe before leaving," Kris stated.

"Couldn't ask for anything more. I'm really grateful, Kris," Riley responded. "I know Wade appreciates all that you've done, too. I expect I'll hear from him later. If he remembers anything else that might help with the case, you'll be the next to know."

"Don't tell Wade this because I don't want him to think he's off the hook," Kris started, "but I do think he's a good guy. Just a little too smart for his own good. I'm hoping working with him will help turn this case around before anything bad happens."

"That would be my preference as well. Take care, Kris," Riley concluded.

Riley placed her cell phone back in its previous spot on the counter and glanced at the pendulum clock on the wall over her pantry. Sam had been gone for well over an hour. A brief frown accompanied her thoughts. It was time for the news. If there'd been an accident or something, a news crew would be on the scene, in spite of the weather. Or rather, they would be there especially because of it. The news media seemed to thrive on the chaos that accompanied a major storm like this one. In some instances, it was possible they even went so far as to create chaos, if nature didn't provide enough to suit the networks.

Riley pointed a tiny remote at the small flat screen television mounted on the wall across from the kitchen island to tune into one of the local channels. All programming had been suspended in favor of storm coverage, and likely would be for as long as there was a cloud still in the sky. She half-listened as the lead meteorologist redundantly reviewed the radar.

There would be rain and wind, and then more rain and more wind. Everyone in the I-4 corridor was getting pretty much the same forecast as the storm tore across Central Florida. The weatherman then suggested they check with their field reporters stationed along the coast in the Satellite Beach and Cocoa Beach area.

Riley glanced up at the screen expecting to see the usual—a rain slicker-clad reporter foolishly battling wind and rain for the sake of their craft. No surprise there. However, this particular reporter was also joined by an unexpected, yet familiar guest.

CHAPTER 24

⸻

Bunny positioned herself so just enough wind could rush beneath her umbrella to push her blonde hair back in dramatic fashion. She had been planning this promo for months. A big part of that preparation included the search for a bright red, storm-sturdy umbrella. It had taken longer than expected to find just the right shade of red for her dramatic backdrop. From her perspective, that time had been well spent. Nothing catches the eye like the color red.

Forecasters had predicted a few major storms during this year's hurricane season. Not all of them would come her way, of course. That was fine. She only needed one. Irrespective of classification or category, as long as Central Florida was in the path of a storm with enough blustery tropical force winds to attract the national media, she was good to go.

By any account, the likelihood of a major storm forming early in the season *and* making landfall in just the right spot was slim to none. For that reason, the forecasted arrival of Adonis had come as something more than a pleasant surprise. He was the perfect storm for Bunny, in every way.

The local news would dominate the airwaves for the next 24 hours, maybe more. With that much air time to fill, they would be actively seeking stories or commentary to bridge the gap between the local radar reports and updates from the National Hurricane Center.

As would any civic-minded professional, Bunny had offered to give viewers some free legal advice on steps to secure their property and belongings for insurance purposes and what steps to take, should they incur losses during the storm. Naturally, she would weave into the conversation the other types of services her firm could provide. Inquiring minds would want to know, especially since she had put herself out in dangerous conditions to bring important information to them.

When she developed this all-too-clever marketing plan, it was premised on the notion that she needed to reach the broadest audience for little or no cost. Things had changed since then. Fortunately, what was once a simple advertising strategy would serve her current purposes just as well. Maybe better. It was important that she be highly visible right now, even if the reality of her show was intended for a select audience.

Annie Tuttle, an eager young reporter Bunny had met at a Chamber of Commerce breakfast, indicated they would be going live in less than a minute. The cameraman made a few technical adjustments and then wiped away droplets of water that had accumulated on the lens over the past few seconds. With the wind blowing rain in every direction, he would repeat that chore several more times during the thirty to forty seconds that preceded their segment.

They were broadcasting from a man-made wooden-plank walkway that ran from the public parking area across the upper dunes of a popular local beach. Annie had spent most of her day on that beach, but the assignment had not turned out to be one she could revel in. The better part of it involved standing in circles of flying sand while waiting for the surfers to return to shore. That enviable endeavor was necessary in order to get their often humorous explanations for risking life and limb on film.

About an hour ago, even the die-hard thrill seekers had abandoned their folly, leaving only Annie, her cameraman, and Bunny to foolishly brave the increasingly ominous elements. At least, they were the only ones braving the elements at this location. There were other teams of reporters, including ones from the networks, stationed up and down the local beaches. But as luck would have it, this young reporter—the one who owed Bunny a favor after Bunny got a few parking violations thrown out for her—had somehow managed to pick the spot the rest of her peers would soon come to envy. She was standing dead center in the predicted point of first landfall for Hurricane Adonis.

Maybe it was beginner's luck or maybe it was fate. Either way, Annie was in the right place at the perfect time and because of it, her broadcasts were sure to get national play. Although most anyone else would not consider being pelted by rain and flying sand a good thing, Bunny grinned widely as she assessed her good fortune.

During the final countdown to air time, Annie braced herself against the wind by standing next to the wood handrails that accompanied the man-made walkway down toward the beach; Bunny followed her lead. On a normal day, the walkway fed into a 100-foot stretch of golden sand that preceded the shoreline. Today, the end of the beach walk was met and occasionally overlapped by some of the powerful waves the 50-mph winds were frenetically sending to shore.

Now that the beach had been completely overtaken by the storm-empowered high tide, their location on the walkway—a spot that was once quite high and dry—was only a few feet from the water's edge. If conditions worsened as predicted, none of them would be high or dry for much longer. Good thing they were about to go on air.

After this segment, Bunny could attend to other things. Annie and cameraman would not be so lucky. They would be staying put, completely exposed to the elements until their station manager, who was probably sipping hot coffee while sitting in a comfortable chair behind his desk back at the station, decided it was time for them to come in from the rain.

The cameraman raised his hand to begin a silent count. Five. Four. Three. Two. One. They were live. Annie started her spiel in the usual fashion by accepting a lead-in from the station.

"Thanks, Wendy. It certainly looks like the storm is closing in on the area. Conditions here are deteriorating more rapidly than we expected. I'm sure our viewers are seeing similar winds and rain. Folks along the coast here are also bracing for flooding that might result from the current high tide."

Annie motioned for her cameraman to turn the lens toward the water's edge at the end of the walkway.

"As you can see, the beach is pretty much gone right now. The only thing keeping the waves from some of the beachfront homes here are seawalls that are still pretty battered from last year's storm season."

On cue, a towering wave crashed over the walkway. Experience told the cameraman to keep his lens on the breaking wave as it approached. Annie turned her back to the water while she waited for the cameraman to get the shot. It was a rookie mistake and one she wouldn't soon forget.

The camera switched back to Annie at the same time the powerful wave—refusing to accept the walkway as a natural boundary—plowed into her from behind taking her footing from underneath her by force. As would any true professional, the cameraman held his ground and the shot, securing Annie's awkward plummet into the water along with her priceless expression for the viewers.

Bunny was also pushed forward by the rush of water. Unlike her young friend, she was able to keep her footing thanks to the counterbalance provided from the force of the wind against her open umbrella. When the wave retreated, Bunny reached out to help Annie back to her feet before the water could carry her with it into the angry ocean.

Bunny was more than a little annoyed the cameraman hadn't bothered to help his colleague. On any other day, she might have given him a piece of her mind. Today there simply wasn't time and more importantly, whether she liked it or not, the unfortunate vignette provided a strong lead-in for her bit on storm safety.

Now a drenched and disheveled mess, the young woman made a quick recovery and scarcely missed a beat before continuing her update.

"As you can see, the wind and water can do a lot of damage during a storm like this," Annie offered with a gamely chuckle. "Fortunately, we were lucky enough to secure an exclusive interview with local attorney Bunny Keiler, who has a few tips for our viewers on ways to protect themselves and their property at times like this."

Annie turned to Bunny and the camera followed. "Bunny, thank you so much for taking on this challenging weather to bring important information to us. I know our viewers will be grateful for any advice you can offer."

"Of course, it's my pleasure. As a citizen and resident of Central Florida, I feel it's my duty to help out in times of need," Bunny said, capping her words with a large, disingenuous grin.

She would prefer to be paid for her time, rather than give it away like this. Nowadays, everyone expects something for free. This also wasn't how she preferred to be seen—with her hair out of place and her expensive department store makeup diluted and made imprecise by the rain. Worse still, everything she was about to say was something anyone with even a half-lick of common sense would or should already know.

Reminding people of the obvious was what the media usually did at times like this, once they finished scaring people with reports on the multitude of other things that were beyond their control. In this case, she would be the one to get credit for stating the obvious. It was only fair that she get something in return for being the only one of the three drenched professionals not getting paid for her time.

The lack of pecuniary return was also made palatable by the knowledge that she was setting the stage for something larger. Bunny had to continually to remind herself of that fact to ensure her growing resentment didn't show through her drenched façade.

"Right now, let's hope everyone has their homeowners and flood insurance in place. As you know, agencies aren't allowed to write policies when there are named storms out there, so it's too late to change any of that. The next things folks need to do, after getting supplies of course, are document the condition of their house before the storm hits and make a detailed list of their belongings. Having that information available will make filing damage claims easier. I recommend using a video camera, or even a cell phone camera for this purpose. Of course, you have to make sure you keep the camera or phone in a secure location and away from water."

"That's excellent advice for the viewers," Annie interjected. "What else should they be thinking of now, from a legal perspective?"

"Well, one other thing people don't tend to think about when preparing for a storm is their important documents. You know, things like your birth or marriage certificates, insurance policies, or even bank and financial records. Losing those can really come back to bite you. Those items should also be stored in a safe, dry place. If viewers haven't already done so, I recommend they take the time right now to locate their important documents and make sure they are secure."

"You're right. I would not have thought about securing paper-work to prepare for the storm. That's a great suggestion," Annie replied. Her job was to keep the segment moving, while asking things a viewer might. She searched the recesses of her waterlogged mind for a quick follow-up query. "Now, if the viewers do have papers or documents they want to protect, what should they do to keep them safe?"

Bunny smiled knowingly. It was a great question. The answer would allow her to send the message she intended to convey to interested parties.

"That's a great question, Annie. Ordinarily, I would suggest they give copies of important records to their attorney. And really, this could apply to any type of records, or even photographs and videos from important events. We are accustomed to protecting things like that for our clients. Unfortunately, if the viewers haven't given those types of things to counsel for safekeeping, it will be up to them to secure the items."

Bunny felt certain that last part should do the trick. The message she wanted to send was out there. The only thing left to do was to cap it with inane advice that appears intended for the viewers.

"One way to protect items from rain or flooding is by using a waterproof container of some sort. If your viewers have boats, they probably have some type of leak-proof storage available. Or, if you don't have anything like that, those little plastic bags folks keep in the pantry for sandwiches work almost as well. Really, it's just a matter of keeping your important information safe, so you'll have it later when you need to use it."

"What great advice," Annie concluded. "Thank you, Miss Keiler, for taking the time to brave the elements with us for the sake of our viewers. This is Annie Tuttle, reporting live from Satellite Beach. Back to you, Wendy."

Bunny nodded a quick thanks to Annie, and then hurried off toward her car. She had parked it on the far end of the adjacent public access parking lot. Under normal conditions the lot was a very visible, high-traffic location. The storm had changed all that, leaving Bunny with the dark, deserted pavement all to herself.

Standing in the empty space next to her car, completely exposed to the whims of nature, had an ominous feel about it. Bunny assigned the responding chill that traversed her spine to the elements, and pushed any thought of it aside. A few seconds more and she'd be out of this mess for good.

A click of her remote disengaged the car's locks. Bunny pulled open the driver's side door and tossed her purse inside first. To protect her car's leather interior, she then turned away from the open door while she struggled to find the umbrella's release lever. If it was on the handle, like every other umbrella on the face of the Earth, it wasn't apparent. Fighting the wind's commanding assault on the open umbrella didn't make the search any easier. Ultimately, when she found the lever, it refused to concede as did the wind. With no time for further delay, Bunny simply gave in.

She shook the umbrella hard to remove some of the excess water before tossing it, still partially open, into the front passenger's seat of her car. The notion that an open umbrella in the wrong place could be a harbinger of bad luck crossed her mind, but she wasn't sure why. Luck was for other people.

ତ୨ତ ତ୨ତ ତ୨ତ

The sound of the garage door engaging was a welcome one. Sam had been gone far too long and Riley had started to worry. She wasn't worried *for* him. The man was obviously resourceful in ways she hadn't imagined, if today was any indication. Rather, she was worried *about* him. He could be up to almost anything, and whatever he was doing that was taking so long, he was doing in her car.

Riley met Sam at the garage entrance with a wary look that didn't last long enough to make its mark. He was soaked–again. Somehow, he still managed to make the look work.

"You got another one of those towels?" he asked, while making a careful exit from the vehicle. "I don't want to leave your seat wet."

"Sure, I'll grab one," Riley responded. "I might even be able to find one for you."

Sam smiled wearily. "Thanks. I could use it."

Not wanting to track water into the house, he stood in the garage next to Riley's car. It took a moment to register; something in the garage was different. For one thing, there was a lot more room than before.

Riley anticipated his query on her return. "I moved the Jag over while you were gone."

"I thought something was different. Why?"

"Just for kicks," Riley teased. "Duh! I thought it would be obvious."

Sam turned to face Riley to get a read. Her motivations were still far from obvious to him. Riley took his expression and lack of lightning fast retort as an indication he might be genuinely confused.

"I moved it so there'd be room for your car. I can't afford repairs on a car like that if it gets hit by a branch or something," Riley said.

"I think it'll be okay for a few more minutes," Sam replied. "I'll dry off a bit and be out of your way soon."

"Like hell you will," Riley snapped. "The wind gusts are nearly hurricane force already and they're only going to get worse. I'm not sending you out in the middle of the storm no matter how much you annoy me. So, pull your damn car in here."

"Really, I'll be fine. I've driven in bad weather before," Sam said.

"I'm sure you've driven in many conditions you shouldn't have, but I can't do anything about your past. At the moment, this particular part of your present *is* up to me and I'm not the reckless type," Riley stated.

The wicked smile Sam liked to taunt her with took a leisurely stroll across his face. "So, what you're saying is that you want me to stay here with you?"

Riley deflected. "I didn't say that."

"Sure, not in so many words. Still, it's the end result if I do what you ask. That's pretty clever of you, Miss Morgan," Sam said, before deciding to take the assessment even further. "I don't imagine you're afraid of a little wind and rain. You simply don't want to weather the storm in this big house all by your lonesome, do you?"

Riley scowled. The man had a way of turning everything around to be about something else. He was way off base; just plain wrong, as usual.

"That's not it, at all. My concern is for you, not me," she shot back. "I know where you live, Sam. You're 24 floors up in the penthouse suite of that hoity-toity building downtown. I'm sure it's a swell place; perfectly designed for entertaining the ladies. But it's not really a safe place to be in a storm, now is it? When the power goes out—and we all know it will—how do you plan to get up and down those 24 flights of stairs? How do you plan to cool the place with no air conditioning and few if any windows that actually open? More importantly, what am I going to do if you get stuck there after the storm and I have to do the depos alone next week?"

Sam's smile spread. He was pretty sure Riley was hoping to make him mad with her harsh words. She hadn't. Actually, much of it had gone in one ear and out the other, with the exception of the part about her knowing where he lived. That unwitting revelation was entirely unexpected.

She had never been to his penthouse, and the topic had not come up in any of their conversations. The fact she knew about it could only mean she had taken the time to look it up online. This, in turn, meant she had been thinking about him.

"All right, Miss Know-It-All, since you insist. You're stuck with me for a while longer," Sam conceded. "I'm going to move my car into your garage. While I'm doing that, perhaps you'll do me the favor of pouring me a drink. I'm going to need it, if I'm spending the night with you."

"I don't take orders from soggy men," Riley advised.

She was distantly aware of the upward shift in her mood. Presumably, the change was a simple manifestation of relief; she didn't have to worry about Sam being out in the storm with her car any longer. The presumptive relief was accompanied by a twinge of nerves, but the reason for that was obvious.

Sam had given in pretty easily. It was possible the nature of her request had given him the wrong impression. This was not intended to be a social visit. She was just being considerate, and practical. It was probably a good idea to make sure he understood the ground rules.

"You can make yourself whatever you want, and then maybe we can get some work done. It's about time you put in some billable hours today," she concluded.

Wait, was she still talking? Sam had watched Riley's mouth move, but he wasn't able to follow. Her words were lost to the vision he had of her naked in front of the fireplace in the den.

CHAPTER 25

Sam's back had stiffened from sitting cross-legged on the floor across from Riley while they sorted through some of the recently produced documents. He casually stretched his arms over his head before crossing them behind it. To complete the shift, he unfolded his legs and settled back against the base of the sofa.

They had been working by battery-powered lamps; the convenience of electricity having left them some time ago. It had stayed on long enough for them to finish cooking the filets Riley had purchased—a small but unexpected blessing for which Sam was uncharacteristically grateful.

Just a few hours ago, he had shared an incredible meal with the most engaging woman he had met in a long time. Strike that, he had actually cooked said dinner with said woman, breaking his generally unspoken rule about engaging in close interpersonal activities with anyone who might threaten his cover. They had talked over dinner, about anything and everything—a real conversation. Not just the bullshit ones he usually had with the women he had to seduce, or con or steal information from.

Tonight might have been as close to a real date, with a real woman, as he would ever get—at least while he was still engaged in a covert enterprise. It had only happened by the chance of the weather. Odd how powerful the forces of nature can be.

Riley reached for another file from the pile of documents spread out on the rug before her and began to filter through the contents. "There's still a lot about this case that seems off-kilter."

Before responding, Sam had considered how to play down whatever anomaly had caught Riley's keen eye.

"Most litigation is off-kilter, don't you think? If things were going smoothly, the parties wouldn't be in court," he said.

Riley wasn't deterred by Sam's dismissal of her assessment. She continued to filter through the documents in search of something that might make things add up.

"That's a little simplistic, even for you," she chastised. "The timing of this case is really off."

"How so?" Sam inquired. She wasn't giving up. He might as well face her questions head on.

While waiting for her reply, he rose from the floor and carefully stepped over the rug and files scattered thereon to examine the fireplace. "Does this work?"

"Does what work?" Riley was still staring at the file. She looked up to see what latest distraction Sam had chosen to employ.

"Oh, the fireplace? I dunno. I've never used it. To be honest, I've never made a fire before, so I haven't tried it out."

"I thought it might add a little light in here. I'm sure I can figure out how to get it working."

"I'm not sure it's a good idea to heat things up when we know we'll need to cool them down tomorrow," Riley advised.

Sam turned to face Riley with a curious expression. Was she still talking about the fireplace?

Riley absently met his inquiring gaze. "What? Why are you looking at me like that?"

"No reason, Miss Morgan. Your point is taken."

"Good, because it's going to be at least 90 degrees tomorrow and without power we won't have air conditioning.

"Right. Right, as usual. What was it you were saying about the case?" Sam asked.

"What's odd is the timing of the litigation. As far as I can see, the pre-litigation process before the agency that investigates employment discrimination claims was commenced almost two years ago."

"Sounds about right," Sam said. "Mikles asked me to handle that stage of the process and deal with the agency inquiries at that time. I had Bunny handle a good bit of that."

"Okay, so why didn't Elson pull the case out of the administrative process as soon as the statutory time elapsed?" Riley inquired. "It's pretty standard for a plaintiff's attorney to go ahead and file suit if they haven't gotten a ruling from the state or federal agency within the allotted time. They don't want to run the risk of the agency issuing a finding there is no foundation to support their claim."

"I can't really speak to Elson's litigation tactics. Maybe he felt the agency was getting somewhere with their investigation," Sam stated. "I know they came back to us several times with requests for inspections and interviews. There was discussion of conciliation, although nothing formal."

"That might explain the initial delay. The government can provide a lot of pressure on an employer in these cases, if they are so inclined," Riley recounted. "They keep a running tab of the settlements they procure. I've heard that information somehow is used by the agency when trying to secure their annual budget. That doesn't explain the rest of it, though."

Sam internally sighed. Riley wasn't going to be deterred, easily or otherwise. He was going to have to employ alternative methods. "Just exactly what have you decided is the rest of it?"

"Don't get testy, Sam. I'm trying to get up to speed here."

Sam stepped back over the files toward Riley and settled into the small area next to her that wasn't covered by folders and papers. "I'm not testy. I'm enjoying working with you on this case."

Riley found the warmth of his presence a little unnerving. Visions of him shirtless on the ladder still danced in her head. She turned to glare at him, hoping it might cause him to move away, at least a little.

Almost immediately, she wished she had chosen a different course of action. Sam's steely blue eyes were locked and loaded.

In an effort to retain composure, she blurted out the only thing that came to mind. "Do you want some coffee?"

Sam raised a single brow. Riley wasn't responding like other women did when he tried his moves on them. Most were putty by now. This challenge was becoming even more intriguing by the minute.

"I thought you didn't drink coffee," he said.

"Actually, I never said that."

"I believe you did, in a manner of speaking. When I asked you what you wanted for the meeting with Bunny, you said you drank tea. In fact, you requested a specific type of green tea."

"Sure, I said I preferred tea, then. But saying one thing doesn't necessarily exclude another. You should know that. Maybe it's a good thing I'm taking Audra's deposition. You seem a bit rusty at the intricacies that abound in the language of Venus," Riley teased.

Sam looked confused for a moment. His face then registered enlightenment. "It was a test, wasn't it? You wanted to see just how closely I would follow your directions."

Riley smiled wryly. A blush might've crept into her cheeks, as well. "Perhaps."

"Shame on you, Miss Morgan. I would've thought the common tactics employed by your gender to be beneath you."

"The common tactics are. Mine are more refined. They managed to elude your skilled detection," Riley chided.

"Perhaps that's because I didn't expect you to be speaking in your native tongue at the time," Sam responded. "We were conducting business, after all. It was a bit out of context, don't you think?"

"You're kidding, right? You've been trying every move from your high school playbook on me from the moment we met. You can't really be surprised that I responded with something from the book of girl?"

"I guess we are acting a little like children, aren't we?" Sam said.

"Maybe we are," Riley admitted.

"Should we try something different to see if that gets us any-where?" Sam inquired.

"I'm not sure what I would change," Riley said. "I'm just trying to keep my guard up. You've made your intent clear more than once, and I've already told you why I'm being cautious. I guess I was hoping you'd fail the test so I could summarily dismiss you from consideration."

Wait. Sam replayed Riley's last comment in his head. *Did she just say what I thought she did?*

"You're implying I am still under consideration for something. What exactly does that mean?"

As far as Sam was concerned, this conversation couldn't get more interesting. He was vaguely aware of the fact he couldn't allow it to go everywhere he wanted it to, but decided not to let that little techni-cality alter the momentum.

"It means coffee. I'll make it," Riley offered, quickly rising to her feet. She stepped past Sam and the files to make a beeline for the kitchen.

Sam shook his head in frustration. Women were far more com-plex than any federal regulation he had ever had the pleasure of defying. Still, he wasn't about to stop trying.

"Of course. The meaning is coffee," he mocked.

Beverage prep took a little longer than usual without the conven-ience of one of those single cup gadgets, a microwave, or even a stove. It was hard to imagine there was once a time when the little pleasures in life were not managed via small electrical appliances. Fortunately, they didn't have to look too far into the past for a resource. Riley was able to locate the battery-powered tea kettle her father had once used to heat water for tea in his chambers. It would probably work with the instant ground coffee she had stored for an indefinite period of time in the back of the pantry.

"I think this is still good. Guess we'll find out," she mused while stirring the coffee grounds into the preheated water she poured in their mugs. "Don't judge me on the quality of this. It's not a representative sample of my culinary skills, limited though they may be."

Sam chuckled. "According to my sources, you don't have *any* culinary skills."

"You've been talking to Dani, haven't you?"

"I'll take the Fifth on that," Sam added with a grin. "Candidly, I really don't care what the coffee tastes like. It's hot, smells great and I plan to spike it with some of that rum I saw in your liquor cabinet in the den."

"That does sound appealing."

"You want some? I'll get the bottle," Sam offered before rising from his new favorite seat—the barstool at the center of Riley's kitchen island.

"Nah, I'm a lightweight when it comes to alcohol. I'd be asleep in no time, and we've still got plenty of work to do," Riley said.

"Suit yourself," Sam acquiesced, "I don't share your delicate constitution. I work better after a few shots of rum."

"Substituting an over-the-counter remedy for your ADD medication?" It was a little mean, but Riley couldn't suppress the barb before it freed itself from her better judgment.

Sam took a sample sip of his newly spiked beverage before acknowledging the challenge. "Nope. I'm substituting it for the interpersonal interaction you made it clear I won't be getting."

Sam was certainly quick with a retort. Riley had to give him props for that.

"If that's what it takes to keep you at bay, you'd better keep pouring," she replied. "This storm is supposed to stall over Central Florida until sometime late tomorrow. There's no telling how many interpersonal interactions you might otherwise have had in that amount of time."

"Let's see. Today was Friday, tomorrow is Saturday." Sam paused and rolled his eyes upward to take an imaginary count. "Four, maybe five . . . ."

"Should I get you a calculator?" Riley quipped.

"That's not a bad idea," Sam replied. "I'm in high demand with the natives of Venus in my off time. Especially now that I'm back on the market."

"Were you ever really off the market?"

"Now who's the one getting shirty?" Sam said. "Whatever you've heard is idle gossip. I would like to think my good behavior today made a small dent in whatever unflattering myth that precedes me."

Sam internally marveled at his ability to make the statement convincingly. The gossip that gave rise to his reputation was of his own devise; another convenient mask for his identity. A known weakness, for women or really anything else, made it easier for others not to perceive him as a threat. People like to put others into narrowly confined categories, the shallower the better, and leave them there. That way they don't have to think too much about what might really be going on.

Aside from a few frat boy encounters with sorority girls in college, he had managed to avoid the usual challenges that come with a serious girlfriend. His cover wives didn't count in the tally, even if he did occasionally enjoy husbandly privileges with them. They were obliged to play nice with him, at least in public. He liked to think they had enjoyed his company but as Riley aptly noted, he wasn't completely in tune with the inner workings of the female psyche.

Riley knew none of this, of course, and he couldn't tell her. He could, however, allow himself to simply be himself in the brief time that he might get to spend with her alone.

"I'm trying, Sam. I'm trying," Riley said. "I have to admit I've been surprised, once or twice. Especially today. I didn't see it coming."

"You really should watch the news, then. They've been predicting this storm for weeks," Sam teased.

"Ha! Very funny. You know, there's radar to track storms," Riley advised. "I'm not sure modern science has created anything yet that could predict your path."

Sam smiled. Riley had no idea how easily she gave away her internal thoughts. Her naked expression of thought was one of the two things he liked about her that included the word "naked."

"You never asked me the other question you had about the case. What was it?" he said.

"I'm still stuck on the pre-litigation aspect," Riley replied. "From the documents and what you've told me, it seems the EEOC took their sweet time investigating the matter, and clearly did something along the way to keep Elson from pulling the charge and filing it in court. So, after all that time and effort, why did they end up issuing a finding of no cause for the government to bring suit?"

"I don't recall them giving a specific reason," Sam said.

"They usually don't. In this case, though, it seems like they wasted everyone's time and resources, including their own," Riley concluded. "Doesn't that strike you as odd?"

"I suppose, now that you mention it," Sam said. "Like I said, I don't routinely handle these cases. Bunny was primarily the point of contact for the administrative stages. I just picked up the ball when the suit was filed in federal court a few months ago."

"There must've been something that caught the EEOC's eye initially," Riley surmised. "And then something like a change in focus or staffing, both of which happen all the time since it's a politically-charged agency, made them decide to punt, in a manner of speaking."

"Maybe. Or it could be their investigators were enjoying taking field trips to Orlando to question strippers. It's possible they took advantage of that perk for as long as they could before Elson and his client caught on."

"I hadn't thought of that," Riley admitted.

"I wouldn't have expected you to. It's a guy thing," Sam said. "It is reassuring to know you need me for something other than the heavy lifting."

"I imagine you'll prove to be imminently useful if we get to a jury. Most likely Elson will try to seat as many women as possible," Riley replied

"Are you saying that somehow works to our advantage? I believe you need to elaborate," Sam taunted. Perhaps he could pull a compliment out of her before the night was over.

"Getting women to swoon is your specialty," Riley quipped. "I'm pretty sure you not only know that, you revel in it."

"I won't deny having some understanding that your kind occasionally enjoys my company," Sam said. "But if our recent interactions are any indication, I'm not nearly as proficient in the art of wooing as either of us imagines. That is, unless I am to consider your protestations in the Shakespearean sense."

"I definitely do not protest too much when it comes to you. In fact, I may have to kick the protests up a notch if you don't help me go through the rest of these documents," Riley shot back.

"On that note, I believe break time is over," Sam said, with a hint of sarcasm. "Don't want the boss to kick me out into the storm."

Sam returned to the den and the paperwork they had left spread out on the floor there. When he reached an open spot near the sofa, he sat back down on the floor and leaned against the sofa cushions. Riley soon followed and settled into her previous spot.

"Returning to your point on jury selection, I beg to differ," he stated a few moments later. "If Elson is smart, he'll seat more men on the jury. Women aren't likely to be sympathetic to the plight of a stripper. Men will be more accommodating."

"What makes you say that?"

"You."

"Me? What are you talking about?" Riley said.

"I took you to The Polling Place for a reason. It wasn't to share the ambience."

"It wasn't? Could've fooled me," Riley replied dryly. "I got the distinct impression you enjoy it there."

"I do. But you didn't, and I didn't expect you would," Sam stated. "The purpose of the visit was to see how deep your disdain might be. Turned out to be deeper than I expected. You could barely curtail your contempt for the waitress, much less the . . . ."

Sam paused to consider a more politically correct term for the dancers. "We'll just call them the *entertainment*," he concluded.

"That's a bit of an exaggeration, don't you think?" Riley said.

"No. Not really," Sam said. "You also don't think much of Bunny, although you tried hard not to let that show during our meeting. You haven't met her before and don't really know whether she is skilled as an attorney or not, which makes your reaction necessarily premised on the cat factor."

"The cat . . . what?"

"You know, the 'I wanna scratch her eyes out for some primordial reason I can't explain' factor."

"I did not want to scratch her eyes out," Riley contended.

"Yes, you did."

Riley took a very cat-like stance. "I most certainly did not."

"I know a cat when I see one."

"So says the biggest dawg in town," Riley shot back. "Anyway, when did this become the battle of the sexes? I thought we were talking jury selection."

"We are, and I am. If Elson seats women on the jury then it's an easy win for us. Women are not going to care whether poor little Audra's feelings got hurt because the big bad man who paid her insane amounts of money to get naked said a few off-color things to her. Long story short, although I am not without certain charms, they won't be necessary to get a defense verdict."

"I see. So, what you're saying is that I don't really need you at all."

Sam laughed heartily. "You're starting to sound like Bunny. Are you trying to steal the case from me, too?"

"I don't want your case, Sam. And I'm nothing like Bunny."

"I'm inclined to believe you," Sam offered with a sly grin, "on both accounts."

CHAPTER 26

R iley awoke to the sound of her cell phone ringing. It wasn't a morning alarm; rather an urgent call. It had to be. For one thing, she had not set the alarm on her phone. Also, there was no reason for anyone to call her twice in the early morning hours during a hurricane unless it was urgent. She hadn't been sufficiently awake to coherently answer the phone when the first call came in. The second call wound up being the charm.

The night's sleep had been fitful once she finally trudged up to her bedroom, her path illuminated by flashlight. She had left Sam in the den with the documents, a blanket and pillow sometime after midnight. He insisted he didn't need anything more when she had offered him any of the several guest rooms.

They had made excellent progress on the documents after their coffee break–sufficiently so that she felt justified in catching a few hours of sleep. The plan they had agreed on before calling it a night was to start the next day refreshed and ahead of the game. Unfortunately, the storm had made other plans.

The wind howled loudly and beat viciously against the house most of the night. The house, in response to the wind's powerful assault, creaked and moaned with equal emphasis. That dissonant chorus was joined by the percussion of torrential rains beating against the southern-most side of the house, interrupted from a vertical descent by the forceful wind.

Riley reached over to the nightstand next to her bed and fumbled around until her hand made contact with her cell phone. She didn't feel like opening her eyes sufficiently wide to check the caller ID, so she just accepted the call.

"Hello."

"Miss Morgan," a breathless, shaky male voice called out, "thank goodness I got a hold of you."

It was Wade. Riley sat up and blinked rapidly to orient herself. Maybe he had good news. "What's up, Wade? Where are you?"

"I'm at my apartment right now. I've been called to go into the office."

"Right now?" Riley stopped for a moment to listen to the still-howling wind. "There's a storm raging outside. Why would they want you to go out in this weather?"

"Not right this second, but as soon as the worst of it passes. It's part of my company's Emergency Preparedness Protocol. All the IT folks take shifts to make sure the backup generators are working and that the data is secure."

"Okay, so how is this a problem?" Wade was talking and Riley was listening, but not much of what he was saying had sunk in. It was still early, and mornings weren't exactly her thing.

"Well, because I thought you said I'll probably be fired and should stay at home. That was before the storm, though. The company doesn't know about what happened to Halston yet because the police held off on making a public announcement. It might be okay for me to go back to work, at least until the word gets out."

"Right. I did tell you that." Riley's brain reluctantly decided to join the conversation. "If your team is working in shifts, will anyone else be there with you?"

"No, not except for a few minutes when I first get there and then when the next guy comes to take his shift. I think my boss has the shift after me. We repeat that schedule until cleared to return to regular office hours."

"So, for the most part, you'll have unobstructed access to anything in the office while you're there?"

"Pretty much. But, hey, I was thinking this could be a good thing."

"In what way?" Riley asked.

"Well, we may not be able to get anything else off of my computer, but Halston might have left some other clues on her computer at work, or even on the network there. I can search historical web data from our routine backups to see if anything's there."

Riley paused to consider where Wade's proposal might lead. A misstep at this level of the game could come back to haunt him.

"I have an idea where you're going with this. I have to tell you that I can't officially advise you to violate the privacy rights of your employer or other employees. I can't do that, officially."

"Uh, uh. Okay. That makes sense," Wade said. "So, should I see if Kristina can work with me on this?"

Riley bristled at the suggestion. Wade meant well. He just didn't quite grasp the legal ramifications of what he was suggesting just yet. To him, the servers and the information they stored might as well be someone's lunch in the break room refrigerator—there for the taking, when no one else was around. It was likely one of the few drawbacks of being too tech-savvy in an overly tech-dependent world.

"No, that's not a good idea. Kris is law enforcement. She can't enter or search a private location without a warrant or permission from someone with proper authority—like an owner, or officer of the company."

"Oh, okay," Wade acquiesced, somewhat disappointed that he hadn't yet figured out the answer Riley seemed unwilling to spell out for him.

"Here's the thing. You have been called in to manage the data. If you happen to run tests or searches for specific data while you're there, to determine whether it is secure and has not been damaged by the storm, I would imagine that to be part of your job. Is that correct?"

"Yes!" Wade replied in a brighter tone. The company had no set procedure for how the data was to be tested, and he could use his own discretion in selecting the search parameters. If he happened to search the server that held web search data, that was his prerogative.

"Then that's all I know you to be doing, and will advise Kris accordingly," Riley counseled. "If you have any other information for me once you've completed your work, you can give me a call. Do not, however, under any circumstance, remove any information from the premises. You can print or copy it according to your company's policies, but it has to stay there. Okay?"

"Got it. Thanks, Riley. I expect my shift will be sometime later tonight or tomorrow, once the streets are cleared and winds take a pill."

"Okay, I'll be here. I'm not going anywhere anytime soon. Call me the moment you find something."

Riley put her phone back on the nightstand and lay back against the pillows in her bed. Saving the world was exhausting, especially after a long night with little sleep. She closed her eyes and started to drift back into a dream that seemed to involve bacon.

"Hmm, bacon . . . that sounds good," she whispered to herself. The wind chose that opportune moment to remind Riley the kitchen was closed. "There's no way to cook bacon without the power on. Why do I always want something I can't have?"

A voice from somewhere in the recesses of her mind answered the hypothetical. *Maybe you want it because there is a way to have it.*

Riley threw the covers aside. Her feet hit the floor with her mind on a mission. Her father used to go on hunting trips with some of his close friends. They weren't the type of men who ventured into the wild without a few conveniences.

She tossed her version of pajamas–yoga pants and stretchy t-shirt– into her hamper, in exchange for an oversized polo style shirt and well-worn jeans. Ever weight-conscious, her wardrobe, including her comfy weekend attire, was usually fitted and flattering to her curves. That look, however, was the last thing she intended to sport while limited to close quarters with Sam. The man was too easily distracted and getting ever harder to contain.

Harder. Riley suppressed a snicker as the sound of Dani's voice echoed in her head. *You said harder in reference to Sam. I know where your mind is.*

Riley attempted to silence the interloping commentary with an internal rebuke. *Shut up, Dani's voice. I'm trying to be a grown-up over here.*

After splashing some cool water on her face, she stopped to check her reflection in the mirror over the vanity. Her eyes looked tired and her face was a bit pale, but otherwise acceptable. A brush of bronzing powder over the highpoints of her cheeks and dot of clear pink gloss on the lips should do the trick. Although many might find it an unnecessary formality, she was raised with the notion that a lady shouldn't start the day without her lipstick. Old habits die hard, if by chance they die at all.

Ready to start the day, Riley took the stairs that led down to the den quietly. She was pretty sure there had been no sound indicating movement in the den, although it was possible the howling winds outside had muffled it. More likely than not, Sam was still asleep, which is what she would be if it weren't for Wade's early wake-the-hell-up call.

When she reached the next to last step, she had a clear view into the den and stopped momentarily to evaluate the scene before her. Papers and files tossed about on the floor gave the impression the storm might've made its way inside on some level. It hadn't. The room looked like that when she left it last night. But the rest of it? That was all new.

Sam was stretched out on the sofa, his feet extended beyond the end of its 6-foot frame. The blanket she had left him was half performing its intended function, having otherwise been relegated to a twisted mass around and between his long legs. He was still asleep, and deeply so if his breathing was any indication. One of his arms was over his head and the other was hanging languidly from the side of the sofa, resting awkwardly there as if he had been reluctant to move it before drifting off to sleep.

Riley quietly approached the sofa to find out what Sam might have been holding before he succumbed to sleep. The sound of snoring halted her approach, until she discovered the sound wasn't coming from Sam. The rhythm and depth of it was vaguely familiar; was it possible, though? Her suspicions were confirmed after she took a few steps closer.

Mason was sprawled out against the base of the sofa, sleeping so soundly in his favorite position—on his back with his front legs curled against his chest and his back legs fully extended—that he had begun to snore. Riley had heard him snore a few times in the past, when snuggled up in the covers on her bed, but never had he slept like that during a storm. In fact, he was usually highly skittish during storms, especially if there was thunder. His present comfort appeared to have been assured by Sam's touch, which must have remained constant during the night. Sam's long fingers were still entwined in Mason's fur, in spite of the fact that sleeping with his arm hanging over the edge of the sofa must have been at least a little uncomfortable.

"Dawgs of a feather. Quite the pair," Riley whispered.

There was no denying the two of them sleeping together like that was pretty adorable. Sam's face bore the makings of a shadow beard—the kind that all-too-hip guys try to grow to mimic the scruffy look of male models or fictional adventurers. Some men could acquire that coveted look overnight, while asleep, without even trying. Sam, of course, was one of those men.

"It's all easy for you, isn't it?" Riley mused.

She quietly left them as they had been found, and went on to fulfill her mission—a hot breakfast. It was the only way to start a day. Neither rain, nor hail, nor hurricane moving slow, was going to stop her from delivering the meal. Deeply rooted Southern traditions mandated it. Besides, if you dream about bacon, there's no way you're going to be satisfied if you don't have it. That was a well-known fact.

Dani's voice interrupted her thoughts, once again.

Does that apply to other things you have in dreams? The voice paired the query with an echo of Dani's laughter.

That does it, Riley internally ruminated. *I'm not telling Dani anything about my thoughts on Sam ever again.*

Unfortunately, just like its real-world counterpart, Dani's voice talked back. *You don't have to tell me because I'm inside your head. I already know.*

Fine then. After breakfast I'm going to use my laptop to get on the Internet and do a web search for "How to get your friend's voice out of your head." There's got to be an app for that, Riley shot back.

The laughter echoed again, but not mockingly. It was more of a knowing laugh.

Silly girl. You realize you're talking to yourself, right? I'm the part of you that you refuse to acknowledge. The part that wants to have a life. You disguise me as Dani because you still can't face the truth.

Riley sighed, suddenly acutely aware that her internal struggle with what she wanted and what she deemed safe was reaching a critical point. It had her arguing with herself while alone in the dark in the early hours of the day. Her internal voice was right; she was keeping too many things bottled up and she had long-since forgotten the reasons why. Today, she would start with bacon; tomorrow, who knows? Maybe she'd start her day with a different type of rebellion from propriety–perhaps one that was less fattening.

Mason stirred at the first sound of something sizzling in the kitchen. His sudden movement spurred a chain reaction, and Sam was roused from his deep slumber as well. It's a lot easier for a dog to awaken fully alert than for a human, which gave Mason the advantage in the race to see what was cooking. Not that Sam attempted to give him much of a challenge. He was awake but his arm and shoulder weren't giving in that easily. Sam tried intermittently rubbing and shaking it to get the circulation going during his short jaunt to join Mason in the kitchen.

"That smells amazing," Sam announced, his sleepy voice deeper than usual. "Is the power back on?"

"Nope. No power, just propane, a portable cooktop and a match. My father had it stored with his other camping gear in the garage. It's amazing what can still be accomplished the old-fashioned way."

"New, old, whatever gets the job done," Sam added. "Any chance you can make pancakes with that thing? I've heard tall tales about your pancakes. Wouldn't mind finding out if the rumors are true."

"Oh no, Mister. You haven't earned pancakes yet. That prize is on a whole other reward level," Riley advised. "You'll have to rack up a lot more bonus points for a stack of those."

Sam conceded to her terms with a sly smile. "Yet another challenge. Fair enough. I'll make the coffee while you finish the bacon."

"Works for me," Riley concluded.

While they sat in silence enjoying the "survivalist" breakfast, Riley ruminated over a few other recent conclusions. This was way too easy, and too comfortable. As if they'd played the scene out a hundred times before. Sam was supposed to be a jerk, plain and simple. He needed to act like he was supposed to so she could disregard him like she wanted to. The man was going to have to stop being agreeable, or she would have to slap him.

"Do you mind if I take a cold shower?" Sam inquired after they finished eating.

There was no other type of shower he could take with the power still out. He simply couldn't resist the obvious taunt. Riley chuckled. It *was* pretty funny coming from him.

"Not at all. Help yourself. You should know where everything is in the guest bathroom off the den, by now."

"I think I do. Thanks. I've actually got a change of clothes in my car. I'm going out to grab those first."

Riley looked at him skeptically. "Did you bring those because you planned to spend the night last night?"

"No. Don't be daft. I didn't plan to stay here alone with you in this big dark house that has lots of rooms two people might enjoy." He smiled wickedly with that last part, knowing it would bother her. He was about to say something else he knew, or at least hoped, might bother her more.

"Of course, that doesn't mean I didn't have plans to stay somewhere else, with someone else, and possibly spend time with them in rooms two people might enjoy."

He was kidding, but he liked the fact that his jest made its mark. From the look of her disapproving expression, Riley was curious and a little jealous.

"I'm just teasing, Riley. I always keep a packed weekend bag in the car in case I decide on the spur of the moment to take off for the coast or go somewhere to play golf. I like to live in the moment. It's part of my charm, or haven't you noticed?"

"Yeah, I've seen that so-called charm of yours," Riley mocked. "Mason has more."

At the mention of his name, Mason padded over to stand by his owner. He leaned against her leg with the full of his weight. Relying on his master for support was the best way for a big guy like him to show his.

"Mason is quite charming although apparently fickle, as you've no doubt discovered. I was certain we were best mates after last night," Sam reflected.

Sam reached out toward Mason with a scrap of bacon in his hand in an attempt to draw him away from Riley. The venture was unsuccessful. Mason apparently knew where the kibble came from.

"Very well. Since something slightly less frigid awaits me in another room, I shall leave the two of you to re-acquaint," Sam teased.

Riley finished cleaning the dishes from breakfast and headed back to face the pile of documents still awaiting review in the den. Sam soon joined her there, fully awakened from the chilly shower. They spent most of the rest of the day finalizing their preparations for the upcoming depositions. It was all pleasant, absent the occasional attempt to best one another on some random issue or point of law.

Sam was quite easy to get along with, when he had nowhere else to go. Riley wondered if he would be like this when the chance to partake of the many choices that otherwise came his way returned in full force. It was the sort of question that only time could answer.

By late afternoon the winds quieted, stopping almost as quickly as they had started. According to the reports received on the small battery-powered weather radio, this was only the eye of the storm. There would be more to come. Still, the moment of calm was a relief following many nonstop hours of nature broadcasting her fury.

Riley took the opportunity to let Mason out to attend to his business. He returned far more quickly than he usually would, apparently not wanting to leave his master unattended with a new male sharing their space. Mason assumed a seated position just inside the back door and waited for Riley to commence the customary towel dry. He had learned the hard way that a well-bred dog doesn't bound into their person's space with muddy paws.

Starting with his left front paw, Mason raised each of his four legs in succession, allowing Riley to towel his legs and paws dry, while Sam marveled at their teamwork. Without a word, man and beast had joined in a coordinated effort for a common goal. It was an impressive display of unity.

"You two should take that show on the road," Sam teased.

"We should, shouldn't we?" Riley tousled Mason's ears affectionately. "I guess it's too much to hope the power will come back on any time soon, isn't it?"

"Nothing wrong with wishful thinking. So, tell me, what would you do if the power was on that you can't do now?"

"Take a long, hot bath," Riley responded wistfully. She rose from her crouched position in front of the door and rotated her torso from side to side slowly. "I'm getting a little stiff from sitting on the floor."

Sam's eyes were briefly lit by mischief. "I'm sure I can help you with that."

Riley turned to face him, her face twisted to reflect the sarcasm in her tone. "I'm sure you could. Thankfully, I'm not in need of that type of service."

Sam smiled. "That's a good thing because I wasn't offering *that* service, although it is reportedly among the many I'm quite good at. I was referring to the hot bath. I believe we can heat enough water to warm your bath using the propane cooktop you used this morning."

Riley's expression changed while she considered his point. "That could work, except my soaking tub is upstairs in the master bath. I'm not sure how many heavy pots of water I could carry up there before the whole endeavor became more trouble than it's worth."

Sam shook his head. He looked down at his arms and then back at Riley. "Have I suddenly become invisible?"

"No, Sam, I can see you. What does that have to do with anything?"

He rose to his feet and offered Riley a hand to steady her rise. "Would you like me to fetch water for your bath, Princess?"

Riley had foolishly taken Sam's hand and was still holding it as the shock of his offer registered. She quickly retrieved her appendage before responding. "You're not serious."

"Yes, I am quite serious. You've been more than hospitable to me in my time of need. I'd be happy to return the favor."

"You would really do that for me?" Riley asked.

"I wouldn't have offered otherwise. Believe it or not, I am a man of my word."

Riley weighed her options. The offer was too good to refuse. She faced Sam head-on and looked him in the eye. "This doesn't mean you can join me."

"Of course not," Sam offered casually. "This time, anyway."

The mischief had returned to his eyes, causing them to reflect shades of green not ordinarily present. He mockingly bent forward at the waist, much like a servant might when attending their master, before heading to the kitchen to fill a few pots.

Riley stood where he left her, still trying to collect her senses. This was dangerous ground, and Sam had somehow found yet another way to advance his position onto it. It occurred to Riley that, at this stage of the game, maybe the best defense was a good offense.

"You'd better watch what you say, Sam," she called out loud enough for him to hear from the other room. "One of these days, I might call your bluff."

CHAPTER 27

R iley ducked into the study, and away from Sam's keen oversight to check for messages on her office voicemail. Client confidentiality wasn't something to be taken lightly. She and Sam might share one client, but that's where their professional relationship ended. With a situation as sticky as Wade's still in the early investigative stages, there was no margin for error. No information could be leaked in advance of Kristina's go ahead. Lives were at stake. Literally.

She placed the receiver back on the speakerphone's cradle and sat back to reflect. If no news was good news, then things were looking up. This was one of the few weekends in recent memory when she hadn't gotten a single call from a client in crisis. Apparently, this weekend, everyone shared the same crisis—a Cat-4 storm. If there was anything good to come from Adonis, it was the fact it bought her some time to consider Wade's options. They were few; each monumental in its own way. Maybe, if they were lucky, the storm had also bought Halston some time. One could hope.

When Riley returned to the den, Sam was waiting there for her with a pot of hot water. He had been up and down the stairs a few times in her absence. This time, he motioned for her to follow.

"This last one should be enough hot water for you. I'm not sure you can handle too much of it at once."

Riley followed him upstairs. "Ha. You have no idea what I can handle."

"I do, actually," Sam replied. "So, are you going to tell me why you disappeared, leaving me to do all the heavy lifting?"

"I didn't know you were actually serious about this. Anyway, I can't tell you. It's a client matter. We're co-counsel on Vince's case only. You know I can't reveal other client confidences."

"That's true. However, I am a more experienced attorney, and the Bar does allow mentoring for young lawyers. There's nothing wrong with me giving you advice on a hypothetical situation."

"I doubt even the incomparable Sam Stone has encountered this one before," Riley said.

A single raised brow reflected the peak in Sam's curiosity, but he decided to let the subject lie, for now.

When they reached her bedroom, Riley was suddenly self-consciousness. Her preference was for everything to be in its place. Exigent circumstances tend to change customs. At the moment, nothing was as she preferred it. To make matters worse, in her rush downstairs to make breakfast this morning, she hadn't even made the bed. None of that seemed to faze Mr. Ladykiller. He breezed past her bed and headed into the master bath to pour the last pot of hot water into the nearly full tub. Undoubtedly, he'd been in many a lady's bedchamber.

Once Sam was safely out of sight in the bathroom, Riley stopped by the bed to fuss with the covers and straighten the pillows. She also managed to kick a wayward pair of shoes under her bed before he returned to the room.

Sam couldn't stop the smile that spread across his face. It was obvious he made her nervous. He was in her bedroom, and she was about to disrobe. That little irony wasn't lost on him, even if the proximity of those events was only semantic.

"I don't mind if you're not a neat-freak, Riley," Sam chided in an amused tone. "In fact, it's been my experience that the messier the room, the better the sex."

Riley shook her head. "I'm not messy. I've just been busy these past few days," she refuted. "But that's beside the point. Why is everything about sex with you?"

Sam responded earnestly. "Because everything is about sex. Not just with me."

"No, it isn't! That's nonsense."

"It's not nonsense. Name something, anything, and I'll show you."

"Okay, fine. See that silver-plated hairbrush over there on my dresser? It was my mother's, handed down from two generations before. Do tell, what does a hairbrush have to do with sex?"

"That's an easy one. An adorned hairbrush is given to a woman to entice her to maintain long hair because men are attracted to women with long hair. It's a primal thing. We like the notion of dragging you womenfolk off to our caves by your hair. I'll wager that particular brush has everything to do with a man, which in turn means it has everything to do with sex."

Riley frowned. When she was little, her mother used to sit with her before bed and brush her long dark hair using that very brush. Thirty strokes on each side. It was a tradition that the women on her side of the family were bound to hand down to the next generation. As the story was told, her great-grandmother's long, dark hair was one of the many things that her great-grandfather had admired about his young bride.

Damn it. "I should've known you could twist that one into your paradigm. One example doesn't prove the point."

"Then, by all means, fire off another challenge," Sam said. "Better do it quickly before your bath cools."

Riley bit her bottom lip while she scanned the depths of her mind for the most benign inanimate object she could imagine. She reached down and picked up a sock from the floor by her bed. *I never leave socks lying around. What's wrong with me?* she chastised herself internally.

"Okay, how is this sock about sex?" Riley heatedly inquired. "Please, share your divine insight."

"That's a cotton sock, right?"

"Yes, it is. So?"

"Then I imagine you put it on after you put lotion on your feet at night?" Sam asked.

"Sometimes. Yes."

"Well, then, it's elementary. That adorable little piece of fashioned yarn is used to keep your adorable little feet soft. You like to have soft feet because men prefer that in a woman, especially when you show off those adorable feet in those adorably expensive shoes you like to wear."

"That's just nonsense, Sam. Maybe I like pretty feet because I like pretty feet. And I like shoes because I like shoes. And maybe I just wear socks to keep my feet warm. It doesn't have anything to do with you."

"I didn't say it had to do with me. I was talking about sex, in general. It's fascinating that you've chosen to associate the two." Sam beamed a victorious grin before he left the room, closing the door behind him.

Riley tossed the sock at the now closed door. "You're wrong, Sam! You're still just all kinds of wrong."

For her own peace of mind, Riley crossed the room and locked the bedroom door before retreating to her bath. Sam wasn't the type to skulk about. If he wanted something, he wasn't the least bit shy about pursuing it. He wouldn't have given her privacy, if he had other intentions. Still, one couldn't be too cautious with a man like Sam. He had a certain sense of entitlement.

Riley's face wore a slight frown while she slipped out of the baggy shirt and pants that adorned the rest of her. That man wanted to dominate everything, including her thoughts. She silently mouthed Sam's earlier comments about sex in a mimicking fashion, and improvised a few of her own while she pulled her hair back from her face and secured it with an elastic band she kept on the counter by the sink.

"I was talking about sex, in general. I know everything about sex. I'm Sam Stone. I am sex."

Riley might've continued to ruminate angrily on the matter and on the troublesome Mr. Stone, if the piping hot water in her bath hadn't felt so amazing. The cloud-filtered light coming in through the shutters of the bathroom window, coupled with a small, battery-powered light that ordinarily functioned as a night-light, created just enough soft glow to give the room a spa-like ambience.

Riley released a long sigh of relief before reclining in the tub. She hadn't felt this relaxed in a long time. This wasn't something she was inclined to do on a regular basis and most of the time, even if she had the inclination, she didn't have the time.

Sam might be annoying, but he was certainly resourceful. The man made things happen. She couldn't completely fault him for that. It was a trait she usually admired in a person. With that in mind, she resigned herself to enjoying the moment, and Sam's gesture of good faith. The next few days were going to be nothing but chaos, especially with *that man* along for the ride.

Less than an hour later, refreshed and revived, Riley prepared to rejoin Sam in the den. Another loose-fitting cotton shirt, this time paired with ankle-length capris, seemed appropriate. She also decided to leave her hair pulled back from her face in a pony-tail, a look she often donned on weekends when Mason was the only male she had to impress. She bounded down the stairs, two at a time, stopping abruptly just before she might've crashed into the tall, unshaven man who suddenly appeared at the foot of them.

Sam took note of Riley's relaxed mood and was highly pleased he had something to do with it. "I like your hair pulled back like that. It makes you look even younger."

Riley tilted her head upward and gave Sam a sideways glance before stepping around him. "I'm going to take that as a compliment, even if it wasn't intended that way. I only pulled it back to protect myself. I seem to recall you saying you like to pull women around by their hair."

"You have nothing to worry about. I stopped pulling girls' pigtails in the third grade. I've learned a few new tricks since then."

"I've no doubt about that," Riley mocked. She turned away briefly, motioning for Sam to hold his thought and mouth for a moment. "I don't hear the wind anymore."

"It stopped a little while ago. The rain is letting up, too. Would you like to venture outside to see if there's any damage?"

"I think we could both use some fresh air," Riley responded with a hint of sarcasm.

Sam followed her to the front door, stepped to the side and opened it. "After you," he offered.

A steamy waft of humidity rose to greet them at the door. Riley waved it off, stepped out onto the front porch and peered into the yard. Sam followed a step behind. A few clouds still darkened the sky, but no longer overpowered the afternoon sun. In the distance, birds were calling out desperately to locate mates separated or lost during the storm.

From her vantage point on the front porch, Riley carefully surveyed the yard. The storm departing while there was still daylight was beneficial to recovery efforts. At least they could take note of and try to quickly address any unsafe conditions created by the high winds and rain before nightfall. Encountering downed power lines in the dark of night was one of the gravest dangers that followed a storm of this magnitude.

The ground was still soggy, and there were quite a few spots where the torrential rain had left large, mud-filled puddles on the lawn. Aside from the puddles, and a single willowy branch from her favorite forbidden tree, nothing was amiss. Riley stepped off the porch and walked gingerly around the puddles to retrieve the branch. It had broken from one of the limbs of the camphor tree she and her father planted years ago.

Although they have many beneficial qualities, camphor trees are considered to be nuisance plants by many. The trees are not favored among horticulturists, who often warn against planting the trees in Florida due to the potential damage the large, heavy branches could cause in a storm. Riley mused at the momentary irony. Her camphor tree was, with the exception of one small branch, still intact while the more popular and much-favored oak trees in her neighbors' yards hadn't fared as well.

As was natural for its species, the camphor tree had quickly grown large and as a result, taken charge of the front of the yard. It provided a great deal of shade during the hot summer months. Mason could often be found sitting under it enjoying that shade when Riley was out pulling weeds from the plant beds. It also attracted squirrels and birds by droves, both of which were welcome guests as far as Riley and her father had been concerned. Humans had displaced Florida's native wildlife from far too many of their natural habitats. It was only fair to give them something in return.

Interestingly, her favorite rebel tree also appeared to have been in just the right place at just the right time. While a large portion of clay roofing tile was clearly missing from her neighbor's house directly across the street from the tree, Riley's roof had no signs of damage. Apparently, the camphor tree had taken the brunt of the hurricane force wind as it tore across the open street between the houses, and turned the wind's roar into a mild whimper by the time it passed through the tree's thick, leafy canopy.

"Score one for the rebels," Riley whispered toward the sky knowing her father, somewhere up there, had to be reveling in the same small victory.

"Did you say something?" Sam had quietly come up behind Riley, any hint of his approach muted by the soggy terrain.

"No, not really. Just talking to myself, I guess. I can't believe how lucky I am."

"Downright jammy, I'd say. I doubt the rest of the area fared as well. We should probably check out the back yard. By the look of things, the wind came in from this side," Sam pointed in the direction of the house across the street that had lost some of its roof tiles. "So, there's likely even less to worry about in the back."

"I hope you're right," Riley advised. "I need to let Mason out, anyway. He's been uncommonly patient during all of this. I think he's trying to impress you."

"It's a guy thing," Sam teased. "We refuse to let other males know we're scared of anything. Apparently, the rule applies to all species. "

They made a quick trip through the house and then, with Mason joining them, went back out through the French doors in the kitchen. As Sam had predicted, Riley's back yard fared even better than the front. Aside from an extra-soggy lawn, it was as if the storm had never happened. Mason bounded out into the yard, lifted a leg to attend to nature, and then went about his customary duty of patrolling the perimeter.

"Looks like Mason's got everything under control out here," Sam announced with a chuckle. He pulled his cell phone from a pocket and turned to go back inside. "I'm going to make some calls to see where everything stands for next week."

When Riley and Mason rejoined him in the den a few minutes later, Sam was muttering something about a Napoleon complex.

"What's turned you sour?" Riley inquired.

"Audra's nut-job attorney. Donatti is insisting we go forward with the deposition on Monday."

"How does he plan to do that if the power's still out?"

"He said he's already made arrangements to hold the depo at his house. He's got a generator and a court reporter already lined up. Says he faxed over a cross-notice to my office late Friday changing the location of the deposition, in the event of a power outage. I'll bet the cheeky bastard served it by email before the power went out, hoping we wouldn't see it."

Riley blinked a few times in disbelief. "Okay, well aside from that just being asinine, why is he so adamant about his client being deposed on Monday? It's really our call whether it goes forward, not his. The original notice was from your office. Why the hell would he notice his own client's deposition?"

"Elson wanted to call the shots and hold us to the schedule. That's the reason for the cross-notice. It's a move I might have used myself in other circumstances—underhanded, but effective."

Riley shook her head in frustration. "Well, it's not something I would do. I don't play games like that. If that's the case and he's going to be anal about the order of the witnesses, why don't we just agree to move all the depos back a few days?"

"I would have rescheduled if it were up to me. It's not. Mikles won't budge on his deposition date, either. He's adamant that his time is too valuable. He's not interested in wasting any more time dealing with Audra's temper tantrum."

Riley peered at Sam with a look she often used when a witness made a statement beyond belief. Although he hadn't previously, this time Sam caved to the look of shame.

"Those were his words, not mine, okay? Don't glare at the messenger."

"Where does this leave us?" Riley asked.

"For starters, we're still on for Monday, with or without electricity. That leaves us at a disadvantage in terms of preparation. The power is still out at my office, so we can't get in there to prepare copies of the exhibits we plan to use, or to finish our preparations."

"The power is still out everywhere, right now. It probably will be for a few days, maybe even a week, if the damage is as bad in other areas as they're saying on the radio."

Sam nodded.

"So, I'm stuck with you for a few more days," Riley concluded the thought Sam was reluctant to express.

"I can go somewhere else. I don't want to be in the way," Sam advised, apologetically.

"Oh, don't even start with that. I know you don't want to ask if you can stay, so you don't have to. We're in this together, and we're already set up here. I've got a copy machine, and whatever else we need to make copies, and I've got one of those backup power boxes that can run the copier long enough to get that much done."

"Wait. You had a backup power source all this time and didn't tell me?"

"Nice way to change the subject on me. Yes, I've got one of those power box thingies you can use to charge or run small electronics for a few hours without electricity."

"Why didn't you mention that before now?" Sam asked, somewhat irritated.

"I don't know why I didn't mention it. I guess because we didn't really need it. And I'm glad I didn't use it for something else, since it turns out we really need it now. "

It was Sam's turn to respond with skepticism, although the twinkle in his eye belied any implication of genuine concern. "What else are you holding out on me?"

"Pretty much everything, or haven't you figured that out, yet?"

"I have. Just wanted to get confirmation," Sam chided.

"Now you have it. Don't expect that or anything else to change over the next few days," Riley retorted before leaving the room with her nose in the air, Mason dutifully falling into place behind her. Before completing the dramatic exit behind his master, Mason stopped and turned back to see if the new pack member was following suit. He wasn't. This new male apparently didn't know how things worked around here.

Mason sat in the doorway on his hind legs, turned his head to the side and studied Sam with curious eyes. Instead of joining them, Sam strolled over to the couch and stretched out on it. He tucked his arms under his head, and leaned back. It was a clear act of defiance, in any language.

"C'mon, Mason. Why don't you join me for a nap?" Sam taunted. "What's the worst she can do?"

Mason covered his eyes and nose with a paw, as if responding to Sam's query. He whimpered a few times to convey his sympathy, before turning to follow his master.

CHAPTER 28

W ade was sucking air by the time he made it up the five flights
of stairs to the floor where his office was located. Housing a
business in an office tower might seem a smart way to present a
professional image; it made a lot less sense when the power went out,
taking the elevators with it. The probability of that occurrence is far
greater when the business is located in an area prone to inclement
weather. When the inevitable happens, as it had today, employees are
left to climb umpteen flights of stairs lit by only a flashlight and the
dim red glow of emergency exit signs.

He was just a lowly geek in charge of the computers right now.
His less-than-exalted rung on the corporate ladder left him subject to
the ill-advised choices of others. Still, he could remember today's
lesson on accessibility and put it to good use somewhere down the
road when he was the man-in-charge. A single-story building with
functioning windows and adjacent, covered parking was the way he'd
go.

A shot of panic recharged his fatigued heart when he reached the
double-door entryway of the office. It occurred to him—at that
moment and not a second before—that he had forgotten his ID badge.
Under ordinary circumstances, RFID-coded badges and an electroni-
cally controlled, magnetic lock determined who had access to the

office suite. The notion of having to trudge back down all of those stairs, in the non-ventilated stairwell, hit hard.

Fortunately, the notion met an equal and opposing force in the voice of reason that had somehow managed to remain cool in spite of his elevated temperature. The power was out. He couldn't swipe-in even if he wanted to. The company's generator only supplied power to the servers, IT and a few other emergency functions. The doors weren't among those few. They were operating on key access only, and Wade was among the few with the key.

He pulled out a key-laden ring from the front pocket of his khakis and located the appropriate piece of metal that would give him dominion over the double-barreled deadbolt lock. Once found, he inserted the key, turned it with ease, and *voila* he was back to the scene of the crime. Well, not the main crime. That took place at Halston's apartment. He was back to the scene of his first crime–the place where he foolishly chose to follow a dream that had since turned into a nightmare.

First order of business was to let his counterpart from the prior shift know he was here. Then he had to wait for him to leave. After that, he could begin the search for anything Halston might've left behind.

Wade made his way back to the IT area, deeming it the most likely place he'd find the other living soul in the office. Sure enough, his co-worker Justin Burlowe, a fairly new hire under his supervision, was sitting in his cubicle fully reclined in a non-reclining desk chair with his feet propped on his desk. Justin didn't move or show any indication he had heard Wade's approach.

"Wake-up, man," Wade called out. No response. "Damn, are you sleeping, dude?"

As Wade approached his co-worker, he noticed the white cords dangling from both of Justin's ears. No wonder he didn't respond. You can't hear shit with those things on. Wade could've arrived with the fanfare of a marching band, and Justin would never have known he was there. Wade reached out with both hands and yanked the cords from his co-worker's ears.

"Dude, that's so lame. You're supposed to be making sure everything is secure. How you gonna do that if your ears are clogged with the sound of some auto-tuned boy band?"

"I don't listen to that sh . . .," Justin started in protest to Wade's flagrant foul, but then thought better of it. Wade could be a smart-ass, but he was also the boss of him. "Oh, hey, didn't hear you come in. Is your shift now?"

"Ya didn't hear me? No shit, dude. Yeah, it's my time," Wade said.

"Sorry, it's so boring and quiet here right now, I had to do something to stay awake. Plus it's kinda spooky when the place is empty. Like a scene from a zombie movie."

Wade wanted to laugh. He might have said or at least thought the same a week ago. Now that his world had taken a turn in an unwanted direction, he was all sense, no nonsense. He had to be.

"Yeah, I get it. Listen, I'm here, and they don't pay extra for you to stay on. So get the hell outta here and find somewhere else to hide from the zombies, okay?"

Justin breathed a sigh of relief. Wade seemed chill, so maybe he still had a job. "Thanks. I'm outta here. You'll let me know if we're pulling the same shifts tomorrow?"

"You'll get a text from Duong. It's up to him. As long as the power's out, and I'm pretty sure it will be for a while, we're on call. Catch you later, man."

Justin waived halfheartedly and made a hasty retreat. Too much time alone had made him antsy. He longed for the comfort of other humans, and for coffee. Maybe somewhere in this town he could find one or the other while waiting for the return of civilization.

Alone at last, Wade ruminated. Unlike his co-worker, he was thrilled not to have the weight of prying eyes on him right now. He plopped down in his chair and fired up his desktop computer along with its accompanying array of monitors. A pad pulled from his desk drawer was next. While he waited for his system to run through the usual boot process and then run annoying software updates, he jotted a few notes detailing the directories he needed to search on the main servers.

He looked back up at his monitors, and glanced down at his watch. This was taking forever. With all the advances in software and hardware these days, you'd think someone would invent an operating system that updated instantaneously. Slow computing–so 1990.

When the operating system finally relinquished control of his computer, he logged in for administrative access and began searching the servers most likely to store information from Halston's computer. He estimated it would take a while for the computer to run his commands given the number of digital packets it had to review. Might as well use his time wisely. He headed out to the front of the office where Halston's desk was located. If he was lucky, he could find something on her desk or computer that could help them find her.

After searching Halston's computer for what seemed like eons, he had nothing other than the same basic information he had download-ed previously. Her cache indicated she had accessed her home com-puter remotely on her last day in the office. He already knew that, and he already had that IP address. It did nothing to further his cause since her computer was no longer sitting on the desk in her bedroom.

It occurred to him that if, by some odd chance of fate, Halston's computer was turned on and connected to the Internet from its new location, he might be able to find it using those same programs that perform the annoying updates he earlier lamented. It was too much of a long-shot for something this important, though. Even if they found the computer, that didn't mean it would lead them to Halston. Ergo, his search continued.

None of the other information saved in the cache seemed in-formative. On her last day in the office, Halston also browsed a few online shoe retailers, probably looking for more of those crazy five-inch heels she liked to wear. Wade winced upon the realization that whatever shoes she might've ordered would arrive unwelcomed at her door. The odds she would never get the chance to wear them were mounting.

Irritated by his lack of success, Wade forcibly pushed away from the front of Halston's desk. The force of his frustration echoed in the force of his push, and was sufficient to send him away from the desk and propel the standard office task chair he was sitting in into a spin. The chair, and he in it, turned a few 360s before coming to a stop facing the return side of Halston's desk.

On that side of the desk Halston kept a few files that housed important things, like the prior day's sign-in sheets and menus from the local restaurants that delivered downtown. Next to the files was a pile of office supply catalogs. The office manager put Halston in charge of ordering office supplies because the salesmen at the locally-based supply company always gave a discount when Halston called in the order.

Of course, Halston didn't know why she'd been given the extra assignment. Technically, Wade wasn't supposed to know either. Being in IT, and having dominion over all forms of internal communication other than the face-to-face whispered exchanges that take place in the break room, he saw and knew a lot of things he wasn't supposed to. He'd come upon that juicy tidbit of information from monitoring email exchanges between the office manager, a surly woman with a thick Jersey accent who liked to make trouble, and one of her counterparts at a satellite office.

Wade had worked in enough office settings to know that office managers, the ones the powers-that-be put in charge of monitoring everyone else, are really the ones upper-management should monitor. They have entirely too much control over the inner-workings of a business, and generally exercise their power with limited oversight because the business managers—most of them men—prefer not to get involved in what they deem to be woman's work. Lost in such thoughts, Wade shook his head with frustration. The view from his cubicle was far more expansive than any afforded to management in a corporate ivory tower.

Wade rifled through the file folders on the return side of Halston's desk briefly, not finding or expecting to find anything of value there. He was about to give up and return to his station in IT when his eyes wandered over to the far right corner of Halston's desk where the return and main desk were joined. That one small area was partially shielded from view by the raised granite-covered counter in front of her desk facing the lobby.

Halston's work station and desk were below the raised granite counter so that her monitor, phones, files and the like could not be viewed by guests who approached from the lobby. Everyone else in the office had cubicle walls on at least three sides to provide a sense of personal space. They could display photos on those walls, post calendars or notes, clutter their desks with displays of humorous cards and bean-bag animals, or even hang colorful drawings from their children in their work space. The receptionist didn't have that luxury.

Halston was always on display; her work area necessarily open to the surrounding lobby. Using someone who looked like Halston to make a first impression for a business was a wise move. Unfortunately, it came with a downside, albeit only to her. She had no privacy at all. Her work area was completely open, with one small exception—the corner on the right.

A shiny object shoved in the far back of the corner caught his eye. It was a matte silver-toned photo frame presently displaying a picture of an overweight cat. When he moved the frame, the fat cat fell from its resting spot. Apparently, Halston hadn't bothered to insert the photo into the frame.

Upon closer inspection, Wade discovered the reason the cat photo wasn't inside the frame—it wasn't compatible, and size had nothing to do with it. The frame didn't accommodate that medium. It was devised for photos of the digital sort.

He flipped the device from side to side to locate its access ports. Despite the cool satin-finished metal exterior, the device was nothing more than a computer's cousin. It was battery-powered, and held information via a digital memory chip. Wade felt the rush. This fancy little gadget was about to be putty in his hands.

He hustled back to his cubicle in IT and pulled a standard USB cord from a side drawer. He connected the frame to one of his computer's USB ports, easily bypassed the device's minimal security protocols, and began to explore the stored files. Most of them were standard .jpg files, or at least they appeared to be on the surface. Wade scratched a spot on the back of his head that had an itch, probably caused by the wild idea bouncing around in his brain. Maybe it was his skewed perspective that prompted the notion; maybe it was desperation.

These days, pictures can hold more than just a thousand words. They can house entire treatises. Hiding information in files that appear to be something else wasn't just for spies anymore. Anyone could do it with steg software readily available over the Internet.

Fortunately, the very same software, or more precisely the high-tech professional version of it Wade had on his computer at home, could reverse the process and find data that had been hidden in files. The rush he'd felt earlier rose into a wave of desire, crested, and then crashed. He had never wanted to be at home in front of his computer more than he did right now. Unfortunately, his computer wasn't at home anymore. It was on a layover at FDLE.

"Kark!" Wade muttered in true *Legacy* style, before posing a follow-up query to himself. "Now what?"

He had access to the Internet though the office's intranet servers. That posed too many risks. Anything typed into a computer there was traceable. But what if this device held the answer and saved Halston's life? Would losing his job really matter then?

The answer eluded him. On one hand, he might save Halston. On the other hand, the search could lead to nothing yet cost him everything. There was still a chance he might not go down for his prior mistakes. He didn't want to make another one. Riley would know. She would know exactly what to do.

Wade pulled out his cell phone and dialed his new favorite number. He forced extra air into his lungs by breathing deeply and then swallowed hard, hoping that would be enough to extinguish the internal fire that was causing his heart to race and temperature to rise.

"Hi, Wade. What's got you up so early on a Sunday?" Riley obviously recognized his number.

Wade swallowed hard again, and then tried to speak.

"I think . . .," his voice rose to a never-before-reached height, and then broke. He stopped to take a few more deep breaths. "I think I've found something."

He was starting to sound more like himself now. "It seems like something. I mean, it could be something, or maybe it's nothing."

"Okay, calm down, and try to speak slowly. What is it that you've found?"

"It's a photo frame. Not like a regular one, but one of those digital thingies that you upload pictures to from digital cameras or your phone. It looked like a regular frame because she had a photo of a cat stuck on the front of it."

"Where did you find it?" Riley asked.

"It was on Halston's desk. I was checking out her computer and then I noticed it. I didn't find anything on her computer, by the way."

"Where is it now?"

"It's here, with me."

Riley sighed. Thankfully, she had a lot of practice pulling information out of someone too nervous to think. "Where are you, then?"

"Oh, yeah, okay. I'm at my cubicle. At work," Wade announced.

"I see. All right, let me think for a moment." Riley looked over at Sam, who was staring quizzically at her.

She whispered an apology before she quietly moved to another room. "It's a client. I've got to take this."

Sam nodded. "Go ahead, I'll keep your spot warm," he teased, while patting the floor beside him.

They had spent the morning in Riley's den selecting exhibits from the morass of documents provided by Mikles for Audra's deposition.

They were working together well, with none of Sam's usual attempts to misdirect the focus until now. Riley rolled her eyes at him before ducking into the study and closing the double doors behind her.

"Okay, Wade. Here's what we need to do." Her announcement was met by silence. "Wade? Are you there?" She heard a clanking noise and a few loud bumps on the other end of the line, before she heard Wade's voice again.

"Dropped the phone. Sorry," Wade advised, breathlessly.

"Okay. First of all, calm down. I need you to stay cool because I'm going to call Kristina." Riley counseled. "She will need to secure this potential evidence from that location. I'm not sure if she can make it there today, so you may have to store it somewhere there for safekeeping. Can you do that?"

"Yeah, I've got drawers that lock on my desk and the whole IT area is also locked. Only me, my boss and a couple of other people have access. So you don't want me to find out what's on this? It could be nothing, and then we'd be wasting Kristina's time."

"Or it could be everything. If it is, and you've accessed it before it's in the hands of law enforcement, then the chain of custody is shot all to hell, and pretty much anything found on it becomes worthless in court."

"Well, okay, that makes sense. I was thinking more about Halston and finding her, not about what happens in court."

"I understand, and that is paramount. However, if for some reason, we can't find her or worse yet, she's been seriously injured or killed, we need to be able to find and prosecute whoever is responsible. We don't want this guy to get away with this, or be free to harm other people."

"Yeah, okay. I get that. But we gotta move fast. Halston's still missing. And now, with the storm . . . ," his voice trailed off momentarily. "I just don't have a good feeling about things, and I think this could be a real lead."

"I'll get Kristina over there as fast as I can. Hold tight and I'll call you back," Riley said.

Wade grimaced when the call ended. Riley was the only thing helping him cling to the remaining thread of his sanity. Maintaining his grasp was exponentially harder when he didn't have something connecting him to her voice of reason.

He leaned back into his chair. Waiting didn't suit him, although it was a better alternative than doing something to screw things up more than he already had. Hacking into Halston's gaming system and computer seemed like a good idea at the time; that time had long-since passed. Now, the whole thing was a waking nightmare. His mind was spinning. In its dizzying flight, it revisited scenes, images and voices from the past few days. For some reason, it settled on Justin's commentary on zombies, maybe because he felt like one right now.

"Heh, zombies. Maybe the pictures on the frame are photos of zombies and one of them took Halston," he mused aloud. It was a stupid thought. It made him smile briefly, though, and the levity calmed his nerves.

He wiped a bead of sweat from his forehead with the back of his hand. The backup generator didn't do much for the air conditioning system. In emergencies, whatever part of the cooling system that received power was directed to the server room. It was more than a little warm in the office, and his fit of anxiety hadn't helped to lower the temperature any.

He began to fan himself with the cat photo from Halston's photo frame. It was on thick photo stock paper, and moved the air in front of him easily. His eyes focused on the picture as it moved back and forth in front of his face. Halston had a cat. He hated cats. He didn't feel bad about that, though, because the feeling was mutual. They hated him back.

Plus, cats aren't real pets anyway. They don't come when called, and they aren't loyal. You could spend years taking care of one, and it would still up and leave your ass in a heartbeat if you didn't feed it one time. Lost in his thoughts, a sneer moved crossed his face. Cats were fickle beasts. Cats suck!

The sneer was soon replaced by a furrowed brow, his mind now filling with new questions. It was bizarre. Bizarre because he hadn't seen a cat when he was watching Halston through her webcam. Although, he hadn't watched for long and couldn't see in every room.

Even so, it was odd the furball wasn't there when they searched the place the other day. It should've been happy to see people after a few days alone. Or it might've seen someone take Halston. Since all humans probably look alike to felines, it could've been hiding out of fear. Maybe it wasn't Halston's cat at all. Although, if it wasn't her cat, why would she have a random cat photo on her desk?

Wade looked more closely at the photo. It wasn't obvious at first. Someone was holding the cat in the picture. The hands were slight. Whoever they belonged to had chosen an obnoxious shade of bright pink fingernail polish. Those were the hands of a girl, and this particular girl was wearing a thick silver ring that he'd seen before. Halston wore that ring. Those were her hands. The cat was Halston's.

Wade picked up his phone and hit the "Redial" button. It rang a few times before Riley answered.

"Hi, Wade. No news yet. I had to leave a message for Kristina."

"There's a cat."

"Yes, I know. You told me about the photo," Riley confirmed.

"No, I mean, Halston had a cat. We didn't find a cat. So, where is the cat?"

Riley paused a moment to consider his point. "That's a good question. Let me try Kristina again."

CHAPTER 29

Riley took one last look in the mirror before heading downstairs. To her knowledge, there was no dress code for attending a deposition at opposing counsel's house. Best bet was to keep it simple. She had chosen a simple black sheath dress, deeming it the most suitable attire for an informal proceeding. It was far more conservative than what she had worn the last time she attended a deposition with Sam. That was then; this was now. Things were vastly different.

She added a bit of sparkle to the fitted frock with the addition of a pearl and diamond brooch set in white gold fashioned in the shape of a dragonfly. The ornate insect appeared to flutter elegantly just above her heart on the left side of the asymmetrical neckline. Dragon-flies are supposed to be good luck. Hopefully, this little fellow would live up to the lore. Combining the dress with a medium-heeled pair of dark snakeskin pumps finished off the look as she intended–professional yet unassuming.

The goal today was not to intimidate Audra, appearance-wise. As a former stripper, odds were more than likely Audra was accustomed to being the most attractive woman in a room. It could unsettle her if she didn't perceive herself to be the fairest of them all today. No need to ruffle her feathers on that front. If anything, Riley was hoping she might appeal to Audra as her gender counterpart—someone who knows what it's like to navigate in a man's world.

Riley had pulled her long, dark hair back in a tight chignon; something she often did when appearing in court. Sam wasn't too far off with his acknowledgment that a woman's hair can be a distraction for men, although in his assessment the distraction was a positive. That did not always hold true.

Outside of the more intimate situations Sam was imagining and the occasional need to disarm an opponent, turning a man's thoughts toward the prurient rarely serves a woman in the legal profession well. Too often Riley had seen judges dismiss the insightful arguments of a female attorney in court for no apparent reason other than the fact she appeared too feminine. Heaven help her on the day Lady Justice chose to wear red or show a hint of cleavage.

In her last moment of solitude, Riley pulled her cell phone from her purse and dialed Dani's number. They'd spoken briefly yesterday, once the storm had fully passed. Dani and her boys had weathered the storm well, with only a few downed branches and a broken window from an errant lawn decoration to report.

Random news updates Riley received via SMS services on her cell indicated the town, as a whole, also avoided any major tragedy of the Greek variety. For an ancient god and a Cat-4 storm, Adonis had come with more bark than bite. It was as if the author of the storied legend's latest fable merely employed the namesake storm as a device to stop the city's inhabitants in their tracks and remind them to appreciate the beauty in little things—like electricity, or a warm bath.

"Hey, Boss," Dani chirped. "The power on over there?"

"Nope, not yet," Riley advised. "Reports say it could still be a few days. Power company doesn't want to turn the juice back on until they're sure the lines are secure."

"That's what they tell people, anyway. I think it's a conspiracy to make the feds think we need more assistance," Dani said.

Riley chuckled. "Nothing is ever dull or ordinary in your mind's eye, is it?"

"No reason it should be," Dani quipped. "You off to tangle with Elson?"

"Just about. Since the deposition could take most of the day, I wanted to let you know beforehand that you might be hearing from Wade. His IT team is doing solo eight-hour shifts to monitor the equipment until full power is restored. His next shift is sometime later today. Thing is, he's going to have a visitor."

"Okay. What's with the dramatic lead-in? You gonna tell me who or let me imagine?" Dani inquired. "You know letting my mind wander can be dangerous."

"I was getting to that," Riley chided. "Kris is going to stop by while Wade's on duty to pick up a digital frame he found on Halston's desk yesterday. We're hoping it might have some useful information on or in it."

"This case is starting to sound like a television crime drama," Dani said.

"It's more like the real-life stories television borrows from. What they're planning to do with the data is a bit over my head, but both Wade and Kristina seemed excited about the prospects."

"Does Wade know Kris is coming? And come to think of it, won't Kris need a subpoena to enter the business?"

"Yes, Wade knows she's coming. We talked about the subpoena. Kris believes it won't be necessary to notify the business because she's not searching any of their records. The frame belonged to Halston. She's now officially missing, although the public announcement has been delayed. The examination of her personal property is part of the ongoing investigation."

"Got it. What do you need me to do?" Dani asked.

"Keep me posted if anything comes up I need to know about. I told Wade to call you directly, figuring you would know better than he what was an emergency and what wasn't. He's a little hyped-up right now," Riley responded.

Dani couldn't help but sympathize. "Poor guy. I'd be surprised if he wasn't. His whole life just went to the crapper. He had no business doing what he did, but I don't think he meant any harm."

"I dunno. I'd be pretty pissed if someone did that to me," Riley stated.

Dani paused to consider the scenario from a personal perspective. "Maybe I'm the odd one out. I think it's kinda romantic. After being married for umpteen years and having two kids, I'd be a little honored if someone wanted a peek at my goodies."

"Leave it you to turn a hot mess into a tale of twisted romance," Riley teased. Their familiar conversation eased her nerves considerably.

"Yeah, that's me. Twisted," Dani acknowledged with a giggle. "You already knew that."

"Yes, I did."

"All right, I've got Wade covered. Anything else I need to know?" Dani asked.

"Not at the moment. I'll call you if something comes up."

"I think you mean *when* something comes up, right? Let's be real. You're going to the deposition of a former stripper at the home of Elson, the Twinkling Toon, accompanied by none other than your buddy, Dash Riprock. If something doesn't come out of that, I'll kiss a frog."

"Point taken. I'll surely be calling you later," Riley conceded.

"Now you're talking. Have fun," Dani teased before ending the call.

Sam stood at the bottom of the stairs, surveying Riley as she descended. He was wearing a stylish midnight blue sport coat over a crisp, white shirt. His tan pants were impeccably pressed, if their sharp crease were any indication. The shine on his cordovan dress shoes was fresh.

"Let me guess," Riley surmised when within range, "you have an entire spring wardrobe hidden somewhere in that little coupe of yours."

"That would be clever, were it so," Sam acknowledged. "Lovely dress you're wearing. One question, though. Weren't you going to amp up the heels to give us a height advantage?"

"Oh no, you don't get to change the subject on me with something as lame as that," Riley challenged.

"Perhaps you should refresh my recollection. What was the subject, again?"

"Your clothes. That jacket. Where did they come from?"

"My assistant. Mona dropped them off a little while ago, while you were upstairs getting ready."

"I didn't hear the door. I can hear the bell, even upstairs," Riley said.

"You've met Mona. When have you ever heard her coming?" Sam inquired.

"That's true," Riley conceded. "I take it I'm not the only one who's noticed that about her?"

"You are not," Sam admitted. "I'm not sure how she manages it, and I'm not sure I want to know. She seems to have a sixth sense when it comes to timing. She's odd, but effective."

"Clearly. Now, as to your other query, I've decided to let you have the height advantage today. You can be the imposing one. I'll be the one who sees things eye-to-eye. Get it?"

A half-smile and a nod signaled he did. "A rather good play, Miss Morgan. Are you sure you don't want to spruce other things up?"

"Spruce up? What the hell are you talking about?"

"You know," Sam continued while gesturing toward his mid-chest with both hands cupped.

"Oh, good lord, Sam. What is it with you trying to undress me in public? I'm not a Barbie doll," Riley rebuked. "This is what I intend to wear. I have my reasons."

"Very well," Sam said. He motioned toward the door that led to Riley's garage. "On that note, shall we?"

"Yes, we shall. But before we do…." Riley popped into the kitchen and returned shortly with two bottles of distilled water. She thrust one of the bottles toward Sam. "Take this."

"Why?"

"Just take it, okay."

Sam accepted the bottle and slid it into the side of his briefcase. Although he wasn't inclined to take orders from a woman, it seemed harmless enough in this instance.

"Anything else you'd like me to take from you?" he teased.

Riley wasn't in the mood for jokes. "Did you get the exhibits?"

It finally dawned on Sam; Riley wasn't in a playful mood and wasn't interested in doing anything to change that. It was possible she was nervous, or maybe just tired. Either way, there was no point in wasting his time trying to keep things light. She would lighten up when she was ready.

Sam adopted a more serious tone. "Yes. The exhibits are already in the car."

"As we should be," Riley confirmed, following an upward glance at her wall clock.

She followed Sam into the garage, closing and locking the door behind them. They rode in silence during the initial part of the drive to Elson's house, partly because they were both surveying the damage in surrounding areas, and partly because Riley was still miffed at Sam's presumption. She might be working with him on this case, but her body wasn't part of the deal. It was hers alone, to do with what she will. Who did he think he was, anyway?

"You might not want to take Robinson Street because it usually floods just before you get to Orange," Riley advised, finally breaking the quiet between them.

"I wasn't planning to," Sam advised. He cast a sideways glance in her direction. "Are you going to pout the rest of the day, Miss Morgan? Surely, you know I've nothing but the utmost respect for you and your various bits and pieces."

"Is that your idea of an apology, Sam?"

"No. I don't believe an apology is in order. I was addressing a point of strategy; one you've employed before, to be exact," Sam advised. "You can't have it both ways. That being said, I also don't think it's good for our client if you're unhappy. I was trying to play nice."

Riley stared out the window. She wasn't as angry as she let on. Mostly, she was perplexed. So many things about Sam just didn't add up, like the one that held her interest now.

"Where did Mona get your clothes from? The power's not on yet downtown. Did you make her climb all those stairs to your penthouse?"

"No. I did not," Sam replied.

"Well, then. What? Does she just keep your clothes at her place in case you get caught somewhere without your pants?"

Sam turned to face Riley with a wicked grin.

"Nope. Don't answer that. I don't want to know. Just watch the road and drive," Riley said.

"It's not what you think," Sam offered with feigned seriousness.

"Sure. Whatever, you say. I really don't want to know."

"Seriously," Sam said. "I'm fairly certain the woman despises me. She's all about business. There's nothing personal to it."

"Let's talk about something more pertinent."

"Such as?" Sam inquired.

"Such as how many questions do you think it will take for me to get Audra to crack?" Riley teased.

"Ah, now that is an interesting topic. Shall we make a friendly wager?" Sam asked.

"Sure, why not?"

"All right, I'll give you twenty questions, aside from the standard introductory sort," Sam offered.

"Ha, you're on," Riley responded. "What do I get when I win?"

"A tad confident, are we?"

"I've done this before," Riley challenged. "I've got a pretty good idea how it's gonna go."

Sam smiled the wicked smile, again. "We'll see. So, if you win what would you like as your prize?"

"How about you peel me some grapes, Tarzan?"

Sam smirked. "That's a good one. You have a deal. I'm sure I can find something from a vine that will suit your fancy. What do I get if you don't win?"

"Not much chance of it," Riley assured. "I guess if I don't have Audra in tears by twenty questions, you can choose something for me to wear. Just once, and it can't be something I can't wear in public."

"I like the odds and the prize. This day just keeps getting better," Sam added.

He turned down a side road to avoid the main thoroughfare which, according to the report he received from Mona this morning, was still blocked by storm debris. A few round-a-bouts and right turns later, he was back on the beaten path, and they were nearly there.

"I heard the neighborhood where Elson lives was built over an abandoned missile testing site," Riley said.

Sam nodded. "I've heard likewise. It's hard to imagine that as a suitable environment for residential development, much less a community geared toward families."

"You haven't met Elson, have you?" Riley asked.

"We met a few times during the EEOC investigation, prior to the lawsuit," Sam said. "The meetings were brief. Donatti claimed his client had no interest in conciliation. Mikles didn't have an interest in it either, at the time."

"If you spend much time around Elson, you'll see it suits him perfectly to nest over potentially live munitions. He gets a charge from playing fast and loose."

"Sounds like a fun guy."

"You would say that," Riley chided.

She rotated in her seat to collect her purse and briefcase from the back seat as Sam pulled into a driveway beside a pale blue Victorian-style row house. The small yard in front of the house was outlined with a white picket fence, a detail undoubtedly intended to augment the crisp white gingerbread-style trim work. The other houses in the area appeared to have been cut from the same mold. Different pastel hues were all that distinguished the replicated façades.

On their way to the front door, Sam assessed the three story structure. "Dreadful and wankish," he concluded. "Did Elson choose to live here or was there a woman involved?"

"Hard to tell with him," Riley responded. "For all I know, he may still live with his mother."

Sam laughed aloud. "I guess we're about to find out."

Following the second ring of an overly amped doorbell, Elson Ortiz-Donatti greeted them at the door. He looked relaxed in a vibrant cerulean short-sleeve golf style shirt and black slacks. Just before he moved back inside with Riley and Sam in tow, nature's spotlight highlighted the luminous fabric of Elson's shirt. For a brief moment, as was so often the case, the slight man appeared to sparkle.

Once inside, Sam and Riley were greeted by Elson's client, Audra Weyland, who all but ignored Sam while turning a keen focus toward Riley.

"Audra, I believe you met Sam during the earlier proceedings. He seems to have a new sidekick today, who you likely haven't met." Elson gestured in Riley's direction. "This is Riley Morgan. We've crossed paths a few times in the past. I presume she is attending today's deposition as counsel for the defense?"

Elson framed the latter statement as a query. He emphasized its nature as such by turning to face Sam with quizzical eyes. Sam nodded an affirmation.

"Very well, then. We're still waiting for the court reporter," Elson advised. "He should be along shortly."

This was the first time Riley had seen Audra, and vice versa. Each woman quietly assessed the other in the way only women can. As the only two women in the room, some sense of competition was inherent regardless of the circumstances of their meeting.

At five feet seven, Audra was possibly an inch, maybe two, taller than Riley. Riley internally applauded her strategy of wearing moderate heels. Not only did the unassuming footwear place her just above eye level with Elson, they very likely had the intended impact or more specifically, lack of impact, on Audra.

Given her height and the stiletto heels she had chosen to wear, it was clear Audra expected to stand a head above everyone except Sam. With that type of height advantage, she wasn't likely to perceive Riley as a threat, which was more than fine. It was easy enough to concede on appearances, so long as Riley had the advantage in the one thing that mattered—pulling information from her unsuspecting opponent.

Unlike some of the other dancers Riley had encountered during her brief visit to The Polling Place last week, Audra had an athletic build. She wasn't overly endowed in any particular direction. Her long, auburn hair was styled in one of those trendy stick-straight, blow-out styles more often seen on college-age girls. The canary yellow sleeveless mini-dress she wore was adorned with a wide gold zipper that ran from top to bottom down the front center of the dress. It reminded Riley of the kind one might find at the mall in those stores that use loud music and exceptionally low prices to draw in teenage girls by droves.

It was possible the zipper had broken midway down the front of the dress, or perhaps Audra had chosen not to fasten it. Either way, a generous amount of the pale, slightly freckled skin of her bodice and décolleté was noticeably exposed. She had, not surprisingly, made the most of the revealing neckline by utilizing a demi-bra or similar undergarment which forced the swells of her breasts upward and out.

All told, none of that would have been an issue if she had purchased the dress in the correct size. Clearly she hadn't. As a result, the bodice puckered on the sides, giving in to the laws of physics that challenged its ability to contain the overload of contents under pressure.

Although hardly a professional style, the frock wasn't unattractive. It just wasn't one you'd expect to see on a woman who, according to the scant records in her personnel file, was over thirty. It didn't help that the way Audra had chosen to wear the dress only served to reinforce the impression of a backward reach. The pairing of the junior-department dress with her youthful hair style made it appear Audra was trying to recreate the glory days of her early twenties. And while the combination did make her appear younger, what she did not appear to be was guileless or wholesome.

Riley had expected Elson to "style" Audra for the deposition, putting her in something designed to appear demure and at least remotely professional. By all outward indications, that didn't happen. Either Audra had not given him a say in the matter, or he'd chosen a different approach. Audra's look was exactly the opposite of what Riley would have advised.

It would be hard enough to garner sympathy for Audra as a plaintiff given her prior employment as an exotic dancer. The last thing someone should want, as her advocate, would be the appearance that she courted men's attention when off stage, and thereby courted trouble. There was only one reason Elson might have allowed Audra to indulge in her usual sense of style today.

"You mentioned a court reporter. Will the deposition also be videotaped? I believe Sam had requested a videographer," Riley inquired, seeking to confirm her suspicion.

"No, not today. We don't have enough power to run that type of equipment," Elson advised. "I believe we sent a letter to Sam's office advising that resources would be limited under the circumstances."

Now it made sense. If only auditory testimony was on today's menu, Audra could dress as she pleased and clearly had done so. On one hand, it gave Riley insight into Audra's personality. She required attention from men—a lot of attention. On the other hand, Audra's overtly sexual style of dress might make it difficult to keep Sam focused on the task at hand, which may have been Audra's or perhaps Elson's intent. Apparently, they didn't know Sam wasn't the one who would be asking the questions today.

It occurred to Riley that, for once, Sam might have put aside his own interest on behalf of his client when he made the decision to put her in the lead. The choice allowed them to circumvent any attempt by Elson to use Sam's proclivities against him. Perhaps Sam had learned a few things when she used the same tactic against his client Tony Giordano. It was possible he came away from that exchange more aware of his own limitations than he had let on.

Riley's eyes rolled in response to the counter-argument that interjected itself into her internal monologue. It was far more likely Sam had asked her to lead the deposition because he wanted to watch two women go at it. That would explain why he was seemingly disappointed she hadn't chosen to dress more provocatively this morning.

During the moment of silence between them, Elson took a position in front of Riley, looking at her admiringly from an inch below her eye level. He seemed to get shorter with each encounter.

"I do have to apologize, Miss Morgan. I only sent the letter to Sam's office. I didn't see your name on the certificate of service," Elson crooned. "Are you on the case full-time now? Or are you just covering for Bunny today?"

Sam answered before Riley could. "We made a last minute personnel adjustment. I told you about it when we spoke, yesterday."

"You did, indeed, tell me you had substitute counsel, Mr. Stone," Elson acknowledged. "What you didn't tell me was that I would have the lovely Miss Morgan gracing my table today. I'm pleased to have another chance encounter, milady."

Elson took a hold of Riley's hand and raised it to his mouth for a wet kiss.

Ewwww. Riley withdrew her hand and quickly surveyed their surroundings. "Do you have a powder room nearby?"

Elson stepped away and motioned for Riley to follow. "Indeedy, I do. Let me show you the way."

He led Riley down a gallery with walls embellished with an assortment of modern art paintings. If Riley had encountered similar art work at a gallery or festival, she would have easily imagined it to be the type someone like Elson might relish. The artists' renderings were abstract; devoid of any recognizable form. The colors employed, red being chiefly among them, were exceedingly bright and almost fluorescent.

The careful placement of each piece along the wall, which included curious pairings of large and ornate paintings with small and demure mixed media, appeared intentional–as if some story was being told. Each work of art was apparently a chapter or verse. Whatever message Elson intended to convey with the art, however, wasn't readily apparent. The story told, true or otherwise, appeared to be one that could only be known to the author.

Elson stopped midway down the gallery in front of one of the paintings. He beamed with pride while he fussed with a speck of dust on the frame only he could see. "They are lovely, don't you think?"

Riley preferred the classics, but the medium did have its place. "Modern art seems to suit you," she commented. "It also goes nicely with your décor."

"I inherited much of it from my Aunt Erma. She was the collector in the family, and the artist. Her porcelain renderings went for a pretty penny after her death at the turn of the century."

Riley nodded as one does when only half-listening. *Turn of the century?* That meant in or around the year 2000–just twelve years ago. Naturally, Elson would find a way to make that sound more dramatic.

Elson cast another beaming gaze at his prized painting before dispensing the remaining directions to Riley. He nodded in the general direction she would be heading.

"The powder room is just around the corner, second door on the left."

"Thanks. No need to wait. I can find my way back."

"Excellent. We'll meet you in the foyer and then we can all go up to the conference room. It's over the garage."

Riley nodded absently, again. The whole setup for this deposition was too surreal for words. She made the short jaunt toward Elson's powder room, leaving him in the gallery to admire his own storytel-ing art work.

Riley twisted the small, round oiled-bronze knob on the second door on the left and entered a dark room. A reasonable expectation would be to find a light switch on the wall, somewhere near the door. She felt around the wall in both directions, briefly encountering several cold, hard objects on inset shelves before she landed on the switch. Then there was light. It was not good.

Even with the lights on, the room was dimly lit. The two-light fixture over the small pedestal style sink was sporting ancient-looking glass bulbs that might have had 15 watts between them, if they had a watt at all. The faint light was enough, however, for her to identify the nature of the cold, hard objects she had encountered on the wall. The objects, and their many companions which filled built-in shelves along the other three walls, were ornate porcelain depictions of outhouses—some with partially-disrobed porcelain inhabitants.

Riley suddenly wished she hadn't left her purse along with her briefcase in the foyer with Sam. A picture of this room would be its own form of art. If given the chance, she would make an excuse to return to the powder room on their way out. Dani was in need of a new addition to her photographic collection of the inexplicable.

CHAPTER 30

"I am Valdé, reporter on courts."

The muscle-laden, darkly-tanned brute had abruptly ended his approach at the top of the stairs that led from Elson's three-car garage to the makeshift conference room above before heralding his own arrival.

Elson and Audra had already taken seats across from Sam and Riley at Elson's custom-made, split-wood conference table. All four had settled into the black and white cow-pattern printed suede leather chairs that surrounded the rustic table, while waiting for the most essential attendee to arrive. Without a court reporter, there wasn't anything to report.

Elson had been quietly whispering advice and assurances to Audra, while Sam checked his phone and Riley assessed the décor. Before the sound of heavy footsteps distracted her, she had come to the conclusion that "suburbanite dude ranch" was the look Elson was going for in this room. By her estimate, he'd likely paid some Winter Park domiciled decorator a pretty penny to come up with the unusual stylings. Love it or hate it, the room made a statement all its own.

As the last to arrive, the hulking court reporter stood fixed in place at the top of the stairs, waiting for permission to enter. All four inside the room stared blankly back at him, wondering why the hell he didn't just take a seat. Not surprisingly, Sam took the lead in resolving the impasse.

Sam rose from his seat to greet the imposing figure. "Please, do join us. We've saved your place at the end of the table."

Permission granted. The floor groaned beneath the man-giant's feet on his approach. He placed his equipment bag on the floor behind his appointed seat, and stood behind his chair looking randomly at each person in the group before him. He was obviously waiting for someone to commence formal introductions.

Sam, still standing and facing Valdé, leaned forward and extended a hand across the table. He ended the announcement with a nod in Riley's direction. "Sam Stone, counsel for the Defendant, and this is my co-counsel, Riley Morgan."

Valdé accepted Sam's salutation with a broad, toothy smile that revealed not only the cavernous dimples in both cheeks, but the wide gap between his front teeth. His smile remained fixed while he extended his hand to accept Sam's with a forceful grip. Valdé's man-paw dwarfed Sam's masculine, more-than-adequate hand in the process—a phenomenon Sam had likely not previously encountered. Riley wondered if it unsettled Sam not to be the most imposing figure in the room. If so, he gave no indication and recovered gallantly.

"I don't believe we've worked together before. What agency are you with?" Sam inquired.

"I work for Valdé."

Sam sent a curious look in Riley's direction, before continuing. "You freelance?"

The large man nodded methodically. Up, down, up, down, stop. Sam waited a few moments after the motion stopped, expecting something verbal to follow. When it did not, he pressed on.

"Do you have a last name, Valdé? We'll need to read it into the record."

"I am Valdé."

"So, no last name, then?"

The six-foot five hulk nodded again. Left, right, left, right, stop. This time he chose to embellish his answer. "Second name hard for America to spell. Easier, just Valdé."

"I see. And how do you spell your first name then, if you don't mind me asking?" Sam had already accepted the fact he was going to have to work for what little information Valdé had to offer.

"It's Vee-Ay-El-Dee-Eh, with special on the 'Eh.' Pronounce like I say, 'Val' and 'Day.' Am from Norway. Is like Sweden, only besser." The man's blindingly white-blonde hair and pale blue eyes had made the latter part somewhat obvious, as did his Muppet-like accent. "I have card with name. I give to you."

"I'm glad you were able to make it on such short notice," Elson chimed in, suddenly deciding to play host again while Valdé searched for a business card. He rose from his seat next to Audra and danced on air in his approach to the end of the table where Valdé stood. "We're all ready, so once you get set up we can get started."

Elson looked up admiringly at Valdé, who towered a good 18 inches or more above him, an amusing juxtaposition that didn't escape Riley's keen notice. Elson almost always made a hasty retreat when in the presence of tall women, yet he seemed unnaturally pleased to see the gigantic Scandinavian. "While you're unpacking, can I get you anything to drink?" Elson offered cordially.

Valdé shook his head to decline. He directed his gaze to the tray in the center of the table that displayed a pitcher of water surrounded by tall glasses. He handed Elson a stack of business cards as he spoke. "I see water on table. Is good for Valdé."

"That's quite accurate," Elson affirmed. He dismissively tucked the business cards into a pant pocket without bothering to review or share them. "I only use water that is drawn and distilled from a local spring. I think it's important to support local businesses, like yours. You run a small shop like me, Valdé. Our friend Sam, here, is from one of those fancy international law firms."

Riley nearly choked on the lozenge she had popped in her mouth. The pectin based pastille was a pre-deposition custom for her. If she was going to be speaking for the better part of the next hour or two, her throat would need to be cajoled into cooperation.

Choking on the very thing that was supposed to appease her vocal chords wasn't part of the plan, but was unavoidable in the face of Elson's blatant pandering. She couldn't tell whether his intent was to curry favor with the court reporter to gain an advantage in today's deposition, or whether he was seeking to establish a rapport on a more long-term, personal level. Either way, his interest in pleasing the man was palpable, humorous, and gag-worthy.

Sam addressed the apparent irony more directly. "That's an interesting philosophy you have, Elson. Of course, Riley's firm is also local, and you know my client, Vincent Mikles, owns and operates a number of businesses here in Central Florida. In fact, this is where his empire started."

Ignoring Riley's earlier implied admonition not to drink the enemy's water, Sam reached across the table and took one of the glasses that surrounded the water pitcher. He poured a glass of the "local" elixir, and took a sip before continuing.

"This is excellent. It's also excellent to know you take the interests of the local economy seriously, Elson."

Elson cast a cutting look in Sam's direction. He wasn't speaking to Sam and held no reverence, local or otherwise, for the interests of his client. He donned an air of annoyance and wore it convincingly on the short walk back to his seat next to Audra. "Speaking of your client, Mr. Stone, where is he? I thought the renowned Mr. Mikles was going to grace us with his presence today."

By the end of the inquiry, Elson had managed to fully replace the pleasing tone he used in speaking to Valdé with one of derision. Sam apparently found the mercurial change amusing, and donned a Cheshire grin to accompany his retort. This was the type of pot he lived to stir.

"Mikles planned to attend the deposition as scheduled. The storm changed his plans," Sam advised. "He is attending to damage and delays it caused to his businesses right now. Vince has quite a few employees who depend on their jobs to feed their families."

Elson pursed his full lips, and rolled his eyes mockingly. "Of course, he is. And I'm sure he alone will be carrying Central Florida on his back during the storm recovery. Be that as it may, I trust you'll remind him none of that will excuse him from appearing for his own deposition tomorrow."

Sam returned to his seat and leaned against the back of his chair nonchalantly while holding steady gaze on the small man sitting across from him. His easy smile and shoulder shrug said what his chosen words did not. He wasn't concerned in the least. "You may want to see what today brings before concerning yourself with tomorrow, Elson."

The rush of impending battle flushed Elson's face. He chose to try on righteous indignation for size. It turned out to be a tad small.

"Is that a threat, Mr. Stone? We've made good-faith efforts to keep this case on schedule, in spite of recent setbacks. I expect you to do the same. Are you planning to produce your client, or not?"

"There was nothing at all threatening about Sam's comment, Elson. He was simply stating a fact," Riley replied calmly.

Without an intervention, Sam might happily toy with Elson the remainder of the day. As amusing as that might turn out to be, it wasn't going to get Audra's testimony on the record. Getting under opposing counsel's skin had its advantages, but at the moment, it wasn't narrowly tailored to their present objective.

Riley cast a sideways glance at Sam and then turned her focus back across the table to Elson. The men's eyes were locked on each other in an apparent "who's gonna blink first" standoff. They were both acting like little boys on the playground, measuring things only little boys value. Riley sent Sam a slight rebuke in the form of a kick under the table before her next action effectively put him in a time-out.

"Valdé is set up now, so why don't we get started?" she inquired.

Valdé nodded. "Ready as you to go."

Elson broke his visual standoff with Sam long enough to note Riley's position in the seat across from Audra. "It appears you're going to be taking the lead today, Miss Morgan. That's good. Audra has been subjected to quite enough manhandling from Mikles and his hired goons."

If Elson thought his characterization might prompt Riley to go easy on his girl, he was mistaken. Rather than respond to the obvious goad, she smiled sweetly and nodded. Elson could interpret the cue however he chose. She wouldn't be bound by it.

Riley knew firsthand the type of things Audra had likely encountered while working for Vince, and how those experiences might have impacted her. The men Audra danced before night after night at Vince's club were just like the men, if not the very same men, Riley opposed in court or from across tables much like the one separating them today. They both danced, in a manner of speaking, on stages for men, in shows owned by men. It wasn't much of a gamble to presume the similarity of their experiences had likely left them both with similar calluses and scars. Riley planned to press Audra hard where she expected it to hurt.

Riley turned her attention to Audra, who had been oddly quiet during the preceding melee. From her expression, it appeared she might rather be anywhere else than in a room above her attorney's garage today. Riley calculated Audra's sentiment to be something worth exploring. Most litigants are eager to tell their side of the story and have often waited years for the moment to come. In contrast, Audra stared intermittently at Sam or at the view through the window behind him.

"All right, Valdé, would you please swear in the witness?" Riley directed.

Valdé nodded. He pointed to Audra and raised his right hand, to suggest she do the same. He pulled a piece of paper from his pocket and stumbled through a broken-English reading of a standard witness oath, having to retreat and repeat a few parts before reaching the end.

Accepting what had vaguely sounded like an obligation to convey some form of truth, Audra responded with a tone that hinted at annoyance. "I do. Is this going to take long?"

"It will take as long as it takes," Riley countered. "I'm sure Elson has instructed you on the process, but I'll go over it again to make sure we're all on the same page."

Once Riley completed giving a standardized outline of the deposition process, she segued into basic questions to determine Audra's identity and fitness to give accurate testimony at this time.

"Would you please state your full name for the record?"

"Sure. Audra, that's spelled A-U-D-R-A, and my last name, is Weyland, W-E-Y-L-A-N-D."

"Thank you. And where do you presently reside, Audra?"

"I share a townhouse in Maitland with a couple of my friends."

Riley nodded, an intentional nonverbal cue to denote unity, prompting the deponent to continue answering questions without reservation. "Can you give me the address? We need it on record for purposes of identification."

"Sure. It's 229 West Keys Avenue."

"Do you and your friends rent or own the townhouse?" Riley continued.

"My friends own it. I rent a room from them."

"How long have you lived there?"

"I dunno, maybe four years or so. I lived there while I was working at the club."

"And what is your date of birth?"

Audra's brow furrowed and she turned to Elson for affirmation. "I don't see what that has to do with anything. I don't see why she needs to know that."

Riley had anticipated the question might ruffle Audra's feathers, which was why she hadn't followed her opening query with it. Age is a touchy subject with most women, especially those who make their living from their appearance. Youth, whether real or the well-preserved perception thereof, was an asset to be carefully guarded.

Elson rubbed Audra's arm for assurance. "It is a standard question for identification. You can answer."

"I got plenty of ID," Audra protested. "She can look at it if she wants. I don't get why I gotta tell my age to the whole world."

Riley calculated this as an opportunity to show compromise in the interest of good will. The more Audra felt Riley identified with her, the more likely she was to give something away.

"Why don't we do this? Why don't you give me the month and day of your birthday on the record, and then I'll look at your license and acknowledge your identity on the record from there?"

Audra eased back in her seat and considered Riley's proposal. "I could do that, I guess."

She pulled a small zippered wallet from her purse and opened it to display her license for Riley. Riley noted the driver's license appeared to be a current, valid Florida license, and that the picture, name and birth dates coincided with Audra's testimony.

"See, I was born on the 19th of June," Audra stated. She pointed at the birthdate displayed on her license. "That was the year."

"Very well, then. I'll note for the record upon review of Ms. Weyland's license that the deponent's identity has been sufficiently verified at this time," Riley concluded. "Now come a few questions I have to ask as precautions. They do not reflect on anything you might have said or done today or prior to today."

Audra crossed her arms in front of her body. "Okay. What is that supposed to mean?"

"It's not as big of a deal as it sounds. Basically, I have to ask you if there's any reason you might be unable to give complete, accurate and truthful testimony today. And by anything, I also mean any medications you might have taken, or any conditions you might be under."

"I object to the phrasing of that question," Elson snipped. "You make it sound like she might be under some sort of coercion on my part, and you're also implying she's lying although you haven't even asked any real questions yet."

"There was no implication and you know it, Elson. The question is standard," Riley argued.

"Even so, I want my objection noted for the record. Did you get that, Valdé?"

All eyes turned to Valdé who, as it turned out, was pecking at the stenograph machine with his two enormous index fingers, one key at a time. "Ja. Words are here."

"Wait, a minute," Riley interjected. "Do you know how to type on that machine, Valdé?"

"Valdé type some," the oafish man responded, accompanying the verbal assurance with one of his mechanical nods. He then picked up a small device he had placed in the center of the table between Riley and Audra when first unpacking his equipment. "Valdé also use recording. Machine type words for Valdé later."

"That's so reassuring," Riley retorted with a smirk. She turned to Sam with a quizzical look, as if to say, "Should we continue with this farce?"

Sam shrugged. "Let's just get what we can, for now."

"Alrighty, then. We'll do it your way," Riley conceded. "Valdé, since Elson has made an objection he wants preserved on the record, will you read it back so we can make sure it's worded properly?"

Valdé sat motionless, staring at Riley with a bewildered expression. "What is Valdé to read from?"

"And that would be my point," Riley concluded. "What can you read from, Valdé?"

"Valdé not understand the question."

Riley sighed. "Of course you don't."

She turned to face Elson just in time to catch the smug expression on his face before it faded into a blank one. It figured. He hired this cartoonish reporter on purpose. He intended for the transcript to be completely useless in court.

"Seems the court reporter you selected missed the objection, Elson. You'll have to repeat it, verbatim," Riley goaded.

"It's not a big deal. I just objected to Miss Morgan's last question," Elson cooed.

"Just to be clear," Riley interjected, "why don't we have Valdé repeat my last question?"

Valdé stared blankly back at Riley, rather than responding to the request.

Riley reiterated the question. "Can you read the last question back to us, Valdé?"

Valdé reached for the voice recorder in front of Riley. "Easier to play for you."

"I take it you will be relying on the voice recording for the accuracy of the record, is that right, Valdé?" Riley inquired.

Valdé nodded an innocent affirmation, clearly unsure what all the fuss was about.

"Hold on," Elson objected, "I don't recall the deposition notice including the right to depose our court reporter. You're out of line, Miss Morgan."

"No, Elson. I'm standing on the line you think you've cleverly drawn. Here's the deal, and it's non-negotiable," Riley stated. "If the court reporter you selected is relying on a voice recording to collect today's testimony, then I am hereby entering that voice recording into the record for this proceeding. The recording is to accompany whatever transcript Valdé manages to provide. If, for any reason, our review of the recording indicates the transcript is flawed, you will be responsible for the costs of either a revised transcript taken from the recording or a re-examination of the witness."

"You can't . . . do that, Miss Morgan," Elson stammered.

"I can, and I just did. Or do you want to try to get a judge on the phone right now to rule otherwise?"

Elson retreated back into his seat and turned his focus to Sam. "You need to explain this process to Miss Morgan, Sam. Audra and I don't take directions from her."

Sam, who had been sitting back watching the entire exchange with much pleasure, casually leaned forward to respond to Elson. "I see no reason for an explanation. It seems Miss Morgan is doing a splendid job at calling you on your bullshit." Sam then turned to Valdé to inquire. "Do you need me to spell any of that for you?"

Valdé dismissed the offer, summarily. "Valdé know of bull-sheet."

Elson alternated display of his shocked expression between Sam and Riley, offering both a full view of his lower molars via a wide-open mouth. He closed his yapper just long enough to form words of rebuke. "I've never been so insulted in a formal proceeding in my life! This is a travesty."

"Indeed," Sam acknowledged. "And it is one of your making. You insisted we go forward under these conditions, and go forward we shall. We're back on the record, Valdé, assuming there is one."

Sam then turned to face Audra. "I believe the question pending regarded your fitness to give testimony, Miss Weyland. Please instruct your client to answer the question, Elson, so we can move things along."

Audra, whose visceral response to Sam's authority was evident from her wide eyes and noticeably alert nipples beneath the thin fabric of her dress, turned to Elson for instruction.

Elson grudgingly nodded. "Go ahead, you can answer. We'll clean the record up later."

"Okay. Well, I feel fine, I guess," Audra stated. "I can answer the questions."

"Good," Riley responded. "Just to be clear, have you taken any medications recently that might impact your recollection of events?"

Audra shook her head.

"You have to answer audibly," Elson advised.

"Oh, right. No, I don't take any prescribed medications, except maybe a sleeping pill now and again. I didn't take one last night, though."

Riley followed up on the missing implication. "Have you ever taken any medications or narcotics that have not been prescribed to you by a doctor?"

Audra looked at Riley like a deer in headlights. "When do you mean?"

"I mean both recently or at any point in time."

"I object to the form of the question," Elson grumbled. "Overly broad."

Audra turned to Elson to clarify. "But, like you said before, I still have to answer, right?"

"Yes, you answer unless I tell you not to."

"Right," Audra acknowledged. "Okay, well, other than what I just said, I have occasionally taken that female Viagra stuff before a show. It helps to get in the mood, you know. All the girls take them. Well, most of them do. But I haven't done any shows since I left the club."

"Where or from whom did you obtain that medication?"

"I dunno. It was just there, if we wanted it, backstage in the dressing room."

Sensing this line of questioning could be filled with land mines detrimental to their client, Riley eased away from it and made a mental note to follow up with Sam on what could amount to a serious problem for Mikles later. Only a few more introductory questions remained, then the count began.

Per her wager with Sam on the ride over, she had only twenty substantive questions to get Audra to crack. If early indications were of any measure, it wasn't going to be an easy win. Riley had been on target with the assumption Audra might be vain. It was evident from her appearance, attire, and from her protestations to the age inquiry. She also seemed to thoroughly enjoy it when Sam took control of things. Neither trait was the sort often found in women sensitive to workplace banter. The dissonance warranted exploration. It was time to turn on the heat.

"You make it sound like you didn't enjoy performing at Vince's club. Yet in all of your employee surveys, you indicated you loved your job. Isn't that true?" Riley asked.

"What? How do they know who said what in those surveys. They were supposed to be anonymous."

"I'm the one asking questions here, Audra. Please answer the question I asked."

"I wouldn't say I loved the job. I didn't hate it either. It paid well, and the hours were good," Audra said.

"You didn't hate your job, but you took recreational drugs while you performed it. That doesn't make sense. Let's be real. You took the drugs so you would be in the mood to let some of Mikles' clients order off the menu. You earned extra money that way, didn't you?"

Audra visibly bristled. "Are you calling me a whore?"

"That is your word, not mine. I'm asking you why you took medication to enable you to do a job you say you didn't hate?" Riley deflected.

Audra glared at Riley with poison-filled eyes. She managed to force her answer through clenched teeth. "I don't know why I took them, okay. All the girls did it. It made things better."

Now they were getting somewhere. Riley leaned back in her seat and took a moment to let Audra's temper reside before asking the next question.

"What things?"

"I don't know. Having to let men paw at me all the time. Having to pretend I liked it when they talked dirty to me, or having to pose for those stupid pictures Vince would use for advertising on the web."

"Aren't those all normal situations one might encounter when employed at a gentleman's club?"

"Gentleman's club my ass," Audra spat back.

"Move to strike," Elson interjected. "Just let the record reflect my client feels strongly on the subject, Miss Morgan."

It occurred to Valdé someone might be speaking to him. "What Valdé need to swipe?"

Elson shook his head in frustration. Seemed his plan to have a less-than-adequate court reporter wasn't his brightest. "Never mind, it's on the recording."

Riley internally calculated how many more licks she would need before she exposed the soft center of this lollipop. Shouldn't be much longer at this rate. "Perhaps your client would like to elaborate on what has brought such strong sentiment to the surface, Elson?"

Elson looked at Audra to get a sense of her stability. She nodded stoically and continued.

"I'm sorry. This has all been very upsetting for me. I don't know why anyone would consider Vince to be a gentleman. He sells sex, which essentially means he sells us, his girls. And he treats us just like his inventory or some commodity. We might as well be a herd of heifers, as far as he's concerned."

Audra's humorous choice of words, given the chairs they were seated in, wasn't lost on Riley. Unfortunately, now wasn't a good time to laugh at the witness.

"Did you expect anything to be otherwise working in a position that requires you to perform nude in front of an audience of men?" Riley inquired.

"Strippers have rights, too, Miss Morgan. We're dancers, not desserts."

"I see. Assuming that to be the case, why don't you tell me what rights of yours were violated when you worked for Mr. Mikles as an exotic dancer?"

"All of them. Every right a woman has."

"Refresh my recollection as a woman, Miss Weyland. What specific rights are you referring to?"

Audra, seeming exasperated, exhaled sharply and shifted position in her seat. "The guys that work there treated the girls like we were fair game, you know. Like they could have a go at us because they saw us naked every night. And they'd say things to me. Vincent would, too. Awful things."

"What types of things?"

"They would ask me if I was 'horny' after my shows. Or if I wanted a 'ride,' and they didn't mean home. Vince would come backstage after my show sometimes, and put his hands on my shoulders like he was going to massage them. He would ask me if I needed anything."

"I'm going to get back to the first part of that, but right now I'd like to understand what you thought was so objectionable about Vince's conduct as you've just described it?"

"I don't know. It didn't seem so bad at first. At first, we got along good. He would even call me at home after my shift to see if I got in all right. Sometimes, he'd come over to check on me."

"Did something give you the impression Mr. Mikles had other intentions?"

"Nothing that he did. Anyway, I was okay with it if he did have other intentions, I guess. He's loaded and not bad looking."

"You do know he's married with children, right?"

"Oh, like that has anything to do with anything," Audra snapped. "He got around. Everyone knew it. And the girls he got around with did real well working for him. You just ask Sam's friend Bunny, if you wanna know about that."

Sam inwardly cringed, but held his surface composure. He wasn't as concerned with Audra's disparaging assertions about his client as much as the impact her testimony might have on Riley. Vince wasn't the type of squeaky-clean, do-gooder underdog Riley usually represented. Riley was impossible to contain when driven to balance the scales of justice. He'd learned that one the hard way. What remained to be seen was whether she'd stick it out in a case where justice wasn't remotely interested in tipping the scale in either direction. His concern lessened with Riley's quick volley.

"Objection. The witness is testifying to matters beyond the scope of the inquiry, and to matters of which she has no personal knowledge. The statements are also inflammatory and serve no probative value. Those last comments will be stricken from the record."

"Not if I can help it," Elson interjected.

"There's nothing about that you can help, Elson. The testimony will be tossed for all the reasons noted."

"You don't get to make rulings, Miss Morgan, just because your father was a judge. We'll let the judge in this case be the judge of that."

Invoking her father's memory was a low blow. Elson was obviously trying to distract her. She had known it was only a matter of time before someone tested that wound in the heat of battle. Someone as inane as Elson might as well be the first to try and fail, and thereby be the one anointed to tell those who followed not to bother.

"I look forward to it," Riley quipped, meeting and holding Elson's gaze with steely eyes. "Meanwhile, I'm going to finish taking your client's deposition."

Riley returned her focus to Audra. "Bunny's not here answering questions today, Audra. You are. And if I understand you correctly, you are now saying you didn't get some benefit from Mr. Mikles. your employer, because he didn't have sex with you. Is that correct?"

"I didn't follow the question. Was the question whether cr not Vince and I had sex?"

"We can break it down into small parts like that if that makes it easier for you," Riley shot back. Audra was playing dumb. She knew more than she let on.

"You don't have to be so mean about it, Miss Morgan. I'm trying real hard to answer your questions." Water started to well-up in Audra's green eyes. She sniffed a few times, before trying to continue her response. "We . . . we didn't . . . I just . . . ." Her voice trailed off.

Elson jumped to his feet. "I'm objecting, Miss Morgan! Look what you've done. Can't you see my client is upset? Have you no sense of decency? We're taking a break, right now!"

Elson pulled Audra from her seat by her elbow and headed toward the stairway with Audra in tow. Their footsteps echoed in the stairwell as they stepped down several stairs to converse in private. Valdé busied himself by making handwritten labels for the deposition exhibits that were likely to follow.

Riley turned to Sam with a satisfied smile and whispered. "Does that count?"

Sam sat back in his chair and rubbed his chin with a forefinger while considering whether to concede. "I'm inclined to say no."

"Of course you are. And why might that be?"

"Well, first of all, she hasn't really broken down in tears, yet. You can thank your pal Elson for putting a stop to that before it started. Also, I think you've had more than twenty questions."

"Have not!" Riley pursed her lips and donned an air of disapproval. "Some of those were the same question twice. The witness isn't exactly working with me on this."

"I can count, Miss Morgan. I think you're over the limit," Sam surmised, coolly.

"You're wrong. You just wait," Riley argued. "When we get today's bang-up transcript hot off Valdé's Gutenberg press, you'll see."

Sam couldn't suppress laughter at the clever retort. Riley had no option but to join him in it. The transcript from today's proceedings was likely to be the worst either had encountered, and that was saying a lot.

Sam pulled his cell phone from his pocket. "Let's table our discussion for now. I'm going to make a few calls to see where things stand for tomorrow."

He rose from his seat and walked over to face the window on the exterior wall behind them. A few moments later, Elson and Audra returned and took their seats.

"We can continue now," Elson announced. "I will be advising Miss Morgan on the record to conduct herself with some sensitivity. These are delicate personal matters we're dealing with here."

Riley kept her lip from curling, but couldn't stop the roll of her eyes. There were so many ways she could have put him in his place for making gender-based assumptions as to emotionality. Better to save that for another day. She quickly read over her notes to get her bearing on the most recent line of questions before returning to the task. Sam rejoined Riley at the table just before she commenced the prior line of inquiry.

"Miss Weyland, your attorney says you're ready to proceed. Is that correct?"

Audra started to nod but was distracted by a beeping sound coming from inside her purse. Audra lifted her purse from the floor and placed it on the table in front of her before diving in to examine the source. She pulled out her cell phone and swiped her finger along the screen to take it out of power-save mode.

Riley turned to Elson to offer an admonition. "This isn't the time for your client to take calls, Elson. We're in session. Please advise her accordingly."

"I'm sorry. I just had a message. I'll turn it off now," Audra interjected. She pressed a button on the top of the phone and turned the screen toward Riley. "See, it's off. We can start."

"Excellent," Riley replied. "Now, I believe just before the break, you were starting to tell us about your relationship with Mr. Mikles. Specifically, we were discussing whether the two of you had been intimate during the course of your employment. Your last response indicated you had not, is that correct?"

Audra swallowed hard and sniffed a few times. "Vince never loved me, not like the others."

Riley recoiled slightly at the absurd response. This circus was getting more ridiculous by the minute. "Okay, not to coin a phrase, but 'what's love got to do with it?' Did you have sex with your boss or not?"

Audra sniffed a few times, and then rummaged around in her purse looking for something she was unable to find. Her lip started to quiver, slightly at first, and then uncontrollably. Moments later the waterworks began. Labored breaths were accompanied by resounding snorts. She covered her mouth with her hand to suppress a wail before moving her hand upward to wipe tears and mucus from under her nose.

"Damn it! Doesn't anyone have a tissue?" Audra pled, between a set of heaving sobs.

Elson pulled a handkerchief from his pocket. "Here, take this," he offered. "You've done it now, Miss Morgan. We're finished here."

"Deponents cry all the time, Elson. I see no reason we can't continue," Riley objected, in a reserved tone.

Internally, she was challenged to suppress rising skepticism at the over-the-top display of emotion. The fact Elson was ready and waiting with something as obscure as a hanky also stretched the imagination. This whole scene was completely contrived.

Audra wrapped Elson's handkerchief around her nose and snorted loudly. She then folded it over and buried her face in it. The thin cloth did little to suppress the sound of her wails. Sam seemed genuinely moved by the display. He rose to his feet, picked up the notes he'd taken during the proceedings and stuffed them into his briefcase.

"We're not done, Elson," Sam said. "We can, however, reschedule for another day. In fact, now that we've encountered this ridiculous roadblock, we will be rescheduling all the depositions. They will be in the same order as the original schedule."

"Oh, you've got to be kidding me," Riley complained.

She searched Sam's eyes for something to explain this sudden turn. He was the last person she would have expected to succumb to such a blatant game of avoidance. Sam's eyes revealed nothing but his intent for a hasty exit. He hurriedly directed Riley toward the exit stairs. Still confused, she stopped halfway down the stairs and turned back to face Sam, who was following behind.

"This is a croc, and by croc I mean those are nothing but crocodile tears. That's bullshit if I've ever seen it," Riley quietly contended.

Sam nodded and winked. He leaned toward her and whispered in her ear. "Pure bollocks. But it's what you wanted, right?"

"Not really. I expected real tears. The kind you get from someone who's been through a very stressful situation. I barely scratched the surface and she's blubbering all over the table. Something's not right."

"You may be on to something, Miss Morgan. Let's discuss it over lunch."

CHAPTER 31

"Hold on," that's my cell. "It may be Dani." Riley took a deep breath and wiped tears from her face before answering the call. "Hey you, what's new?"

"Everything. But first, are you okay? Your voice sounds a little strained."

Riley coughed a few times to clear her throat. "I'm fine. It's all Sam's fault."

"What's he done, now?"

"He's making me laugh so hard my sides hurt, that's what. You'll have to ask him to do his impersonation of today's court reporter for you. It's a killer."

"The man has hidden talents. Who knew? Anyway, I'm glad you're having a good time. Unfortunately, that may be the last laugh you'll have for a while."

Riley's broad smile faded. The outward change Sam observed in her demeanor was dramatic enough to warrant inquiry.

"Is everything all right with Dani?" Sam inquired.

Riley turned to acknowledge him with a concerned expression, and shrugged. She covered the voice receiver on her cell phone with her hand and mouthed, "It's work."

"First of all, did I just hear Sam in the background? Second, are you sitting down? If not, you may want to," Dani advised.

"I was sitting and yes, that was Sam," Riley said. "We were on the patio having a glass of wine. The depo ended earlier than expected so we came back here for a late lunch. He's been entertaining me with his impressions ever since. I'm headed to the study now. Let me get behind closed doors before you ruin the rest of my already absurd day."

When she reached the study, Riley shut the heavy wood door behind her and took a seat in the high-back leather chair in front of the desk that had once been her father's favorite relic.

"Okay, Dani, fill me in."

"Sure thing. So, here's what I've got so far. Kris went by to see Wade this morning at his office. His IT group is still doing the skeleton crew thing while the power's out like you said," Dani stated. "Wade gave Kris the photo frame and showed her Halston's work area. They didn't search anything else because, as you know, Kris didn't have a warrant. Anyway, so Kris went back to FDLE and their techs started working on the photo frame. There were a bunch of photos on it that sounded a lot like the ones Wade described having seen on Halston's personal computer."

Dani stopped briefly to catch her breath. She had a long way to go and only a short supply of air to get her there.

"So far, so good," Riley added. "We were expecting all of that. What, if anything, did the pictures reveal?"

"That's where it starts getting good. Or weird, I guess, depending on your perspective," Dani said.

"I'll go with good. Spit it out, already."

"Wade told Kris I would be relaying messages to you, so Kris emailed the pictures over to me. She recognized some of the men in the photos partying with Halston as public officials, both local and national, and others are apparently well-known foreign venture capitalists. Given the high-profile people involved, she wants to tread lightly in this part of the investigation. Before this goes any further, she wanted to know if you or I or Wade recognized any of the other men in the photos," Dani advised.

"You know pretty much everyone I know," Riley said. "Do we know any of them?"

"One of them will ring a bell or something like it, for sure," Dani replied.

Riley was genuinely confused. "What's that supposed to mean?"

"I'll send you the pictures, and let you decide."

"Okay, send them to my phone, I guess," Riley said. "I don't have power yet, so I'm running only essential equipment right now."

"Same here. I'll try to get into the office tomorrow if I can to check on things and grab some files."

"Don't be silly, Dani. If the power's out, there's not much we can do there. We can be just as effective remotely, if we have to."

"I know. I also have, or had, an appointment scheduled at Florida Memorial. It's not too far from the office. I may still stop by to check on things, assuming the hospital doesn't reschedule. If it will make you feel better, though, I'll neither confirm nor deny that I'm going," Dani offered.

There was no point in argument when Dani made up her mind about something. "As you wish," Riley said. "Is this a follow-up to the appointment you had last week?"

"Just running tests. You know how it is. We get all the joys of womanhood, and then have to pay extra for male doctors to examine the parts of us they can't remotely comprehend."

"Sadly, I am aware. While I'm thinking about it, did Kris mention whether they found Halston's cat?"

"Talk about a quick change. You'd think I'd be used to your rapid turns by now," Dani quipped. "To answer your question, yes, she did. I'm glad you brought it up."

"So, they found the cat?"

"No, but she mentioned it," Dani said. "Geez. You, of all people, know the importance of semantics. I would imagine you had a refresher course on that very subject today, with taking Audra's deposition and all."

"Semantics were the least of it where this morning is concerned," Riley recounted. "I'll fill you in, or better yet, you can hear it for yourself when we get the audio transcript."

"Listen? But not watch? Wasn't it supposed to be videotaped?" Dani asked.

"It's a long, sordid tale. Don't worry though. Sam and I can re-enact relevant parts of it for you. So, what did Kris mention?"

"FDLE searched Halston's apartment and the surrounding area, but did not find the cat," Dani said. "They did find cat food at the apartment, which leads them to believe Wade is correct in assuming the cat was Halston's. Wade also remembered that Halston's boyfriend was working as a vet tech somewhere locally. They're gonna canvas the local vets to see if they can find the cat or Halston's boyfriend. Or two for the price of one."

"I hope they can find it, whether or not it offers any clues. I'd hate for an animal to have been caught out in the storm without shelter."

"I thought you were a dog person?" Dani recalled.

"I am. Doesn't mean I wish ill upon their feline 'frenemies.' Besides, I know you're a cat person, and I'd suffer vicariously if the animal's suffering bothered you."

"Ha! Still got that symbiotic thing from childhood going on, do we? If you're so in touch with my thoughts and feelings, what am I thinking now?"

"You're thinking I should take liberties with a ladykiller," Riley deduced.

"Damn! You're good."

Riley added an obvious follow-up. "You also know I'm not going to."

"Yes, right again. I know you well enough to know that," Dani added. "Still, as your sym-sister, I can't help but want for you to have someone else to share things with. I may not always be around when you need me."

"All things in their own time. That's what my Dad used to say."

"I recall. On another note, since I'm so great at what I do, I've managed to send you the photos while we were talking. They should be in your email now."

Riley switched the screen on her cell phone to verify. "Yep, they are in my inbox. Thanks."

"Take a look at the fourth one, and let me know what you think."

Riley opened her inbox in the email app on her phone, selected the recent message from Dani and opened the fourth attachment. In it was a picture of Halston sitting on the lap of someone quite familiar. Riley's jaw dropped slightly with the realization.

"That's Vincent Mikles. So . . . Halston knew Mikles? Great. This case just took a swan dive into a mud bog."

"Pretty much. From the look of things, Halston knew him well. Kris is in the process of getting access to Halston's bank records. It's possible she was on his payroll in some way. Many of the other girls in the photos have been identified as dancers at one or more of Mikles' clubs."

"If Mikles had anything to do with Halston's disappearance, or is in any way considered a person of interest, it could put my representation of him in Audra's case in conflict with Wade's best interests. I don't have a choice. I am going to have to bring Sam into this," Riley conceded.

"You never know, he could turn out to be useful. He's been representing Mikles for a while. He may have met Halston or know something about what she was doing for Vince. Sam also seems to know everyone who's anyone on the shady side of things."

Riley took a moment to consider the possibility that, just like his client, Sam also knew Halston. The notion was anything but far-reaching. She was exceedingly attractive and apparently ran in many of the same questionable circles.

"Let's see, we've got a gorgeous, leggy blonde working for a sex peddler whose businesses Sam frequents. Having seen the pictures of Halston, I don't see any way she could've escaped Sam's notice," Riley said.

"True, although it's also possible for a guy to notice a woman, appreciate her aesthetically, and leave it at that." Dani added. "I've been married long enough to know that sort of thing happens all the time. They're men. They can't completely rewire their brains, but some do manage to trip a circuit breaker once in a while."

"Good analogy, although you may be likening apples to oranges when comparing Jack to Sam. Sam's history with women, at least what we know of it, is vastly different from your husband's. I'm not sure Sam comes equipped with a surge protector."

Dani chuckled. "That might not be all bad. Some high-end equipment is designed to work best under extreme conditions."

"Sometimes, it's pretty obvious you have nothing but men in your house. You're starting to sound like that shop teacher you used to talk about in high school," Riley recalled.

"Hey, don't dis that guy. I met Jack in his class."

"Yes, I remember," Riley said. "I often wonder whether you'd have chosen to be the only girl in a classroom full of guys if we'd gone to the same high school. Perhaps it was fate that we didn't."

"I dunno about fate's part in any of it. But I learned a lot of useful things in that class. Not many women can fix their own carburetors."

"I certainly can't," Riley admitted. "I wouldn't even recognize one if it fell out of my car and I ran it over."

"They're not pretty. You're not missing much," Dani said. "Anyway, let me know what you find out from Sam and where you want to go with Wade's situation from there. Kris says they can't sit on Halston's disappearance much longer if they don't turn up more leads. They're going to have to go public to see if someone out there knows something that will help find her. And when this goes public, Wade's part in it will probably get out, too."

"Right. I imagine Kris plans to start questioning the people in those photos soon, starting with Mikles and his dancers," Riley said.

"That's where I'd start. If those interviews lead to any information, she can avoid putting any of the real big wigs on the spot."

"Yep," Riley agreed. "You know, I really didn't think this day could get any more twisted. Boy, was I wrong. Thanks for the update, anyway. I'll take it from here."

Riley ended the call and sat in silence for a few moments to collect her thoughts. There was no clever way to present the convoluted dilemma to Sam. It was probably best to just start with the photo and then fill in the back story with only the information he needed to know. It wasn't necessary to reveal Wade's part in it to Sam. At least not yet.

The fact of the matter is that if Halston had fallen prey to some type of ill will, which was looking more and more likely by the hour, she wouldn't be around to press charges against Wade. More to the point, if he hadn't been in the wrong virtual place at the right time, the authorities would have no idea at all what might have happened to the girl. Among the plethora of bad guys in this sordid affair, Wade didn't rank anywhere near the top. So, for the moment, the details of Wade's involvement could remain confidential.

Riley returned to the back patio to find Sam still reclined in one of her deep cushioned patio chairs with his feet propped on a nearby ottoman, and Mason sitting devotedly next to his chair. While she was gone Sam had rolled up the sleeves of his crisp white dress shirt, and loosened a few buttons at the neck. With just that small change, he'd somehow transformed himself from high-powered corporate counsel to the poster boy for classic Ralph Lauren casual. He and Mason both looked unnaturally comfortable sitting there, as if they'd spent many an afternoon in that very spot watching birds on the lake.

Riley decided it was best not to sneak up on them, so she announced her return with an obvious revelation. "It's still cooler out here than it is inside, isn't it?"

Sam smiled broadly and reached for the bottle of wine sitting on the round iron patio table in front of him. "Yes, it is. Should I refill your glass, or should we switch to something with ice?"

"A nice glass of sweet tea does sound pretty good right now," Riley concluded. "I've got some in the fridge that should still be slightly chilled, and I guess the ice from the cooler can do the rest. I'll pour a couple of glasses."

Sam started to rise. "I don't expect you to wait on me just because you're stuck with me as a houseguest."

"I know, but I'd rather you stay there. I know where all the glasses and such are located. I'd be mortified if you found my stash of chocolate while searching for the tall ones."

Sam shook his head and sank back down into his seat. "That's nonsense, but I'll oblige. Mason and I won't mind spending some more quality time together."

He reached down to tussle with Mason's ear, and received a wet nose of gratitude in response. "Mason talked me into tossing one of his balls around with him while you were gone, until we both decided it was too hot to play games," Sam advised. "It is, you know."

"It is what?" Riley asked.

Sam wondered if Riley understood he wasn't really talking about Mason. "Too hot to play games."

"That it is, even with the breeze Adonis left behind," Riley concurred. "Anyway, I want to run up and change clothes. This dress isn't the best choice for a hurricane after-party. I'll be right back."

Riley disappeared into the house and returned in a few minutes wearing a comfortable combination of purple denim capris and a white t-shirt. She brought along two tall glasses of iced tea. She placed one of the glasses in front of Sam.

"Here is your beverage, sir. If you want something else, I'd advise that you absolutely *not* tweak me," she teased.

Sam's wink implied recognition of the throwback to their waitress from The Polling Place. He picked up the glass and took a long draw. "Best iced tea I've ever had, following a hurricane," he apprised his hostess.

"I'm honored," Riley said, wryly. She placed her own glass on the table in front of the chair next to Sam, and reclaimed her seat there. "I'm glad you and Mason had some time to play earlier because it looks like we may have more on our plate than just deposition preparation tonight."

"Really? Does it have to do with the call you just took from Dani?"

"As a matter of fact, it does." Riley paused for a moment, and pulled her cell phone from her pocket. "I have some questions for you, and I'm not sure where to start."

"This sounds serious," Sam noted. He had been casually recumbent in the chair with his feet propped up, but abandoned the ottoman to assume a more alert position. "Whatever it is, I'm pretty sure I can take it. Besides, after the day we've had, I feel certain we're partners in some type of crime by now."

"Funny you should say that," Riley added. "I'm going to show you a picture and I'd like you to tell me if you recognize it."

Sam laughed aloud. "If I didn't know better, I'd think you were deposing me, Miss Morgan. Should I be sworn in first, or are you going to take me on my word?"

"I expect there will be sufficient indicia of reliability from your admissions."

"Admissions? As in admissions against interest?" Sam raised a single brow to accompany the inquisition. "Should I have a lawyer present for this?"

"Oh, stop it, you are the lawyer. We both are," Riley scolded. "As it turns out, our professional interests have now collided in more ways than one." Riley called up the pictures of Halston she had downloaded on her cell phone, selected the one of Halston sitting with Vincent Mikles, and handed the phone to Sam. "Recognize anyone?"

Sam glanced at the picture and nodded. He handed the phone back to Riley. "Of course. That's Vince Mikles, obviously, and I don't recall her name, but I've seen that girl before, too. Either at the club or at one of Mikles' parties."

Riley pushed. "Do you know her name?"

Sam shook his head. "No, I don't think we were introduced, although I can't say I would have objected if we were. She's not unattractive, if you like blondes."

"At least two of your wives were blonde and so is Bunny, who by all indications you've also made acquaintance with, so I think your preferences in that regard are well established," Riley said.

"What's the big deal about Mikles knowing this girl?" Sam asked, decidedly ignoring the challenge. "He hangs around beautiful women all the time. He's cleverly made that very thing part of his job. Nice work if you can get it."

"The big deal is that the girl is missing, and has been for several days. A client of mine works with her and has been helping the authorities try to find her, but so far they've reached dead ends."

Sam's expression changed to one of genuine concern. He reached over and took the phone back from Riley to get another look at the photo. "Is she just missing? Or missing and presumed . . . ?"

He wasn't sure why he couldn't just say the word "dead." It's not like he hadn't been there and done the types of things that lead to that—more than once. Maybe it had something to do with the growing knot in his gut. His gut rarely filed a false report.

"Yes. They believe she might have met with foul play," Riley advised.

"Do the authorities have any leads?"

"Not really. There's some indication she might have been abducted from her apartment, but that's about it. She doesn't seem to have had any enemies, and other than hanging out with your pal, Vincent, she didn't run with the wrong crowd."

"What about your client? Is he or she a person of interest?" Sam asked.

"I think my client is probably a little of both right now. He hasn't been charged with anything and has been working with FDLE, but he's the only person who knows anything about Halston's disappearance."

"Halston. So that's her name?"

"Yes, her name is Halston McKinley. She worked in the same office where my client does downtown. My contacts at FDLE also think she might've been on Vince's payroll in some capacity."

"That's easy enough to find out," Sam assessed. "Mikles still owes us copies of his payroll records in response to Elson's discovery requests. I can stop by to get those from him and advise him that we're rescheduling at the same time."

He rose from his seat and headed toward the house. He stopped just outside of the French doors that lead into the kitchen. "I'm not sure how long this will take."

"Just like that? You're gonna go pick up info FDLE has been working all day to get?"

"Sure, why not? He's my client and if she worked for him, he's got a vested interested in finding her. Not to mention, he's got to turn over those documents anyway. I, for one, would like to know why he's been holding those back. Wouldn't you?"

"Yes, I would," Riley admitted. "I guess I'm just surprised you're not a little concerned about the fact your client might know something about her disappearance or worse yet, be involved."

"It doesn't sound like something Mikles would do," Sam advised.

Sam outwardly dismissed the possibility with ease. Inwardly he wasn't so sure. Both he and Bunny had only recently advised Vince Mikles about the damage corroborating witnesses might have in Audra's case. During the early stages of the investigation, the EEOC hadn't managed to uncover any, but their search had been limited to employees of The Polling Place. Mikles had hundreds of people working for him at his other business ventures. Bunny had been particularly concerned with the possibility of corroborating witnesses and given her history with Vince, she likely knew better than anyone which corporate "ponds" he preferred to fish.

"There is someone else we might need to bring in on this," Sam added reflectively.

Riley's brow bent with curiosity. It didn't seem wise to bring anyone else into the loop just yet. "Who?"

Sam winced slightly before the name passed his lips. He probably could've handled things better during their last encounter, and Riley was sure to remind him of it.

"Bunny. She knows the ins and outs of Vince's clubs, and during the early stages of the case, she was in charge of interviewing the female employees at his other businesses to see if anyone would corroborate Audra's claims," he said.

"I hadn't thought of that," Riley replied. "How likely is it that she'll cooperate now? You kinda hosed her during our meeting the other day."

"It's Bunny," Sam added, with a shrug. "She'll cooperate as long as she gets something in return."

Riley didn't know the woman as well as Sam did. "And that something will have to be . . . ?"

Sam donned his annoying half-smile and winked. "I'll take one for the team, if I have to."

"You think a little attention from you is all it'll take after you yanked the rug out from under her the other day? I don't think so," Riley disputed. "I think she'll want more. I expect you'll have to clear out a drawer for her at that fancy penthouse of yours, at the very least."

Sam laughed at the amusing image spawned from Riley's rebuke. "I doubt it. I don't think I'm high enough on the food chain for her taste any more. It's more likely I'll have to send some clients with deep pockets her way. That's what she really wants. That's easy enough."

Riley collected the glasses and wine from the patio table and followed Sam inside. "I'm coming with you."

"No," Sam corrected, and confirmed his intent to leave alone by outpacing Riley's steps toward the garage two to one. When he reached the door that led from the house into the garage, he turned back to conclude his missive. "I need to handle this with Vince, and Bunny, if possible. We've got history. Besides, if this goes south, your client and my client might have a conflict. We'd better keep things separate and compare notes later."

"So, you want me to just wait around for you to call me?"

"I would never expect that of you," Sam replied, mostly in jest. He then adopted a more serious expression. "Maybe you could do me a favor and prepare the revised deposition notices, resetting all of the depositions to next week? We should get those over to Elson before the end of the day."

"Fine. I can do that." Riley conceded. She followed her words with a physical concession by halting her approach to the door. He did have a point about the potential conflict, and the notices for Elson.

Sam pulled his keys from this pocket and headed into the garage. Before closing the door behind him he added, "This may take a while. Best to not wait up."

"Like I would," Riley retorted, knowing the sound of her voice was lost behind a closed door and the roar of a Bentley coupe's engine.

CHAPTER 32

"I wondered when you were coming up for air."

"Don't be an ass. You know I was working on the Mikles case with Riley," Sam objected.

"Right. That's your story. Doubt anyone will buy it." Kent matched his tone with the sarcasm of his words. Sam needed to know a lecture would likely be forthcoming. "So, to what do I owe the honor of your call?"

"I've got to talk to Mikles about a girl. Figured you'd know whether he was at the club."

"Yeah, he's here. Everyone's here," Kent advised. "He called everyone in as soon as the storm let up. I thought it was to assess damage, but turns out it's something else."

"Something else, like . . . ?"

"He's on a tear about something that's missing. Apparently, it was taken just before we shut down for the storm. He's calling everyone into his office for questioning, one by one."

"Any idea what it is?" Sam asked.

"Dunno. Something he kept in his office, so I imagine it was a file or something like that," Kent surmised. "Could also be money, but the deposits are made nightly and he doesn't keep a lot of cash on hand. Plus, I get the impression he would handle simple theft in more of a 'bust your kneecap' style. He's taking a less direct approach on this. Looks like he's trying to smoke out the rat who found his stash of cheese."

"And he has no idea what cage to rattle. Interesting," Sam opined. "You sure are speaking freely for someone in the thick of it. Where are you?"

"In the parking lot. Vince asked me to record the make, model and license of everyone's car. Not sure what he's gonna use the intel for, but the possibilities don't give me a warm fuzzy," Kent said.

"He doesn't care much for the notion of privacy, especially when it belongs to someone else. I've advised him more than once on just how far he can go before his need to know crosses the line."

"So, he knows he can't secretly search their cars, right?" Kent asked.

"We're talking about a guy who uses infomercials to sell vibrators," Sam snarked. "What he should do and what he does are obviously two different things."

"Of course. Stupid question. He who knows no shame, abides no law."

"Exactly. But what's the downside?" Sam inquired. "You were sent in to procure something without a warrant. Somebody got to it before you did. If you happen to recover it while doing a different type of illegal search, guess that puts you back in the game."

Kent didn't see the world in quite the same way Sam did. "Your concern for the balanced pursuit of justice is overwhelming. Got any other questionable takes on morality you'd like to share?"

"Not at the moment. I'm sure something will come to me," Sam taunted. He paused for a moment to consider how to use the situation to his advantage. "This could be good."

"There's a silver lining?" Kent sounded more surprised than he was. Of course, Sam would find one. "I'm only seeing the cloud. Enlighten me."

"Mikles is desperate and his guard is down. If he thinks the law can help him, he'll tell me what it is he's got, or had, that everyone wants."

"He spends every waking hour around naked women."

"Yeah, aside from that," Sam admitted with a chuckle. "Do you know if he called Bunny in on this?"

"I know he's been trying to call her," Kent said. "Last I heard, he was hurling expletives in the direction of his speakerphone because his calls were going straight to her voicemail."

"If he's that hot about it, I wonder why he hasn't called me, yet?" Sam inquired.

"Again, dunno. Haven't been inside long enough to read the guy's mind. You've been running your game on him for a lot longer. I'm surprised you don't already know what he's thinking."

Sam chose to ignore the jibe in favor of more pertinent considerations. Kent was right about one thing: Vincent Mikles was a person of interest to someone with high-level clearance in the federal government. Whoever that was put Mikles on Sam's to-do list a few years ago. Sam's assignment was the usual one—obtain confidential information from the target that could be used to promote the interests of justice. As Mikles' personal counsel, Sam had been consulted on many of his highly confidential financial transactions and business arrangements during the past few years.

Thus far, Sam hadn't come across anything a shade darker than he had encountered representing any other large corporation with global interests. But that simple truth wasn't inherently telling. It was possible he hadn't yet earned Mikles' complete trust. Actually, it was more than possible. It was fact, evidenced by the occurrence of something he wasn't yet privy to. That fact pointed toward one conclusion—since Sam was on the inside for Mikles' business dealings, whatever was going on wasn't business related. Sam considered the options before settling on the one he deemed likely.

There had been no inordinate public outcry in recent years over the colorful way in which Vincent Mikles had chosen to make his vast fortune. There were always a few vocal members of the self-proclaimed Moral Majority who would take the skin trade to task from time to time, mostly for locating a club or business too close to schools or churches. But those concerns no longer resonated widely among the populous. If skin could win, it had a long time ago.

With no one on the outside particularly concerned with the fact Mikles profited from sex-ploitation, there was only one reason Sam and Kent were inside: Vince was on someone's personal 'watch-list.' Someone had a bone to pick with Mikles, and had released the hounds to corner him. That someone was also either running another set of dogs from a different pack, or a third party had their dogs out hunting in the same field.

It was possible Kent had reached a similar conclusion, or already knew who was pulling their leash, but that seemed unlikely. This kind of thing wouldn't sit well with Kent. If the two of them were the government's lap dogs, they weren't of equal comparison. Kent was a loyal family pet, and Sam was the flashy show dog. One was trained to prance on an open stage, performing on cue for whoever grips the lead. The other is kept in careful confinement, and expected to answer only a chosen master's call. At the end of the day, one's value came down to stud fees while the other's was immeasurable. Whoever carefully chose Kent from the rest of the litter planned to keep him around for the long haul.

"He probably decided I had my hands full with Audra's deposition today," Sam concluded, hoping to deflect attention from the matter and his growing concerns a while longer. "Anyway, could be Bunny's phone is turned off because of the storm, or the battery could be dead. The power's been out for a few days now."

"Maybe, but what lawyer doesn't have a car charger for their cell?" Kent snipped. "I've never seen one of your kind not glued to their damn phone."

"Some of us are in high demand. Try not to take it personally," Sam chided.

"Some of us are undercover," Kent shot back. "Can't fly under the radar and keep an active social calendar at the same time. Besides, you know I hate cell phones or any other device that allows any idiot with access to the Internet to track your every move."

"And yet you're talking to me on one right now. That's my kind of irony," Sam crowed.

"Job requirement. I don't own a personal one," Kent replied sharply. "You know that."

"Yeah, yeah. I know. With that antisocial disposition of yours, it's a miracle you have any communication skills at all."

"Never claimed to," Kent acknowledged. "I do well enough where it counts. Some women prefer strong and silent."

"That, my friend, sounds worthy of a wager. Believe I've won the last three. Who knows? Maybe your luck will turn around," Sam taunted.

"Whatever. Only an idiot would take the short game with you when it comes to picking up women. Besides, I don't need that bait."

"Really? You got a side-game I don't know about?"

Kent had let Sam avoid the Riley subject for long enough. "Nope. Just doubling-down in the current one. You're all-in, and it's only a matter of time before your ass is torched for bringing Riley in with you. You know domesticated animals lose their killer instinct, right?"

"Good thing I'm higher on the food chain than that," Sam chuffed, dismissively. The subject of Riley was off-limits for the moment, maybe permanently. He was playing with fire, but it does no good to warn a moth of the heat that accompanies a flame.

"Oh ho . . . hit a nerve," Kent surmised with amusement. "How 'bout that? Didn't think you had one. Since this is new for you, let me fill you in on how it works. That stinging sensation might stick around for a while. You'll get used to it. In the meantime, we've got more important things to focus on. My gut says this new development is going to churn up more muck than the fucking storm just did."

"I'm getting the same feeling," Sam admitted. "I'm headed your way. Will be there in about ten minutes. I'll call ahead to let Mikles know I'm stopping by with an update on Audra's case. If anything changes on your end before I get there, text me."

"Sure. By the way, the x's and o's will be for your sore spot."

Sam smirked and cut the line. Nothing he could say to that. Kent was right. Things hadn't gone quite as planned, and his initially benign decision to involve Riley was starting to cause genuine concern. He'd chosen not to fill Kent in yet on the fact that, due to the missing girl, Riley was in deeper than even Sam anticipated. It was too late to turn that clock back.

While en route to The Polling Place, Sam tried a few times, in vain, to reach Bunny on her cell and office lines. All calls went to voicemail. Following the third attempt, Sam left a quick message on Bunny's cell phone, asking her to call for an update on Audra's case. If nothing else, he imagined Bunny's curiosity about what went down at Audra's deposition would motivate her to return the call.

When he turned into the parking lot at The Polling Place, some of the dancers and other employees were heading for their cars. They were apparently among the lucky few who had survived the inquisition and had been released. He expertly navigated around a small amount of storm debris that had accumulated in piles at various points in the parking lot, pulled his Bentley into a VIP parking spot near the entrance, and headed inside.

Nearly three hours later, Sam emerged and returned to his car. During that span of time, he'd managed to garner marginal insight into what had put Mikles into such a rage. Vince confided that he was missing a computer flash drive containing some sort of encrypted records. He wouldn't say more. It had taken careful coaxing to get that scant info out of him.

Sam convinced Vince that, as his attorney, confidentiality was ensured. That was true, sort of. From the Bar's perspective, as long as there was no ongoing criminal activity there wasn't any reason for Sam to betray the confidence. For the moment, at least, there was no indication Mikles was involved in an ongoing criminal enterprise. In that case, and as long as Mikles' interests didn't run counter to the interests of whomever it was in Washington pulling Sam's strings, the white lie was more of a colorful truth.

Mikles had also confirmed Halston was on his payroll, and had been for a few months. He recalled having encountered Halston on the elevator at the downtown office tower when doing a site visit to his call center. Mikles immediately recognized the attractive blonde's potential in his line of work, and had requested she do some modeling for a product he was developing. He had also utilized her, along with some of his popular dancers, to attract investors for the venture. Beyond that, he claimed to know little or nothing about her.

Sam hadn't told Mikles all the details because he wanted to gauge his reaction. He didn't seem at all stressed when Sam inquired, which could mean he had no idea she was missing. Or he could have been wearing his world-class poker face. Either way, Halston's disappearance at or around the same time the flash drive was taken from his office didn't bode well for Mikles.

Everything Sam thought he had a handle on had been put into a tailspin. There were obviously unidentified forces at play. These new developments changed the game, and particularly the part of it he had been running. He accessed the voice control for his cell phone and barked a command.

"Call Riley."

"Calling Riley." The device, given life and assigned gender through a digitized voice, acquiesced without inquiry, something a real woman would never do.

Riley answered, following the first ring. "What's new?"

"You were waiting by the phone for my call. Admit it," Sam teased.

"I was, but only because I set my phone on vibrate."

Sam laughed openly. "If that's what gets you going, I'm happy to oblige. Should I hang up and dial you again?"

"Maybe later. I'm good for now," Riley advised. "So, did Vince know anything about Halston?"

"Yes, he did. Halston was working for him on a new business venture, along with some of his other girls. From what I can tell none of the others are missing, though. I had a chance to talk to all of them, and none have seen Halston lately or have any idea where she might be."

"Wow! You got all of that information that quickly? I guess I should be impressed."

"You should be," Sam mocked.

He wanted to enjoy the rare moment. Riley wasn't easy to impress. But the pleasure would have to be fleeting. He hadn't really worked as hard as she imagined for the information and he had another stop to make before it got too late.

"I have to confess, I did have a little help," he added.

"Really? I thought we agreed to keep Halston's disappearance close to the vest. But from the sound of it, you went and immediately spilled the beans to some secret associate who does your work for you," Riley chided. It occurred to her there were two sides to it. "I guess I can't complain, though. You got the job done. I just hope whoever you told will keep Halston's disappearance quiet for a while longer."

So much for his good impression. Sam chuckled. Riley would probably never know how right she was about his associate. "I'm handling this one, just like we said. Vince had all his employees at the club, so I didn't have to work too hard to find the other girls. That's what I meant when I said I had help," he confessed. "Mum is still the word for now."

"I see. Well, you got the ball rolling and it's a good start. I guess I should thank you. My friend at FDLE will appreciate the help."

"You're welcome, as is your friend," Sam replied. "But before you lead a parade in my honor, I'm in this as much as you are now. Mikles is my client, and it's my job to protect his interests."

"I know. We're stuck with each other until this thing shakes out," Riley acknowledged. "So, if no one at the club knows why Halston might have been targeted or taken, where do we go from here?"

"Let's not get too far in front of this. I'm not ruling out the relevance of Halston's association with Mikles, just yet. There may be more to it. I've still got a couple of other things to follow up on. Like I said earlier, it may be late before I'm done."

"Somehow, I imagine this to be the type of call your wife got tired of getting," Riley responded. "No need to apprise me of your comings or goings, Sam. The power's still out downtown, and as long as it is, you're welcome to stay. The sofa's here if you need it."

"You may be right about my ex. She didn't understand my dedication to work," Sam recalled. That was true, even though there had been no romantic entanglement between them to complicate the matter. "You've been more than gracious, Riley. I appreciate it, and probably don't deserve it. I'll have to make it up to you somehow."

"I'm almost scared to imagine what that might entail," Riley replied. She hoped the sarcasm in her voice would mask any sound made by the rush of blood to her cheeks. The thought of what that man might do if given the chance was a little unnerving.

"Imagine away, and then sleep on it," Sam teased. "Perhaps your subconscious is more equipped to handle the possibilities."

"You're not getting any further in my dreams than you do in my days, Sam. Call me if you uncover anything else and for God's sake, try to stay out of trouble."

He couldn't promise that. Trouble had chosen to favor him a long time ago. He paused before ending the call. There was more he wanted to say, but couldn't. "Sleep well. We'll talk again soon."

There was one other call to make before he reached his next destination. She needed to know he was coming. Hopefully, she would take the call in spite of their recent encounter.

A woman with a sleepy voice answered the phone. "Hello?"

"I need to see you," Sam said.

"Oh, it's you. You have some nerve. What time is it, anyway?"

"It's too early to be in bed, at least by yourself."

"I was taking a nap. It's been a long day. Are you offering to join me?"

"I'm coming over now," Sam announced.

"Good. You've got a lot of explaining to do."

CHAPTER 33

A mostly naked woman dangling handcuffs from an index finger answered the door. "Should we start with these, or finish with them?" she inquired.

Sam leaned on one shoulder against the door sill and smiled mischievously. "Which would you prefer?"

"I'd prefer to keep you in them the whole night. That way you have to stay where I put you."

"Very well. Before you chain me to your bed post, you have to let me in," Sam advised. "I trust you've got the place to yourself tonight?"

"Du-uh," she replied. "Come on in, handsome, and then take off your shirt, and the rest of it while you're at it. You're much more interesting naked."

"So I've been told."

Sam took a deep breath and crossed the threshold. He had expected a different type of heated reception. This could complicate things. But if a cheap thrill was what she wanted, he could give her that.

As he entered the room, he noticed all the curtains were drawn and the room was lit by what appeared, on quick count, to be dozens of candles. They filled the already-warm air with a floral fragrance, their flickering light wantonly piercing the darkness, free from the challenge of any man-made counterpart. His companion was taking the power outage in stride.

He was barely inside the room before the woman pounced, throwing one arm around his neck for leverage while she hoisted herself up. With her long legs wrapped firmly around his waist, she met his face. Her eyes smoldered with an internal fire that appeared to have been freshly fueled; her hungered expression the kind a lioness might give its prey before the kill. The bite she gave to his neck may not have been as deadly as a lion's, but it was still going to leave a mark.

"Hold on, now," Sam cautioned, as he gently pushed her back. "You know the rules. Nothing where it shows. I don't want to have to come up with some silly explanation for the girls at the office."

"Screw them."

"I can if you'd like," Sam offered.

"Not like that. You're such a shit. You know what I meant."

"A gentleman always takes a lady at her word. Therefore, I am obliged to presume you said what you meant," Sam said. "Guess I'll have to screw them all, just for you."

"Ha! You a gentleman? That's hilarious. Almost as funny as you calling me a lady. Although, you do clean up nice, and you've sure got that little lawyer friend of yours fooled."

Sam bristled. "Let's not talk about Riley. I'm here for you."

"All right, then. Prove it." The challenge was followed by a barrage of wet, open mouth kisses.

Her next advance was in the other direction. With her arm still around his neck, she pressed her breasts against his chest firmly and then tightened the hold of her legs around his waist. She forced the full wet, warmth of her womanhood against his midsection and rubbed against him suggestively, the thin filmy fabric of her sheer panties doing nothing to mask her growing heat.

"See what you've been missing?" she whispered in a husky tone.

"You certainly make a convincing argument," Sam conceded, his breath starting to quicken.

"I'm getting the impression the feeling is mutual. Let's see."

She lowered her free arm toward Sam's waist and then wedged her hand between their bodies in search of his belt. Once the belt gave way, his zipper was the next front to fall. From there, her wandering mitt found what she was looking for in his pants, and she claimed it with a firm grip.

"Forget what I said. Forget all those bitches, and just fuck me. I'm tired of waiting. It's been forever since you've been inside me."

"Let's take this to another room, shall we?" Sam whispered.

"You know where it is. If you're going to take me there, make it fast."

"Very well, then," Sam said. "You're going to have to let go long enough for me get there."

He carefully pried her fingers, one by one, from around his currently not-so-little friend, and pushed her reluctant hand away. He retained a firm grip on her hand, and all five of its roving digits, to ensure they were unable to reclaim their prize. With his fervent tormentor still joined at the hip, Sam covered the short distance across the small living area toward an open doorway on the other side. A few long strides carried him into the bedroom and to the foot of her bed. He turned his back to the bed and bent slowly into a sitting position on the edge of the bed, allowing his passenger to rest against his lap.

"This is better, don't you think?" he soothed.

"It doesn't get better until you take off that shirt," she moaned. She fought against his steely grip and forced him to release her hand. "I need both of these for the buttons."

Sam conceded and leaned back against the bed, propping his torso halfway up by his elbows. His eyes surveyed the taut flesh and generous curves that were dominating his line of vision while feverish fingers worked to release him from the pressed cotton prison.

"While you're doing that, let's talk about your case, Audra," Sam suggested.

"What about it?" Audra inquired, with a hint of annoyance. Talking wasn't on her agenda right now. Her agile fingers continued their southerly excursion down the front of Sam's shirt while she spoke. "I thought it went pretty well. I did what you said. Everyone bought it."

"Yes, you put on quite the show, but I think it's time for the curtain call."

Audra's hands ended their journey a few buttons short. She straightened her posture and met Sam's face with a quizzical gaze.

"What do you mean? Elson seems to think we're on to something big. Bigger than the harassment thing. He's talking about a class action, and big bucks."

This was unexpected news. It was Sam's turn to return with a query. "On what grounds?"

"He says it has to do with the payroll records Vince is refusing to give us. Something about us dancers not being as independent as Vince thinks we are. I don't know. Elson just goes on and on about it. I don't really listen," Audra advised.

Her flushed lips curled into a little girl's pout while she settled into a more comfortable position on Sam's lap. "But you said I didn't have to understand what it was about, anyway. I'm just supposed to say what you tell me to. I've done that, for like forever now."

"Yes, you've done what I've asked of you. It has gone on longer than we expected. You've been patient, like a good girl," Sam replied softly. He gently brushed back a wayward strand of long coppery colored hair from Audra's face, and stared deep into her emerald eyes. At the moment, he had a view few men would mind.

"That's right, I have. Now, it's time for a treat," Audra announced with childlike glee. "I think you're going to have to stay the whole night this time. I've earned at least that. Not everyone can cry on cue like I did today."

Sam's agile mind, masked behind a practiced look of seduction, began to flesh out the available options. The plan had always been to have Audra suddenly change her mind and drop the lawsuit once he had what he needed on Mikles. Unfortunately, things had not gone according to plan. Until he had a better idea of exactly what went wrong and who was responsible for it, he was going to have to improvise.

He lifted his upper body from the partially reclined position to meet Audra's face. Audra's baited breath quickened with anticipation.

"I don't have any other plans for tonight. Might as well stay here," Sam confessed.

He then gently brushed his index finger against her cheek before moving his hand down to the base of her neck. He stroked the side of her neck gently, looking for just the right spot. When he found it, he wrapped his full hand around the back of her neck, his long fingers coming to rest on one side and his thumb on the other.

Audra leaned into the caress to signal her submission. She expected Sam would draw her to him. With the full of her neck in the palm of his hand, Sam tightened his grip and pressed fiercely on both sides with his fingers and thumb. She tensed at first, surprised by the intensity of the pressure before she succumbed. There wasn't much choice. Lack of oxygen to the brain will do that to a person. It was simple biology.

Sam slid out from under Audra's limp body, leaving her to lie alone on the edge of the bed she had intended them to share. He then stood up and turned around to face the bed. Audra was out for now, but she could wake up at any time. Fortunately, that was a problem he could solve.

He reached into his pocket, pulled out his key ring and separated a long silver-colored cylindrical object from the multitude of keys sharing space there. He turned the ends of the cylinder in opposite directions until they gave way, the top half remaining attached to the key ring and the bottom releasing into his hand.

He bent over Audra's body, lifted her head and tilted it back slightly. He parted her lips with a finger just long enough to empty the small vial of pungent mint scented liquid into her mouth. The stuff might smell like mouthwash; it had a far different impact.

Tomorrow, Audra would wake up after having slept like a log, with little or no recollection of his coming or going. If she remembered he was there and asked, and it was possible she might, he'd say they did even though they hadn't. He'd tell her it was a night to remember. Her ego would likely keep her from inquiring further.

Sam took hold of Audra's arms at the wrists and pulled her further up onto the bed, leaving her to rest in a more natural position. He tucked a pillow under her head and pulled the edges of a bed sheet over her bare skin. She'd wake up in the morning with a slight headache; otherwise no worse for the wear. He'd be long gone by then.

In the meantime, he'd check out her fridge. A sandwich and quick review of the news and weather via wireless mobile sounded like a good way to end what had turned into a hellish day.

Back in the living area of Audra's three bedroom townhouse, Sam made the rounds to the various clusters of lit candles, extinguishing most. This wasn't his first visit to Audra's humble abode. Minimal light was all he needed to find his way around the kitchen and living area. What he didn't need was to have excessive heat or smoke from the candles' flames set off the fire alarm.

That mission accomplished, he then headed into the kitchen and pulled open the refrigerator door. With the power out there was no internal light, which made foraging for the makings of a sandwich largely impossible. He again resorted to his ever-useful key ring, this time for the small halogen flashlight on the other end of the ring. He pressed the button to engage the light. As fate would have it, another button was pressed at or around the same time.

Bzzzzzt. Boom.

The internal light in the fridge illuminated, as did the overhead lights. The power was back on, at least for the moment. After a few of storms, you become accustomed to the drill. In rare cases, once the power came back on in an area it stayed on. More often, however, following a storm like Adonis, the power would come back on for a few hours and then go back out a few more times before it returned for good. In those instances, the power company was cycling it to different locations until all the grids were back up in a benevolent attempt to give residents a brief taste of relief from the humidity and heat.

It wasn't likely something as simple as an overhead light would wake Audra up, but Sam didn't want to take the chance. He ventured back over to the bedroom to check on her. She was still sleeping soundly, if the occasional snorting noise she made upon exhaling was any indication. He closed the bedroom door quietly, and headed back to the kitchen.

Over the past few days, he had spent time in close quarters with both Riley and Audra. The two women couldn't be more different with the exception of one thing: neither knew how to stock a fridge. He shuffled around a few bottles of salad dressing to see what was hiding behind them. Near the back of the shelf he found a jar of strawberry jelly. He pulled it out and checked the expiration date. It had a few good days left. If he was lucky, he might also find some peanut butter and some bread in the pantry. If he was less lucky, there would at least be crackers. Everyone has crackers.

He pulled open the small pantry door beside the refrigerator and was met with a welcome discovery. Luck had decided to be a lady tonight, after all. With the makings of a meager snack sitting on an ottoman before him, Sam settled into an easy chair in Audra's living room and turned on the television via remote.

According to the weather report, the western part of the region was still experiencing a few squalls from the now-downgraded storm. It was headed toward Tampa, where it would exit the state and enter the Gulf Coast. All indications were that it wouldn't be strong enough, once it reached the gulf to re-intensify, but the announcer conceded that was speculation. Storms were unpredictable which is probably why they had originally been assigned only female monikers. The precept of equal protection was the impetus for that change, and nothing more.

The weather reporter returned the focus to the evening news anchor who was just receiving details on a breaking story. Sam's eyes widened with recognition at the picture displayed on the screen. He turned up the sound as the anchor outlined newly discovered details in the search for what appeared to be a missing person.

His assumption that the less-than-stellar day had turned a corner as it neared its end had been off base. If the report was accurate, things had just gone from hell to whatever existed that was worse. He muttered an incoherent expletive, pulled out his cell phone and dialed.

"Not sure I want to know what made you drop whoever you're doing and call me," Kent said.

"I wasn't doing anyone. At least not at the moment," Sam responded, flatly. "I believe the operative question is, are you?"

"Shagging the assets isn't part of my cover. That's your gig."

"So, you haven't turned anyone and sequestered them since we last spoke?" Sam inquired.

"Uh, no," Kent responded with annoyance. "Is that your bassackwards way of implying I should have?"

"When was the last time you saw Bunny Keiler?"

"Thursday night, when she scuttled out of the club in a big hurry," Kent recalled.

"Have you seen the news?"

"No. The power's still out here," Kent retorted. "Stop with the twenty questions already, and get to wherever the fuck you're going with this."

"The power's back on the east side of town. I just caught the evening news," Sam responded.

"I thought you were staying with Riley. She's not on the east side of town. Where are you?"

"Never mind. That's not important," Sam declared. "What is important is that Bunny is missing. They found her car near Satellite Beach, parked in a beach access lot. Her purse and an open umbrella were inside. No sign of her."

"All valuables in place?"

"Looks like it. The report said law enforcement is treating it as an abduction without robbery," Sam advised.

"When you came by the club earlier you said you were looking for another girl that had worked for Mikles. Did you find out anything else about her?" Kent inquired.

"Nothing useful. She apparently went missing last Tuesday. Mikles said she was still on his payroll, but he hadn't heard from her in about a week."

"So, two girls who worked with Mikles have gone missing in less than a week and neither disappearance was of our doing," Kent surmised. "What are we missing, other than the two girls?"

"Don't know. That's why I called you," Sam quipped. "If a backup was assigned to the case, I think we'd know. I'm going to call Washington and press some buttons to see what gives."

"I'll get with my contacts on the force and find out what they're not telling the reporters," Kent advised. "Are you somewhere I can get back in touch with you?"

"Yeah, just call back on the number you've got. It'll get routed to me," Sam said. "Make it quick. It won't be long before Riley hears about this. I'm going to have to tell her something."

"Yet another reason why she shouldn't have been involved in the first place," Kent preached.

"What's done is done. I can't undo it, now. Besides, she'd be involved anyway. Her client is the one who reported the first girl missing."

"Yeah, about that client. Where'd he come from?"

Sam stopped to consider the question. The only place Riley would have met someone who knew Halston would've been in the building where Halston worked—the same building where Sam had sent Riley to conduct the training seminar. He hadn't asked Riley much about her client before, but it was starting to add up.

"Shit," Sam muttered. "He works in a building downtown. Mikles has a call center there."

"You mean the call center where you sent Riley to teach the employees about sex, don't you?" Kent concluded.

"That's the one," Sam responded, reluctantly.

"Sending her over there was 'all in good fun,'" Kent mimicked. "Isn't that what you said? Doesn't seem so funny now, does it?"

"Do you hear me laughing?" Sam snapped. "This case was supposed to be an easy in and out. Get whatever goods there were on Mikles and move on. Not the kind of thing where assets drop like flies. There's obviously a helluva lot more to this than we've been told. If I'd had any idea, I wouldn't have brought her in on it."

Kent sighed audibly. As much as he wanted to give Sam grief it wouldn't serve any purpose, and it wouldn't likely be anywhere near the grief he knew Sam was already giving himself. "Yeah, I know. But I did warn you. That's all I'm saying."

"Just find out what you can and get back to me," Sam directed. "Once I know what we're up against, I can figure out how we all get out of it."

CHAPTER 34

Sam waited in painful silence for Riley's response. Two years of careful staging had gone into the Mikles operation. All of that work was about to go down the drain, possibly taking Sam's reputation with it.

The plan he had hatched during the sleepless night at Audra's and just spent the past forty minutes briefing Riley on was a good one, considering the dearth of alternatives. Riley's role was pivotal. Sam needed her to play the part, at least long enough for him to determine whether Mikles was responsible for the disappearance of Halston or Bunny . . . or both. He also needed to act fast, before the local authorities got more deeply involved. Once they did, it would be almost impossible for him to recover the information he was sent in to secure from Mikles without raising too many suspicions.

If Mikles had nothing to do with the missing women, there would be less reason for law enforcement to center its focus on him or his businesses. In that case, Mikles would only be a cooperating witness, adding whatever basic information he had on Bunny and Halston to the investigation. That was the outcome Sam was actively seeking. If it turned out Mikles was involved in the disappearances, the job Sam was sent in to do had somehow managed to become easier and harder at the same time. Obviously, that was not the preferred resolution.

On one hand, the information Sam was supposed to procure from Mikles—information that, like the two women, had also recently gone missing—was far less important if Mikles was responsible for the missing women. Kidnapping and murder trump financial crime on any government scale. Either misdeed should be more than enough ammunition for whoever it was in Washington that had Mikles in their sights.

On the other hand, if Mikles had nothing to do with the disappearances, and was as much a victim as the missing women, Sam was duty-bound to use whatever means available to find the women and recover the information stolen from Mikles, all without blowing his cover. That was a tall order. He had managed to fill more than a few of those in the past, but this one might exceed even his expansive repertoire. Right now, only two things were certain: Sam needed to find out what he was up against, and he needed Riley's help to do it.

"I just have one question," Riley started.

"Ask away," Sam responded. If one answer was all that was left to seal the deal, things were looking good.

"At what point in all of this do you plan to bring in Shaggy and Scooby?" Riley inquired. Her somber expression remained unchanged despite the absurdity of the question. "I can already hear Vince, at the end of all this, telling the cops he 'would've gotten away with it if it weren't for those meddling attorneys.'"

Sam was standing in front of the sofa in Riley's now-familiar den, facing Riley who was seated on the sofa. He had paced back and forth in front of her while he made his case, much like he might when arguing before a jury. The pacing had continued while he waited for Riley to acquiesce. Her unexpected query stopped him in his tracks.

"I'm not sure how to respond to that," he declared. "This isn't a joke, Riley."

"I know it isn't," Riley confirmed. "But this grand scheme of yours sounds like something straight out of a Saturday morning cartoon. Which is why I'm left to wonder what the rannygazoo you're proposing is supposed to accomplish?"

"It's supposed to give us some insight into whether Mikles is involved in Halston's or Bunny's disappearance. I need to know that in order to know what information I can give the authorities and when I can give it to them."

"I get that part of it," Riley admitted. She hadn't intended to sound facetious. Sam was obviously concerned and possibly even frustrated. Bearing witness to uncertainty in a man who had previously seemed unflappable had her on edge as well.

"What I don't get is how your plan gets us from where we are to where you want to be," she continued. "I guess, in that regard, I was exaggerating about only having one question. I have a few."

"I expected you would. We don't have much time, though. So, start asking," Sam replied, his impatience starting to show.

Riley rose from the sofa, stepped around Sam and headed toward the front door. She opened the door and walked out onto the covered entryway to get another look at the expensive new sport sedan parked in her driveway. After confirming she had not imagined the car that was personally delivered by the dealership an hour earlier, she stepped back inside to direct her query to Sam.

"First, you can tell me how you managed to get a brand new BMW 550i that just happens to be the same make, model and color as Bunny's delivered to my door while most of the city is without power and still reeling from the impact of a major storm?"

Sam crossed the space between them and joined Riley at the door. "That's easy. The dealer is a client of mine. Next question," he coaxed.

"Of course," Riley replied. "All right, then. Do you really think a BMW, blonde wig and oversized sunglasses is all it will take for Vince to mistake me for Bunny?"

"That's the beauty of the plan," Sam crowed. "The way Mikles responds to you in that getup will answer everything. If he had something to do with Bunny's disappearance, he'll know it's a bluff and quickly conclude he is under suspicion. I'll be able to see if he's sweating it. If he wasn't involved, he will show some indication of relief. He and Bunny have a history."

"You said I'm just supposed to stay in the car. How is he going to see me and mistake me for Bunny?"

"Let me worry about that," Sam assured. "Mikles has got high-tech security on the property. There are cameras everywhere. If he wants to confirm what I tell him, he'll find a way to get a closer look."

"So, all I need to do is follow you to his estate on Lake Vineland and park in an area where you think he'll be able to see me wearing this ridiculous get up?" Riley inquired.

"Yes. I'll take it from there," Sam said. "Once I'm able to gauge Vince's reaction, I'll call you and let you know you're free to go. I'll come by later to get the car. We can decide then what, if anything, we can take to Kris."

"Just so I'm clear, tell me again why we can't take what we already have to Kris and let the experts run their own investigation?" Riley rebutted. "It seems like we're playing with someone else's fire."

"Vince is my client," Sam answered. "I have to protect his interests the same way you have to protect your client. The fact your client came to you before going to the police gives me a pretty strong suspicion he or she is also holding a few things back as well."

It was plausible enough, mostly because it was true. Sam did have to protect Vince's interests, at least long enough to get what he needed out of the arrangement. Riley didn't need to know the real reason; she just needed to accept his word on the observable part.

Riley nodded in agreement. He was finally speaking in terms she understood. "You're right. My client, whose name is Wade by the way, did come to me to protect his interests. He had reason to be concerned the police might misconstrue the information he had to provide."

"I expected as much. Are we good to go now? If so, I'll put in the call to Mikles and let him know I'm on the way," Sam said.

Riley stepped back into the house and pulled a platinum blonde wig and sunglasses out of the bag Sam had brought with him. She turned to face a mirror on the wall near her foyer to fix the wig in place. Once it was secure, she donned the large-framed sunglasses, turned to face Sam and struck a pose.

"How do I look?"

Sam studied the result. "You make a pretty convincing blonde. As long as you stay in the car and don't say anything, I think it'll work."

Riley smirked. "Right. I get it. What you're saying is, as long as I don't launch into a verbose soliloquy about the world's injustice and society's deepening moral decay, I might fool someone into believing I'm a bleached-blonde. Of course there's nothing at all stereotypical about that presumption."

"Naturally, there are exceptions," Sam conceded, "but right now we're working with the rule. For the moment, Bunny is the type of woman who should be seen and not heard."

"Having met Bunny, I can't exactly argue the opposing point," Riley admitted.

"Good, so the discussion part is over and we can move into the implementation phase," Sam directed.

"Yes," Riley reluctantly responded, "let's get this over with."

"Have you ever driven a BMW before?"

"Nope. Too trendy for me. I'm partial to my well-worn Benz."

"In that case, it might be a good idea for you to get familiar with the car while I'm setting the stage with Vince. It's a new model and has a lot of bells and whistles, but it's an automatic. You shouldn't have too much trouble with it," Sam advised.

Fifteen minutes later Riley was behind the wheel of the BMW and carefully tailing Sam's Bentley along the winding, suburban streets that led to Vincent Mikles' palatial estate. Most of the debris and tree limbs downed by the storm had been cleared from the roads, but unfortunately they had been piled on the shoulder so close to the thoroughfare that Riley feared the sharp edges of fragmented branches might scratch the borrowed car's perfect paint. She held her breath each time she passed one of the piles hoping that slight retraction might make a difference.

Once the entrance to Mikles' estate was within sight, she slowed down and pulled off the side of the road to wait for Sam's signal. The plan was for Sam to arrive first and meet briefly with Mikles to lay the groundwork. Riley, now playing the role of Bunny, was to arrive a few minutes later, seemingly on cue.

While she was waiting, Riley took her cell phone from her purse to check messages. Dani indicated she would be stopping by the office today to see if the power was back on and make sure everything came through the storm unscathed. Once Dani finished surveying the damage, she was to call Riley with an update. Riley was also eager to hear more about the medical appointment Dani had this morning. Dani was the quintessential super-mom, which meant she generally scoffed at physical frailty. If she was going to see a doctor, something was up.

After checking and finding she had no messages, Riley placed her cell on her lap to wait for both Dani's call and Sam's signal. When her cell vibrated to indicate an incoming call, Riley assumed it was Dani. She answered it without checking first.

"Hey, you."

"Um . . . hey," Wade responded, hesitantly. "This is . . . Riley Morgan, right?"

"Oh, sorry. Yes, Wade. It's me. What's up?"

"I haven't heard anything from FDLE and was wondering if you had," he started. "Now that the power is starting to come back on, I figured they would start to release the details of Halston's disappearance."

"You're right. I imagine FDLE will be taking the case public very soon. I'm sure Kris will call you or me before they do that so we can prepare," Riley advised. "Are you scheduled to go into work today?"

"I'm actually in the office now. IT's still on skeleton crew until the rolling power outages are over, per company policy. I imagine the schedule will return to normal by tomorrow. I guess. . . ."

Wade's voice trailed off. It suddenly hit him that if the announcement of Halston's disappearance was made today, this would probably be his last day on the job. The wave of sadness that followed the realization of impending loss came as a surprise. Some clichés are true—you really don't know what you've got until it's gone.

"How long is your shift today?" Riley inquired. She could sense what she couldn't hear of his rapidly sinking emotions. It wasn't unusual for a client to be overwhelmed by the weight of their dilemma. It happens more often than not. In the past, she had found that providing detailed instruction on the course of things to come usually helps. Hopefully, that pattern would hold.

"I had the 2:00 a.m. to 10:00 a.m. shift. I've got about an hour left, and then my boss comes in. He gave himself the prime daytime hours, of course."

"Okay. Here's how I imagine this will go down," Riley continued. "Kris will call me and give me about an hour's notice before the story goes public. I'll give you a call as soon as I hear something. At that point, we will need to meet to go over the details and strategize. I don't know yet if we have power at the office, but if it's back on we will meet there. If not, we will meet at my house."

"Do you think I'll have to give a statement to the press or something?" Wade inquired.

"Not initially. Right now, you're a material witness. While the case is under investigation, your part in it should stay confidential." Riley didn't have the heart to include the unwelcome truth: Wade's role would only remain confidential if he wasn't charged with a crime. If FDLE decided to charge him with any of the multitude of offenses they had to choose from, everything he had done would become fair game for public scrutiny.

Wade sighed audibly. "That's a relief, I guess. I mean, if talking about the case would help in any way, then I want to do that. I'm just not good with crowds and television cameras and all of that."

"Not to get off point, but you might want to work on that," Riley added.

"What do you mean?"

"I'm not an expert, but don't you think your tendency toward introversion is kind of what got you in trouble in the first place?" Riley asked. "If you had just bitten the bullet and asked Halston out, or at least tried to make friends, you might not be in this mess."

The long silence that followed the query made Riley wonder if Wade was still on the line. She didn't mean to offend him. It was hard not to "mother" clients sometimes, especially when the client so desperately needed to grasp the wisdom that seems only to reach them with hindsight.

After a full minute, Wade responded. "I know you're right. It's just hard to think about it now because I can't exactly go back, can I?"

"I know. That's the worst part," Riley replied, her voice soft with understanding. "While I've got you on the phone, I do need to tell you about something that might be a break in the case."

Wade's tone brightened considerably. "Seriously? There's a break? Why didn't you tell me that first?"

"I was getting there," Riley defended. "I'm still trying to decide how much you need to know. Not all of this involves you, at least not directly."

"All right, tell me what you can," Wade pled.

Riley mentally prepared a quick synopsis of recent events to guide the rest of the conversation. "Another woman is missing. Her name is Bunny Keiler. She had a connection to Halston in that they both did work for a man named Vincent Mikles. He's a very wealthy local businessman."

"Yeah, I've heard of him. He owns that business on the eighth floor. The one where you did the seminar," Wade said.

"That's right. Okay, good. You have a frame of reference then," Riley said. "It seems highly unlikely the two disappearances are unrelated, and it seems more than likely the connection to Mikles is relevant."

"Yeah, there's like almost no probability of that if you do the math. I can give you the exact stats if you want. It's a pretty easy algorithm."

Riley shook her head in disbelief. It wasn't hard to imagine the many ways in which Wade's immeasurable intellect had kept him isolated from the rest of society.

"That's okay. I can work with the general assumption for now. Anyway, there's more to the story."

"I've got plenty of time and nothing to do here," Wade responded. "I'm all ears."

"Okay, well I've been working with Mikles' counsel on another case," Riley added. "Bunny Keiler was working with us on the case, at least until right before her disappearance. I'm helping Mikles' attorney to determine whether Vince knows more than he's letting on."

"Isn't that like a conflict or something? I mean, the guy's attorney is supposed to be on his side," Wade surmised.

"Yes, he is under normal circumstances. But as you know, none of this is normal. If there's an ongoing crime, then an attorney has a duty to report or at the very least withdraw from representation. Finding out whether or not you're being used to aid in a criminal enterprise is the only responsible thing to do. Trust me, I wouldn't be involved in this charade otherwise."

"What do you mean by charade?" Wade asked, his seemingly limitless curiosity fully peaked.

"I can't go into all the details. Right now I'm waiting outside of Mikles' house disguised as Bunny. The idea is for Sam, that's the other attorney, to see how Mikles responds when he thinks Bunny isn't really missing and is about to turn over evidence."

"That's like something out of a spy novel." Wade's quick mind calculated the open-ended contingencies. "There are a few flaws in the paradigm."

Riley's forehead wrinkled. "I didn't know we were involved in a paradigm."

"It's just a figure of speech. What I mean is that the chosen course of action might not be the best course to achieve the result. For example, the same result could be achieved without your involvement."

"How so?" Riley asked, genuinely intrigued with the fact Wade had so easily found flaws in Sam's grand, if not cartoonish, scheme.

"For starters, this Sam guy could have just had a text sent to Mikles from a number that spoofed Bunny's. The spoof dialer could be programmed to send the text at or around the time Sam was meeting with the guy, so he could watch the reaction."

"That makes sense. I'm not sure why Sam didn't think of that," Riley added. "Although, not many in my profession are as adept with technology as you are. Knowing Sam, I imagine he was going for the easy sell. It's harder to disavow something that's standing right in front of you. Or, in this case, sitting in a car outside your house."

Riley's cell phone beeped. She pulled it away from her ear to review the message.

"Great."

"What? What is it?" Wade asked nervously.

"My cell battery is dying and I don't have my charger. I'm not in my car. Sam has me driving a car that looks like Bunny's."

"What type of car is it? If it's decked out, it probably has a dock or cradle for a smartphone," Wade advised.

"It's a 2012 BMW 550i. What would the dock look like?" Riley asked.

Wade decided against chiding Riley on her lack of techno-savvy, mostly because she had plenty of other grounds on which she could return the favor. He did a quick online search for the information he needed.

"The dock is a cradle with a plug sticking out of one end that fits into the bottom of your phone. Open up the console between the seats. It should be in there," Wade advised.

"Okay. Hey, I think I found it," Riley said gleefully.

"It may be made for a particular type of device, so try plugging it in to see if it fits," Wade instructed.

Riley wiggled the phone onto the docking jack until it snapped into place. "Looks like it fits. It says it's charging."

"Great!" Wade replied through a fog of static. "Hey, it's kind of hard to hear you. The car should also have Bluetooth. You know what that is?

Riley huffed loud enough to make sure Wade heard it. "Yes, I know what that is. Got it in my Benz. But someone else set it up for me. Tell me what I need to do."

"First of all you have to change the settings on your phone so it will be discoverable," Wade advised. "Then you need to turn on the Bluetooth in the car and enter the code to accept the connection."

"That sounds easy enough, but I don't have a code."

"Some of them are universal, depending on the make of the car. Is there like a manual or something in the glove compartment?" Wade asked.

Riley reached across the dash and opened the glove compartment. "No, I don't see one."

"No worries. I can find one online and push it to you."

"I'm going to guess that means you're going to send it to me, right?"

"Yeah, it's kinda the same thing. I mean, it can be uploaded to the cloud, if your phone syncs that way, or I can just send a link in a text."

"Let's be super old-school here and go with a text," Riley quipped. She was pretty sure she didn't have anything stored in the atmosphere.

"I can do old-school. It's probably just as fast as new-fangled in this case," Wade said.

Within a matter of seconds, Riley's phone beeped again, this time to notify of an incoming SMS message.

"You should have the link to the manual now," Wade announced. "I linked you to the page where the Bluetooth information is located, so you wouldn't have to look for it."

Riley was impressed. "I appreciate that. So, I just need to click on the link?"

"Yep. Although, I've already read it so I can just tell you what it says."

"There is that," Riley remarked. "What do I need to do?"

A few minutes and detailed instructions later, Riley's cell was paired with the BMW's phone application and she was now talking with Wade handsfree.

"Seems to be working. Thanks," Riley said.

"That should also increase the signal strength on your phone some," Wade noted. "That Beemer has some awesome features. It's got cameras and sensors that connect to the steering so it can basically park itself."

"Well, I haven't read the manual like you have, so I don't know all the features," Riley said. "If the dashboard is any indication, the car might be able to take flight."

"Not to change the subject," Wade started, "but when is that Sam guy supposed to get back to you?"

"I would imagine any time now. I don't know exactly what he's telling Vince, or how he plans to bring up the subject of Bunny. He may be building up to it."

"We could always speed things along," Wade offered.

Riley wasn't sure it was wise to intervene, although Wade had already come up with some good ideas. It wouldn't hurt to hear him out. "How so?"

"I could send that spoof text from Bunny, to get the ball rolling."

"I'm not sure. That could be dangerous," Riley replied. "We don't know whether Sam has gotten around to that part of the conversation yet."

"That's easy enough to find out," Wade answered.

"Really?"

"Yeah, aside and apart from the eavesdropping part, it's not a big deal."

"Hold on. That's all I want to hear about whatever it is you have in mind," Riley stated. Seemingly, she stood alone in her resolve to uphold privacy laws.

"Do you have Sam's cell number?"

"I do. I'm not sure I want to give it to you," Riley said.

"Umm. Not to be all cyber-creep and stuff, but I could get it anyway. You telling me just saves a minute or two."

"What are you planning to do?"

"Do you want to know all of it, or just the legal part?" Wade asked.

"Stick with the legal part, for now. I really don't think it would be a good idea for you to cross Sam."

"I'm just going to let him know that Mikles guy is about to get a text from Bunny. I figure he should know there's been a slight change in plans," Wade added.

The plan he was quickly putting into place went quite a bit further than that. He didn't want to drag Riley any further into his quagmire, but since he was already in a shitload of trouble for the incident with Halston, one more little black hack wasn't going to make much difference for him. If it helped to find Halston, it was worth all the trouble in the world.

"That sounds reasonable enough. I'll text you the number." Riley picked up her cell phone from the car's cradle and typed in the information for Wade.

"Got it. I'm going to have to call you back. This next part is going to tie up my phone," Wade instructed.

"Fine. I don't really want to know the rest of what you're up to anyway," Riley confessed. "Call me back when you're done."

CHAPTER 35

Sam was seated in Vince's study, talking with his client about the weather, the storm's aftermath, and pretty much anything else but the day's hot topic. Vince's wife, Cayren, popped her head in the room to interrupt.

"Do you boys want anything to drink?" she asked.

Vince nodded. "Yeah, Babe, pour me a shot of that Grey Goose on the rocks. You want one, Sam?"

"Sure," Sam replied. He wasn't on the clock, technically.

Cayren walked over to the built-in bar in the expansive study to pour the drinks. She moved with cautious deliberation while filling the glasses with ice, so the sound of it clinking would not interrupt the men's conversation. At the moment, they weren't discussing anything that appeared to be of import, but she wasn't taking any chances. She could be as silent as a ninja and Vince would still yell at her for making noise.

This time, Vince couldn't blame her for the interruption. It came from a different source. Sam's cell phone chimed, causing both Vince and Cayren to abruptly turn and face him.

"Do you need to get that?" Vince inquired. "I can give you some privacy if you do."

Sam glanced down at his phone to retrieve the message. It appeared to be a text from Riley.

"No, it's not important. Just a woman I know," Sam added with an air of annoyance. "You know how it is."

Vince chuckled. "Yeah. I work with 'em all day long. Although, now that I've got my Cayren and the family, the girls at the club only bug me about work."

The sudden recollection that his wife was still in the room had prompted Vince to add the last part. A vague smile accompanied the reference to his family. He glanced over to the wet bar where Cayren was standing, and then turned his attention back toward Sam.

"I know you didn't come all the way out here to talk about the weather, Sam. And I sure as hell ain't gonna pay your fee for that type of talk," Vince stated. "What did you want to tell me about that missing girl and the lawsuit?"

"Have you been watching the news?" Sam inquired.

"Nah, it's all back-to-back weather reports right now with a bunch of loons reporting next to dead trees that fell on live electrical wires," Vince said.

"I see. So, you haven't heard the reports that Bunny Keiler now appears to be missing? That makes two girls with ties to your club."

Vince did an apparent double take. "Come again?"

Cayren had finished pouring their drinks. She walked over to Vince's desk, handed him the drink and then crossed over to the other side of the desk to deliver Sam's. She started toward the door but stopped just before leaving.

"I heard about Bunny," she advised, in a timid tone. "I'm really worried about her, V. You know she's been a good friend to us. I didn't hear anything on the news about another girl, though. Is someone else missing?"

"Just some gal who worked for me on the side," Vince bristled. "She seemed like the type that followed money. I wouldn't be surprised if she's just holed-up in some swanky hotel with one of my customers."

Sam surveyed Vince's demeanor for any indication of anxiety. Outwardly, there was none. Vince appeared to be genuine in his belief that Halston would turn up soon. His response to Bunny's disappearance was not as easy to read.

"What are they saying about Bunny? When did this happen?" Vince inquired.

"The reports have been sketchy on details," Sam conveyed. "It appears Bunny hasn't been seen since she filmed a live newscast over on Satellite Beach last Friday."

"Friday? It's Tuesday, now. That's half-a-fucking-week ago. Why is this only being reported now? Why are you only telling me this now?" Vince demanded.

The classic and anticipated display of outrage over the ineptitude of law enforcement didn't reveal much, but maybe Vince's jab at Sam did. Sam was going to have to prod some.

"Don't get untethered just yet," Sam counseled. "The reports of Bunny's demise may be premature."

"Demise?" Cayren blurted. "They think she's dead already?"

"No, Doll, that's just a figure of speech," Vince soothed. His next comment was couched in a less comforting tone. "What are you saying, Sam?"

"I have it on good authority that Bunny isn't missing at all."

Vince's eyes followed the movement of his thoughts. He shifted positions in his seat. "That's good news, right?"

"Not exactly," Sam responded. "If she's not missing, then there's a reason for the news reports declaring that she is, don't you think?"

"Fuck! I don't know. Those hacks get shit wrong all the time. They usually get half-a-whiff of a tall tale and run with it," Vince brayed.

"I've seen this type of thing before. It appears to be misdirection," Sam added, his comportment unchanged despite Vince's intemperate turn.

"Okay, then, what is that trifling whore up to?" Vince asked.

Cayren cringed. "Don't call her that, V. You know I hate that word."

"If the word fits, Cay, it fits," Vince shot back.

The barb drew water to Cayren's eyes. Sam intervened. "Maybe we should discuss this in private, Vince. It is a legal concern, after all."

"Good idea," Vince concluded. "Why don't you go check on those two furry rats you like to call dogs, Cay? I'll bet the rodents are chewing up another twenty-thousand-dollar Turkish rug as we speak."

The moment Cayren left the room, Vince's cell bleeped. Sam surmised it was the presumptive text from Bunny as indicated in Riley's earlier message.

"Looks like you're right," Vince concluded, after staring at his phone for an inordinate amount of time. "According to this, Bunny's on her way over right now. Says she wants to talk."

"That's unexpected," Sam lied. "Why would she do that if she's working with the authorities?"

"Dunno. Buns and I go way back. Maybe she's coming over to give me the heads-up."

"Maybe," Sam assessed, with a slow nod. "Or maybe she's wearing a wire and planning to get you confess to something on tape."

"Buns would never do that," Vince stated.

"Are you sure? If there's one thing I've learned in my business, it's that people are capable of just about anything," Sam said. "I don't think it's worth the risk to find out the limits of her loyalty. My advice, as your counsel, would be that you not speak with her. Turn her away at the gate."

"What if she's coming to make a deal?" Vince questioned. "Don't know why I didn't consider it before, but she could be the one who stole my files. Maybe she wants to trade 'em in for something green."

"Still too risky, in my opinion," Sam noted.

"Maybe so, maybe no. I need those fucking files," Vince declared. "If there's a way to get them back, it might be worth the risk."

Vince was not going to be easily herded in the direction Sam desired. "Listen. Since keeping you out of trouble is part of my job, let me meet with her. I can find out what she knows and where she's going with it," Sam suggested.

Vince rubbed his jaw. "That could work. Yeah, let's do that. I'll tell her to wait outside. You go see what she wants."

At this point, Mikles hadn't revealed as much as Sam had anticipated. He didn't seem too surprised that Bunny might show up at his door, which meant one of two things: either he had nothing to do with her disappearance or, if he did have something to do with it, at least she hadn't been fed to the fish. Yet.

Sam pulled his phone from his pocket and hit the "Send" button. The message advising Riley that it was time for Bunny's grand appearance was on its way. Except that it wasn't.

ଠୀଠ ଠୀଠ ଠୀଠ

Wade rushed over to the IT storage closet and pulled out an unassigned laptop. What he was about to do exceeded the capabilities of his cell phone, no matter how smart it claimed to be.

After sending the text to Sam, he had been listening in on Sam and Vince's conversation via some extra oomph he had added to the spoofed SMS message from Riley. Sam's phone had an excellent microphone on it, which had performed quite well under Wade's direction. That little trick didn't quite approach the level of magic, but it worked like a charm.

It didn't occur to Wade until after he sent the spoofed message from Bunny that Vince or even his wife, who sounded pretty lame from what he heard over the phone, might try to get in touch with Bunny. If they called the real Bunny while Riley was impersonating her it could screw things up. It was best not to leave that detail to chance.

While connected to Sam's cell phone he had managed to sniff out surrounding WiFi and Bluetooth signals. The house had a wireless router with a number of devices connected, the most interesting of which was a commercial quality treadmill. Based on the treadmill's recorded statistics and use records, Vince's wife was a bit of a freak when it came to working out.

Less interesting, but more useful devices connected to the WiFi included a tablet that used an Android operating system, and a couple of computers. Wade had secured the MAC addresses for each of those devices, just in case he needed to exploit them later.

Wade fired up the company's laptop. It took a minute or two for the device to boot-up. Once it finished with all that and was ready to get to work, he connected to the Internet through the company's server. Using an unsecured connection was risky, but there was no time for a mask. If he got caught, they could just add it to his tab.

He connected to Vince's wireless router via the router's IP address. The command he entered next should have the router transmit 802.11 management frames which would cause surrounding wireless clients to disassociate from the access point. He had read about this type of thing, but had never tried it before.

"What are you working on over there?" Duong inquired.

Wade had been so focused he didn't hear his boss enter. Wade glanced down at his watch. It was almost time for Duong's shift.

"Just making sure the reserve laptops connect to the new server. You know how management gets when they're on the road and their shit doesn't work," Wade advised. He had tested the unassigned laptops weeks ago. They had the required programming, were charged up and ready to go, but Duong didn't know that.

"A few more minutes and I'll be done here," Wade announced.

"I can finish that," Duong offered.

If Duong got any closer, he would be able to read the screen and see Wade was doing something quite different from what he claimed to be doing. There weren't many options. He could abort or destroy. Wade opted for deflection.

"Hey, I heard they're giving away ice cream at that place down in the lobby," Wade coaxed. "It won't stay frozen with the power going off and on. They're just giving it away to anyone who wants it."

Duong's eyes expanded to accommodate newly widened pupils. Ice cream was a terrible thing to waste. He pulled his cell phone out to check the time. There were a few minutes to spare. If he left now, he could make it back down to the lobby and grab a few scoops before Wade left.

"I guess I could go down and check it out. I'd hate for them to have to throw it out," Duong reflected.

"You were the first person that came to mind when I heard about it. I told 'em I'd let you know when you got here," Wade said.

"You want anything?" Duong offered. "I'll bring something back if you want. Just don't blame me if it melts on the way back up the stairs."

"Nah. I can grab some on the way out," Wade said. "Take your time, though. Like you always say, I'm 'not hourly.' There's no overtime if I work late."

"It's good to know you've been listening," Duong jibed on his way out the door. "I'll be back."

"I'll be here," Wade called out. Once his boss was out of earshot, he completed the thought. "If they don't haul my ass off to jail in the meantime."

Wade picked up his cell phone and dialed Riley's number.

"Hey, Wade, I'm kind of busy right now," Riley answered. The noise in the background indicated she was still using the handsfree connection.

"You're supposed to go to the entry gate now to let them think Bunny is there," Wade advised.

"How do you know that?" Riley asked.

"I'm going to ignore that question on the advice of my attorney. You said you didn't want to hear the gory details."

"Great. That's just great," Riley grumbled. She pressed the ignition button and shifted into drive. "While you were doing whatever it was you were doing, I got a call from Kris. Turns out they found Halston's cat at a local vet. It seemed fine but they're going to do a thorough exam."

Wade's tone brightened. "It's pretty lame that I'm glad to get news about a friggin' cat. I guess it's probably the only good news I'm gonna get for a while."

"Don't sell the day short, yet," Riley stated. "It's just a little after ten in the morning."

"Did Kris say anything else?"

"Yes, she did. FDLE will be making Halston's disappearance public around noon."

Riley winced as she spoke. She imagined the news would hit Wade hard. By noon today, his life would become chaos and wasn't likely to return to normal any time soon.

"Okay," Wade replied in a distracted tone.

That wasn't even close to the response Riley anticipated. "You don't sound worried anymore," she replied.

"I'm trying to keep busy with other things right now."

"Other things?" Riley did not like the sound of that. "Like what?"

Things like keeping this jacked-up plan of your friend's from getting you both in trouble, Wade thought. "It's complicated, and kinda technical," he answered. "Are you at the gate, now?"

"Yes. I'm about to press the call button," Riley advised. She was surprised Mikles, who certainly had the means, didn't have a guarded entry.

She pressed the button and then turned to face the wall-mounted security camera instead of speaking into the box. She waived at the camera and smiled. That was all that was necessary to do the trick, according to Sam. She looked down to the speaker again as it crackled to life.

"Hello, Buns." The voice was Vince's. He wasn't amused. "I'm not interested in whatever bullshit game you're playing. Sam Stone is here, though, and he apparently is. He's gonna come down there to hear you out."

Riley nodded and then waved at the camera again. She engaged the electronic control to roll her window back up.

"You still there, Wade?" Riley asked, once the window was closed.

He was still on the line, but was busy running calculations to determine the distance at which their connection might fail. If she entered the gates and proceeded closer to the house, the code he had just sent to disrupt cell service in the house might disconnect them.

"Yeah, I'm here," Wade eventually answered.

"Since you seem to know what's going on in there, clue me in. What am I supposed to do now?" Riley asked.

"Stay there. I'll try to find out."

Wade could probably return cell service long enough to get a message to Sam, without running the risk that Mikles or his wife might make a call. He sent a quick text message to Sam that appeared to be from Riley and waited to receive confirmation the message was transmitted. Whatever response Sam sent would go directly to Riley's phone, not his. Hopefully her cell still had enough juice for her receive it. Wade waited a few minutes and then called Riley back.

"Did you get instructions from Sam?"

"Yes, he just texted me and said he was coming out to meet me at the gate," Riley answered. "I guess he wants to make sure Vince buys the complete package. Personally, I think he's selling past the close."

The remote mechanism that controlled the entry gates sounded. The heavy iron gates groaned loudly as they began to part.

"Someone's coming," Riley whispered.

Tap. Tap. Tap.

Riley had been watching the gated entrance, and had not seen Sam's approach. She presumed he had chosen to use the pedestrian exit on the other side of the entrance, rather than wait for the tortoise-injected motor to open the heavy gates. Wade listened to the sound of the car window receding.

"What the hell are you doing, Bunny? I've been going out of my mind here," a high-pitched voice shrieked over the whirr of the automatic window.

The shrill voice sure as hell wasn't Sam's. Riley turned away from the window and tried to engage the electronic control to close it. It refused to deploy while there were fingers in the way.

"Listen, Bunny. I don't have long before Sam gets here. You need to tell me how you got here and what it is you want," Cayren insisted.

She was not pleased that her friend was giving her the silent treatment. She yanked on the door to open it, only to discover it was locked. "What the hell, Bunny?"

Suddenly it was obvious. "You're not Bunny, are you?" Cayren hissed.

She knew something was off when Sam said Bunny was on the way over. The last time she saw Bunny, she was enjoying the ameri-ties of the yacht Vince kept docked in Clearwater. Vince always said it was a good practice to move a vessel out to sea when a storm was approaching. For the sake of convenience, mostly her own, Cayren had volunteered to oversee that part of their overall storm prepara-tion.

She and Bunny had set sail on smooth waters just before the storm hit the eastern coast of Florida. The conditions later changed as the storm crossed over land to meet the Gulf waters. The water had been far more agitated when she returned with the boat. The choppy ride had left Cayren feeling almost as nauseous as she felt right now.

Cayren had left the house in disbelief of both the notion that Bunny was back and that she had somehow turned traitor. Then again, it was also just like a bitch to be like that. Somewhere in the back of her mind, she always knew Bunny was capable of it. That's why she had come prepared.

Cayren reached into the front pocket of her sleeveless cotton vest and pulled out a hypodermic needle. With the speed of a cobra, she struck with the needle extended. Riley was caught off guard. She didn't have time to move out of the way. Time wasn't her only disadvantage. With her seat belt still attached, she could not have gone far anyway.

The strike found its mark. When Cayren felt the needle pierce Riley's clothes and break skin, she pressed the end to deliver the contents. It was powerful stuff. Mere seconds later, Riley was slumped over the steering wheel.

Cayren reached through the window to unlock the door. With the car door open, she disengaged the seat belt and lifted Riley's body just enough to push her over the console and into the passenger seat. She jumped behind the wheel, shifted into reverse and took off, putting the sedan's powerful engine through a few autobahn-level paces in the process.

"Riley?" Wade's voice reflected the severe uncertainty he felt. From the way things sounded, he wasn't expecting to get a reply.

"What the hell!" Cayren exclaimed. Either this was a talking car or the bitch pretending to be Bunny had been on the phone.

"Riley can't talk right now," Cayren snapped, before pressing a highlighted button on the car's touchscreen display to end the call.

She looked around to find the cell phone that must be connected to the car's phone system. It was in the floorboard by her feet, displaced during the transition of drivers. She grabbed the phone and tossed it out the open window. If this car worked like most late models, the connection would be lost within seconds.

It occurred to Cayren that she also had her cell phone on, which presumably could be used to trace her location. At the moment, the priority was to put real distance between her and whoever might have been close enough to give pursuit. That priority brought the need for excessive speed. The car was more than capable of it. Cayren struggled to match its ability, requiring both white-knuckled hands on the wheel to keep from losing control. She would have to dig out her phone and toss it later.

She made quick time over familiar back streets on her way to wider lanes. While en route, her thoughts raced to conclusions almost as fast as the car. Sam was pulling a sting on Vince. He had to be working with law enforcement, which meant they would be on her tail soon enough. The ruse had caused her to reveal herself, which was never part of the plan. She had played coy to this point, letting Bunny take the heat while she enjoyed the shade. It had all played out so well, until now. No one had even imagined she might be the one pulling all the strings. If it weren't for that meddling attorney, Sam Stone, she might've been in the clear.

ojo ojo ojo

Wade was struggling against the same wave of panic that crashed over him when he witnessed Halston's abduction. This time, he refused to release his sense of reason to the undertow. The disorienting effects of duress were starting to lose their advantage to both time and repetition.

He typed a command into the laptop to release the lock he had put on cell connections. Next, he dialed Sam's number, this time without a cloak.

"Who the hell is this?" Sam demanded. "And how did you get my number?"

"That isn't important," Wade responded. "Here's what you need to know. That Cayren chick did something to Riley and is now behind the wheel of the BMW speeding off to God-knows-where, taking Riley with her."

"How do you know that?" Sam inquired.

Sam was becoming less and less certain of his command over things with each passing minute; his demeanor and tone reflected the same. He hastened his pace toward the entrance gate to verify the unknown caller's information.

"We don't have time to get into that," Wade confessed. "Listen. I might have a way to slow Cayren down. Someone needs to go after them or call the police, or something."

Sam reached the open gate. He stepped out to where the call box was located and visibly scanned the surrounding area. Neither Riley nor the BMW was anywhere in sight. With limited resources at his disposal in the face of what appeared to be an epic fail, he had little choice than to work with what he was given.

"Have it your way. We can do formalities later," Sam stated. "Since you seem to know so much, tell me where the BMW is headed. I can get there before the police."

Wade considered the request. "I don't have that information. I'm pretty sure I can get it, though. It may take a few minutes."

"Whatever you need to do, just do it! Call me back when you have the location," Sam directed. His next call was to the cavalry.

"Where are you?" Sam demanded.

"I'm where you told me to be," Kent responded. "At the call center downtown. Why?"

"Remember when you told me not to get Riley involved?" Sam started. Ironically, a lightbulb appeared to be going on in Sam's head at precisely the same time the lights came on in the office building where Kent was standing.

Kent hated being right about something like this, but he almost always was. "Do I remember every day for the past few weeks?" Kent responded. "Yeah, I remember them all too well."

"Riley's in trouble. I need your help to get to her. Now!" Sam implored.

"What happened and where is she?" Kent inquired in a calm tone. From the sound of it, Sam was frantic enough for the both of them.

"Vince's wife, Cayren, has her. She's headed somewhere in a late model metallic gold BMW. I don't have a lock on their location yet, but I will."

Sam had no idea whether the unknown caller who just promised him the world could actually deliver. Believing he could was the only acceptable choice.

"Call me when you get it. I'm on my way," Kent said.

Kent was currently standing beside the double glass doors that fronted the call center for Mikles' sex toy souvenir business. He had arrived on the eighth floor of the downtown office building where the business was headquartered no more than fifteen minutes ago. At the time the power was out, leaving the building, with the exception of the lobby, hot and dark. A few battery-operated emergency lights were all that illuminated the stairs and hallways.

In a phone call earlier this morning, Sam suggested searching the business for information that might link Vince to Halston's disappearance. Since Halston and Mikles had originally crossed paths here, it wasn't a bad idea. It also made sense to go in now, before the staff returned and before the police connected all of the dots between Halston and Vince. At Sam's request, Kent agreed to search the office while Sam took care of something he claimed he wasn't at liberty to discuss. Whatever that something was, Sam apparently had not taken care of it.

Kent had taken the stairs on his way up, mostly because the power was out, although that wasn't the sole determinative factor. He also wanted to avoid the security cameras. It had only taken a minute for all of that to change. The power was back on and, after Sam's call, avoiding detection was no longer high on the list of priorities. It was replaced by two new contenders–speed and convenience–both of which had just experienced a meteoric rise of import.

Kent was pleased not to have to retrace his earlier path. He marched down the newly lit hall and into the elevator lobby. The floor indicator showed the elevator car was heading his way. To ensure it didn't pass his floor, Kent assaulted the "Down" button, more than once. When the elevator doors finally opened, he stepped inside and pressed one button to hasten the rejoining of the doors and then another that would return him to the parking garage.

Kent found himself alone behind the closed elevator doors which prompted a brief, uncharacteristic display of emotion. He pounded his fist against the metal wall and muttered a few choice words. Frustration with Sam's lack of focus was starting to take a toll. They had worked together many times before. It simply wasn't like Sam to make this type of mistake. In their line of work, one mistake is all it takes for someone to get hurt–or killed.

When the elevator doors opened, Kent bolted like a greyhound chasing a mechanical rabbit. He didn't have far to go. The number of cars parked in the garage when he arrived could have been assessed by a finger-count with a digit or two to spare. With so many open parking spaces, it had been easy to secure a choice one just a few strides from the elevator and stairs.

He was about to jump inside his Ford F-150 when inspiration struck. A masterfully restored yellow and black 1972 Chevelle SS hardtop was parked beside him. It wasn't there when he first arrived or he would've noticed it. It was the kind of vehicle that demanded a second look.

He jaunted over to the driver's side and peered through the window. By the look of it, the car was a sleeper. It had a shift kit with a staple shifter between the seats—the kind that probably allowed for manual shifting without a clutch—instead of the standard "three on a tree." That alone was a pretty good indicator the car was race-ready. The upgraded headers and exhaust system implied the same.

He anticipated the car's owner, who from the look of it clearly knew a thing or two about giving a car muscle, might have paired that shift kit with a torque converter. It's what he would have done. With that type of transmission, the converter would be necessary to ensure the engine didn't shift until the RPM's were high enough for the gear to take off without lagging.

No doubt about it. The car was a blower—a meticulously restored and then genetically-altered throwback from the time when the American auto industry made something worth keeping. If what the car had under the hood was as hot as the exterior suggested, the engine would easily put his truck to shame. It could probably rocket to illegal speeds in less than 60 seconds. Imagining the car doing just that after a burn out in third gear sent a thrill down Kent's spine.

It didn't take long to make the decision. Desperate times call for desperate measures. He pulled a metal device out of a tool box in the back of his truck. Leaning against the window to absorb any sound, he slid the device between the driver's side window and the window seal to disengage the lock. It was the kind of thing prepaid auto clubs did all day long at the request of stranded drivers. He wasn't stranded, but his need to get inside the car was just as urgent, perhaps more.

Fortunately, whoever owned this car was too confident to install a tacky, aftermarket alarm system. The lock gave way easily. Kent opened the door and slid into the driver's seat. He reached under the dash, disconnected a few wires and then connected them to each other while he gently pressed on the gas. The beast roared to life.

When he no longer needed it, Kent planned to leave the car somewhere safe and give the police an anonymous tip as to its whereabouts. Whoever owned and maintained a vehicle like this deserved at least that much respect. Hopefully, he would be able to return the car in the same condition it was when he found it. That good intention, however, was somewhat beyond his control.

He barreled out of the unattended parking garage and onto Orange Avenue. Ordinarily, the downtown thoroughfare would be filled with weekday traffic, but like most everything else, the storm made today an exception. With almost nonexistent traffic, Kent estimated he could make good time to wherever it was he ended up going. That optimistic calculation was quickly dashed.

Less than a block from the parking garage, Kent found himself stuck behind a car driven by a woman in no particular hurry. She was driving so slowly that, even though the light was green when Kent moved into the lane, she somehow managed not to make it through the intersection before the light cycled through yellow and on to red.

The street they were on had four lanes, two in either direction. Ordinarily, Kent might have passed the woman using the outside lane. Today, because of the storm, a large electric company vehicle had set up shop in the outside lane just before the intersection. The truck's fork lift was raised and a disheveled-looking worker, who had probably been on duty for the past thirty-six hours, was inside the lift checking the pole-mounted lines.

While waiting for the light to turn green, the woman in the car in front of Kent made a huge mistake. She started applying mascara. When finished, she made matters worse by slowly outlining her eyes with dark liquid eyeliner. By the time she graduated to lipstick, Kent had completely lost his cool. There was little he despised more than women putting on makeup while driving.

The light in the opposing lane turned yellow, which meant his light was going to turn green any minute now. Kent pressed the gas to rev the vintage car's engine. It responded with a hearty roar befitting its heritage. That should have been enough to make the point. It wasn't. When the light turned green, instead of moving forward the woman leaned over into her passenger seat. She appeared to be searching for something in her glove compartment. Enough was enough.

Kent shifted gears and let the car lurch forward until it made contact with the rear bumper of the woman's car. He then hit the gas. The makeup-obsessed woman probably wouldn't be smart enough to just hit the gas so she could get out of the way. But, if he caught her off guard, she might release the brakes. At that point, the force from the muscle car would be enough to move her car into the intersection. There would then be an opening in the outside lane large enough for Kent to maneuver past the truck, the annoying woman and whatever else stood in his way.

David Duong was sitting at his favorite table in the lobby of his office building. It was in a remote corner, next to a window that faced Orange Avenue–a perfect spot for people-watching. Joining him at the table was a triple serving of rapidly melting mint chocolate-chip ice cream and a bottle of water.

His taste buds were about to deliver a favorable critique on the first spoon of minty goodness before they were rudely interrupted. His ears had breaking news. They recognized the sound as easily as a mother recognizes the cry of her child. That was his engine. Those were his tires screaming with each rotation that forced them to leave rubber on the pavement.

Duong looked up and out the window facing the street just in time to see a flash of yellow and black speed past. Hoping to catch another look before the car sped out of view, he pressed his face against the glass like a child drooling over a department store's holiday window display.

It wasn't his imagination. There was no mistake. His ride just left without him.

CHAPTER 36

"You're not going to believe what just happened," David Duong exclaimed between heaving breaths.

It had been about ten minutes since full power cycled back on in the building, but the timing could not have been more provident. That small miracle afforded him the luxury of an elevator ride back up to the office. In the state he was in, he would not have made it otherwise. Just running the length of the office to reach the IT department had left him gasping for air.

Wade didn't acknowledge his boss or respond in any way. Whatever he was doing on the laptop was commanding his full attention.

"What are you doing?" Duong demanded. He followed the query with a stern command. He wasn't in the mood for Wade's typical trifling at the moment or to be ignored. "Your shift is over. You can leave, now."

"I'm not leaving," Wade barked. His fingers continued to move feverishly over the laptop's keyboard. "I'm in the middle of something that can't wait."

"No you aren't," Duong dismissed. "Syncing those laptops can absolutely wait."

Wade looked up. The intensity of his glare stopped Duong in his tracks. "You're not syncing the laptops, are you?"

"No. I'm not," Wade replied, forcefully.

"Is this work related?" Duong asked, his voice rising with confusion and growing concern.

Wade's focus had returned to the device in front of him. His fingers continued to fly. "Not even close."

"Then you need to stop what you're doing right now," Duong insisted.

Wade shook his head, and continued typing. "Can't."

"Have it your way. I was on my way to call 911 because someone just stole my car. I'll have the police deal with you too, when they get here." Duong really didn't want to go there, but he would if Wade didn't shape up fast.

Wade didn't respond. Instead he started cursing at the laptop. "Hurry up you good-for-nothing, grandma fucking piece of shit. I don't have time for your lame processor to churn butter."

Duong had never seen anyone act like this, especially not at work. Wade appeared to have lost most, if not all, of his marbles somewhere between their earlier conversation and the time it had taken for Duong to get ice cream. First his precious car was stolen, and now his prized employee was possessed. He had heard people could get stir crazy during storms, but the storm was long gone and the crazy was just getting started.

Duong walked over to Wade's desk and reached out to retrieve the laptop. He imagined that action to be sufficient for Wade to get the hint and abandon his folly. It wasn't. Wade leaped up with the laptop in his hands and moved away–crossing half the room in record time. Wade settled back down at another cubicle once he was well outside of Duong's reach.

"Don't you fucking touch me or this computer!" Wade bellowed.

This wasn't storm-crazy. This was real crazy, Duong decided. Whatever was going on in Wade's head was apparently very real to him.

"Listen, Wade. I don't understand what's going on but I can see it's important to you. Why don't you let me help you?"

"You can't help," Wade insisted. "You can't do what I'm doing."

"I might be able to," Duong offered. "Tell me what it is."

"It's the kind of shit you only dream about!" Wade shouted.

Duong blinked rapidly, his mind struggling to process the rebuke. Whatever was going on with Wade was obviously going to continue regardless of his admonitions. No sense in wasting precious time trying to stop it. There was another crime in progress that was of far more importance to him.

Duong stepped into his office and called 911. Once he had outlined the little information he had about his car being stolen and described his car in detail for the emergency operator, he hung up and returned to the IT cubicles to deal with Wade's situation. He did not report that yet, mostly because he had no idea how to describe it without sounding like a loon himself. If Wade was still acting like this when the officers responded to the call about his stolen car, they could deal with him then. Duong liked to wear black; he did not like to be the bad guy.

Duong slowly approached Wade, who was now mumbling to himself incoherently. He pulled a chair from a nearby cubicle and sat down close enough to Wade to observe whatever it was Wade was doing on the laptop computer. A window that flashed on the screen indicated Wade had successfully downloaded some type of software from the Internet.

"I know you're there, Duong," Wade said. "I told you I'm not leaving. I can't. Someone is in trouble and I've got to help."

"Okay. I'm not trying to stop you now. I've got my own problems," Duong advised. "I just wanted to see what it is I supposedly dream about."

"You ever hacked a car?" Wade asked. He looked away from the computer and toward Duong to receive what he knew would be a negative response.

The near maniacal look of intensity in Wade's eyes caused Duong to sink back further into the seat cushion of his adjustable task chair. "No. Can't say that I have," Duong responded, quietly.

"Well, I'm about to do something that's never officially been done. Watch and learn," Wade announced.

When Duong left the room to make his call, Wade had called Sam back and requested him to go back inside Mikles' house and gain access to one of Mikles' computers. Wade could do that remotely, through the connection he had created earlier with Sam's cell phone, but it was easier and faster if someone sitting at the computer just followed his instructions.

Wade was using a Bluetooth headset so he could talk to Sam handsfree. He needed all ten digits to command the keyboard.

"Are you in yet?" Wade inquired.

Duong looked around the room, and then back at Wade. "Are you talking to me?" he inquired.

Wade shook his head. "No, dumbass, I'm on the phone."

Wade paused for a minute and then spoke again, this time to the person on the phone. "No, I wasn't calling you that. My boss is here. Tell me when you get in."

A minute later, Wade got the answer he was seeking.

"I'm in," Sam advised. "Mikles is here with me. He'll give us the password if we encounter anything that's locked."

"Good. I don't need a password right now, but when we get there that'll save us some time," Wade said. "Right now, I need to know what model of cell phone his wife uses."

Wade heard a conversation going on in the background before Sam's response. "He says she has a Singtec Smartphone."

"Good," Wade said. "That makes this easier. Does his wife sync her phone with that computer or another one?"

Another rush of voices in the background preceded the response. "She uses a different one. He's not sure where it is."

"Do they back up to a server, either locally or remote?"

No voices this time. Wade figured that meant either the guy didn't know or was simply shaking his head. Sam confirmed the suspicion, but in a good way. "He says yes."

"Yes, to what part?" Wade countered.

"You're starting to sound like a lawyer now," Sam responded before redirecting the question to Vince.

Wade speed read a .pdf file he had opened on the laptop while the men on the other side of the line reached a consensus. He had to assimilate a great deal of information in a short span of time to make this work.

"Vince thinks they have a local server. It should be connected to the router," Sam announced.

"Okay, here's how this needs to go down. I'm going to send you a request to pair with the computer you're on. When I'm in, I'm going to access the server and find the backup from Cayren's computer. I'm going to remotely restore that to the computer I'm on. That'll take me a couple of minutes."

Wade worked in dead silence while those waiting for him to save the day nervously held their breath.

"I'm in," he announced, a lot sooner than anyone expected. "What's her password?"

Sam responded in a sardonic tone, likely due to the absurdity of what he had to repeat. "He thinks it's 'PinkVelvet.' That's the one she uses for everything else."

Wade smirked. Women have the dumbest passwords. He could've brute forced something like that in about an hour. He didn't have an hour. It was possible he didn't even have the five to ten minutes this was going to take. "That means she probably uses the same one on her cell phone, right?"

"Most likely," Sam responded, after a short wait. "What do you need me to do now?"

"Just wait. If this works, I should be able to nail down their location and direction in a few," Wade advised.

"Brilliant," Sam responded. "While we're waiting, how about telling me your name and how you got my phone number?"

Wade gave his response in staccato. "Riley gave it to me. I'm her client. Wade Warner."

"You're the witness to Halston's disappearance, aren't you?" Sam asked.

"Yeah, that's me. Hold on, okay. I can't really chat while my brain's in overdrive."

Wade had a duplicate version of the desktop screen from Cayren's computer on his laptop monitor. He accessed the program that served the dual function of digital music storage and device synchronization for the cell phone Cayren used—the phone he was hoping she had on her at the moment. With the application launched, he signed into Cayren's account using the user information automatically populated by the program and the password Vince had provided.

The program accepted the inputs, giving him full access to the account. He then accessed the online mobile application store and typed the word "coupon" into the search box.

Duong, who had to this point been watching with great interest, interrupted with a query in keeping with his nature. "Is this really the time to shop for discounts?"

Wade's arm shot out in Duong's direction, his hand extended in the manner often utilized when commanding a sock-puppet. To emphasize his point, he closed his fingers as the puppet might to close its lips.

"Zip it, Duong. I'm looking for a rogue app I heard about. It's a destination-based coupon locater that comes with a few freebies like a spyware trojan linked to a botnet."

When the search response rendered a link to the app he was looking for, Wade accessed it and downloaded the program.

"This is gonna show up as a charge on your client's account," he advised Sam.

Wade listened with appreciation while Sam easily silenced what sounded like Mikles' inane request for the amount of the impending charge. "Bore off, Vince. That's the least of your worries right now," Sam barked.

A moment later, the computer signaled affirmation that the app was fully loaded. Wade then went into the administrative panel of the synchronizing program to confirm Cayren had it set to automatically push new downloads to all devices. Cloud computing was a beautiful thing, for a hacker. Infect one; infect 'em all.

"What's happening now?" Sam inquired nervously. "We can't wait much longer. My guy in pursuit is gonna be driving in circles if I don't give him somewhere to go."

"Most of these devices sync automatically if they're on. It won't take long to push the program to her cell phone. When it does, I can access her phone by putting her cell number into the web-based control panel set up by the bot master."

"I get all the latest security updates. I haven't seen anything about an app having malware like that," Duong advised. "Where did you hear about it?"

"Caught some chatter about it in a web forum for hackers. It's a new bug. The antivirus wonks haven't picked up on it yet, which is why *you* haven't heard of it," Wade responded. "By the time something like this hits their radar, the damage is done. That's why I like to get my information at the source."

Duong's expression aptly indicated his appreciation for Wade's enterprising effort. "Is that how you caught the virus that was slowing down the servers last month?"

Wade nodded. "I catch stuff that could shut down your beloved servers every day. That's what I'm doing while you're finishing your morning coffee and reading the newspaper online."

Wade stared intently at the monitor. He had accessed the malware's control panel and was now examining it to determine user protocols. The panel didn't take long for him to decipher. He located the appropriate field and typed the required information into the blinking text box. Seconds later, his fingers started to fly over the keyboard again.

"I'm in," he announced. "I'm going to use the location services on the phone first. That should tell me where they are. I'll have to use something else to get an idea where they might be headed."

"I need to put you on hold and call my colleague who's in pursuit," Sam said.

"No problem," Wade stated. "I'm accessing the coordinates now. I should have them by the time you get your guy on the phone."

⚭ ⚭ ⚭

After peeling away from the stoplight on Orange Avenue, Kent headed south toward the closest ramp onto the expressway. It was the best location to commence pursuit given the limited knowledge he had on the matter. Cayren started her trek in the southwestern part of town; he was starting his from the north.

If he was lucky, she was headed his way and would be crossing paths with him in no time. The chase would be a little more challenging if she had chosen to go south or further west, toward Tampa. Even so, the numerous exits from and ramps to the expressway, as well as the limited traffic, would make it easy enough for him to change course as necessary.

Kent turned on to the ramp leading to the expressway, the monster he was driving requiring everything he had to handle it. Naturally, with both hands fully engaged, his cell rang. It was most likely Sam; he was supposed to call with directions. In anticipation of the call, Kent had smartly placed his cell phone in the passenger seat.

The car's shift kit allowed him to shift gears without use of a clutch. To accelerate from the ramp, Kent shifted into second and then reached over for his phone. "Where am I headed?" he inquired.

Wade's predicted timing for retrieving the information was on the mark. Sam had just received what he needed to convey.

"Cayren's on the Turnpike," Sam answered.

"That doesn't tell me a lot. Where on the Turnpike and going which way?" Kent demanded.

"In Lake County, around Clermont. Looks like she's headed to I-75."

"I'm about ten miles from there. If I don't hit any traffic I can make up the time," Kent said.

"Is your truck making all that noise? Sounds like you're in a tractor," Sam stated.

"I borrowed something faster."

"Borrowed? Does the owner know?" Sam asked.

"If not, he will soon. I'm sure to pick up some heat driving this thing and going the speed I'm about to. You may have to call this one in. I don't want to get stopped before I get to them."

"If I do that we lose the advantage of our cover," Sam reminded his friend. "Try to stay under the radar."

Kent scoffed. "I'm on a toll road in a bowtie that flies like the wind and looks like a bee. The only radar I won't be pinging is The Weather Channel's. How'd you get their location without calling it in?"

"I'm not sure. When I find out, I'll let you know," Sam quipped. "Listen. There might be a way to slow them down. I've got someone working on it now. Just get there before anything else happens."

The silent ending to Sam's advisory was understood. Kent needed to get there before anything happened *to her*.

"I'm on it," Kent responded.

He tossed his cell back in the passenger seat, took hold of the shift handle and shifted it as far back as it would go. The four-lane road in front of him was open; he intended to make good use of it.

While Sam was on the phone with Kent, Wade had gotten down to business. The program he downloaded earlier was a black hat reiteration of cutting-edge software designed a few years ago by a couple of professorial types. The theory underlying their prototype had been simple. Cars, like most everything else these days, are run by computers. The computer that constitutes a car's brain is comprised of a large number of electronic control units, otherwise known as ECUs. Interrupt, fuzz or reverse engineer the workings of the ECUs and thereafter whatever function they once controlled could be obstructed or even commandeered.

Existing automotive systems are exceedingly vulnerable to hacks, some more than others. That warning had already sounded in the tech industry, but it had not reverberated far beyond it. Thus far, the consensus among experts was that there was no need to alarm consumers, yet. One reason underlying the consensus was that the range within which exploitation of an automotive system could transpire was ordinarily very limited. Another reason was the perceived lack of motivation for the so-inclined hacker. Simply put, there wasn't any money in it.

Money wasn't today's objective. This hack, if Wade managed to pull it off, was the ultimate for a white hat. This one was to save the life of someone he hoped could restore his.

The app he had pushed to Cayren's cell phone through the standard sync operation gave him complete control over her phone. He remotely activated the Bluetooth on Cayren's phone and then coupled the device with his laptop to allow the software to run remote packet sniffing commands. With a complete reading on the multiple CAN packets that were utilized by the BMW for system diagnostics, he could then observe or reverse-engineer the packets using the black hat software interface. The next step was to alter the packets to send modified firmware updates to the car's ECUs.

Once he isolated the packets for the functions he wanted to control, Wade paired Cayren's cell with the BMW's Bluetooth using the same code he had given Riley for the earlier pairing with her phone. From this point, dashboard pwnage was almost a given. The car's advanced onboard computer system was a hacker's dream. Wade had just made that dream a reality.

CHAPTER 37

The adventure had not started with a plan. The morning's unexpected turn of events compelled Cayren to act without forethought. She glanced over at the limp body in her passenger seat for the first time since she started her hasty escape across Central Florida. The woman looked nothing like Bunny. Sam could've done a lot better in choosing a doppelganger.

Her neck was getting stiff from holding all of the morning's tension while also supporting a formal 10-and-2 driving position. Cayren lowered her shoulders and stretched her neck from side to side. She followed the linear stretch with a circular one. Slow subsequent release of the deep breath that had accompanied her movement helped clear her head.

She may not have started out with a plan, but the one she was quickly developing was a good as any. At this speed, she would make it to the yacht in Clearwater in record time. There was little traffic on the road to slow her progress. Hopefully that would continue, as would the absence of any random member of law enforcement trying to meet a monthly citation quota.

The ocean was a good place to wash away the past—exactly what she needed if she was going to make a fresh start. The Turnpike would feed into I-75 before long. That's where anyone who might be giving chase would think she was going. If she exited the Turnpike in one of the more isolated areas, well before I-75, she could double back toward the Tampa Bay area by taking Highway 33 down to I-4 or wait a little longer to cut through the Green Swamp before cutting back over to I-75 South. The swamp sounded like a good idea. It might be possible to ditch the car there.

"You're getting a little ahead of yourself," she mused aloud.

The announcement followed the realization that before she dumped one car, she needed to have a replacement. She rose up slightly from her seat to examine her reflection in the rear view mirror. Getting a new set of wheels wouldn't be too hard. Her body and face had managed to get her pretty far over the years. They had a few more miles in them; enough to secure a junker.

She took a second look into the rear view mirror, this time to utilize its intended purpose. Still no one behind her. With that confirmation and the early makings of a plan in place, she was confident enough to settle back into her seat. There was no longer a dire need to worry about being followed. She had too much of a head start and too fine of a vehicle for anyone to catch up to her now. She could afford to slow down and breathe easier.

She reached into her pocket for her cell phone, and pressed the button that was supposed to turn it off. It took an inordinate number of tries before the screen went blank. Presumably, turning it off was enough to keep anyone from tracing her by its signal. That was assuming it was off at all.

It occurred to her that the car might also have some sort of navigation system that could send and receive information from a satellite. She looked over at the touch screen display in the center of the dashboard to examine the options. There had to be a button somewhere that turned the nav system off.

The rain sensing wipers suddenly deployed, as did the mechanism that lubricated them with wiper fluid. The combination of water and wiping, when mixed with the bounty of lovebug guts already on the windshield, blurred her view. She scrambled to find the switch to turn the wipers off. She found it, nowhere near the dashboard touch screen. The confusing series of events which followed caused her to ease up on the gas.

"There is no way I pressed that button," she announced. "Why the frick won't these things turn off?"

She repeatedly tried the switch that was supposed to turn the wipers off, but to no avail. They refused to stop their cut-time cadence. Her attention was then directed to the windshield where the mileage, speed and other information was projected. The projected information started to change from numbers into letters. The message it now displayed–SELF DESTRUCT–was far more ominous than the excess speed that was previously shown.

"Dang it! I must've hit the wrong button," Cayren exclaimed. She continued to press on the touch screen console, but it didn't respond.

She was fairly certain the car was not going to explode. The manufacturer would get their ass sued off if they put a feature like that in the car. The message had to mean something else, like a security system had been armed. That could be bad. She pressed the screen a few more times, harder than she had before.

"Ouch! Stop that." The car spoke in a pleasant feminine voice.

Cayren nearly leapt from her seat. "What did you say?"

"Stop pushing my buttons," the car said. "Oh, and stop the car while you're at it."

Her speed vacillated between 40 and 50 mph during the melee, which was a far cry from the breakneck pace she had previously employed. Even with the fluctuations, she was still making forward progress too quickly for Kent to catch up.

"Cars don't talk. You better shut up, bitch, or tell me who's doing the talking for you," Cayren shrieked.

The car's entertainment system began to blast heavy metal guitar music at an ear-splitting level.

"That's not funny! Stop it right now or I'm going to bank this foreign-made tank into a tree," Cayren declared.

The car's voice returned through the sound system, this time preceding its taunt with a maniacal laugh. "Bwaahahahahahaha! Go ahead and try."

Cayren gripped the steering wheel and tried to turn it to the left, then right. Nothing happened. The dashboard instruments indicated cruise control was engaged. If this was cruise control, it wasn't anything like the type she had previously encountered. Ordinarily, that function just maintains a pre-established speed. In this case, the possessed car appeared to be driving itself, and doing so at the preferred pace of a snail. Cayren screamed and kicked the dash from underneath. She could take a spiral down-ramp in a parking deck faster than this.

Kent was racing down the Turnpike at a speed any street racer would envy. He studied the make of the few cars that he came upon and easily passed. So far, none met the description. If Sam had actually managed to do the impossible and slow Cayren's car down, he could be coming up on her any time now. Holding tightly to the steering wheel with one hand, he reached over to grab his phone.

He voiced dialed Sam and launched into his query as soon as the phone established a connection. "I'm on the Turnpike, heading toward I-75. Where are they?"

"Mile marker 280," Sam stated. "She's not going anywhere fast. I'm somewhere behind you; headed your way."

"Okay. Listen, I don't want to know how you're doing it, but can you stop her car when I get there? Don't do it before. I don't want her to run," Kent said.

"I think so," Sam said. "I'll have to ask. Hold on." The line went silent.

Kent was afforded extended visibility by virtue of an intermittently overcast sky and a straight stretch of pavement. A flash of gold appeared on the horizon about a mile ahead of him. Sam needed to come back with the right answer, and fast. Otherwise, Kent was going to have to improvise.

The BMW was within plain sight in a matter of seconds. Kent slowed down to the speed limit on his approach, hoping not to spook Cayren. He also wanted to confirm it was the right car before he took further action. He approached the slow-moving BMW on the left, taking note of the driver's blonde hair and manic behavior as he passed by. This had to be the car, but he didn't see Riley. He drove a few hundred yards ahead while he waited for Sam's reply.

"C'mon, c'mon, c'mon already," Kent harped.

Sam's voice cut the tension. "I think we can slow the car down some more. We don't want to stop it yet, because that might cause the air bags to deploy. We need to confirm where Riley is in the car to make sure stopping it wouldn't do more harm than good."

"I passed the car a minute ago. I didn't see anyone but the driver," Kent stated.

"It's possible Cayren released her," Sam said, with a hint of optimism.

"I wouldn't get my hopes up," Kent advised. "If Riley's not in the car, it likely means Cayren dumped her body on the side of the road somewhere."

Kent's astute observation was met with silence. He didn't have time to wait for Sam to break it. "Suck it up, Sam, and get me some damn information. Is Riley in the car, or not?"

"Hold on. We're checking."

Sam was in his Bentley, using one hand to vacillate between calls with Wade and Kent, and somehow managing to use the other to steer the car. The balancing act was made all the more impressive by the fact it was performed while he raced against time at full throttle. He had already made the Turnpike and was approaching Cayren's location fast.

The BMW's verbal taunts had Cayren too hysterical to notice the side view mirrors shift position. The mirrors retracted toward the car as they might when called in to avoid damage at a car wash. The mirrors then made an awkward horizontal twist that turned the bottom of their casing upward to face the vehicle. The small cameras that were imbedded in the bottom of the mirror casing were part of the vehicle's parking-assist package. Normally, the cameras served to aid the driver in parallel parking, among other things. Wade was using them for an entirely different purpose.

The feed from the cameras displayed on the screen in the car's dashboard. It wouldn't do them much good there and he didn't want to alert Cayren to his surveillance, so Wade redirected it to his laptop. There was no sign of Riley near the front or back of the driver's side. Wade turned his attention to the passenger side.

"What was she wearing?" Wade called out.

Sam had Kent on hold, and was waiting with shallow breath on the other end of Wade's line. He searched his recollection for the answer. Riley looked as fetching as ever this morning, but he had not really taken notice of how she accomplished that feat. Something she had said before they left on their regrettable mission echoed in his head.

"She's wearing a coral jacket," Sam advised. He recalled her stated reason for choosing it was that it seemed like the kind of thing Bunny might wear.

"That doesn't tell me much," Wade replied. "Coral reef, in its natural habitat, comes in many colors including ones on the far reaches of the visual spectrum."

Sam exhaled with frustration. Only a complete weed would know the color spectrum of coral reef. "It's orange! A bright orange."

Wade examined the screen again. The resolution wasn't much to speak of, but a bright color like orange should be evident. Following a close examination, he clapped his hands victoriously.

"I see orange. It looks like she might be bent over in the seat and floorboard of the passenger side of the car. All I can see is a blob, but it's definitely orange."

Sam swallowed hard. It was good news, sort of. He knew where Riley was now. Unfortunately, the flip side of that was the realization he had somehow managed to have a woman he cared for reduced to an orange blob on the floorboard of a stolen car.

Kent had slowed down to a crawl, not wanting to get too far ahead of Cayren. When he got the go ahead from Sam, he hit the gas and made a hard left. The sudden change in course caused the responsive machine he was in to briefly spin out before it regained traction on the pavement. When the rotations ended, the Chevelle was facing the opposite direction from where it had started, almost as if it knew where Kent intended to go next. In mere seconds he was racing back toward Cayren—approaching her slow-moving vehicle head on. It was an unusual matchup for a game of chicken, and one that could end badly if Sam couldn't deliver on his promise to stop the BMW.

Inside the BMW, Cayren watched the unfolding scene in front of her with horror. The sight of a flying yellow monster rushing toward her was almost as unfathomable as the inexplicable action taken by her own car. A sudden trigger of the stop-and-go feature in the Active Cruise Control caused the BMW to automatically apply the brakes without any assistance from her. Wade had managed to slow the car down sufficiently before the brakes engaged to avoid a jerking halt. Kent wasn't quite as lucky. He down shifted on his approach and hit the brakes, but not soon enough. He had to swerve to the right to avoid crashing into Cayren.

The Chevelle came to a tire-smoking stop a few yards behind the BMW. Kent jumped out and approached Cayren's car slowly and deliberately from behind. She was still in the car, apparently having a full-blown meltdown. Sam had indicated Cayren's door would be locked and could not be opened from the inside. He had also indicated the lock on Riley's side would be disengaged as soon as Kent gave the signal.

As he neared the car, Kent crouched below the BMW's windows and moved to the passenger side door.

"I'm in position," he whispered into his phone.

A single thump indicated the passenger side door had unlocked. Kent raised his head slightly to confirm Cayren's whereabouts. She was still in the driver's seat, having chosen to scream obscenities at the car rather than try to escape. Kent reached up and pulled on the passenger side door handle. He opened the door swiftly, grabbed Riley's limp body with both arms and pulled her out of the car.

Somewhere in the background, Kent heard the screech of another set of tires. In an instant, Sam was in front of him. "How is she? Does she have a pulse?" Sam demanded.

"You may not have noticed, but my hands are a little full. There wasn't time to check," Kent shot back.

Sam took hold of Riley and rushed back to his Bentley carrying her in his arms. He fully reclined the passenger seat and laid her in it. His cheek, pressed lightly against Riley's face, was welcomed by a rush of warm air. Still seeking confirmation, he pressed two fingers against the side of her neck.

Riley was breathing. She had a slow pulse. By outward appearances, she seemed to be in a deep sleep. Whatever it was Cayren had used on her did not appear to be fatal, at least not yet.

On his way back around to the driver's seat Sam glanced in the direction where he had last seen Kent just in time to watch Cayren make a run for it and Kent rush her like a linebacker. Cayren hit the pavement hard. The landing was definitely going to leave a mark.

CHAPTER 38

A bright light caused Riley's eyelids to flutter. She attempted to avoid the glare by turning her face to the right, to no avail. The sun was nearing its peak. Its commanding light filled the windows over her bed, and then some. The beams that overflowed the silk draperies cascaded down onto her king-sized bed, bringing unnecessary warmth along for the ride.

Heavier than normal lids continued their struggle against the inevitable, but eventually succumbed. Now awake, and with eyes opened, Riley turned back toward the light. First into focus was a familiar patch of ceiling. Many nights had been spent staring at that very spot while deep thought frustrated any attempt at peaceful sleep. Last night was apparently not one of those nights. Rather, it seemed she was awakening from what had been her most restful night in years.

The night had been so restful, in fact, that she couldn't recall the day before. Riley tried to scan her memory for a recent recollection, but was thwarted by the sensation that someone was pounding her temples from the inside. She freed her hands from the twisted covers and raised them to rub her forehead.

When the sheets moved against her body, she came to a surprising revelation. What she had on was a far cry from the soft, stretchy type of thing she preferred to sleep in. She was still dressed in street clothes.

What the hell? You don't sleep in your clothes, her logical mind reported.

This was starting to feel oddly similar to a dream she once had. Of course, she had a co-star in that dream. Not just any co-star; a preposterous one, even for a dream. The recollection would have brought a chuckle, if her throat had been capable of it. She tried to swallow, unsuccessfully. Juice or water or most anything wet would be the perfect way to wash the night away.

She pushed the covers off and started to rise when she felt something next to her stir. Her body went on full alert. The sensation of someone or something next to her in bed was not one of recent memory. Mason usually slept at the foot of the bed, but he was nowhere to be seen.

Riley caught her breath and turned to face the culprit lying in wait next to her. Apparently just awakening himself, he stared at her with eyes half-open. His expression warmed when their eyes met. He had that same crooked little smile on that he had worn in her dream but thankfully, unlike her dream, he was wearing something else.

It took a great deal more effort than it should have for her to speak. "Sam, what are you doing in my bed? And why are you wearing pants?"

The crooked smile changed into a wide one. "I can take them off if you'd prefer."

"No! Of course not. It's just . . . nothing happened, right? I'm dressed and you are, sort of, so nothing happened," Riley firmly stated, trying to convince herself.

"You don't remember? I'm not sure how to take that," Sam teased.

Even with the layer of fog that clouded her mind, Riley couldn't resist a taunt. "Guess you didn't make that much of an impression."

Sam pulled himself up into a sitting position and leaned back against the headboard. "Oh, it was more than memorable. Some might say it bordered on life altering."

Riley attempted to swallow again, this time more successfully. She searched her mind for any recollection of what had happened and why she was waking up to find Sam Stone, of all people, in her bed. She sat up straight and turned back to face him.

He looked so smug sitting there–like he knew a secret he had no intention of sharing. It would be easy to be angry at him for whatever advantage he might have taken. Although, probably not for long. Riley's gaze foolishly wandered away from his eyes and moved down to the spray of dark hair that covered his chest and stomach. He was tan, dark-haired, and lean with muscles. Throw a doughnut into the mix and she might as well be staring at the only things on the planet that made her weak in the knees.

Sam reached toward her. He brushed her hair away from her face and then held his hand to her forehead as a parent might to a child. The contact at first, then the nature of it, startled her. She thought about moving away but chose not to.

"You're acting like I have a fever or something. What's up with that?" Riley asked.

"Just checking," Sam replied. "The doctor said I needed to keep an eye on your breathing and temperature."

The pounding in her temples was starting to expand. Sam had no right to make her work this hard for an answer. "What doctor? I don't remember a doctor. I don't remember inviting you to sleep with me, either."

"It was your doctor. He agreed to make a house call," Sam advised. "And I confess. I did take the liberty of assuming you would invite me to stay with you, had you been able."

He stared at Riley with a look of genuine concern. Teasing her was fun, but only to an extent. It was entirely possible the sedative Cayren had used had left a genuine gap in Riley's memory.

"You really don't remember anything, do you?" he asked.

Riley's eyes moved upward while she surveyed her limited recollection, and then returned to Sam with resolution. "No. I really don't. I feel like I've been out of it for a while. What time is it?"

Sam looked down at his watch. "It's around 11:00."

Riley's confusion and growing anxiety were apparent. "So, it's Wednesday, then? Yesterday was Tuesday. We were going to go do something yesterday morning, but I can't remember if we did."

"Actually, it's Thursday," Sam said. "You have been out for a while."

"A while?" Riley recoiled. "That's two days, Sam. How is that possible? What in the hell happened?"

Spelling all of it out could take some time. Sam had a better idea. "I imagine you're hungry."

"According to you, I haven't eaten in two days. So, yeah. I'm starving," Riley answered.

"How about I get you some breakfast? We can work through the details while we eat." Sam started to rise. "I've got doughnuts downstairs. I'll bring them up with some coffee."

ৡ৹ ৡ৹ ৡ৹

Kent hastened his pace over the tropical terrain. Another day, another rabbit to run down in a hole he'd prefer not to be in. He was trying to move quietly, but the underbrush that littered the hiking trail wasn't cooperating. This would have been so much easier if she had parked herself by the ocean like all the other beach bunnies.

The storm had not hit the Caymans, but had come close before taking a wide right out toward the Atlantic. The same tropical trough that had pulled the storm back over land, and across the state of Florida, was keeping the humidity levels in the Caribbean near a hundred percent. After nearly a decade in Florida, the heat was something he should be used to. He wasn't.

He stopped to wipe beads of moisture from his brow with his sleeve. The sound of fallen palm fronds cracking underfoot somewhere ahead encouraged him. Not much further to go. He stepped off the path, intending to follow it from behind the cover of the lush, green foliage growing along the perimeter. Quickening his pace, he expected the mark to come into view any time now.

Bunny was moving slowly along the trail, enjoying all the bountiful colors of nature. She preferred the tree-lined trail and its natural canopy to its alternative—an uncomfortable seat under an umbrella on the beach. The smell of the sea was nearly as evident along the trail as it was by the shore. Here, however, there was the additional advantage of a fragrant mix of flowers.

This was where the island's real flavor could be found. Naturally, this being the best place on the island also made it the place where the island's vermin preferred to hang out. She placed each step carefully, looking down periodically to ensure the ground below her wasn't slivering. There are only a few species of snakes in the Caymans, and none are reportedly threatening to humans, but Bunny didn't know that and wouldn't care. Snakes make great shoes, and that was as close to one as she wanted to get.

She looked up when she heard the footsteps of someone walking toward her. The approach struck her as odd since there were no other cars parked in the public access parking when she arrived and she had not seen anyone in front of her on the trail before now. Her eyes met a familiar pair.

"Hello, Ms. Keiler. Fancy meeting you here."

Bunny smiled. This was not an entirely unpleasant surprise. She had not spoken to anyone for about a week. She reached out to shake Kent's hand. "I've seen you before at the club, working the door, right? Did Cayren send you with the supplies?"

"Not exactly," Kent responded. He took her hand, and then reached further to take hold of her wrist, firmly.

"Hey, not so rough. At least not out here. I don't like sand in my hair," Bunny advised.

Kent paused to place the comment. If he wasn't mistaken, she was hitting on him. That was a new one. "No worries," he answered. "I don't like the sand anywhere. This won't get dirty unless you make it."

A guy with a nice butt *and* a quick wit? Cayren sent the right one; this guy was just her type. Bunny was about to take the verbal foreplay further, but stopped short. Something about this didn't feel right. She tried to withdraw her arm from Kent's firm grip.

"All right, hot stuff. I'm game. Just loosen up a little on the appendage. I bruise easy."

"I wouldn't be doing it right if it didn't hurt a little," Kent taunted. "If you want this to go easy, though, why don't we head back to your car?"

He stepped closer and reached out for Bunny's other arm. Her eyes met his with an unexpected look of longing. She really did like it rough. The look faded as an alternative thought took passion's place.

"You're not really a bouncer, are you?" Bunny sulked.

"No ma'am. Not today," Kent replied. He was almost sorry to disappoint her.

Kent held both of Bunny's arms with one hand while he reached into his back pocket for his cuffs. With his preferred implement of bondage in hand, he turned Bunny around, pulled her arms behind her and secured the cuffs on her wrists, taking more care in the process than he might with a less fascinating catch. Most of the criminals he dealt with did not have legs like hers.

Bunny didn't struggle; there was no point in it. Her thoughts raced back to Criminal Law 101. If she talked, and fast, there might be a deal. "I don't know what she told you, but I had nothing to do with what happened to that girl."

Kent shook his head at the irony. Bunny and Cayren had supposedly been close friends for over a decade. "Funny. She said the same thing."

"That bitch! I can prove she's wrong," Bunny stated. "She's not the most incandescent orb in the fixture. I've got her on tape."

Kent turned Bunny to face the direction from which she had come and directed her to start walking. "I've got an officer searching your suite. If he hasn't found your stash of evidentiary goodies by the time we get back there, you can show me where it is. You also have something else I'm going to need you to hand over."

Fuck! They knew about the flash drive. "I'm not sure I know what you're talking about," Bunny said. "Still, let's say . . . for the sake of argument . . . that I did have something else. What's it worth to you?"

"Depends on what it is and what you've done with it. We've got a mile or two of trail ahead of us. Why don't you start at the beginning? I imagine you're better than most at weaving a good yarn," Kent replied.

"None of it was illegal, at least not the way it was planned," Bunny started. "The plan . . . my plan . . . was to hit Vincent financially, coming and going. He was supposed to give that blasted case to me so I could make sure he got hit with a seven figure verdict. I found that girl, the one that disappeared. She was one of the girls I interviewed early on, even before the case went to court. Met her at her office. When I saw the picture of her and Vincent on her desk, I knew. That dick was boning her just like he did a lot of the others. Only there was more to it with her. It was a good bet they were making plans toward something more serious, so I told Cayren about it."

"I don't imagine Cayren took that lightly," Kent opined.

"Actually, she wasn't as surprised as I thought she would be. She was on board and eager to help right away, or so I thought. Anyway, the girl would have been the perfect corroborating witness. Then Cayren started to extemporize. She went totally off script. I didn't find out about what she had done until days later, when she spilled the beans to me outside the club."

"Did she tell you what she had done with Halston?"

"Do I look like the kind of cow that gives free milk? You're going to have to put me on a greener pasture if you want me to put out," Bunny protested.

"I'm not the one you need to talk to for that. I'm just the guy that does the dirty work," Kent replied. "I am curious about something, though. How was this plan of yours supposed to help Cayren?"

"It was genius, if you ask me. Which you did," Bunny gloated. "When the case went to court, I clued Vincent in on ways he could protect his assets from a judgment creditor. You know, just in case things went south. I had him make me a list of his assets so we could decide together which ones to transfer. It needed to look legit."

Kent had spent enough time on assignments with agents going through contentious divorces to know the value of that list. "You did that so he wouldn't be able to deny those assets later, when Cayren filed for divorce."

Bunny turned back to reward Kent with a look of appreciation. "You're pretty smart. I'm smarter, though. That was just the backup plan. Once I had the list, I went over it with Cayren to see what she wanted to keep. Then, to lay the groundwork, I advised Vincent, sort of offhand, about the law in Florida that protects assets if they are held by a spouse. I knew once the other girl came forward to testify in the lawsuit he would realize he might lose the case. At that point, with a little nudging, he would decide to transfer everything to Cayren's name before the trial date so Audra and that coruscant little attorney of hers won't get their grubs on it."

"So, why get rid of Halston?" Kent asked. "For your plan to work, you needed her to testify, didn't you?"

"I know, right?" Bunny mused. "That was all Cayren. And that's all I'm going to say about that right now."

"Fine by me," Kent said. "There'll be plenty of time to talk on the flight back to the States, if you change your mind."

CHAPTER 39

⸺◦⟡◦⸺

Riley grabbed a handful of fabric to lift her floor-length skirt. The layers of lavender chiffon were chafing against the rhinestones imbedded in her shoes. If the rub continued the fabric was likely to thread, and that would be entirely unacceptable.

It was quiet in the long corridor just outside of the hotel's grand ballroom. The animated conversations of guests and live music from the ballroom were still audible, albeit muffled behind the doors she had just walked through. If the waiter she had spoken to on her way out advised accurately, the restrooms were at the end of the corridor that led to the hotel lobby. It was a bit of a jaunt to be taking in heels, but a necessary one. After a good hour of eating, drinking and merriment, her lipstick needed a do-over.

When she neared her destination at the end of the corridor a tuxedo-clad gentleman approached from the direction of the lobby.

"Aren't you the height of fabulosity?" Riley said, with genuine admiration. It was no surprise that he cleaned up nicely.

"Thank you. You aren't so bad yourself," Sam replied.

"I didn't expect to see you here. Did your firm reserve a table for the gala?"

"No. We made a private donation instead," Sam advised. "Dani asked me to come, though. She couldn't get away tonight."

Riley was genuinely surprised. "I wondered where she was. I tried to call her several times, but the line's been busy."

"I got the impression she had a number of calls to make," Sam said. He continued to admire the way the bodice of Riley's dress did her and any man with an eye for aesthetics justice.

"She talked to you tonight, and not me? What's up with the two of you being thick as thieves these days? I don't get it."

Sam settled against a long table that was placed along the back wall of the corridor, and fidgeted with his yet-to-be tied bow tie. "She knew I would see you tonight. I guess she figured I would convey the message that she couldn't make it."

"That's not at all like her. I'm gonna call her again later and get the real scoop," Riley challenged.

"Be my guest," Sam responded, as if he surely had nothing to hide.

Riley found the story incredibly suspicious. She took a step towards Sam, who was now sitting on the table. The intent was to study his eyes for any indication that he wasn't telling the truth. She discovered something else during the course of the examination. It was the type of thing that required immediate attention.

She pushed Sam's hands away from his collar. "Here, let me tie that. You're making a mess of it."

Sam gladly relinquished the reigns. Allowing her to fix his neckwear meant she would have to move closer—not the kind of thing that warranted an objection, at least not from him. While Riley untangled the knot he had made and proceeded to refasten it more appropriately, she stood between his straddled legs. The moment felt intimate, prompting them to share it in silence.

Riley took a step back to observe her handiwork. She reached out to tug on the ends of the bow a few last times to perfect the tips before signaling final approval. "There you go. That's how it's supposed to look."

"Much obliged, Miss Morgan," Sam said. "Are you leaving, already?"

"No, just taking a breather. I'm still a little wobbly from the whole Cayren caper," Riley confessed. "Which reminds me, I saw on the news that Mikles put up a reward for information on Bunny's disappearance. Have you heard anything? Kris said something about Bunny being found, but she couldn't give me any details."

"I did hear that the rumor of Bunny's demise was of her own making," Sam offered. "Beyond that, I don't know much more than you do. What about your client? Is Kris taking it easy on him?"

Riley smiled. Wade's dilemma had turned out far better than she could have imagined. "Kris says the feds have taken over the case. They did tell her it's unlikely Wade will be charged with anything. He's getting a lot of credit for whatever it was he did to help stop Cayren."

Riley glanced down at her watch to check the time. Unfortunately, the bejeweled trinket had already stopped keeping it. She rewound it for the umpteenth time and fiddled with the dial before returning her attention to Sam. "What the hell?"

Sam smiled roguishly as Riley examined his newly unfastened bow tie. "It must've come loose," he explained.

Riley stepped toward him and revisited the issue. "You are such a little boy, Sam. This is the last time I'm fixing this. Next time, you're going to have to go find whoever untied it the first time and have them fix it," she declared.

"That wouldn't be nearly as much fun," Sam said. "By the way, Miss Morgan, is your dance card already full or do you have a few spots still open?"

"This isn't exactly the type of dress one dances in," Riley quipped.

"I see. That's too bad," Sam assessed. "Still, I'm sure you would have many offers if you were so inclined. Like that gentleman you were talking with earlier."

Riley met Sam's eyes with a question. "Gentleman?" She paused to reflect on the evening. "Oh, you mean Representative Grayling? Kris introduced us. I was hoping to get him to sponsor legislation to increase protections for victims of domestic violence. He seemed really interested."

"I'm sure he was," Sam said.

"What's that supposed to mean?" Riley inquired. She tugged on his collar, tightening it uncomfortably in retribution while finishing off the bow tie.

Sam exacted a greater return. He moved forward abruptly, catching Riley by surprise. One sturdy arm encased her waist while the other moved upward, permitting his hand to weave into the length of her hair. Her lips were parted, likely with surprise, when his found them. Sam took full advantage of that circumstance, and then somehow managed to take even more. A faint, muffled protest escaped from Riley. It fell away quickly, when startle lost hold to the rise of other emotions. The embrace and its accompanying display of passion lasted longer than either had imagined it might.

Riley's knees threatened to give way. If Sam had not been holding her as tightly as he was, the threat might have become a reality. She braced her arms against his chest and after a few attempts managed to pull away. She stared at him, still agape while internally searching for some semblance of resolve.

"I . . . I need to go," she whispered.

"Please don't," Sam pled. "You don't have to."

A part of her mind that still had some measure of control had made the choice between two options. Flight had won by a nose. "I do," Riley stated. "I should be somewhere . . . else."

ᦂ ᦂ ᦂ

Sam leaned back against the soft leather car seat. He had chosen the quiet, secluded spot beside an old orange grove thinking it would be a good place to park while he collected his thoughts. It was also a good spot for keeping an eye on Riley. The grove was directly behind her house. From here, he could see the lights that were still on along the back of the house.

Riley had practically run from the gala; immediately returning to her safe place. He wondered how safe that place made her feel now that she no longer shared it with her father. What was it that made her run? If she still had feelings for Evan, it didn't show. She hadn't mentioned his name at all during the time they spent preparing for Audra's case. Sam considered that it might be his reputation that was making her skittish, but his ego wanted him to believe it was something more. He didn't scare easily. Still, the way she made him feel had taken a toll. It was distinctly possible she was feeling the same pull.

A chime sounded from his dashboard, indicating an incoming call. Sam answered, reluctantly. He had intended to sulk a while longer.

"You back from your island vacation?" Sam quipped.

"A vacation? Is that what they're calling running down miscreants in remote locales where the native bird is a giant mosquito?" Kent retorted. "If so, then it was *awesome*."

Sam ignored Kent's bite. He wasn't in the mood. "I heard they both confessed. Although, each with a different version of events."

"They did. Between the two of them, we managed to get enough to piece it together," Kent replied.

"So, Bunny and Cayren were running some kind of con to get back at Mikles. I got that much of it," Sam stated. "Whose idea was it to go after the other girl?"

"According to Bunny, it was Cayren's idea. Bunny claims Cayren was the one Wade saw in Halston's apartment that night. Looks like Bunny might be telling the truth on that much of it. She turned over a tape she had of Cayren confessing to the murder and telling where she dumped the body."

"Has that information been confirmed?" Sam inquired.

"Yep. They pulled the body from the small lake behind Mikles' club earlier tonight. Cayren apparently got the inspiration to unload it there just before the storm hit. Before that, she had it wrapped in plastic and stashed behind a week's worth of meat in the club's refrigerated meat-locker."

Sam shook his head in disgust. "I never imagined Cayren was the kind to have that in her. How was the girl killed?"

"Not sure. They're waiting for the medical examiner to confirm. My guess is that it was the sedative," Kent answered. "They tested the syringe Cayren used on Riley. It wasn't something you can get over-the-counter. Wade also indicated that Cayren had Halston in a mean choke-hold for a while. So, it could have been that, too."

A troubling realization followed Sam's assessment of the new details. "Cayren used the same sedative on Riley. How did Riley manage to come out of it if Halston didn't?"

"Don't know. Maybe Cayren didn't have enough of it left," Kent surmised. "It's a controlled substance. They think she might have stolen it from the vet that treats her dogs. In fact, that's where the story gets interesting."

The story was already interesting, although not sufficiently so to hold Sam's attention. Something more compelling drew his notice elsewhere. He watched with a twinge of regret as a trail of dimming lights announced the end of Riley's evening. First to go were the outdoor lights on the lanai, and then the ones in the kitchen. The one in the den went next. She was probably turning on her alarm system now. In a minute or two she would be upstairs in her bedroom. Before long, she would slip between the cool sheets of her bed, alone.

Sam wondered if she was still wearing the lavender gown she had on earlier, or if she had changed into something less formal. The fabric seemed delicate; like something Mason might damage should he decide he wanted to play tug-of-war with her. Riley was too practical-minded to take a chance with something so beautiful.

Kent was talking about something, but Sam had forgotten he was supposed to listen.

"Hello? Are you even remotely paying attention? Or is it already past your bed time?" Kent huffed.

"Sorry. I got distracted," Sam confessed. "What were you saying?"

"I was saying . . . Where the fuck are you?"

The abrupt turn in the conversation drew Sam back in. He was busted. "Nowhere, really."

"Bull! You're doing something you shouldn't be, like you always do," Kent said.

"I am not," Sam replied in all honesty. The exact spot where he was parked did not have a formal address. Technically, he was nowhere. And he wasn't doing anything but sitting in his car, at the moment.

"You're with her. Or you're watching her, aren't you?"

Kent's instincts were far too good for his own good, sometimes. "Weren't you in the middle of telling some kind of fish tale from your Caribbean vacation? How big was the one you brought in this time?" Sam snarked.

"You know...whatever. Do what you want. You're going to anyway. Just don't call me to save your ass tonight. I'm off the clock," Kent responded, his frustration apparent.

"I believe it was you who called me," Sam taunted. That one was too easy to let pass.

"Yeah, well, I didn't know you were on a date with yourself," Kent shot back. "I called to give you an update and that's what I'm doing, whether or not you choose to listen."

"I'm listening. Get on with it," Sam replied, reluctantly.

"So here's where the story takes a wild turn," Kent said. "Halston was sleeping with Mikles, but she wasn't planning to replace Cayren. She was just keeping Vince distracted while she stole from him. When FDLE picked up her cat from the vet and examined it at the lab, they found it had a couple of microchips under its skin. One of them was the usual type vets put in animals to track them. The other one had something entirely different on it."

"I can't even imagine," Sam sighed. He wasn't really trying. "What was it?"

"Mikles got some of his billionaire buddies to finance the design of a virtual reality sex game. They were using girls like Halston as models. The girls were fitted with digital motion sensing receptors and put in front of a blue screen so Mikles' people could record them performing in ways that simulated, umm . . . personal contact."

"Don't be a girl. You don't look good in pink," Sam snipped. "They were simulating a good fuck."

"If that's what you want to call it. I regard human interaction with a little more reverence," Kent shot back. He paused to retrace his account. "All right, where was I?"

"When last I was listening, you were mumbling something about a sex game."

"Right. So, Halston knew about the project because she was part of it. Somehow, she managed to get her hands on a copy of the software prototype along with all the schematics, tapes of the girls and pretty much everything else. She had it all transferred to a microchip and had her vet tech boy-toy unwittingly inject it into her cat for safe keeping. I'm guessing she was going to sell it on the black market. There are tech companies in China that could produce the final product a lot faster than Mikles."

"How do you know it was *unwitting*," Sam inquired. "He could have easily been in on it."

"The vet tech? He doesn't seem the type. He's here from Australia on a student visa. When not giving pet enemas he's taking acting classes and auditioning for parts. Had a spot in a reality show called *Mussel Men* not too long ago."

"Pleased to say I've never heard of it," Sam announced.

"Too bad. Sounded to me like it was right up your alley," Kent remarked. "The show takes a bunch of 'roid enhanced guys out on a boat where they compete in slimy seafood challenges."

"I'm terribly sorry to have missed that enchanting opportunity," Sam quipped.

"There's always next season," Kent said. "You might be more successful than Halston's beau. I heard he was voted off the boat in the third round, following a Cajun-style cook-off. His mussel etouffee wasn't all it was *cracked* up to be."

Kent laughed at his own joke, since Sam wouldn't. "C'mon. Get it? Because mussels are in a shell?" Kent explained.

Sam stayed silent. Ordinarily, he wouldn't have let Kent get away with a lame joke like that, which made it more and more obvious to Kent that whatever Sam had going on inside was really eating at him. No amount of worthless humor was going to draw Sam out of tonight's funk.

After a long pause, Sam summarized his thoughts. "Bunny and Cayren were using Halston to set Mikles up for a fall, not knowing that Halston was shagging and stealing from him at the same time. Almost makes me sympathize. Mikles was surrounded by beautiful women, all of them pure evil," Sam opined. That assessment led him to another. "Cayren must've found out what Halston was up to."

"Exactly. Glad you've decided to join me," Kent applauded. He picked up the story where he left off. "As luck would have it, Halston's boyfriend worked for the same vet Cayren and Vince used. Cayren must've been there with her dogs at some point and overheard Halston or the beefcake she was dating talking about their plan. Hard to say, for sure. Cayren didn't fess up on that part."

"Makes sense that she wouldn't," Sam surmised. "From a legal perspective, Cayren getting that information firsthand lends to Bunny's claim that Cayren acted alone. Bunny needed Halston for the case. Cayren didn't have much use for her."

"Right. That's the point where the story gets even more twisted. When Cayren killed Halston, it threw Bunny's plan into a tailspin. In order to salvage anything, they had to change course. Bunny decided they should make it look like Vince was responsible for Halston's death by disappearing herself. Cayren was supposed to implicate Vince by claiming she overheard him arguing with Bunny about the case right before Bunny went missing. That would lead the authorities to consider Mikles a prime suspect given his connection to both missing women."

"Of course," Sam said. "Halston's body would be discovered behind the club and Vince would take the fall. It would just be assumed Bunny had met a similar fate."

"Yep, leaving her free to start a new life somewhere else under an assumed name," Kent added. "My sources indicated Cayren took the yacht down to Captiva Island to get behind the storm while it passed over Central Florida. Bunny was along for the ride. When Cayren and the yacht returned to Clearwater, Bunny stayed behind. From there, Bunny must have hitched a ride on another boat to Mexico. Found out from some locals in Cancun that Bunny had picked up a new ID and passport there before hiring another boat to take her to Cayman Brac. That's where I found her. She was planning to work from there anonymously, siphoning off assets into shell companies for Cayren while Vince was behind bars."

Sam rubbed the stubble that, in spite of a recent shave, had started to return to his chin. "Something doesn't add up," he stated. "Cayren must not have known where Halston hid the prototype. That's why she took Halston's computer. Was that what Bunny was trying to find in Vince's office, or was she after something else? A video game seems like a small prize in the face of everything else Cayren stood to gain with Vince out of the way."

"I don't think so. Bunny didn't know about Halston or the video game at that point. I'm not sure what she was after, but she handed everything over," Kent said. "We logged in a couple sets of duplicate accounting books. Mikles had more than a few offshore accounts with several million in each. But you're right about it not adding up. When Mikles found out the stuff was missing, he didn't say anything about the books. The flash drive was what set him off."

"Was the game prototype on that drive?" Sam inquired.

"Don't know. I was directed to turn it over to Central Intelligence as soon as we got our hands on it."

"Unless things are slower than usual right now, the boys in D.C. wouldn't be interested in a video game even if it did have naked women in it. Whatever's on that drive is the reason we were sent in," Sam concluded.

"Good thing I made a copy of the drive before I turned it over," Kent touted. "That hot potato is all yours."

"I knew I liked you for some reason," Sam said. He looked down at his phone. "Gotta go. I've got a call coming in."

Sam picked up the incoming call with anticipation. The light had stayed on in Riley's bedroom longer than he had expected it to. She must have gotten the news. "Wasn't sure I was going to hear from you tonight. I'm glad you called."

Riley didn't speak at first. When she did, her voice was broken. "Dani's got cancer. Stage 4. You knew, didn't you? That's why she sent you."

"Sounds like you need to talk," Sam said. He engaged the Bentley's ignition and shifted into gear. "I'm coming over."

CHAPTER 40

W ade tore open the manila envelope the courier delivered from Sam's office. He had a few days before he started his new job with the NSA. Taking on an outside challenge seemed like a good way to pass the time.

He flipped the envelope over allowing the contents to fall into his hand. One USB flash drive, as expected, and a note from the sender. He turned the note over to read it.

Figure out what's on this, Genius. S.

"Good morning to you, too," Wade snarked.

He pushed the drive into his computer and started to examine the contents. There were several files on it; all of them encrypted and password protected. He commenced the program that would perform the busy work of brute forcing the passwords while he engaged in the type of analysis no computer could yet accomplish. He knew where this information came from, so he might be able to speed the process along. If his wife, Cayren, was any indication, that Mikles guy wasn't a genius. How hard could his passwords be?

Wade played around with a few options. It didn't take long before he had a hit for one of the files. He typed the password into the command field and the file opened. It took a little while longer to crack the encryption, but it too wasn't complicated. If his new job was as easy as this, he was in for a good ride.

Wade started to speed read the information that filled the screen before him. A few lines in he stopped reading. His mouth fell open at about the same time his eyes bugged.

"Kark! This isn't a game."